THE TRANSFORMATION OF HARLEN VOSTESK

The Transformation of Harlen Vostesk
Copyright © 2021 Samantha Duke

D1607867

Written By:
SAM DUKE

PART ONE

CHRYSALIS

CHAPTER 1

The rain never stopped in Wakefield. The gray sky poured itself out endlessly, only ever pausing long enough to part its clouds and take a deep breath of salty air before closing up again to add more and more to the black waves. They lapped at the worn docks beyond the small town, docks that had stood at the edge of the sea for a thousand years. The little wooden buildings all huddled like a flock of birds, hunched underneath the perpetually dark sky.

Harlen had spent the first two decades of his life watching the town from a distance behind the wrought-iron gate that stood black and pointed all around the outside of Vostesk Manor. It was a world unto its own: a hulking creature of mossy, gray stone worn smooth in places by years and years of pounding rain. It was a relic of a hundred years gone by and stood larger than any other house Harlen had ever seen. Far too large for the four people who lived in it.

When he had been very small, it had seemed impossible to him that people lived in the town. It had been real to him as a village drawn in the pages of a storybook. Like specks in the distance, the people he saw only seemed real when they walked on the cobblestone street below the window. Only then could he make out their faces and hear their voices. But even still, they were only to be observed. The only exceptions were the few that came into the house, invited by his father.

Of course, he understood differently now. The world beyond the manor was teeming with life: loud, intense, and vast. So vast that a person could vanish into it forever if they wanted.

Harlen stood behind the window, looking through the glass at the town and the street below; he began fiddling with the cufflink on his left wrist. It was small, silver, and nearly worn smooth on the inside from his relentless twisting each time he felt that familiar unease gnawing at him. His wide, dark eyes behind his thick glasses were trained on the black iron fence.

The longer he watched, the more he felt anxiousness bubbling up in his chest. *What time would he return? How long had it been? How many hours?*

He swallowed, staring at the rivulets of rain twisting down the glass, and stepped up hesitantly to the window made foggy by the faint warmth of the house. He raised one long-fingered hand and pressed it against the smooth surface, tracing downward and leaving tracks in the dampness.

Two lines upward. Two circles outward. One arch for each ring reaching outward. He had the pattern well-memorized and traced it slowly so he could be sure he'd done it right. He adjusted and smoothed each curve where his shaking hand caused a line to be imperfect or where the moisture began to collect again because he'd done it too slowly. That wouldn't do. It had to be perfect. If it were perfect, it would work.

He finally completed it, an exact replication of the runes he had seen in his studies. He stood back and took a deep breath that caught in his chest as he tried to concentrate. *Visualize what you desire.* That was what the book said. *Visualize what you desire and open yourself to what is within you. Eliminate distraction. Let the magic flow through you.*

It should be easier this way; at least, that was what he tried to convince himself. Runic magic does not require much natural talent or energy. Those with the most moderate magical inclination can perform it. It's only a step above alchemic magic, which requires the least innate ability of all, but Harlen knew his father wouldn't dare let him stoop that low. The one time he had tried to suggest it, the man had made that quite clear.

He attempted to calm his mind, pressed his fingers to the rune he drew, careful not to smudge it, and closed his eyes, visualizing the ice he wanted to crawl up the glass. He imagined stopping the rivulets of water in their place. He imagined it spiraling outward from his hand, a frost that would spread like lace and capture the drops like a spider catching insects in its web. He concentrated. He visualized it so clearly, he could swear he felt it. But when he opened his eyes, nothing had happened.

Nothing. Just like always.

He dropped his hand to his side, feeling the same sinking disappointment he felt every time. It had been twenty-two years, and nothing ever happened. Still, he was sure that if he could do it correctly, if he could only focus properly, it would change.

Harlen shook his head, blew out a shaky breath, and began tracing the rune in the fog again. And again. And again. Nothing each time.

Not good enough. Do it again.

He could almost hear his father's voice speaking behind him, and he worked faster, unable to stop his hands from shaking as he drew. He started over and over, but he couldn't get the lines straight anymore. His fingers were twitching, and everything came out looking wrong.

Again. Do it again. Do it until you get it right.

If he could make it perfect, it would work. That was what all the books said. That was what his father said. He had to perfect it. And he had to do so quickly. His father was growing impatient. This decision was an indicator that he had lost patience with him long ago.

Vostesk Senior had always been adamant about keeping his children's lack of magical talent a secret. It was why they had remained within the confines of the manor. He would not make his offspring's feeble magic common knowledge. He had insisted he would not. But suddenly, he was bringing some of his friends and colleagues into the equation.

Harlen couldn't decide if this was a last-ditch attempt to try and reach out to see if they could provide his son with what he couldn't seem to give or if it was just another way to humiliate him in hopes that it would be a motivator to try harder. If the latter was the case, he had certainly succeeded.

That morning Vostesk Senior had taken him to what was referred to rather fondly as "The Academy" by his father and his father's friends. Harlen had been expecting some grand palace of a building from the way they spoke about it.

He had visions of polished marble halls, rows of desks in lecture halls, and stern but kind professors who dressed immaculately. But from what little he had seen of it earlier that day, it seemed his only correct assumption was about the professors. Even then, only half so.

Of the ones he had seen, none of them seemed very kind. They all had stern faces set firmly in frowns and eyebrows perpetually raised as though everything around them had failed to live up to their expectations in some way.

The Academy itself turned out to be nothing more than an old guild house for fishermen. Harlen had seen the remnants of it, as well as all the attempts to hide it.

The entire building smelled like saltwater, and the sharp smell of kerosene lamps that fought to keep the place brightly lit under Wakefield's perpetually gray sky couldn't completely block out the faint smell of fish. The sea had sunk into the wood itself, and nothing short of tearing the place down to the ground and starting over could have gotten it out. There were also a few lingering fish hooks he'd spotted here and there, pressed so hard into the floor by the constant tramp of shoes that they were practically part of the woodgrain.

His father hurried him into one of the back rooms that he supposed the public didn't see as often, and he saw that there was still one brass plaque on the wall that read "The Silver Sturgeon Fisherman's Guild." He had sat in that back room for the better part of an hour, alone, with nothing to occupy his thoughts but the little brass plaque and the one fishhook pressed into the floorboard beside his shoes.

As he sat, he wondered why an entire building had been dedicated to educating the noble children and those magically gifted when there couldn't be that many in Wakefield. Not nearly enough to justify the use of such a large building or so many professors.

There must have been at least one for every student, judging by what little he had observed. Based on what he had heard from his father and his father's friends, it couldn't be too wild of an assumption. With a good deal of pride, every one of them claimed to have been privately educated.

Eventually, five of those stern-looking professors filed into the room. None of them acknowledged him, but he recognized nearly all of them as those who occasionally came calling at the manor. The only one he didn't remember seeing was a young man who couldn't have been much older than he was with curly copper hair and a patch freckles beneath a pair of green eyes, and who looked uncomfortable in his stiffly pressed suit.

They all sat at the long table pushed against the room's far wall, adjusting their coats and talking to one another in hushed mutters, occasionally casting glances at him that made his heart jump up into his throat. He stared at the fishhook embedded in the floorboards and tried glancing at his father, who stood in the corner beside the door to see if he would tell him what was going on.

His father had his arms folded, his stern face set, and his pale eyes glittered coldly. As soon as he caught him looking in his direction, his firmly set mouth curled into a frown that said he was stupid for not having figured it out. Harlen had gone back to staring at the fishhook, feeling those cold eyes boring into the back of his head.

He was almost glad when one of the professors called him over to the table. He stood up and shuffled over, not knowing if he should smile or mimic their stern expressions until one of them gestured to a glass of water set in front of them. That was when he understood what they wanted, and it made his heart drop into his stomach.

He had looked back at his father again; sure there had been some mistake. But he was met with a long, cold stare and was left alone to face the table of five stern men and their impossible request.

He felt like each set of eyes was slowly pulling him apart while he set his hands on either side of the glass and stared down at the water inside. Peeling back clothing, skin, and muscle, dissecting him to see if they could discover what was wrong as he tried desperately to concentrate.

This time it will be different. Don't panic. Concentrate. Clear your mind.

But he *was* panicking. It felt like any coherent thought he ever had vanished while he stared down into the little glass of water that should have been turning to ice. He tried to envision frost forming on the water, creeping down into the cup like fog, but all he could think about were the eyes on him. And the seconds were ticking slowly by in complete silence.

There was no clock anywhere he could see or hear, so he had no idea how much time was passing, but he could feel the time stretching on and on. Why was nobody saying anything?

He knew he shouldn't have needed to vocalize the spell. He could feel his father's glare burning through the back of his skull as soon as he began to recite it. But as more time passed, Harlen knew he needed every ounce of help and concentration he could muster.

He had memorized so many spells by heart that he could have recited an entire lexicon of them in his sleep but had to force himself to remember as he, slowly and clearly, spoke each word. But every moment, he was able to focus less and less on anything but his face burning, and the staring, and how agonizingly long it had been.

He managed to keep himself together reasonably well until he fumbled the words. His tongue was beginning to feel numb, and he heard one of the professors give a bit of a chuckle. The man tried to disguise it as a cough, but the damage was done.

Harlen's hands had begun to shake, and his chest and throat closed up tight. His face must have been blazing red, and he could feel sweat breaking out on his forehead. He fumbled the words again. Then again. He couldn't remember which spell he was supposed to be using, and there was more silence, and he had just wanted it to be over. Why were they still waiting?

He had risked looking up at the professors just in time to see them all exchanging either smirks or pitying glances. He also saw the one with the coppery hair reach forward when the others weren't paying attention to nudge the glass off the table.

They all froze and seemed startled by the sound of the cup smashing on the floor, and the copper-haired professor said something Harlen couldn't entirely remember about stretching too far.

"I suppose that's the end of that then, isn't it?" he said and gave a meaningful glance towards the door from beneath his red brows.

Harlen hadn't needed to hear it twice. He hurried out of the room into the relative safety of the hallway, his heart still pounding, his face still flushed. He was given a few curious glances by those passing by, but it had been mostly empty by then.

His father hadn't followed him out, so it allowed him a moment to steady himself, to catch his breath and still the shaking in his hands. Unfortunately, his relief was short-lived and was overtaken by shame as soon as Vostesk Senior emerged.

The man refused to look at him. He made his way towards the door without saying a word, leaving Harlan to scramble after him.

If standing in front of that table had been bad, the walk home was far worse. His father hadn't said a word or so much as offered him a glance for the entire trip. Shouting would have been better. Waiting in silence for whatever he would do to repay him for embarrassing him in front of his colleagues was agonizing.

When they'd gotten to the wrought iron gate outside the manor house, and his father had finally turned to him, Harlen had flinched out of habit. His father's lip curled at his reaction; disgust written all over the harsh angles of his face.

"I trust you can manage to find your way inside from here. I understand it's asking a lot from you," he said. His stare was so intense that it was nearly impossible to meet his eyes.

Harlen had mumbled a quick yes and had seen himself inside. The iron fence he had shut between them had given him little comfort.

Since then, he had been unable to do anything but dread his return. So he drew runes on the window until his fingers were stiff. As though that would change what had already happened.

He only stopped when he reached the end of the hallway. Harlen hadn't realized he had been moving down so far but looking back; he winced to see he had left the tracks from his hands all up and down the glass that ran the length of the long hall.

He really should clean them off before anyone saw it. His father would not be happy to see he had ruined the work the goblins had done earlier that day. Vostesk Senior held no particular fondness in his heart for the little scurrying creatures, with their big, luminous eyes, moving silently around the house, keeping out of sight, and ensuring everything was spotless. Still, Harlen knew that upsetting what they had already cleaned was unacceptable.

He pulled the handkerchief from his pocket and began wiping away the marks on the window. When the glass was clear, he was again offered a clear view of the front yard and gave in to the temptation to spend another moment staring at the front gate.

His fingers twitched unconsciously to twist at the cufflink on his left wrist once again. The yard was empty. The street beyond it was empty. The gate shut tight.

It was no use watching. Besides, Harlen knew what his father would say if he returned home and caught him up there doing nothing but staring. At the very least, he should set himself to something useful. Maybe that would make what was sure to come later less severe.

CHAPTER 2

Harlen made his way down the grand staircase, the sound of his shoes echoing first on the creaking, polished hardwood steps, then on the marble of the black and white chessboard floor of the foyer. His footsteps were the only sound aside from the grandfather clock's ticking that grew fainter and fainter as he left the upper hallway.

There were only a few of the glass kerosene lamps left sputtering here and there along the walls, and outside the rain was falling straight and hard, no longer beating against the windows but turning the streets to shallow rivers of mud and cobblestone with no sign of letting up. If anything, the clouds had only grown thicker and darker, casting the entire house into a dim twilight.

It made the light coming from the library's fireplace visible as soon as he reached the bottom of the stairs. The small, slanted path created by it shining out from the space beneath the door seemed like a brilliant beacon of orange and gold.

He had no idea how he had failed to notice it on his way in. He was probably too preoccupied with his worries to see it when he entered. Unless he had been upstairs staring out that window for far longer than he thought. Either way, he turned towards it and walked down the brilliant path towards the library.

"Mother?" he called as he pushed the heavy oak door open. The wave of heat that wrapped around him was heavenly; the smell of burning wood and old books even more so. But the room appeared to be empty.

Perhaps she had lit the fire and wandered back to her room. Or, she was warming herself and heard the door open. That would have made her retreat deeper into the house without thought for anything but hiding. He considered going back upstairs to knock at her door to let her know that it was only him, but depending on her mood, it could just frighten her more. No. It would be better to let her come out of her own accord, despite his concern. At least he was there to keep an eye on the fire.

Harlen looked up at the high-ceilinged room: the shelves crammed with books and artifacts collected over the many centuries that the Vostesk family had existed. Many of the metal and stone trinkets gleaming between massive volumes were from far, far away from the rainy coastal town where they had settled in the end. Nobody had added to the collection in his living memory.

In his mind, it gave the room a peculiar feeling of otherworldliness. Whether it was the books, the objects from distant places that perhaps never saw a drop of freezing rain, or even just the fireplace that curbed the dampness as the fire seemed to do in the rest of the house—he could believe he was almost anywhere else when he stood in that room.

He stood beside the fireplace for a moment, warming the stinging chill from his hands and looking up at the shimmering golden constellations painted on the ceiling. It was rare to see a clear night sky in Wakefield, so he had learned their names by lying on his back on the green and white carpet for hours on end, picking out their gilded shapes.

He had memorized the story behind each one. It was one of the few things he seemed to have a mind for devouring and remembering anything put in front of him. He could remember every spell, who discovered it, the how and why behind what lead to its creation.

That was never the problem. The problem was with some other part of himself that he couldn't seem to master, no matter how hard he tried or how badly he wanted it.

He was still standing at the fire when he heard the door creak open. He turned, expecting to see his mother standing there, the reassurance that it was only him halfway out of his mouth before he realized it wasn't her. Even in the shadow cast by the slant of the door, he could see that the hair was too dark, and the figure was too tall.

His heart was already in his throat by the time she stepped fully into the light of the fire. The long, loose hair like mahogany, warm gray eyes, and soft features were unmistakable.

"Millie," he said, fighting to swallow the nervous ball tightening in the pit of his stomach that only clenched tighter when she smiled. She had a crooked smile that pressed a single dimple into her right cheek and lifted the corners of her eyes.

"Hello, stranger. I thought I heard someone come in."
She glided through the door and shut it behind her to bar out the
cold. Her long, pale dress with the delicate red, green, and
yellow flowers embroidered on the hem swirled above her
ankles. The draft carried the gauzy material easily.

All of her clothes were like that: breezy and airy and far
too light for such a cold climate. Supposedly his father planned
to have new clothes commissioned for her, but that promise was
made two months ago.

He was amazed she hadn't gotten sick yet. He had been
born in Wakefield and had spent the majority of his childhood
horrendously ill. He couldn't imagine how someone who had
grown up in the sunny, southern mountains managed unless
being born in such a climate made her health incredibly robust
by nature.

He hoped that was the case. He was well aware of her
dislike of the constant cold and dreariness here and would hate
for her to fall sick in a house of strangers.

She came to stand next to him, and he became aware of
every inch of space he took up. She wasn't as diminutive in size
as his mother and sister, but she was by no means a large
woman. The top of her head would have reached only the
middle of his chest if they stood across from one another. He
felt too big next to her: all long limbs and sharp angles, whereas
there wasn't a hard line on her body.

He folded his arms while she glanced into the crackling
fire, hoping to make himself less of an imposition on her space.
Harlen stole glances at her, wondering if she felt nervous in his
presence as he did in hers.

He shouldn't be so nervous around her. Not still. They
had, in law at least, been married for nearly three months. But,
unfortunately, they had only known each other for about as
long.

There had been no courtship for them. Harlen hadn't
even known his father was arranging for him to be married,
though he supposed he should have known it was coming
eventually. He didn't expect his father to be incredibly romantic
about the affair, but he did wish that he and Millie could have
had some time to get to know one another before the wedding.

He hadn't even learned her name until their introduction
the day before the ceremony.

He should have tried to get to know her then, but he'd been too painfully shy even to manage to hold a conversation with her. He had never had the chance to interact with many people outside his immediate family or his father's friends and had been at a loss for how to speak with her or how to act in her presence. She was so pretty and bright, and her smile came so readily that he had felt like a fumbling idiot, just struggling through his initial greeting.

He had gotten somewhat better as they spent more time together, and luckily for him, she had been patient so far. And she had been kind enough not to voice the disappointment she must feel. He was well aware that he was hardly a catch. He couldn't be anything like she might have imagined her future husband would be. But she was more than he had dared hope for: she was kind. She hadn't raised her hand or even her voice to him once.

"I've been stealing from the kitchen," she announced to break the awkward silence that had formed. She pulled a small pale pink sugar pastry from the little cloth napkin bundled in her hands. She offered it to him, and Harlen took it gingerly. He was far too nervous to eat it, but he didn't want to reject her offer that was an attempt to put him at ease. He gave her a smile he was sure was awkward, but it seemed to please her well enough.

"So, where have you been all day?" she asked.

"Oh. Well." His fingers found the cufflink again and began twisting. "My father took me to be evaluated. At The Academy."

She raised an eyebrow and cocked her head to the side, and he had to remember that she would have no idea what he was talking about. Despite how its previous attendees spoke about it, The Academy wasn't well known outside of Wakefield. Based on what he had seen today, he would even venture that it probably wasn't known at all outside of town.

He explained it in the best way he could, trying but failing to make it sound as illustrious as his father did, in the end summing it up as he had seen it: a former fisherman's guild where they had decided to teach magic. She seemed incredibly underwhelmed by the whole thing but did ask how it went. He winced at the thought of explaining the disaster to her and settled on saying, "Not well."

"Well, who would want to go somewhere like that anyway?" she asked. Harlen could feel her watching him worry at the cufflink on his left sleeve. "Sounds pretentious if you ask me."

That did bring a little twitch of a real smile to his face. Millie's lack of interest in the place was oddly comforting. "Well, my father thinks it's amazing."

Millie grimaced. "He would."

Harlen glanced toward the door out of habit and felt his stomach twist. He wasn't home. Harlen was sure he would have heard the main door open and shut if he had returned. But he was still half-convinced he would look up to see those cold eyes watching from the entrance to the room. There was nobody there, of course, but his discomfort must have been visible. Millie was giving him a concerned look, and he quickly changed the subject.

"I came in to look through some of these. To see if I missed something today," he said, indicating one of the shelves closest to the fireplace.

The books inside it were far more worn and ragged than what usually would have been on display, but in the case of spellbooks, signs of being heavily used were a mark of pride. Wrinkled, yellow pages, smeared ink, and crumpled scraps of fabric left to mark specific places inside the banged-up covers were all ways of showing that the person who used them had put it through its paces before leaving it behind for others to learn from. Most, if not all, of the spell books on this shelf, were from former Vostesk family members, though not in proper order. If the books were arranged in order of use, it would have been all too easy to see how the spines' condition improved as they moved towards the present day. Instead, he had learned the order by heart and knew exactly where to look for his preferred volume.

"Adrian Vostesk wrote this," he said as he pulled the book from the shelf with great care.

It was well-used, but not in the same way as the others. It wasn't worn from years of being lugged around in bags, pulled out in the heat of some disaster or adventure. It was stained from spilled ink bottles, marked by burns and drops of wax on pages where candles used to write by night had burned too low. "I tend to find his work the most helpful."

Millie was still studying him closely, the concern remaining on her face, but she went with his eager change of topic. "Any particular reason?"

Harlen took the book and set it down at the long, gleaming table in front of the fireplace. He pulled out one of the high-backed chairs for Millie before sitting down himself in the one beside it.

Millie had no magical talent herself. But she did like the look of the spellbooks. He could hardly blame her; some were centuries-old with elaborate drawings in ink or liquid gold and silver. She seemed to enjoy any of the books so long as they had beautifully illustrated pages and exciting stories. She would frequently sit nearby when he was deep in his reading, occasionally glancing over to see what he was engrossed in or doing something of her own. Simultaneously, she waited for the inevitable moment when he found something he thought she would enjoy and wanted to show her. He wasn't sure if it counted as an activity for couples, but it was a small habit they had managed to form and that he enjoyed.

She sat, curling her legs up underneath her and propping her elbows on the table while he explained.

"He's the easiest to understand. Figuratively and literally, I guess. A lot of the ancient ones are in other languages, and I have a bit of trouble with the technicalities of some of the older. . ." he trailed off and cleared his throat. He was probably boring her. "He was the first. The first one born without magic in the family, almost two centuries ago. He spent his entire life studying the nature of magic, breaking down spells, trying to find out why. Half of the book isn't even spells. It's his journal as well."

He was rambling. He knew he was, but Millie just shifted to get a better look at one of the pages cramped with Adrian's uneven handwriting. "Huh. What's he like?"

"Well. Honestly, he was. . .he was a bit of an. . ."

"Ass?" Millie asked, surprising him enough to get a laugh out of him that was half a cough. She grinned while he pushed his glasses back up where they had slipped down his nose.

"Yes. Sort of," Harlen admitted. "He was frustrated. The first child born without magic is the beginning of the end for a bloodline, and he was seen as this living embodiment of a bad omen. He wrote this entire thing because his family sent him to live in this tower on an island away from the rest of them so they wouldn't have to live with the shame."

"That's horrible." Millie grimaced. "I suppose that means he's allowed to be a little bit of an ass."

He couldn't help the little smile that tugged at the corner of his mouth. "I suppose. I think you would like him. He's quite witty. Like you."

Millie smirked. "Oh, I wouldn't go that far. I'd hardly call myself witty. Funny, absolutely. But I don't know about witty. I think I hid from my tutor too much growing up for that."

"I don't think that disqualifies you," Harlen said, and the little impish grin she gave him made his breath stick in his throat.

He wanted to say more. To make some attempt to be charming because he liked that playful spark in her eyes, but then he heard the front door open.

He was on his feet without even thinking of it. His heart pounded painfully in his throat as he listened to the familiar sound of the heavy front door banging shut, followed by a sharp surge of fear when his father's voice called his name.

"Let's just see what he wants," Millie said. He hadn't heard her get up, but she was standing beside him now and had lightly touched his arm in an attempt to bring him back down from the heights of panic he had leaped to.

"I'm sure it's nothing," he said, trying to sound relaxed despite the reaction he had just had. His voice was shaking.

They made their way out of the library, the cold hitting Harlen like a punch once he stepped across the threshold. He could see his father beside the door, shrugging out of his soaked coat, the long tails leaving matching puddles on the marble beside the door.

As soon as Vostesk Senior saw the two of them, he began speaking, too impatient to wait until they had come all the way over. "I was just finishing arrangements with the school board," he said in his clipped, curt manner. "One of their officials will be visiting later this evening, and I want you at your best, do you understand? Wash up well and get your mother out of her room. Make sure you get her cleaned up and presentable."

What arrangements? Harlen wanted to ask but knew better. Instead, he gave a quick agreement and gladly took the opportunity to retreat into the house as quickly as possible with Millie close behind.

"Oh, and Harlen," his father said, stopping him in his tracks and turning him back around as effectively as a hand on his shoulder. "Do at least try to hold a conversation tonight. I know it's a struggle for you, but I am trying to convince this man that you have promise."

Harlan felt his face grow hot and tried hard not to look at Millie. He knew that this was one punishment for disgracing him earlier. He had embarrassed him in front of his colleagues. His father was simply returning the favor.

He made some kind of agreement so that he could leave, and the quiet was much heavier than before as he and Millie trudged up the stairs towards their room.

CHAPTER 3

The room was the same one from his childhood, and he couldn't help but feel a bit more relaxed when he closed the door.

The sound of the lock on the outside made its telltale rattle against the thick wooden frame, letting him know it was fully shut. Walls surrounded them painted a green-blue, one entirely covered by a line of bookshelves jammed to their maximum capacity so that several of the shelves were beginning to dip in the middle with the weight of what they held. Unlike the books he buried himself in in the library, these were his companions. His safe places. Books of stories and poetry. Most of them were saccharine sweet with characters who were far too kind and with thoughts far too romantic, but it was always nice to pretend for a moment that things could be so gentle. Especially while the other side of his room was dominated by his desk, stained in ink and covered in crumpled papers showing more of his failed attempts at magic.

"I don't know how you let him talk to you like that," she said as soon as they had reached their bedroom, and he had closed the door securely behind them.

"It's just how he is." Harlen didn't know how else to explain it. He had never seen his father act any differently and doubted there was any other way for him to be. In all the twenty-two years he had lived with his father, Harlen never once saw him crack a smile that wasn't some form of a cold smirk.

"I don't care if that's how he is," Millie muttered to herself. She did it quite often, under her breath but somehow still loud.

"I know. I'm sorry," Harlen said, not knowing why he was apologizing, but it felt necessary. At the very least, it felt like he should say something to relieve the new awkwardness between them, and it was all he could think to say.

She had turned away and begun the process of taking out the little diamond earrings she wore while talking to herself but paused with only one off to look back over her shoulder at him. "It isn't your fault that he acts that way."

Her voice was stern, and her gaze intense, and he had to look away. She was right. He knew she was. But he still couldn't convince himself of that entirely. He wouldn't be in such a mood if the board meeting that morning hadn't been such a disaster.

They lapsed into silence, and Harlen let her go about her business undisturbed. Harlen opened his wardrobe, planning to take his things to the washroom to offer Millie some privacy, his eye catching as always on the inside of the door.

He'd scratched little tick marks there. Marking away the hours chimed by the grandfather clock, he used to hide in the far corner like a fox in its hole. The polish inside the closet was nearly worn away in its entirety from all the times he had done it when he was still small enough to fit in the wardrobe and wasn't ashamed to crawl inside to feel safe.

Now, he had another place. Though, the feeling overall was the same. Once he collected his clothes and retreated to the washroom attached to the bedroom and clicked the door shut, he felt the same nearly dizzying sense of relief. The small lock—the only lock on the inside of any door he had ever been allowed—felt like sliding a shield into place as he pushed it closed.

There, he felt safe undressing. As the water ran and filled the air with steam, he caught blurry images of himself in the mirror. His skinny body with his ribs showing like a starving dog, and the scars that marked it made him wince. Some were white and silver. Some were pink or red and still looked gnarled and angry as they pulled the skin around them. There were straight lines, curves, and burns. All formed a patchwork over his body.

Sometimes he thought he saw a pattern in them, but he knew that wasn't right. They were just the result of him not living up to expectation—marks of weakness. A symbol of the lack of magic in his blood was so horrifying to his father he had tried to carve it out with knives and tongs.

As he sank into the water of the bath, the freshest of the marks on his upper arms stung. But he scrubbed at them all the same. They were already a few days old, and it wasn't that bad. It was far better than the alternative. His wounds had infected before, and it was better to endure the temporary sting than the fever that came with infection or having to cut away rotting flesh. Both of which he had had the misfortune of experiencing in the past and was not eager to repeat.

He washed meticulously. He found the process calming, and it released the tension that had been building in him like a coiled spring all day. It would begin to turn itself taunt again once he left the room, but he knew how to take his moments of peace. And though he'd never considered himself attractive, he was careful about his grooming.

He dressed with care before returning to his main room, where he gave himself one last look in the full-length mirror beside his door—a great, round mirror surrounded by polished black wood.

The suit he had chosen was black and fit slightly better than most of what he wore. All his clothes seemed to hang off him in some way, and he supposed nothing could be done about that. A little extra fabric had to be used to accommodate his long limbs, and he simply couldn't fill it out.

He adjusted the bluish-green tie and gave his face a lingering look, raising one hand to his hair that was chopped short around the chin. For all his trying, he still hadn't been able to get it to be even.

His father had cut most of it off shortly before Millie's arrival. He was always saying that they had elves' blood in them. Long hair was a mark of pride in that blood that he didn't deserve.

Harlen himself had hair down almost to his waist before and still wasn't used to the change. It always felt wrong and ugly.

When Millie had first arrived, he kept trying to hide behind it. He would tug at the ends as if that could make it longer again, and he was sure she would know it was embarrassing for him to have it cut so short. But if she did, she didn't say anything. On the one occasion where he had alluded to his father's long hair and its meaning, she only looked at him in confusion. So maybe she didn't know. But there was no use worrying about it. It wasn't as if he could make it grow back faster.

"That looks nice," Millie called from across the room. She had undressed and re-dressed into a silky gray gown that very nearly matched her eyes. It was trimmed with beautiful white lace and did suit her, but it left her arms and shoulders bare and had been made for warmer weather.

He knew her compliment was just courtesy, but he would be lying if he said it did not affect him. He stopped tugging at his hair and smiled at her in the mirror where she was struggling to tie her own back with a little jeweled pin wedged in the corner of her mouth.

"Do you need help?" he asked.

"Do you have much experience with hair pins?" she asked.

"Yes, actually," he said, and when she shrugged and nodded for him to come over, he took both the silky ribbon and the hairpin from her and set to work.

She turned away from him, and he pulled her hair back over her shoulders. It was long and thick and seemed by nature to want to be left to its own devices. He knew she had lost her pins on more than one occasion inside it and that she had a bit of a struggle trying to get it to remain in place, but it was lovely to touch. Despite its unruliness, it was soft, and it was warm where it had been lying against her neck and back. He would be lying if he claimed he didn't find its wild nature charming.

"I feel intimidated. You're better at this than I am," Millie said as he finished, raising a hand to the simple work he had done. In some way, he hoped it helped redeem him for being so cowed by his father's comment earlier.

He offered another sheepish smile and said, "I've had a lot of practice."

She gave him another curious look but didn't ask for an explanation.

"You can go ahead downstairs if you want. I'll be there in a minute," Harlen said. He needed to take care of just one more thing, and he didn't want to make her late. It had been about an hour. And if the guests his father had invited before were any indication, they would be arriving shortly to chat before the meal.

"Are you sure?" she asked.

"I won't be long," he promised. Millie agreed and gave him one last parting glance he couldn't quite read as he stepped out of their room into the hallway.

His mother lived behind the upper hallway's last door beside the one window that stood at its very end. Day in and day out, it let in watery light and the sound of rain tapping glass into the long, narrow hall filled with portraits of the staring, stern faces of his ancestors and a few low-glowing, sputtering lamps that smelled of stinging kerosene.

She didn't share a room with his father anymore. The last time he could remember them doing so was when he and Tansey were very young, and they had separated without a word of explanation.

Tansey was the only reason why he ever found out that had come to an end. When the argument that proceeded the split had happened, it was far worse than their usual bouts of screaming. He retreated to his room as soon as he heard the first dish in the dining room break and had holed up in his place in his wardrobe. Through its closed doors, he almost couldn't hear them anymore. He tried to get Tansey to join him, but she wanted to sneak downstairs and listen to what all the fuss was about.

If she had been caught, they would both have been in a world of trouble. Harlen had tugged on her sleeve and begged her not to go, but there was no convincing her of changing course once she made up her mind. She had gone anyway, returning after a very anxious hour in which he had listened carefully to his parents' muffled voices to make sure they didn't leave the dining room where Tansey was likely hiding right outside the door. He couldn't understand what they were saying but hoped their yelling meant his sister hadn't been noticed.

To his relief, she returned unseen but with tears in her eyes. She'd spoken in a rushed, choked voice.

"He said she's like us because she can't have kids anymore."

Harlen hadn't known what that meant at the time or its implications. He only understood that she was more upset than he had ever seen her. She crawled into the wardrobe to sit with him, and he had done his best to comfort her, but it was years later that he came to understand what she meant. Their father had been saying she was useless—like both children born without magic in their blood.

His mother had never been a particularly spirited woman. She had always struck him as someone who was deeply sad and detached from everything. After that argument, though, any life and resilience left inside their mother had been swept away. She never so much as raised her voice at his father again. It was rare she ever raised her voice at all above a trembling whisper. He felt sorry for her. He always had.

"Mother?" Harlen knocked at her bedroom door softly. From inside, he heard her give a soft, listless sound of confusion, and he braced himself for what he might see as he pushed his way into the room gently.

Her room looked the same as his and all the others. Same creaking wooden floor and blue-green walls. She had a lovely dressing table in one corner made of dark wood and silver carved into the shape of foam-capped waves around the round mirror, but it always sat with a thin layer of dust on it. Each crystal bottle of perfume and round box of powder wrapped in a pale gray film. In the opposite corner, her wardrobe, also trimmed in silver waves, stood with one door hanging open like a slack jaw. Several dresses in soft white and pale green silk trailed out from it across the floor like a lolling tongue.

She laid on the bed, sideways, one hand still splayed outward toward the little dark bottle that was always at her bedside. Opium. She'd been taking it for her pain after her last failed pregnancy, and Harlen supposed it did its job and then some. His father claimed he kept her supplied with it out of care for her condition, but Harlen couldn't help but feel his stomach turn at the state it left her in.

She was a beautiful woman. She was in her fifties, and the white that was beginning to show mixed well with her pale blonde hair. Tansey had had her hair. And her eyes. Large and a pale blue like the sea in a place that wasn't so dreary, but unlike his sister's, hers were hauntingly vacant. She had a ghost's eyes.

She was painfully small as well. She didn't eat much anymore—the only thing she seemed interested in consuming was her water mixed with the opium drops. The few bites of food they could coax her into eating left her small and frail like a little porcelain doll. Her skin was white and colorless; the fine lines around her eyes were delicate as spider webs. He was always afraid he would hurt her when he touched her.

"Mother?" he repeated, approaching slowly. Sudden movements tended to startle her when she was in this state.

She was laid back across the bed, half on her side with her petticoats pooling around her like seafoam. Her pale, cream dress was half on, half off—unbuttoned in the back over her layers of underclothes and unfastened at one hip. Either getting dressed or undressed, she had slumped in a pile, and it looked as though she hadn't moved in quite some time.

"Do you need help?" he asked, keeping his voice as quiet and gentle as he could.

She kept staring at the ceiling for a moment, then turned her head towards him with a slow blink. She looked confused, so he reached down and touched her shoulder lightly as he could.

"Mother, it's me. Harlen."

She blinked again, perplexed, then finally said in a dreamy voice, "Oh. Yes. Right. Harlen, dear. Ah—what time is it?"

She looked out the window, clearly disoriented. Harlen kept one hand on her shoulder to keep her attention so she didn't drift off again and said, "It's almost dinner, mother. I came to get you."

She looked up at him again and seemed frightened. "Oh. It's later than I thought. I must have nodded off again."

"Right." Harlen forced a calm smile and nodded. "Why don't I help you? So we can go faster?"

"No, no, no. We have that woman. Don't we?"

"Agatha?" Harlen asked.

"Yes, her. She can help me. You don't need to."

Harlen forced another strained smile. Agatha had been a nurse his father had hired to assist in his mother's care. She was a grandmotherly woman who was strict and stern but overall kind. Unfortunately, his mother tended to. . .forget who she was. She'd flown into a panic no less than five times within the month she'd been hired, and Harlen had had to calm her down from her panic while she screamed and kicked and demanded to know who this person in her room was.

Eventually, Agatha had lost patience with her and left. His father had said he would find her a new nurse, but as with his promise to get Millie warmer clothes, Harlen doubted he ever planned to follow up on it.

Explaining all that to her, however, could upset her. And Harlen didn't want to have to quiet an episode of screaming before dinner, so instead, he said, "I've already called her, but why don't I help you until she gets here?"

She looked conflicted, then nodded. Harlen helped her stand up, fixed her skirts, fastened her dress back in place, securing all her little buttons, and with experienced hands, he carefully pinned her hair. She selected her jewelry with wandering fingers when he guided her over to her dressing table, and he put all of it where it should be. By the end, she seemed to have forgotten all about Agatha.

"Thank you, dear," she said with a smile, her eyes still distant. She touched the side of Harlen's face, and he had no idea if she was seeing him or not, but he felt his throat tighten. It tightened even further when her eyebrows drew together, and she asked, "Where are we going?"

"Dinner," he said, staring into her face. He gripped the hand she'd put on his cheek and squeezed, searching for some spark of life in her eyes. "We're going to dinner. Remember?"

She looked confused as a child, and he felt angry pain twisting in his chest. At what, he wasn't sure. But there was no time to concern himself with it. Being late would only cause trouble for both of them. So, he pushed the feeling down as far as it would go and smiled at her.

"Come on. I'll take you."

CHAPTER 4

Millie braced herself as she stepped out of the bedroom and into the long, dark hallway. The sharp smell of kerosene from the lamps on the walls stung her nose. Above each lamp, there was a noticeable black mark on the wall where the little glass bulbs coughed smoke. The guttering flames cast a strange, dim light on the portraits that lined the walls.

She hated this hallway: really, she did. She felt like she was being watched by a hundred faces, none of them smiling. Out of every picture in this house, there was only one with a smiling face. It stood at the end of the hallway, at the top of the grand staircase.

It was a family portrait of the current Vostesk clan.

It was tempting to believe it was painted at least to scale if not larger. Vostesk Senior stood straight-backed and severe at the back next to a small woman with blonde hair and sky-blue eyes that even in paint seemed strangely vacant.

A younger Harlen, she guessed he had to be about thirteen or so, looked almost the same as he did now but with longer hair. It seemed to her that all that changed about him since then was him growing like a weed, his face losing the last of the child's fat that had offered it any kind of softness. It left him sharp and bird-like, but he had kept the big, round glasses and the sad eyes behind them. He looked miserable in the picture—the only one of them who didn't was the girl.

She looked like a younger, far more alert version of the woman. She had the same delicate features, pale yellow hair, and big blue eyes, but she stood as though she had as much a right to be there as her father. Her small shoulders were squared, her back was straight, and she had a little, what Millie could only describe as a sly, smile on her face.

Millie wondered who she was. A sister, she assumed. Millie had done a bit of looking around in the house when Vostesk Senior wasn't around and had found what looked to be a girl's room. She hadn't gone inside—after all, she had no idea why in all the time she'd been there, Harlen hadn't mentioned a sister. She assumed something must have happened.

She had it in mind to ask Harlen when she felt she had the right to bring up what might be a very personal topic. For the time being, the smiling girl would have to remain a mystery.

"Berkley, good of you to make it."

Millie saw Vostesk Senior standing at the open front door as she descended the stairs, helping a man dressed in a wet suit and jacket through the door.

The man was wearing possibly the most ridiculous top hat Millie had ever seen that was as white as the rest of his clothes. She also spotted an expertly curled mustache that somehow withstood the rain and wiggled and twitched as he returned the greeting. Millie thought he reminded her a bit of a rabbit as she hurried down the steps and off into the dining room before they could spot her. She would rather skip the stiff introductions at the door. Instead, she made her way into the dining room.

It was a place that could have been beautiful; the black and white checkerboard floor didn't look as severe with the crystal chandelier that hung in the center of the long room reflecting glittering light onto it. There was a long, polished, mahogany table directly beneath it large enough to seat twenty, though Millie was sure there were never more than five people seated at it at once.

There was a fireplace, the beginnings of a blaze flickering to life on the opposite wall, and in the far corner, there was a piano she had never seen touched. It sat beside a door that opened to a charming sitting room she considered escaping to but thought better of it. Instead, she perched herself on a green-padded mahogany bench near the wall and watched the door to the kitchen in the far corner swing open and shut as the goblins scurried in and out.

There were ten at least; small creatures no more than a foot tall in varying shades of blue and grey with tiny, squished noses, tails nearly as long as they were tall, and ears half as long as that. She thought they dressed adorably in doll-sized clothing with their huge, lamp-like eyes.

Back home, she had lived in an area that was far too open for goblins to find it accommodating; from what she understood, they preferred the closeness of thick forests or cities.

She had been thrilled at the prospect of getting acquainted with them when she first saw them, but unfortunately, none of them spoke the common tongue. They talked to one another in small, squeaking voices and seemed to avoid interacting with the others living in the house. Millie wouldn't be surprised if Vostesk Senior scared them into such behavior.

At least she had managed to become familiar enough to sit in their presence without unnerving them. Millie hoped that, eventually, she would be able to speak to them. Maybe then she wouldn't be so lonely, and they wouldn't have to feel so afraid.

She watched them run in and out of the room, sometimes walking on two legs, sometimes dropping to all four to hurry a little faster. One with scruffy brown hair was standing at the center of the table, squeaking directions to the others. Vostesk Senior paused to look at her when she came into the room, but once she sat and made no move to interrupt him, he continued with his work.

"I must thank you again," came the voice of the man she'd heard addressed as Berkley. It sounded fittingly posh for a man who wore a top hat, and when he hurried around the corner, she saw that he was brushing off the front of his coat primly."Your donation is appreciated greatly, as always. Honestly, I'm not sure the school would run without the likes of you."

"Oh, please. Every family in town with anything to offer is practically under obligation to do so. But I will accept the praise, nonetheless. And I do hope it's properly appreciated."

He noticed her as he finished speaking. Millie pretended she wasn't listening and fixed her attention on the goblins again, setting the last of the table and hurrying off to disappear into the kitchen. She wished she could join them.

"Ah," he said with a distinct chill in his voice. "Millana."

Millie grimaced internally. She hated her full name but stood for introduction to the rabbit-man Berkley all the same with as pleasant a smile as she could manage.

"Chairman Berkley, this is my new daughter-in-law. Millana Conwell."

Vostesk Senior put a hand on her back as she stood up and made her way over to them. It made her shudder. It didn't feel inappropriate; it was squarely in the middle of her back, and he wasn't eyeing her. But she always got the impression that any touching on his part was in some way a threat. His wife and Harlen flinched and went pale whenever he so much as brushed against them.

"Pleasure to meet you, Chairman," she said, trying her best to ignore the pressure on her back and to remember the manners her tutor had taught her as a girl. "And, please, Millana is so formal. Millie is just fine."

Vostesk Senior's fingers pressed into her back. It wasn't hard, but it was so sudden that it made her jump. The chairman didn't seem to notice. He kissed the back of her hand, brushing it with his twirled, twitchy mustache.

"Certainly, my dear, certainly," he said with a bright smile. He removed his top hat for the introduction and saw that his hair was white and pressed into perfect waves. "I do apologize that I wasn't able to make it to the wedding. Unfortunately, some matters simply cannot be put on hold. But I assure you that I much rather would have been there to congratulate the both of you than locked up in that stuffy record's room. I swear we need to hire someone to dust in there."

"I'm sure Millana doesn't want to hear about the dusting," Vostesk Senior said sharply. The chairman shrugged, and Millie was relieved to notice Harlen coming into the room with his mother in tow. He had his arm looped around hers so that it wasn't entirely obvious that she was leaning on him.

"Ah, Harlen! Good to see you again, my dear boy!" the chairman said brightly, again, apparently oblivious to the tense atmosphere and to how Mrs. Vostesk was looking at him. The poor woman seemed terrified of him. And her husband. Overall, she just looked frightened and confused and kept glancing up at Harlan as though he could explain what was happening. Millie felt awful for her and was glad that Harlen kept the greeting short and hurried to help her into her chair.

"Why is he here?" his mother whispered, looking at the chairman while Harlen put her napkin on her lap.

"He's visiting," Harlen explained quietly while Vostesk Senior ignored both of them and fell back into conversation with their guest. Millie took the chance to slip away from the two men talking business and hovered close to Harlen and his mother. He was smiling but tense. "Just for dinner."

Harlen moved to step away and find his seat, but the frail woman caught his hand. She looked up at him imploringly, like a child afraid of being left alone, and half-stood. Her napkin fell to the floor, and where she bumped the table, her crystal glass shook. "Where are you going?"

Harlen turned back to her and gently guided her back down in her chair. He knelt so he could be at eye level with her. Her lip trembled, and Mille could see tears welling in her eyes.

"I'm not going anywhere. I'm going to sit right here at the table with you, alright?"

She nodded and let go of him, folding her shaking hands in her lap. She still looked like she could cry but instead trained her eyes demurely on the floor.

Harlen searched for the napkin, but Millie bent and picked it up before he had to crawl around looking for it. She held it out to him, and he seemed surprised to see her standing there. He took it from her with a thank you and put it back in place.

"Is she going to be okay?" Millie asked as he stood up and slowly stepped away from her. She risked a quick look over at Vostesk Senior and Chairman Berkley and couldn't believe that neither of them had noticed what had just happened.

"She should be," Harlen said. But he didn't move far from his mother.

He sat in the chair beside her, pulling out the chair opposite himself for Millie to sit. As they both settled into their places, she tried to be polite both in her silence and in her brief attempts to contribute to the general conversation, but she couldn't keep her gaze from Mrs. Vostesk.

"Once she gets her bearings, she's usually alright," Harlen whispered, taking note of her curiosity. Luckily, he didn't seem to think it was rude. "She just gets a bit confused sometimes, and it frightens her."

"It's good that you help her," Millie said. Vostesk Senior and the chairman hadn't even spared the woman a glance since she had entered the room.

Harlen looked surprised again and moved his eyes to the floor in a way that, she realized, was quite similar to his mother. The gestures were almost identical.

She saw the faintest of smiles pull at the corner of his mouth, and he gave her a fleeting, shy glance out of the corner of his eye that vanished as his father and Chairman Berkley scraped out their chairs, took their seats, and began speaking over drinks as though nobody else was there.

Millie didn't pay much attention to what the two men were discussing as dinner commenced. She kept her attention mostly on her plate and Mrs. Vostesk.The tiny woman was staring dazed at her untouched food that Harlen carefully pushed in front of her. She would occasionally take the smallest of sips from her glass of champagne, lifting it to her lips with a trembling hand.

She at least seemed to have calmed down somewhat. However, Millie wasn't sure if being vacant was better than being outright confused.

"So, my dear boy." Chairman Berkley broke away from the conversation with Vostesk Senior at long last and turned towards them.

Harlen must not have been addressed in company often because he started, then tried to compensate with an overly attentive expression as the chairman pushed on. "It is so good that you'll be joining our ranks soon."

Harlen blinked. "I will?"

"Of course you will," his father said curtly, shooting him a look over the top of his glass that put Harlen's eyes back on the ground.

"I-I only thought after today. . ." Harlen spoke so quietly Millie could hardly understand him. With a glance at his father, she understood why; she had never seen such a cutting stare directed at anyone that wasn't despised.

Berkley waved one hand, shaking his head. "Oh, just a bit of stage fright, I'm sure. You're hardly the first student to get cold feet when it was time to be reviewed. It's a rare occasion indeed that a student shows their true potential under scrutiny. It's why nobody volunteers to go before the board."

He dabbed at his curled mustache with a napkin, wiping up the drops of drink clinging to it while he smiled fondly. "I think the only occasion we had a volunteer was that one time— she was hardly older than twelve and came running up to me once when I was here and begged to be evaluated—that sister of yours. Tansey."

Tansey. So that was the smiling girl's name. Millie wanted to ask about her and glanced at Harlen to see if it was alright. He had his eyes fixed firmly on the chairman and was sitting up straight for the first time all night.

"She did?" he asked, his voice tight.

"Oh yes, poor dear. She heard me talking about student examinations, and I think she was feeling a bit left out. Not that there was anything I could do for her given the circumstances, but she was very enthusiastic. Refreshing to see."

Harlen looked as though Berkley had slapped him across the face. He was staring and kept opening his mouth to speak but couldn't seem to form any words. Millie watched him and saw out of the corner of her eye that Mrs. Vostesk was sitting up straight too. She looked present again, and tears were spilling down her cheeks.

"Tansey?" she asked, a painfully hopeful note in her voice. Harlen heard her speak and turned around, standing, reaching out to touch her shoulder.

"Mother it's alright—"

"Where is she?" She looked at the chairman with her big, wet eyes, apparently not even feeling Harlen's hand on her arm. "Where is my little girl?"

Vostesk Senior hit the table so hard that the silverware rattled. Millie jumped so severely she nearly fell out of her chair. Mrs. Vostesk let out a little cry of surprise, then put a hand over her mouth and folded right back up into herself. She stared at the shaken table, tears dripping off her face. Harlen had sat back down so quickly that Millie had hardly seen him move. He was white and rigid and was staring down at his plate. Berkley even seemed startled.

"I told you that we weren't to discuss her at family gatherings," Vostesk Senior said in his smooth, even voice that was somehow more intimidating than shouting. "Look how much you've upset everyone. Look at my wife."

Berkley's rabbit-like features flushed bright red against all his white. He took a moment to smooth his suit's vest before turning to the table and saying in a far less cheerful voice than he had been using, "Yes. Well. My sincerest apologies. I seem to have forgotten myself."

The dining room was horribly quiet. The chairman smiled at them all awkwardly, then sank back into his chair and quickly lifted his glass back to his mouth. Millie sat stunned, gripping the edges of the seat hard where she had grabbed it to keep from falling.

The only sound was the noise of Mrs. Vostesk's quiet sniffling that she had both hands pressed to her mouth to suppress. Vostesk Senior had fixed his pale eyes on her, and after a moment of staring like he was trying to will her to stop crying, he said, "Harlen. Take your mother to her room. Clearly, she's having an unpleasant time."

"I can help," Millie added quickly, jumping at the chance to get away. Harlen didn't seem to need any further prompting either. He was already kneeling, trying to coax her hands away from her mouth while she shook her head violently. Over her shoulder, Millie glanced in time to see Vostesk Senior standing and motioning for the chairman to follow him towards the sitting room.

Millie almost felt bad for the man. He looked like he wanted to follow the rest of them in their retreat into the house, but he stood and followed Vostesk Senior's long, pale brown ponytail.

"He said her name," she was saying through her fingers. "He said her name; why would he say that? Where is she?"

"Mother." Harlen was trying, but he was obviously as shaken as she was. His hands trembled while he attempted to get her to stand up, and he seemed at a loss for comforting things to tell her. "I know. I know it's been a long time, but please. Please, you need to follow me. We can talk about her upstairs, mother, please—"

She wasn't listening to him and was getting more agitated. Her voice was slowly rising. "No! Where is she? I want to see her!"

Harlen looked anxiously back at the door his father had just gone through. Millie didn't know what to do. She was hovering close behind Harlen, looking around the room, hoping that something would show her what to do. And when it didn't, she just said the first thing that came to mind.

"Mrs. Vostesk—did you want anything to take upstairs with you?"

Mrs. Vostesk turned to look at her. Millie blindly reached onto the table and picked up one of the thick white rolls from its dish, and held it up where she could see. It was a stupid idea, but she didn't want Vostesk Senior coming back into the room.

"I wanted to ask. You didn't have dinner. I wanted to know. . .if you wanted to take anything with you." She rambled on for a moment and watched the brightness in the woman's eyes slowly fade. It sent a chill through her, and she stopped speaking while Mrs. Vostesk once again looked at Harlen in confusion.

"We're going upstairs, alright? I'll take you," he said, a smile meant to be comforting that showed nothing but the pure, jittering nerves behind it plastered on his face.

She nodded, once again vacant. Harlen helped her to her feet, and Millie stood on her other side, just in case, and together they took her upstairs.

Harlen sat her gently on her bed, and she sat on the edge of it, staring ahead at nothing. Harlen tried speaking to her for a moment, but his mother didn't seem to hear him. He settled instead for slipping off her shoes, earrings, and necklace before turning her on the bed so she could lie down. She let him move her, and it reminded Millie hauntingly of how she used to dress her dolls.

Millie stood back and watched this process from the doorway, feeling like an intruder. She wanted to offer some help but wasn't sure if that would be right. Millie felt like she was watching something private. That perhaps she shouldn't even be there. But when Harlen finally got back to his feet and pulled her bedroom door shut with a sigh, she was glad she stayed. Because once he was safely back out in the hallway, he finally put one of his still shaking hands to his mouth and closed his eyes momentarily. He looked as though he might be sick, and she reached up to place a reassuring hand on his arm.

At first, she felt him flinch at the unexpected touch. His eyes snapped open, and he tensed like a scared rabbit, then; as he looked at her and realized the gesture was meant to be comforting, she felt him relax ever so slightly.

"I'm sorry about all this," he said once he had gathered himself enough to speak. "It's ah—a lot. I know."

It was. It was, and Millie was nodding before she could stop herself.

"My father is. Well." Harlen swallowed.

That didn't need explaining. Instead, Harlen gestured back to the room where his mother was likely still lying and staring blankly at the swimming sharks in churning waves painted on the ceiling. "And she's alright. Really. She just gets. . .a little dazed sometimes. She's harmless. I promise. I'm sorry if she might have scared you. She doesn't mean to."

"She didn't," Millie assured him. And she hadn't. Mrs. Vostesk didn't unsettle her because she was frightening. She unsettled her because she seemed so unbearably hollow. If the evening made her feel any way about her, it had been to make her feel pity for the frail woman. "And your father is. . .well. . ."

Millie allowed her sentence to trail off as well, and Harlen smiled in a way that didn't quite reach his eyes. "But I do like to think it takes a bit more to scare me than one bad dinner party."

That was minimizing matters, perhaps. But it did make Millie feel a bit better to at least sound brave. And that time, when Harlen smiled, it did reach his eyes.

He reached up and very briefly touched the hand she'd put on his arm. A little gesture of thanks that was quick but sincere before he said, "Even so. Why don't you stay up here? I know it's miserable down there."

"What will you tell them?" she asked, then urging him on with a bit of a smile of her own, she said, "That my delicate, feminine constitution had been exposed to too much business talk for one night?"

Successfully, she had managed to make his eyes a little brighter. "I wouldn't say that so loud. They might believe it if they hear you say it."

"That sounds tempting if it means I would be excused from all family dinners in the future. Shame you can't use the excuse."

She was glad she managed to help push away some of the heaviness hanging over him. She was sure she hadn't managed to clear away everything bothering him or that she even understood everything going on enough to do so, but for a moment, he seemed lighter.

He gave the small, breathy laugh that sounded nearly like a cough she'd slowly been getting used to—she hadn't managed to get a real, full-body laugh from him yet—and stepped back from her.

"Are you sure you don't need me to come back down there?" she asked, admittedly relieved when he shook his head.

"I'll be alright," he said.

She wasn't entirely sure about that. She lingered in the hall, watching him make his way back toward the grand staircase. He looked back only once and gave her one last strained smile before descending out of view.

CHAPTER 5

Once Harlen left, Millie let the door close softly. As always, the sound of the lock that bumped against the door frame was jarring. There was one on the outside of every bedroom except for Vostesk Senior's. She guessed it was because he was probably the one who had put them there. Though for what reasons, she'd only been able to imagine. And she had had plenty of time to speculate.

Ever since she had arrived, she'd felt a constant sense of unease. At first, she'd contributed it to nerves. She was well and truly away from home for the first time in her life, separated from her family by miles and miles of grassy fields and dusty roads.

Millie had only found out about her impending marriage a month before it happened. She felt like she hardly had the time to say goodbye to the place where she had grown up. And she only had that small amount of time because she had realized that something strange was going on.

Her father had been spending a curious amount of time in his office, meeting with far too many strangers for it not to provoke curiosity in a household with four girls. Millie and her sisters had been speculating about what he was doing for quite some time and were suspicious that it had something to do with either death or marriage—one of the only two things that could be the reason for such secrecy.

They had debated among themselves to try and satisfy their curiosity once they realized they had all been wondering about it. Their debate lasted only a day before they chose Rhoslyn to eavesdrop on one of his meetings. She was the youngest and, as such, got in the least amount of trouble for anything.

She had come tearing through the garden like a fox with its tail on fire to find them all afterward. The verdict was a marriage for Millie. To someone in the Vostesk family. She had felt her heart drop once the words were out of Roslyn's mouth.

The Vostesk family was known for two things: having a powerful magical history and being the coldest group of unsmiling people anyone had ever met. The very thought of leaving the sunny, flower-filled mountainside where she had grown up to live on the rainy coast away from her family and everything she had ever known terrified her. But here she was, all the same.

She had been living under a perpetual gray cloud that never seemed to stop drizzling rain down on the dreary little town like the sky itself was crying over the small bent buildings beside the sea—a city where she knew nobody, least of all her new husband. But as time had worn on, she realized that her nerves had far more to do with her husband's father.

When she first laid eyes on Vostesk Senior, she had thought for one horrifying moment that he was the one she was supposed to marry. He looked markedly young for a man in his fifties, so she was inclined to believe that his claims of having elf's blood in his lineage somewhere were valid. He had a rather unlined face and wore his hair slicked and tied neatly back into a long ponytail. She remembered thinking that he looked like someone who had never smiled in his life and that he had the most unsettling, pale eyes she'd ever seen.

Her relief at discovering that he was not, in fact, the Harlen Vostesk she was going to be marrying had been enough to make her legs go weak. Instead, it was his son. Who, by contrast, was one of the most skittish looking people she'd ever seen, with the saddest pair of brown eyes she had ever seen.

He was so tall and so skeletally thin, and he'd kept twisting at that little button on his sleeve. All during their first meeting, he reminded her of a starved, wild cat with the way he kept darting his eyes around and flinching. He had been red as a rose for their introduction and stumbled over his words so severely he was hardly understandable.

She'd felt sorry for him but assumed that it was just a result of being introduced to his bride hours before the ceremony. She wasn't the most articulate herself that day, she was sure, for the same reason. She had been laughing too loudly and making a joke out of too many things to try and make herself less anxious in the hope she could somehow make the situation less awkward.

During the ceremony itself, when it had come time to kiss her, he had missed her mouth entirely. She had been so nervous she'd let slip a giggle that she was sure hurt his feelings. He didn't try to kiss her again and sat wordlessly beside her for the rest of the night.

She had been sure she'd managed to destroy everything on day one. She managed to make him hate her from the outset. But once they were out from the public eye in their bedroom, he'd admitted that he was just, well, terrified is what she thought fit the lengthy, rambling apology he went off on best.

He was wringing his hands and looked like he thought she would reach out and strike him at any moment while explaining himself, apologizing for the attempt at a kiss and about seemingly everything he'd done since their meeting. She hadn't even known what to say. She had just stared at him thinking he might faint at any moment.

There was, unsurprisingly, no consummating the marriage. It had taken Harlen a few days even to look her in the eye, and she'd been sure he was either terrified of her or despised her until she'd finally gotten him to laugh one afternoon. She couldn't even remember what she had said. She was so surprised to hear such a thing from him, and he looked like he'd startled himself.

Only then, like she had shoved him over some invisible hurdle, had he spoken more. He would situate himself near her to read or write, casting glances at her when he thought she wasn't looking.

He looked at her like she was some great curiosity and always seemed to be afraid of interrupting her before he spoke. At least, he would talk to her now and didn't seem quite as timid as before. And much to her relief, he seemed harmless. Extremely awkward, to be sure, but he wasn't frightening. As such, she could no longer convince herself that it was her new husband, causing her unease.

The house had an unsettling air to it. It was so quiet. Even the little goblins who staffed the place managed not to make any noise unless nobody else was around. She wished she could understand the little chirping, squeaking sounds they made to one another. She wanted to make sure she wasn't the only one who felt like there was a distinct wrongness in the air.

She knew Harlen's father mistreated him in some way. That was no mystery. He flinched too much at sudden loud voices or quick movements and seemed like he was about to crawl out of his skin every time Vostesk Senior was around.

And every time Harlen thought he had offended her or done something wrong in her presence, the fearful look he would give her had her wishing they were closer so she could breach the topic enough to let him know she wasn't going to hurt him.

She wished she knew what to do about any of it. She had been writing letters home, but they were coming along slowly. She got far too sick at heart, asking how everyone was doing and would have to put her pen aside to do something else to keep from crying. She was sure that she would never stop if she let herself cry once over her lost home and family. But she desperately needed advice and had no idea where else to get it.

So far, she had completed three letters but had mailed none. She didn't like the idea of handing off her things to Vostesk Senior and kept them tucked carefully in her trunk, determined to post them herself when the rain stopped. She didn't know her way around town but convinced herself she could find anything with a few hours of wandering. Everything here was so cramped together she couldn't imagine it would take longer.

The rain, however, seemed to have no end. It hadn't stopped for more than a few moments to take a breath before pouring down a new, torrential wave, and she was beginning to consider throwing caution to the wind and going out searching anyway. She was going to get sick eventually with how bone-cold this dreadful place was.

More than anything, she just wanted to hear from them. She had never gone longer than a few hours without one of her parents or siblings speaking to her, and now it was like they had never existed at all. She missed her mother, who would listen with at least feigned concern while she complained about the weather, and her sisters, who would commiserate with her and tease her about her husband's shyness.

Even her father, who she had been determined to hate forever for sending her here, she couldn't manage to think about without wishing to see him again. She missed the rolling fields of trees and flowers. She missed the sun. She missed home.

She stared at herself in the black-framed mirror and saw her eyes begin to well up. She bit her lip and took a deep breath, blinking hard. She wouldn't let herself start. She wouldn't. Instead, she tried to admire the work Harlen had done on her hair. It was very simple but pretty, pinned up carefully on one side but still left mostly loose. She couldn't have done it better herself.

She tried to tell herself that this showed there was some measure of care he had for her. She would have to take comfort in that for the time being.

CHAPTER 6

Harlen heard his father and Chairman Berkley speaking in murmuring voices on his way back through the dining room. The goblins had emerged from the kitchen again and were whisking plates away, unperturbed by his presence as he slowed his steps and listened to see if his father was still agitated.

"It has been a long time Berkley. Years and years of trying everything I can think of with no result." His father's voice sounded tired and weighed down.

There was no trace of the anger that had been there just moments ago, only frustration that held no real bite. "Sometimes, I feel as though I've tried everything there is to get that boy to show some sign of what's in him. I know it's there—I do. It has to be."

Harlen slowed even more, reluctant to step into the room. How many times had his father reminded him of their family history? How many times had his father gone on about the fantastic magical feats of their ancestors; while shaking with rage, claiming his son must have that same power inside of him? As though he didn't remember his great ancestors enough every time he looked at those portraits lining the hallways and every time he had to read yet another spellbook that was useless in his hands and bore the name Vostesk on its binding. He had been under their eyes and in their shadow for his entire life, and not for one moment had he ever forgotten.

Harlen had tried giving himself a better outlook on it. Telling himself over and over that their blood was inside him; he just had to work hard enough, and it would make him better. But deep down, in some part of his mind that he tried hard to ignore, there was a thought he could never quite shake. The idea that his blood didn't matter. The magic he knew had been waning for generations had simply decided to vanish before it touched him.

"My dear friend, don't look so down," Berkley said as Harlen forced his mind back to the present. The chairman evidently bounced back from the outburst earlier and was back to speaking in his enthusiastic manner.

"The Academy has coaxed magic out of the most hopeless of individuals for decades. And believe it or not, that wasn't the worst introduction I've ever seen. There was one incident quite some time ago—back when I was a new member—when a fellow with an inclination towards fire got so nervous, he set the table itself ablaze. That was a gruesome affair."

"You aren't helping," his father grumbled.

"Well, how about this, then? We already have one of the board who has volunteered to oversee his lessons."

"Is he that new fellow?" his father asked as Harlen finally decided it was safe to step into the room.

He walked in quietly, slipping in unnoticed beneath the cover of the sound of rain on the window. The entire wall of the room that faced the front of the house was nothing but glass, floor to ceiling. It let in the gray light from outside and offered a view of the pitiful garden. A garden that was nothing more than a few sad bushes Tansey had planted long ago. He hadn't thought they would survive the first real rainstorm, but somehow years had passed, and still, they refused to die.

The rain beat against the window like a thousand tapping fingers. Against the other room wall, yet another fireplace crackled and popped in its vain attempt to keep the air warm. Harlen's father stood leaning on the polished mantle with a glass of brandy in hand while the chairman stood separated from him by the spindly refreshment table, pouring himself a full glass.

"New fellow he is, indeed," Berkley said, carefully raising his cup in agreement. "And he's got wonderful talent."

His father seemed unimpressed. He had finally noticed Harlen's entrance out of the corner of his eye and fixed him to the spot with a long, cold look. He let the silence stretch just long enough to become awkward before saying, "Did your wife find us too dull?"

"She wasn't. . .feeling well," Harlen managed, sure that the lie didn't hold under that icy stare. Luckily, Berkley seemed to have taken in enough drink to jump right in without hesitation, clicking his tongue.

"Probably frightened, the poor thing," he said. Harlen wasn't sure if he had forgotten his father's outburst or if this was just another slip-up of his, but much to his relief, his father merely shrugged.

"If she's so easily put off, she has no business in serious conversation."

"I understand I shouldn't have brought up—the subject. But perhaps a kind word or two wouldn't go amiss?" The chairman was tilting his head, trying to catch his father's eye. "It might help her feel more settled."

His father glared at him. "That's my son's concern. Not mine. And stop with the staring Berkley; you know that doesn't work on me. Try it on her if you want her to feel settled so badly."

That was the end of that. Berkley flushed at being caught and took another quick sip from his drink. Harlen thought he should be grateful his father hadn't backhanded him for trying to use his little magical talent on him.

"Apologies," Berkley muttered.

His father rolled his shoulders with a sigh. "Just tell me more about this new fellow."

Berkley cleared his throat and resumed conversation with his father, for which Harlen was grateful. He was glad to place himself near the window in one of the twin armchairs and stare at the softly glowing light atop the candles that sat on the table that divided them. He kept his eyes on the little, dancing flame but kept his ears trained carefully on what his father and the chairman were saying.

The entire situation seemed strange to him. As far as he knew, his father had always been intensely secretive about his offspring's lack of magical talent. He had gone as far as barring both him and Tansey from leaving the house beyond the bounds of the black wrought-iron gate.

The only ones who knew about their condition were his father's closest friends. The ones who could be trusted not to spread the word around. The sudden change of heart in releasing him to attend an institution separated from the house, out in the relative public, confused Harlen. It seemed like the perfect setup for a public embarrassment to the family. Was his father growing *that* desperate?

He couldn't understand the reasoning to it, try as he might. However, that could have been because he was a bit distracted. Of all things, he hadn't expected Tansey to come up in conversation at dinner.

The mention of her had thrown him. Ever since she had vanished, nobody inside the house had been allowed to speak about her. Outside his mother's mutterings when she was too out of her mind on her opium to even know where she was, he hadn't heard her name said aloud by anyone in years. Not since that morning when he was seventeen.

CHAPTER 7

He had woken late that day. Far later than he had ever been allowed to sleep in. He had opened his eyes to the chiming of the grandfather clock and remembered lying there, counting its rings, hoping that it was still early enough that he would have time to lay in bed before the day began. But as the chimes kept sounding, he realized that it was nearly noon.

He sat up as the eleventh and final chime rang out and faded, leaving emptiness in its wake. The sensation that filled the house raised the hair on the back of his neck.

Something was wrong. Harlen knew in his heart; something was deeply wrong.

He had burst out into the hall, still in his nightclothes with his heart in his throat. In his mind's eye, he could see with perfect clarity what had greeted him as soon as he came flying out of his room: the long line of closed doors with Tansey's at the end hanging open like a slack jaw.

He had approached, calling for her with growing panic, and had thrown it open to see her room just as it always was. Her bed was unmade. The vanity was a mess of bottles, crumpled pages of drawings she started but didn't like, and books discarded face-down. It all framed her wide-open window. The curtains fluttering with a mocking calm on the morning breeze.

She had been sneaking out for years by that time. She had always pushed the bounds of their father's confinement, a venture he had never been brave enough to join. However, he knew she went in and out through her bedroom window once their father locked himself in his study each evening. So Harlen's first thought on seeing the window left open was that her luck had run out. Their father had caught her. And the idea terrified him.

He had warned her. He had warned her a hundred times that if their father or one of his friends ever found out, there would be hell and more to pay. She always laughed, saying he worried too much in a tone of voice that suggested she was speaking to a worried child. He was frustrated that she never listened, but he never wanted her to get caught. Not when he knew what would happen if she was.

The sound of voices pulled him down the stairs at a run, and he sprinted to the dining room where they seemed to be coming from. He knew she would be there and that their father would be hurting her. He was punishing her for what she had done.

He had no plan or idea of what he was going to do to stop it. He only knew he had to help her. He had torn into the room so fast he slammed into the doorframe but hardly noticed he had bloodied his nose. He expected to see his sister being beaten within an inch of her life. Instead, he had been greeted by his father talking to some stern-looking town guardsmen in long black coats.

They delivered the news in a far too detached and clinical way for the weight of what they said. She was gone. Missing. Vanished into thin air.

It seemed impossible. Harlen always believed if anything happened to her when she slipped out of the house, he would know. Twins were supposed to be able to sense that sort of thing about each other; he had read that somewhere. He thought of it when he lay awake, waiting for the sound of her window sliding shut to signal she had returned safely and unnoticed. But that night, he hadn't heard it.

She must have left later than usual because he had fallen asleep before he even heard her go. Try as he might, he couldn't remember hearing the distinct click of the window's latch pushing outward that signaled her departure.

He had been sitting up at his desk and nodded off over some writing, and when he had woken up for just long enough to roll himself into bed, it had been nearly two in the morning. He could have sworn he still heard Tansey walking around in her room and had thought nothing of it and so went right back to sleep. He was mistaken; the result of his moment of carelessness was devastating.

He had never gone with her to protect her. He had only ever stayed up to listen to make sure she came back. That was all he ever did for her, and he had fallen asleep the one time she might have needed him to notice something was wrong.

That had been the last day anyone had said her name inside the walls of the Vostesk house. He always thought the day someone would say it would be when they finally received some news of where she was or what had happened to her.

Or perhaps one day, she would simply walk back into the house as though she'd never gone, with as little fuss as she'd left. Speaking about her would be of no more consequence than it had been six years ago.

Since the day she disappeared, he had not been expecting her first mention to be such a nonchalant statement by a man who hardly knew her. It felt wrong, and it still unbalanced him.

Sitting in the armchair beside the window, he tried settling his mind while his father and Berkley chatted, apparently forgetting he was in the room at all. Ordinarily, it would have left him feeling awkward and struggling to find some way to place himself into whatever they were talking about, but tonight it gave him some time to collect his thoughts. It wasn't until the time his father began to escort his guest to the door that he felt he had regained his composure as much as he could.

The chairman put on his white top hat and coat at the door, rosy from the champagne and brandy. As Harlen approached to say the proper, polite goodbyes, Berkley did not scrimp on the niceties and that they simply must do this more often. He shook both of their hands with great enthusiasm and assured them many times over that The Academy was going to be lovely.

Harlen feared his feigned excitement might not be convincing, but in the end, Berkley seemed satisfied that he convinced them both that this was the most beautiful thing in the world, and he strolled out the door with a spring in his step like he had just been to a party rather than a family dinner.

"I think that man is a might too optimistic," his father said once the door was closed, peering out the long, thin windows that stood on either side of the massive oak frame.

The silver moonlight streaming through small spaces in the clouds turned his father's pale eyes nearly white as he watched Berkley walk off in the rain that had slowed to a drizzle, which in Wakefield passed for pleasant weather.

Harlen followed his gaze out of courtesy but kept a careful watch on his father. He had no doubts in his mind about what was coming and flinched out of habit when the man turned his gaze on him suddenly.

"What do you think about this?" he asked. The moonlight made half of his father's severe face glow in a way that could have been soft were it not for the stern set of his brows and jaw.

Harlen knew it wasn't a question. Not really. It couldn't be. It was a test of some kind. It always was. His father expected him to say something, and he scrambled in the far corners of his brain for something to meet the expectant gaze fixed on him. "He seems optimistic."

"I didn't ask about him, did I?"

Harlen swallowed and tried again. He felt a familiar coldness in the pit of his stomach. "No. No, you did—you didn't. Um." Despite the cold, he knew he was beginning to sweat. That stare was unbearable.

"We both know you don't believe in this," his father said. "I saw the way you looked at him when he started talking about it."

His voice was calm, and Harlen knew that meant danger. He said nothing, hoping there would be less of a chance for him to say the wrong thing that way.

With his eyes on the floor, Harlan felt rather than saw his father's face fill with disdain. It descended like a physical weight, and he knew what was coming before he heard the dreaded, familiar words.

"Meet me in the basement," he said. "Your lessons are long overdue. If today has shown me anything, it's that we have a lot to work on." There it was.

Harlen nodded and began his walk toward the door at the back of the kitchen. He felt the familiar wave of nausea that always accompanied his trips through the small, cramped kitchen where the goblins lived in their little beds on the shelf above the stove. Ten pairs of their glowing eyes he was sure held sympathy watched him as he passed by to push the wooden door open with shaking hands and descended the narrow, creaking steps with numb legs.

CHAPTER 8

If it was chilly upstairs, then the basement was bitterly cold. The air smelled like damp earth and of the dust that settled on the shelves where food in jars, crates of old clothes, and a hundred other things were stored and forgotten.

The only thing not covered in dust when he reached the bottom of the stairs was the battered tin lantern that he lit with a practiced hand. It spat bitter-smelling, jumping flames that cast twitching shadows on the walls once the fire caught. It somehow only made the basement seem darker as he made his way through the rows of shelves to the back room.

It was a room where things like salt, sugar, and wine were stored once upon a time. Harlen still had some vague memories of it the way it used to be, but looking at it in the pulsing light of the lamp, it seemed impossible that it had ever been anything but the place in all the world he hated most.

The hook in the center of the ceiling was waiting for him to hang the lamp upon it. He did so and let it bring everything else in the room into view.

The chair: the rough wooden chair with leather straps on the legs and arms. The table laid with gleaming instruments and the long, leaping shadows they threw across its surface—small, sharp blades for biting into the skin. Little bits of metal to be heated inside the sputtering flames of the lamp and pressed against flesh. The long straps of leather for leaving welts and bruises that would last and ache for days. And the book. The book that was the cause of it all in the center of the table.

He had never been allowed to read it, which had struck him as one of the cruelest injustices of all. If he was to be subject to what it said, he should at least be allowed to look at it.

Not to say he had no idea what was inside its pages. His one, small act of rebellion had been sneaking looks here and there where he was able. He still did not understand it entirely. But he knew its general meaning.

It was an old book. The kind that gets passed down in noble families for generations. It was full of diagrams of bodies. Human, elvish, goblin, and many, many more.

It had passages on observations concerning the development of magical talent, from strong natural-born magic to the faintest touch needed to perform higher alchemy. How to watch for it in children, how to encourage it. And, when none was observed, how to draw it out.

"I have observed invariably in all forms of magic, no matter how small, one common trait that remains persistent. Magic dwells in its host's blood and will, without fail, rise to protect the host. Even in cases where the magic lies sleeping, dormant, or seemingly non-existent, I have proven that so long as it is present, it can be drawn out with the proper encouragement."

The passage remained blazed in Harlen's mind, so clearly, he could have recited it while sleeping. It was the cause of what he had to experience. The reason for this room. The reason his father spent hours poring over the pages and its diagrams, finding new ways to inflict pain. To do whatever it took to draw the magic out of his blood.

How long had he been doing this? Almost twenty-three years now. No. That wasn't quite right. His father hadn't begun these desperate measures until he was sure that he and his sister had no magic. He was eight then, but it was long enough for it to feel as though this had been going on for his entire life. Long enough for it to feel normal, but not so normal that he didn't feel terrible shame at the prospect of others knowing what happened down here.

He turned away from the book. He began removing his jacket and shirt as he had done countless times, leaving him shivering. His patchwork of deeply scarred skin looked even more inhuman, with the flickering light casting its bizarre shadows. He took his seat in the chair with a steadiness that came after years of resignation, knowing that a fight would only make the inevitable moment when the leather straps tightened worse.

Tansey would have fought this, he thought, startling himself. Then, he surprised himself even more with the thought that responded. *Tansey never had to.*

He shook his head to clear the thoughts away. That wasn't fair. Anyway, it wasn't as though he had never tried.

He had tried for years. He had begged and cried and even tried to run. But what could he do against his father? He was larger and far more physically capable. And above all, he had magic. There was no way for him to combat that.

He felt nausea and dizziness tilting the room on its axis as he heard his father's footsteps descending the stairs. They drew closer and paused for a moment in the doorway, his shadow looming like a vision from a nightmare before saying, "Very well. Let's begin. We don't have all night."

And begin it did. And once it did, it seemed to have no end. What felt like hours passed beneath the flickering lamp in a haze of failed concentration and pain, uttering spells that began to make less and less sense in his mouth and his head as the smell of blood and burned lamp oil blurred together. Pains melted into one another until he couldn't remember why parts of his body hurt and why others didn't. He only understood that there was one way to make it stop, and it was something beyond his reach no matter how hard he strained to take hold of it.

His father's eyes burned bright in the dark, the pain of a sharp knife sinking into his skin while his bare arms strained against tight leather straps that bit into him.

"Focus. Focus your pain! You're not trying hard enough!"

Harlen panted, his half-naked body shivering in the cold dampness of the cellar. With the chill of his sweat clinging to him and the coldness of the blood dripping down his arm. The rune drawn on the paper shoved under one of his hands was illuminated by the flickering lamp, staring up at him like a mocking smile.

You can't. You can't do it.

Harlen focused on the rune. He stared and focused until he saw spots swimming in front of his eyes. He repeated the words of the spell over and over until he felt pain blossom behind his eyes, and a new trickle of blood ran down from his nose. The rune remained unchanged. Just ink on paper. Nothing more.

Then, far more suddenly than it had begun, it was over. Harlen's father let out a long, sharp sigh of frustration and shut the book with a bang.

"Get out," he snapped.

Harlen's vision was blurry as he struggled to free himself from the chair, but he managed. He stood and gathered his clothes as quickly as he could, hastily putting them back on as he hurried up the stairs and shut the basement door at the top. His father always wanted his solitude after their lessons and likely wouldn't be up for hours. He would be pouring over the book in misery, trying to discover why it wasn't working.

Harlen could never understand why he persisted, whether it was pride or shame that drove his insistence that he couldn't be wrong about magic being in his son's blood. But Harlen had no energy to think about it any harder than a passing consideration.

As soon as he closed the basement door, the fear that had kept every sense heightened for what must have been hours began to ebb away; he felt exhaustion welling up to fill the space it left in him. It seeped into his bones, and he wondered if he would even be able to climb the steps of the grand staircase that would take him back to the relative safety of his bedroom.

Perhaps he would sit on them and rest for a few minutes. The chilly air drifting under the front door always seemed to pool around the base of those stairs. Perhaps that would help clear his head.

He stepped out of the kitchen, through the dining room, and into the main entrance. All the lamps had gone out, and each fireplace had burned down to embers. The house was dark aside from the dim moonlight creeping through cracks in the heavy curtains. There was no sound aside from the rain on the roof and the ticking of the grandfather clock.

He struggled up the grand staircase, every nerve in his body begging for him to collapse against the railing. He knew if he did allow himself to sit, he wouldn't make himself get up again. So he struggled to the top, and then to his bedroom, where he opened the door with shaking fingers.

Harlen eased the door open carefully and was glad that he did when he saw Millie sleeping. She was lying on top of the blankets, curled like a sleeping cat in her nightdress, her evening gown draped over the desk chair. Her hair was still half up where he had put it earlier, but it had come loose on the side where her face pressed into the bed.

He briefly considered waking her up to let her know he had returned but thought better of it. Instead, he sank onto the far edge of the bed for a moment and ran his hands back through his hair that was damp with sweat, enjoying the dimness and silence of the room aside from the sound of Millie's breathing. It was soft and low, nothing like the metallic scrapes and rattling in the basement.

It was something he had never considered: the sound of another person aside from himself sharing the space the green and blue bedroom had to offer. It had been one of the more pleasant surprises that came with the sudden matrimony. He liked the sound of her moving around during the day, of her breathing and turning over at night. It gave his thoughts less free reign. And made the room seem far less lonely.

Even if she didn't know what happened in the basement, it was nice not to come back to an empty room.

The sound helped him relax his breathing from the shaking gasps he had been dragging into his lungs and helped ease the lingering twitching of his hands. It didn't make him feel calm per se, but he did feel better than he had. Somehow it helped him pull himself together enough to stand and pad into the washroom.

Silently as he could, he shut and locked the door with its satisfying click and stripped off his rumpled, sweaty clothing while the tub filled with water. He washed the sweat and blood from his body and pressed his fingers over his eyes as he lay in the water, trying to ease some of the lingering pain behind them.

He had suffered from a bout of migraines a few years back, around the time Tansey vanished. He had guessed it was a side effect of the stress, but they had gone away after a few months. These teaching sessions, however, seemed to aggravate the throbbing pain that still lurked in his skull. Luckily, most of the time, he could get them to go away with some hot water and some firm pressure.

When he got out, he cleaned and bandaged the new wounds with an expert hand that only shook a little. He dressed slowly, carefully, wincing at the tender places in his flesh that were sure to leave new marks on his body. He did his very best not to look in the mirror as he did so,

By the time he finished, he had finally managed to calm down or to become as close to calm as could be, and all he could think about was falling into bed. The thought of the thick blue-green blankets and crisp white sheets had never sounded so inviting. But there was one last thing he needed to attend.

He was never afforded much privacy in his life. His bedroom offered only the illusion of solitude; a shut door meant nothing when the only lock was on the door's outside, and only his father had the key. Everything he ever did, read, or wrote would somehow be found out.

His father had made it very clear over the years by bringing things up in casual conversation that he should not have known about, that there was nothing in this house that was truly a private matter. But there was one small thing Harlen had managed to create, that as far as he knew, was entirely his own.

Harlen reached into the back of the cabinet beside the wall-mounted mirror over the sink where he had gotten his soap and bandages and pressed on the wood panel at the cabinet's very back until it gave with the smallest of scraping sounds.

From there, it was easy to pry off the wooden board to reveal the small space he had created inside the wall. It was no bigger than a shoebox. But it was the only thing that was undoubtedly his—one of his small rebellions.

He had read about the idea in some story or another, and one day he had been mad enough to try it for himself. He had no idea how he had been bold enough to carve a simple rectangle out of the wall itself and felt a mix of excitement and dread every time he remembered it was there. It was his own, but if his father ever found out about it, he would be livid.

Fortunately, only the little goblins ever stocked the cabinets. Harlen's father considered such things beneath him, which in this case, worked to Harlen's advantage. As did the fact that though he couldn't communicate with them verbally, he knew enough about the goblin's passing glances and body language around the man to see that they had little love for his father. He couldn't imagine them showing it to him if one of them found it.

He never had much to keep there. Over time he had collected a small stash of his own money, but nothing substantial. He had a small poetry book and a little seagull carved from polished wood that Tansey had brought him from one of her nightly excursions. It was hardly larger than his thumb, but she had been so excited to have what she called "a real present" to give him for their seventeenth birthday. The last one they had together.

There was one other thing in the wall he had kept from her, and he breathed a sigh of relief when he found it still in its place. A folded piece of stationary slowly growing yellow at the edges: Tansey's list.

Every morning after she would return from her trips, she would tell him about all the places she'd visited and the people she'd met. She would sit on the floor for hours with him, weaving the night's events into art with bright words. She made every place sound enchanted, every person blazingly alive. He was sure she had to have exaggerated certain things, but her telling of it had been so beautiful that he never cared.

After she disappeared, he was careful to remember and write down each one. Every place, every name. He had always had an excellent memory. He hadn't forgotten a thing.

He didn't know why he kept the list and knew even less about what he intended to do with it, especially all these years later. He had thought to give it to those guardsmen if they ever returned, but he had seen no more of them after that first day. He had tried to pose the idea to his father, but there had been no room for suggestions with him.

It just felt too important to let go. Harlen hung onto the possibility that there was something there: that she had somehow known or planned what would happen and had hidden some kind of trail for him to follow.

He knew it was childish and unlikely enough to be impossible, but it was all the hope he had that her vanishing hadn't merely been, well, that. Her disappearing with no reason or explanation. Maybe forever. He needed to hold on to something.

CHAPTER 9

A footstep in the bedroom sounded, and in a second, he had the list back in its place and wedged the panel back into the wall. He stood, heart, beating in his throat, staring at the locked door.

He expected his father to open it, somehow knowing what he was doing, but instead, there was a soft knock.

"Harlen? Are you in there?"

Millie. He crossed the floor quickly and opened the door for her. She had the kind of dazed look about her that said she had just woken up, and she blinked her big, gray eyes at him slowly. The other half of her hair had come loose and tumbled over her shoulder, fully wild again.

He had never been so relieved to see her. "Sorry. I didn't mean to wake you up."

"You didn't—I was just resting my eyes," she said, though she had been fully asleep when he had sat down across from her. She looked half asleep still—and cold. She was hugging her bare arms and standing rigidly. It was getting late, and any lingering heat from the fireplaces burning that day had long since gone.

"Here." He unhooked the dressing robe he'd hung on the back of the door and held it out to her. She stared at it for a moment, putting her hand on the thick, dark gray fabric. "This might help."

She didn't need further convincing. She took it and pulled it on, and while it was big enough to reach nearly her ankles and positively swallowed her hands, she didn't seem to mind. She seemed to enjoy it. Her eyes grew brighter, and by the time she had finished folding herself into it, she looked at him with a smile.

"Not to be too forward, but this smells wonderful." She brought the sleeve up to her nose, a spark of teasing in her eyes. "Do you perfume your dressing gowns around here?"

Harlen felt his cheeks turn red, and a hand jumped to tug at the ends of his short hair. When it had been longer, he would have twisted it around his hand, but as it was, he could only tug on the ends and wish he could turn his face into it. He was suddenly aware of how tangled and unkempt it must have looked and wished he'd thought to brush it. He was also aware of all the space he took up in front of her and wondered why he had to be so horrifically tall and unwieldy.

"Uh. No. I just got out of the bath, and, well, I might have gotten a bit carried away with the oils."

The sharp smell always helped ground him. It reminded him where he was, not in the basement but safe behind a locked door. Even when he closed his eyes and could swear he still felt the sharp press of metal on his skin, but the strong scent of the oils never failed to keep it at bay.

"No, no. This is wonderful. Keep doing that," Millie said, still pressing the side of the robe to her face while she walked back over to the bed and plopped down. He blew out the lamp in the bathroom before following to the bed's opposite side, smiling to himself a bit despite his shyness.

"You won't mind if I wear this to sleep, will you?"

"No, no, not at all," He said, and decided to be a bit bold and added, "It. . .it suits you."

She grinned and hugged it around herself a bit tighter. "Why, thank you. I'd have you try mine on, but I'm not sure it would cover much."

They tugged back the heavy blankets, and Harlen felt his aching muscles breathe a sigh of relief when he was no longer on his feet. He collapsed into his place near the bed's edge and was sure he wouldn't be able to summon the strength to move position even if he had wanted to.

On the other hand, Millie struggled for a few moments to find a place in the mattress that suited her properly. He had seen cats on the street outside on the rare sunny days searching for the perfect spot of ground to lay on to soak up the warmth, and he couldn't help but be reminded of it as she molded the blankets to accommodate her.

It was strange, sharing a bed. Harlen had never done it before, and at first, he had been so self-conscious about every movement and so afraid he might snore and wake her up that he had hardly been able to sleep at all. But he had been getting used to it and had come to enjoy the added warmth of her body, not close enough to touch but close enough to feel the small dips and rises in the mattress when she moved.

She finally settled in on her back with her hands folded over her stomach, her fingers drumming against each other with barely audible taps. Harlen couldn't make out too much of her. Only the outline of her soft profile and her eyes gleamed in the dark. As his eyes slowly adjusted to the lack of light, he watched her study the ceiling and the underside of the window ledge above her, her roving gaze stopping when she noticed he was watching her. She turned her face towards him and offered another impish little smile, chuckling when he looked away.

He hadn't meant to stare. He tended to be up early and went to sleep quite late; there hadn't been many occasions when they were both awake in bed at the same time. He had been trying to decide if Millie seemed comfortable or not.

"Dinner wasn't too bad after I left, I hope," she said, breaking the silence.

"No, no, it was," he said, adjusting his glasses, "It was alright.

"That bad?" she asked.

He let out a breath of a laugh and again saw her grin in the dark.

She returned to staring at the window ledge above her, and he watched while she shook her head with an air of amusement. He wondered what it was she was thinking. What had brought on the curve of a smile that dimpled her cheek and was wondering about how he should go about asking what she found so funny when she said, "You know, I don't know how much you care about this sort of thing, but you know, the first time I came in here I was a bit surprised. After I saw you, I thought your room might be a little more. . .intellectual, I guess? Fussier."

He knew his desk and shelves weren't exactly neat, but he didn't understand why she was grinning at him the way she was or what was causing the glint in her eye until she raised her hand brushed the window above the bed.

"What I'm saying is, I definitely didn't expect you to be drawing on the walls."

He knew what she was talking about and reddened immediately. At first, he had hoped she couldn't tell in the dim light, but then she laughed.

He glanced over at the window frame where, in the place where the frame met the wall, he had a small constellation of scribbled stars that one could only see when laying directly underneath them. He hadn't even thought of Millie noticing their presence, and now he wondered how long she'd known.

"That's from when I was young," he said, which wasn't entirely true. He had started it when he was sixteen, and now and then, he would carefully scratch a new one into the paint.

As if she could hear his thoughts, she gave him a knowing smile. "Sure it is."

"It is."

"Well. *If* that's the case, young, you and I might have gotten along. I used to draw on the walls all the time. Though mine weren't nearly as discrete."

He suppressed a nervous laugh that was in large part due to relief that she hadn't thought it too strange. He thought he might be pushing his luck with the conversation, but he couldn't help asking, "What were they?"

Millie made a sweeping gesture with both of her arms. "A big vase of flowers. I'm very proud to say that they did vaguely look like flowers. Lavender, to be specific. My mother had a few lavender plants out in the yard that were attracting all these fuzzy bees. And when winter came along, the flowers died back, and the bees stopped coming. My toddler understanding was that if I made more flowers, the bees would come back. I was a real intellectual."

"And did they?" Harlen couldn't resist a little smile tugging at his lips while she illustrated every word with waves of her hands.

"Unfortunately, no. My mother caught me before I could draw those."

"She wasn't upset, was she?" he asked, his humor dying as soon as the words were out of her mouth. He twisted part of his blanket between his fingers, his stomach suddenly twisting along with it. He shouldn't have laughed.

He couldn't imagine what his father would have done if he'd caught him doing something like that. He supposed he would have had bruises for weeks.

"Well, yes. I had to sit in my room for the rest of the day, but she loves joking about it now."

"Oh," Harlen said, simultaneously relieved and surprised.

His sudden change in demeanor hadn't escaped her notice. Millie caught the expression on his face from the corner of her eye and slowly dropped her hands back onto the bed. He sat in quiet contemplation for a moment, and he wasn't sure what the look on her face meant. Concern perhaps.

"Sorry," he apologized. He should have just let her keep talking. He shouldn't be so difficult.

It was silent for a long moment. Harlen could hear the rain tapping the window, and the clock at the end of the hall ticked by second after second. He felt Millie watching him even as he kept his eyes on the bit of blanket he was twisting between his fingers. They had been having such a pleasant conversation—why did he have to ruin it?

"Harlen?" she asked eventually. He felt the bed shift. She'd become more serious, but there was a softness about her voice that helped to ease the nervous twist in his stomach when he risked glancing up at her.

She had rolled onto her side to face him; her cheek pillowed on one arm. "I do have one question I wanted to ask. You don't have to answer this if it's too serious, but after dinner, I was wondering."

She pulled at a loose thread on the robe's sleeve as though she had suddenly taken on some of his nervousness. Like she was afraid of asking whatever was on her mind. She looked and sounded like he did all too often. The realization filled him with a rush of tenderness towards her. He turned over onto his side as well to face her better and nodded.

"Of course."

"Who is Tansey?"

The question didn't shock him. It was strange to hear her name mentioned for the second time in one night, but he had known she would come up eventually. Or, at least, questions about the portrait and unoccupied bedroom would.

He had been wondering how he would answer those questions out of his father's earshot when they inevitably came up—how he would word it exactly if the man happened to be listening. But in the dark, closed bedroom, he could talk about it in relative privacy. The space between them, if he kept his voice quiet enough, could be as secret as his space in the wall.

"My sister," he said, easing the words out slowly. He listened, half expecting his father to burst through the door once she was mentioned. But there was silence. It was just the two of them. "My twin, actually. She. . .went missing. A few years ago."

"Oh. Oh, I'm so sorry," Millie winced. "I shouldn't have—"

"No, it's fine. I don't get to talk about her," Harlen admitted. He realized he hadn't had anyone to talk to about her since she'd disappeared.

His father wouldn't hear of it, and his mother broke down in hysterics every time anyone mentioned her. It felt surreal to be doing it now, but not unpleasant.

"We used to be pretty close, so it's nice to be able to bring her up."

"What happened to her?" Millie asked hesitantly.

"We don't know," Harlen said. "There was an investigation, but nothing ever came of it."

"I'm so sorry," Millie said, sounding for all the world like she meant it.

Harlen opened his mouth to thank her and again had a realization that made him pause. He had never had anyone tell him that.

"Thank you," he whispered, the words only coming out on the second try and coming out far more hoarsely than he would have liked.

What followed was silence. As it drew out longer and longer, Harlen couldn't keep from anxiously twisting at the button on the wrist of his shirt in the absence of his suit's cufflink with fingers that had once more begun to shake. He felt he might have said too much.

He might have burdened her with too many things, telling her so blatantly the truth about his sister. There were better ways to say it, gentle ways of alluding to it. Ways that wouldn't make her feel like people simply disappeared without a trace here in a place he knew she already hated. He wished he had thought about that before he'd told her. He wished he knew how to speak.

"Thank you for telling me," she said.

She reached for him and gently placed a hand over the one twisting the button on his sleeve so forcefully his knuckles had gone white, and he flushed with heat realizing he hadn't been near as discrete as he thought.

He let go of the button immediately and began to pull away with a mumbled apology, but she intertwined her fingers with his and held them so tightly that they stopped trembling. He felt the pressure in his chest begin to ease, and his heart stopped beating quite so fast as he focused on the sensation of her warm fingers and how steady she was. And slowly, he remembered how to breathe again.

"I'm sorry," he said as he regained himself. "I didn't mean to get so worked up."

"My little sister Roslyn is a lot like you," she said, giving his hand one last, comforting squeeze as he self-consciously pulled his away from hers, balling it near his chest.

"She gets nervous fits pretty often. None of us are sure why, but I've always left the knowing why to my mother. She's a lot smarter than me. I just worry about knowing how to calm her down."

"I would say figuring that out is pretty smart," he said, pushing up his glasses.

"You give me too much credit," she said, but he saw her smile in the dark.

"They must miss you," he said without thinking.

Her smile didn't vanish, but it became distinctly sadder. "I hope so. This is the longest I've ever been gone."

"I'm sure they do," he said, wanting to be brave enough to squeeze her hand in return.

He watched her grip tighten on her pillow and wished he knew if it was only courtesy that made her say thank you before she rolled back away from him and went silent.

Harlen found himself lying on his back once again, the hand she had squeezed feeling somehow warmer than the rest of him. He could swear he still felt her fingers between his.

The sensation was comforting. Soothing enough to make him feel like sleep was within his reach due to something other than exhaustion.

He didn't know how to thank her, but when he drifted off, it was to the thought of lavender out in the garden. It was probably small and soggy with the rain, but perhaps he could find a way to dry it. It wouldn't attract her any bees, but maybe it would make her feel like she was a bit closer to home.

CHAPTER 10

The sound of thunder rumbling in the distance like a mountain lion growling kept Millie awake long after Harlen had fallen asleep beside her. She heard his breathing change to the soft, purring snore that was hardly any louder than his whisper of a voice, and he shifted around far more freely than he did when he was awake.

She always expected to get smacked by an errant elbow in the night, but somehow even in sleep, he managed not to touch her. It was like he built up some invisible barrier; even unconsciousness didn't let him cross.

She sat up, still enveloped in the softness of the dressing robe he'd offered her. It was beautifully warm and did smell incredible. It was the same clean, woody smell that covered him after his baths every night that seemed to have worked its way into every part of the bed. She was greeted by it every time she laid down and had begun taking some kind of comfort from it. Unfortunately, it couldn't ease her mind enough to let her fall asleep after what she had just seen.

She hadn't been fully asleep before Harlen went into the washroom. She had woken up just as he had stood up from the side of the bed and managed to get a brief glimpse of him as he walked away. He had been ghostly white and covered in sweat with deep shadows under his eyes, and no amount of bathing or scented oil was going to cover that. She had never seen a man look so worn.

He hadn't even taken off his glasses when he laid down; he was so exhausted. They were knocked crooked from pressing his face into the pillow, and Millie couldn't imagine it was comfortable.

Carefully, only wondering if the gesture were too familiar when she already had her hands on the heavy frames, she lifted them off his face as gently as she could. The poor man was so deep in sleep already that his breathing didn't even change.

They were incredibly thick. Round, gold-rimmed, and heavy as a stone, they looked ancient as she folded them in her hands carefully. She imagined he must be practically blind without them.

He looked younger without them. His tousled hair, slightly parted lips, and relaxed features gave him a boyish look while his hollow cheeks and the dark smudges beneath his eyes aged him when he was awake.

It was easy to forget he was hardly twenty-three when he was up and moving. And that wasn't even mentioning how frighteningly thin he was. He was mostly beneath the blankets, but he had shifted enough in sleep for his upper half to be open to Millie's curious eyes. The thin white shirt did little to hide the press of his bones.

There were other things beneath the shirt as well that she could see faintly. What appeared to be bandages. On Harlen's arms, his shoulder. She was reasonably sure she could see the shadow of several angry pink scars, too, though she couldn't be sure without lifting the shirt to see. And she wouldn't do that. He seemed painfully shy: after months of marriage, she hadn't seen more skin than what was on his face, neck, and hands. She wouldn't violate his trust while he slept, no matter how curious and concerned she was.

She didn't even know how to approach the fact that she knew they were there in conversation with him, let alone start wondering and asking about where he had gotten them. However, she had plenty of suspicions.

No matter what Vostesk Senior seemed to think, she wasn't completely ignorant. She had noticed the trips to the basement he and Harlen took when they thought she had gone to bed for the evening. She hadn't been blind to how exhausted Harlen seemed when he slipped into bed while she pretended to be asleep every one of those nights aside from the first when she hadn't known better.

The first time it happened, she had been so alarmed by his labored breathing and trembling that she had all but jumped upright and asked what had happened. He had been startled at first, then seemed wildly uncomfortable. He'd pushed up his glasses and flushed from the neck up and seemed so deeply ashamed that she had backed off and hadn't asked since.

But between the bandages, the locks on the doors, and everything else she had seen so far, her morbid curiosity had only grown. Her suspicions grew wilder every day, spiraling out into the kinds of stories her sisters would tell each other about the monsters lurking in the fields beyond their house. She half expected to see something with claws peering at her from the half-closed door of Vostesk Senior's perpetually dark office every time she passed it. It never failed to make her walk a bit faster past the door.

It was a stupid thing to imagine. Vostesk Senior would probably send any kind of monster skittering away in fear with one stern look. She had no idea how Harlen had managed to live under the same roof as the man for so long without having a complete breakdown from the constant tension of his presence. She wondered where he'd found the resilience, and she wondered how long he'd been hurting him.

Millie turned over on her side to look at Harlen, heaving a heavy sigh as she did so. He remained fast asleep, and she stared at the bandage she could see most clearly, trying to imagine how someone who drew stars above their bed and blushed at prolonged eye contact could be the same person who grits their teeth and bore whatever wound it covered. As well as whatever others there were marking him.

It didn't seem possible. Millie had been trying to convince herself for weeks that she was imagining monsters where there were none and was jumping to conclusions about the entire situation. But the way he had flinched when she had put a hand on his arm after dinner kept coming to mind.

He had always flinched whenever she made any sudden movement in his presence, but she had so far chalked it up to merely being a part of his nervous demeanor. The trouble was that it hadn't been her movement that had startled him earlier. It had been the touch. Putting her hand on his arm had, for a fleeting moment, brought panic to his eyes. So, it seemed that in this case, it was possible she wasn't just imagining a monster at all.

Millie made it the better part of an hour before she could no longer stand laying still with her thoughts.

She wasn't going to press Harlen for answers, and she wasn't going to sneak a look at him. However, if something was going on that she needed to be worried about, quite literally beneath her feet in the lowest level of the house, she wanted to know what it was. Perhaps if she found out what it was, it would make bringing it into the conversation somehow easier.

She pushed back the blankets and got out of bed with as little movement as possible even though Harlen was sleeping like the dead, and she doubted anything short of screaming would have woken him up. She winced as her feet hit the cold floor, but thankfully Harlen's robe kept out the worst of the chill while she moved toward the bedroom door.

She held her breath as she twisted the handle, wondering if Vostesk Senior had decided to use that lock on the door's other side. She had no idea what she would do if he had, and as it swung open with ease, Millie thought she had never been so glad to see the emptiness of the dim hallway.

Millie saw nothing but silver moonlight spread across the chessboard floor as she tiptoed downward, staying close to the railing of the grand staircase to keep the steps from creaking and announcing her descent. She didn't know where Vostesk Senior was in the house, and she had no desire to let him find her first—especially if her suspicions that he had everything to do with Harlen's injuries were correct.

She knew it was still nothing but an assumption, but she didn't put it past the man to follow through on those threatening gestures he was so fond of. An angry fist on the table. That menacing grip on her back over something as small as her preference for a nickname. All of Harlen's flinching and everything about his mother's demeanor hadn't come from nowhere.

Her eldest sister Beatrice's first suitor had been similar. He was a well-dressed, well-bred young man with impeccable manners. He presented nicely in front of the family, but there had been something about the way her sister had looked at him that never sat right. Beatrice was always incredibly strong-willed, but with him, she would say or do something then look back at him with the same nervousness Harlen had shown when she made a joke about his father.

That young man had had quite the talent for cutting looks as well. And words edged just so to make simple, passing remarks sound like threats. It hadn't taken him long to escalate to putting hands on her.

But that had been different. Beatrice had been so shocked she had slapped him in return, and she had three fiercely protective little sisters who didn't let that snake in dress clothes near her once they found out. Social graces compelled him to leave her alone once she declared publicly that she no longer wished to see him.

He hadn't been her husband. He wasn't her father. But Vostesk Senior had no such barriers and was free to make good on his threats.

Perhaps that made snooping around stupid. Maybe it would be better, in her situation, to remain ignorant. But she knew herself well enough to know that that wasn't an option. It would be so much worse to wait and wonder, hiding beneath the covers. It was better to rip off the blanket and see what was in the house with her.

The goblins were snoring when she crept into the kitchen. Little whistling noises that sounded like tittering birds. One opened a bright, lamp-like eye that shined in the dark, but it quickly closed again, and they ignored her. She crept across to the basement door, painted white but chipping and grayed around the handle. Like all the other doors, there was a heavy lock hanging from the handle, but it clicked with ease when she touched it.

This is a bad idea. Millie could hear a voice like her mother's speaking in the back of her mind to accompany the way her stomach dropped when she realized the door was indeed open. *It would be best if you walked away.*

She had no magic. She'd heard that magic was like another sense that could warn those who had it of evil and danger, but she didn't need it to feel the thick sense of wrongness that drifted up the stairs.

The only person in her family with the slightest inclination towards magic had been Beatrice. That was the other key difference between the situation with her sister's former suitor and Vostesk Senior. If Beatrice's suitor had gotten more aggressive, he could have been overpowered like any other man. Magic gave Vostesk Senior a far superior advantage, and she still hadn't decided what she would do if he chose to use it on her.

Millie craned her neck to better look down the stairs and saw a light flickering somewhere down there. She hadn't taken a candle of her own just in case she ran across Vostesk Senior and needed to make a speedy and unseen retreat in the dark, so the faint, dancing glow seemed incredibly bright. It seeped through the shelves and threw jumping shadows on the walls.

She could make out only shelves and storage from where she stood, but there had to be something else. There had to be more. She needed to see. She gripped the painted doorframe with both hands and swallowed hard, hesitating.

One foot on the top step: that was as far as she got before the light illuminated the unmistakable figure with a long ponytail. It was just his shadow, but that was enough for her to throw herself back from the doorway. She stood in the kitchen for a few breathless moments and strained her ears, glad she had had the sense not to push the door open entirely as she heard the footsteps growing closer. It was coming towards the stairs.

She practically flew out of the kitchen. The same unexplained but undeniable fear that had filled her as soon as she'd opened the basement door was screaming inside her as she ran as quickly and quietly as she could, trying to put distance between herself and Vostesk Senior. She let the feeling carry her through the dining room and entrance hall, through the heart-stopping openness of the grand staircase where she would be all too easy to see. All the while, hearing the man draw closer.

As soon as she was in the upper hallway, she could hear him on the grand staircase behind her. She didn't know if he was chasing her or just walking, but she wasn't going to slow down to listen and find out.

The handle of the first door she touched in the hallway was the one she opened. She wouldn't take the risk of trying to make it down to Harlen's room. She pushed open the door and threw herself inside, pressing it against the frame behind her.

Inside, she crouched and held her breath. He was in the hallway. He was getting closer to the door. And she felt her heart stop as he paused outside the door.

Again, she let fear carry her. She followed its direction and scurried away from the door to the bed with a speed she didn't know she was capable of. She rolled beneath it just as the door creaked open, ignoring the dust and cobwebs, glad that the dark gray of Harlen's dressing gown would cover the bright white of her nightdress. Millie pressed a hand over her mouth to muffle the sound of her panicked breathing and squeezed her eyes shut. As if that would do any good with her facing away from the door.

It felt like an eternity that he stood there. Behind the closed lids of her eyes, Millie could see the soft light of the candle he must be carrying. But the room was deep and dark, and, hopefully, the light wouldn't be enough to let him distinguish her from any other odd shape in the darkness.

Eventually, he muttered something to himself about being paranoid and shut the door. Millie uncurled from the ball she'd bunched up into and sprawled out under the bed, panting with relief. She laid there, letting the hot wash of panic ebb slowly away, and only then did she wonder where she was.

She crawled out from under the bed, stifling a cough from the dust in the crook of her arm. It was the same as the other bedrooms in the house: the same blue-green walls, the same singular window over the bed. The bed had been left unmade with one yellow slipper tossed on the floor beside it. The bookshelves were full of books with cracked bindings and little glass bottles of beads and buttons, and brightly colored quill pens.

Millie wandered over, picked up one of the small bottles, and pressed the crumpled label smooth with two fingers. In loopy handwriting, "Water from the sea," accompanied by a scribbled drawing of one of the seagulls that sailed through the sky outside, screaming to themselves.

Carefully, she set it back on the shelf and peered over at the desk. There was a little trail of pale blue wax down the side where the owner let the candles drip, but the surface itself was immaculate. Unlike Harlen's desk, there were no ink stains, and the bottles of black, blue, and gold ink lined up neatly like little soldiers beside a stack of envelopes and stationery. There was a stack of closed envelopes in the desk's drawer, which had was hanging slightly open.

Curious, she reached down and pulled the top one off the stack, only to find it sealed. She considered breaking it open, but in the end, decided against it. She put it back, the wax stamp unbroken, and instead flipped through the pile until she found one that was already open. It looked like the seal had broken of its own accord, and Millie took the little envelope in her hands.

It felt heavy. Inside were three folded paper sheets that Millie removed carefully, and only when trying to get the pages appropriately smoothed on the desk did she realize her hands were shaking. She knew who had written the letter before she read the name in loopy blue ink.

"Dear Tansey," the letter said in the same handwriting that was on the bottle of seawater on the shelf. *"I know you know this, but I went down to the book shop today! Donnie saw me in the window and came in to say hello. He's a nice boy. Cute too, but honestly, sometimes I feel like nothing is going on inside his head."*

She was writing to herself.

Millie folded the paper back up without reading any further, feeling sick. She stuffed it quickly back in the envelope and shoved it back in the drawer, then sat down heavily in the chair in front of the desk because she was sure that if she tried to keep standing, she might fall.

The locks on the doors, the basement, the letters. The more Millie saw of this place, the colder it felt. She wanted to go home. She wanted to go home now. But there was no way of getting home.

She had no money of her own, no way to make the two-week journey it would take on horseback alone. No idea of even what direction to take other than somewhere south. Even if every one of those obstacles was removed, this was her home in the eyes of the law now. If she were found, caught more like, this would be the place they would return her to. No matter how little she wanted to be here.

She pulled her knees to her chest and leaned her cheek down into the soft gray fabric of Harlen's robe. She hadn't realized she'd started crying until she felt her face press wetly into the soft material. She could still smell the woody scented oils, and it offered some measure of comfort, even if it wasn't much. At least she wasn't completely alone.

She wasn't alone, and she wasn't the only one trapped here. She imagined that Mrs. Vostesk and certainly Harlen would have gone long ago if it were a choice. Maybe they had tried already and failed. Perhaps Tansey's disappearance and Vostesk Senior's subsequent anger was because she had somehow managed what neither of them had.

Millie felt sorry for them. She felt sorry for herself. And she felt sorry, for a moment, about wondering if Tansey's vanishing had perhaps been the only good thing that had happened here.

Millie dried her eyes on the dressing robe and made herself uncurl her legs. She couldn't sit there forever. She could let fear move her, but she couldn't let it freeze her in place. Besides, maybe everything wasn't lost. She couldn't let herself think that it was.

After all, Harlen wasn't his father. From what she'd seen of him, he was a far cry from it. She was his wife, not Vostesk Seniors. He was the one she was law-bound to. If he ever found a way to get out from under that horrible man, she would be free of him as well.

She could only imagine Vostesk Senior must have something keeping Harlen tied to him. Fear, without a doubt, but other things too. His mother probably. Money tied up in contracts, perhaps something to do with his magic, maybe a thousand other things. Constraints far tighter than locked doors. But anything could be broken. Anything. She had to believe that, or she would never have summoned the will to climb out of the desk chair and return to her bedroom.

Harlen woke partially as Millie returned to bed. She hadn't been careful enough sitting down, and he stirred, peering at her through half-closed eyes.

"What's wrong?" his voice was blurred at the edges, heavy with sleep and coated so thickly with grave concern that it was almost comical. It brought the smallest, bitter smile to Millie's face despite the ache in her chest. She wished that there was no cause for that concern at all.

There were a thousand things she could say. Something she could tell Harlen eventually, but not then. Not when he was half asleep, and she could see the bandages under his shirt.

"Just having a hard time sleeping," she said as she hoisted herself into bed. She faced Harlen as she lay down while trying to get his deep brown eyes to focus on her. She wondered what distant relative he'd gotten them from since both his mother and father's eyes were so pale. "The thunder's pretty loud."

"Mm," he hummed and nodded, and she thought he had gone back to sleep. But instead, he said, "I always listen to the rain on the window. Or count the stars."

He reached one lanky arm up and pointed to the constellation he'd drawn in the seam of the window. Somehow, despite being half-awake to the point he sounded drunk, he still felt enough self-consciousness for a blush to creep up his neck. "I might. . .still add to them sometimes. So, there are more for you to look at."

She smiled without bitterness then, though, for some reason, it came with a fresh sting of tears to her eyes. She was glad she'd taken off his glasses so he couldn't see them.

Like her hair and the dressing robe, it was small, but it was caring. Millie hadn't realized how desperately she'd missed small gestures like that until she held Vostesk Senior and this house, in contrast, poking at the pain she'd been trying and failing to forget tonight.

"You're an artist," she said, keeping her tone light and joking because if she didn't, those tears were going to escape again.

He chuckled sleepily and half-buried his face in the pillow. "Hardly. I was never ambitious enough to draw any flowers on my wall."

She had no idea he'd even been listening to her silly story from earlier. She shifted the blankets and hoped that he wouldn't notice she wiped her eyes with his blurred vision and tired mind.

"Thank you," she said with more sincerity than she'd dared before, cutting off the tremble in her words by pressing her mouth shut tight.

He was sliding into sleep again. His voice was fading and trailing off, and his eyes had drifted shut. "I wouldn't mind if you put them in here. Anywhere you want. . ."

She would have teased him for that if she had the voice or mood for it. Instead, she let him drift to sleep, then rolled onto her back and stared at the constellation in the seam of the window.

Chapter 11

Millie was still asleep when Harlen woke early the next morning. He found her buried deep in the blankets with nothing visible except the very top of her head and a bit of dark hair splayed across the pillow.

He was glad; from what he could vaguely remember, she had been having some trouble sleeping until late last night. It was good for her to get some rest. He got out of the warm bed reluctantly and dressed as quietly as he could, trying to ignore the dryness of his throat at the prospect of what the upcoming day was going to bring.

He had never been allowed out of the house unescorted. His father had taken him to The Academy yesterday, but as far as he knew he had said nothing about doing that today. Would he be able to find his way there alone? If he didn't arrive on time, he was sure one of the professors would inform his father. After all, they were all colleagues.

He also had no idea how similar their teaching methods were to his father's. He hadn't seen much of the building yesterday. Most of what he saw was nothing but desks and books, no signs of anything sharp or chairs with braces. Even so, the thought of an entire building dedicated to what his father did in the basement left his fingers numb. He struggled and fumbled with the buttons on his shirt.

He made his way downstairs, wondering if his father wanted to give him some parting words or directions before he left, but he found both his father's office and the dining room to be empty. Harlen stood uncertainly for several minutes as the distant ticking of the grandfather clock counted off the minutes, listening for his familiar footsteps, and was quite surprised to hear that the house sounded quite empty.

He must have already gone for the day to attend to one thing or another. He rarely told any of them when he was going somewhere or at what time he would return.

It usually set Harlen on edge, but he found some small relief in it on this morning. It gave him some time to try and slow the pounding of his heart, to clear his thoughts, and when an idea suddenly struck him, it gave him the time and privacy he needed to slip outside into the small garden.

Of all the sad but enduring little bushes that grew along the house's side, two were lavender bushes. He remembered when Tansey had started tearing up the grass for her flowers; she had said something about wanting to plant things that would attract butterflies.

He had wanted to tell her that he had never seen a single living butterfly anywhere in the city, but she had been so excited he had decided to keep his mouth shut. So when she asked for his assistance, he had nodded along and spent an afternoon digging through the library for ways to care for the flowers she'd selected, hoping he could find some way to keep them alive.

He wasn't sure she had ever done more than glance at the stack of books and papers he'd found, but she had been happy he appeared enthusiastic.

"It's going to be perfect." She had said confidently. He again wanted to warn her about how plant life and the frost-prone weather of the coast did not tend to mix well from what he had read. He didn't want her to be disappointed when the flowers died. But her soaring optimism was blazing away, and he didn't want to be the one to dim it. So, he instead silently wished for the garden to survive for just a few months. Every time he would pass the window, he would tap the glass quietly as he could, two quick raps to remind them to hang on just a bit longer.

Evidently, it had worked because years later, they still refused to die. Harlen did tend to them now and again when he could in case Tansey ever came back, but not nearly with as much devotion as she had. Yet they had survived several harsh winters and endless rain, remaining living as he continued his ritual—two taps on the glass at least once a day.

Tap tap. *Stay alive.*

It was still late winter in Wakefield, and they wouldn't start showing their flowers for several weeks. He knew how the long, willowy branches would bloom. They'd grown into his memory so firmly he could practically see the round, grey, and purple petals beneath his fingertips as he made his selection.

Very carefully, he removed a tiny section from the ground, roots and all. He hoped that inside the house next to a window and perhaps a fireplace, it would grow eventually. It certainly wouldn't be anything like the rolling fields of vibrant flowers he had seen in the mountains where Millie came from, but it was something. Hopefully, something that would make the world a bit brighter for her.

He doubted Tansey would mind. She would probably have told him to let Millie take over caring for the whole lot before he killed them on accident.

There were no flowerpots or vases in the house—he checked just to be sure—but there was a place in the kitchen where the goblins hid old, cracked cups that had broken and wouldn't be missed.

Harlen had known about the collection for years but had never said a word regarding it knowing how livid his father would be. Harlen was afraid of what he might do to them if he found out they'd broken something.

Eventually, he found a teacup with only a little chip on its porcelain edge. He pressed the handful of dirt that cradled the flower's roots into it— he had read it gave the plant too violent a shock if the roots were yanked free all at once when it was moved—and inspected his efforts.

It was not the most romantic gesture ever conceived. As Harlen stood back to look at it, in fact, he very nearly changed his mind. The bumpy green stems in a chipped cup were not the sort of things he imagined would make it into poetry.

He set the cup on the ground. He considered putting it back in the bin. He closed his hand around it to do just that but hesitated.

Millie loved flowers. She had spent her life surrounded by them. It wasn't much to look at, but he wanted to give her something that might feel even the smallest bit familiar.

She wasn't comfortable here. In all fairness, neither was he. But this was all he had ever known. She was pulled away from a life very unlike his. She had a family she loved and a home she adored and had had to leave behind for him. And although he had had no say or even knowledge that such the arrangement of their marriage had been taking place, he couldn't help but feel guilty that he was the reason she was sad.

And she was sad. No matter how well she hid it, Harlen could recognize it well enough. He only wished he knew of a more direct way to fix it. Because in truth, he liked her. Very much.

She was witty and kind, and he had never had anyone take off his glasses when he fell asleep wearing them. He wasn't sure if she would ever consider herself at home here, or even consider herself happy to have married him, but he hoped she could at least find some kind of comfort in his companionship.

So, he clutched the teacup in his hand and left it beside the bed in the same place she had left his glasses. He scribbled a brief note for her to find as well when she woke that he tucked beneath the cup's edge, just in case she found it a bit odd.

The thought of her finding it made him nervous, but the prospect of it bringing a smile to her face gave him something to focus on rather than his apprehension as he returned to the front door of the house and cautiously stepped through.

Chapter 12

It felt strange walking out of the black wrought-iron gate alone. It felt wrong. It was unlocked, which was unthinkable in and of itself. And when Harlen closed it behind him and started walking down the street, he fully expected someone, anyone, to stop him.

He had only ever tried to leave the house on his own once, after the first time his father had taken him down to the basement, long before Tansey had started her nightly escapes. He hadn't been more than ten, but the result had been enough to keep him from ever daring to try again. He'd been spotted by one of his father's associates and caught before he got even a few blocks away.

He thought for the longest time the flaw in his plan had been running through the upper districts of town. If he had run into the lower and trade districts, perhaps it would have gone differently. His father and his friends would consider such places beneath them, and he might have gone hours without being found out.

Harlen always assumed that was how Tansey had avoided being caught for so long. But as he grew older, he realized that a child stumbling around, crying, and bleeding was not challenging to spot.

Regardless, he had been promptly returned and had lost his last baby tooth as a result of the rage that followed. He still flinched when his father raised that cane of his.

As he moved through town, more people than he thought could have fit in the entire city moved past him, huddled under coats and shawls, speaking, and carrying boxes and baskets of their goods. Nobody paid him any mind as he tried his very best not to be an obstruction to anyone, muttering profuse apologies every other step as he brushed into a body, or someone had to step out of his way as he moved up the street.

It was almost a relief when he reached The Academy just because he was able to step out of the jostling crowd. The tall, white, and gray building was imposing behind a massive wrought-iron gate, not unlike the one around his own home. The difference was that this gate stood open.

Even here, there were more people than he had thought there would be. They were standing in groups outside the steps that lead into the building, talking and laughing amongst themselves like gargoyles guarding the doors. He kept his eyes trained on the ground as he walked past them and hurried into the small entrance hall.

There were iron hooks on the walls for coats, and a long, mud-stained carpet was spread on the wooden floor for shaking off the water from outside. Though judging by how the wood warped and swelled along the seam of the wall, leaving the doors to the main building hanging loosely ajar in their frames, he could guess it didn't do much. Over time, nothing here could do much against the sea and rain's constant onslaught and the continual frost in the salty air.

He discarded his coat on a hook, pretending to be preoccupied with digging something from one of the pockets to keep facing the wall as a group of four chatting students passed through like a windstorm. They spoke without pause, and they all seemed to know each other.

That was rational. Harlen knew that where actual numbers were concerned, there were very few students, so it was understandable that they would know one another very well. It just seemed like there were so many. It was a bee's nest of swarming bodies.

It made him dizzy, as did the realization that nobody seemed to be alone aside from him. He stood out in his isolation—he was sure of it. He couldn't shake the idea that any one of these friendly people with magic in their veins who glanced in his direction knew that he didn't belong there.

He risked a glance over his shoulder at the group still chattering in the hall behind him and saw that they were all smiling, playfully elbowing one another, or making friendly, sarcastic remarks to each other.

It was like something from a painting, and he wondered how all of them managed to look so perfectly calm. Not one of them appeared to be the least bit uncomfortable or awkward.

It was a curiosity that became particularly surprising when he recognized one of them as one of the professors he had seen the other day—the one with red hair and freckles.

As he watched, the professor raised his hand as one of the group was putting his coat on a hook. A sudden gust of wind snapped through the room, blowing it back in the student's face. The rest laughed, and the young man quickly tore the coat off and threw it at the professor and brazenly called him a bastard. Nothing about the exchange was unfriendly, and it quickly devolved into more good-natured laughter.

Harlen stared at them, feeling a strange sort of jealousy. They were so casual with each other. There was no trace of uneasiness in any of them. They spoke to each other with ease, and they simply looked as if they belonged here and never gave such a thing a second thought. He wished he knew how to feel so calm.

"Everything alright there?" the red-haired professor asked suddenly, and Harlen glanced away, his breath catching and burning in his throat. He hadn't realized he'd been staring. He also hadn't had the presence of mind to consider that the professor would, beyond a doubt, recognize him from his spectacular failure.

Harlen thought frantically, but his brain was all white noise as he stood, frozen in place even as his mind shouted at him to move.

He fixed his eyes on the wall and gripped his coat, hoping the man would ignore him if he said nothing. The feeling of wrongness he had felt since he left the house was coiling tighter and tighter in his chest.

He hadn't been paying any attention to the actual topic of the group's conversation. Perhaps the professor had been telling them about his appointment with the board. Maybe everyone already knew he didn't belong here, in fact rather than feeling.

You're nothing, and everyone knows.

"Hey," the professor's voice came again, closer. He was walking over, Harlen realized. His blood ran like ice in his veins as he dragged his eyes up slowly and saw the young man was right beside him.

"You alright?" he asked, both coppery eyebrows raised.

This was a trick. Right? A test. Something was coming.

Harlen's muscles felt like steel, braced for some unknowable threat. He tried to speak, but his voice died in his throat, and he dropped his eyes to the floor. Out of their corners,

Harlen saw him nod to the rest of the group, and he braced for the worst. When he felt a hand on his shoulder, he jumped so severely that the professor looked startled and let out a laugh.

"Easy there," he said, taking his hand off him and instead of shoving it in his pocket. Harlen saw the group of other young men moving through the doors into the rest of the building, leaving the two of them in the entrance hall. "Damn, I thought you were pretty nervous the other day, but I figured it was just because of the exam."

He fished in his pocket and withdrew a small, crumpled, paper cigarette that he proceeded to stick in his mouth. He then rummaged in another pocket and produced a match, striking it on the heel of his shoe. He held the flame up to the end until it shone a brilliant, crackling orange, and Harlen watched as he blew out a small cloud of smoke that smelled like burnt paper and cheap tobacco. "You smoke?"

He hadn't. He'd only seen his father smoke cigars, and he had never been permitted to partake. But before he could explain himself, he found one placed in his hand. The professor lit the end, and Harlen didn't see a way to politely admit that he hadn't the faintest idea of how to use it.

He tried to mimic what he had just seen as best he could and immediately fell into a coughing fit. It seemed like the smoke came from his mouth, his nose, and even his eyes. While he gagged, he could hear the man laughing uproariously next to him until Harlen came back around, at which point he said with a grin that turned up the corners of his green eyes, "There you go."

"Sorry, Professor." Harlen stood up and made to hand the cigarette back to him, but the man raised his hand and shook his head.

"Nah. You've got to finish that now. And do it quickly—we're not supposed to have these on school grounds. And please, spare me the professor business. It's Jacques. Jacques Martin."

Martin. Harlen searched his memory. He knew all the noble families in the area, as well as all the moderately wealthy. He had never met most of them in person, but it was expected he learn their names in the event his father decided to bring him into the public circle, so he didn't embarrass the family.

"I'm. . . I'm afraid I don't know that name," he admitted tentatively, but to his surprise, Jacques burst out laughing.

"I'd be surprised if you did! My father tends the cemetery grounds. The family's a bunch of undertakers and morticians by trade. Not exactly glamorous work."

"Really?" Harlen asked, hoping his surprise and curiosity didn't come off as rudeness. Luckily, Jacques seemed to note his genuine interest.

"Yep." He nodded and reduced his cigarette to ash with a single, long drag. He let the ash fall onto the wet, muddy floor and kicked at it with his scuffed boot, grinding out any faintly glowing embers. Harlen took it as an excuse to follow suit. "But I'm not in the business of cutting people open before they're dead, so you can stop looking at me like I'm about to slap you on my table. Or like everyone you walk past is going to put you there."

Harlen winced and apologized quickly, his eyes sliding back to the ground. There was still a single orange ember glowing on the floor beside his shoe. "Is it that obvious?"

"Well. A kind person would say no. But I'm going to say, yeah. Yeah, you kind of look like you want to throw up. Though, so long as you don't do it on me, I'm not going to stop you."

Perhaps there was something to be said for honesty, at least. Jacques turned his attention back to the rest of the building and nodded for Harlen to follow, which he did without question.

If what the chairman said had been correct, Jacques was the person who would be overseeing his lessons. From what Harlen had seen so far, he seemed alright. But he didn't exactly trust his social skills to tell him otherwise. He had seen far too much of the company his father usually kept not to be at least a bit cautious. So, as they moved into the main building, Harlen took in his surroundings but kept a careful eye on the man in front of him as well.

It was a beautiful building. Or perhaps had been at one time. In the central area, it seemed they had worked hard to remove any traces of the guild house it had been; still, the floors were made of wood that had been warped by age and showed countless ink stains and cracks where the coast's dampness had split them. The walls were painted a neutral shade of gray and hung with elegant portraits of former headmasters and influential attendees, and they did manage to look rather regal despite the black soot stains above the lamps that framed each picture.

There was an open staircase leading to the second floor and a banister overhead where those up at the top could look down on the masses milling around on the main floor, and there was a grand chandelier hung with lamp bulbs that looked quite magnificent. However, one of the glass bulbs was shattered.

Jacques directed him to a glass-paneled door on the ground floor, and once the door shut behind them, it blocked out a good deal of the buzz of activity outside. It sounded like the distant drizzle of rain and would have been relaxing had the shutting of the door to the small room not made him tense.

There was a single table at the center of the room with a chair on either side. Harlen eyed both chairs warily but saw no sign of leather straps on either. Though there were several books stacked on the table, none of them appeared to be the one his father poured over.

He saw no sign of sharp instruments anywhere. Just ink bottles and quills were gleaming in the faint gray light coming in through the single window.

Even so, Harlen hesitated in the doorway. If Jacques noticed, he said nothing and breezed past him to sit in one of the chairs. He pulled it out from the table and sat in it how Harlen imagined one might sit on a barstool: sideways, with one leg on the floor, and the other propped up on the rungs. Not at all like he had been sitting with the other professors.

"You coming, or are you taking in the décor?" Jacques asked.

Harlen took a deep breath and sat down at the desk across from Jacques. As was his habit, he began twisting at his cufflink at his wrist while the room settled into an uncomfortable silence.

He pretended not to be watching Jacques out of the corner of his eye, acting as though he was occupied reading the spines of the books stacked on the table, watching for any sudden movement. Perhaps that was a pathetic thing to do. Cowardly even. But if violence were coming, he would rather be able to brace for it than be caught off guard.

As he watched him, Harlen noted that he wasn't dressed at all how he had been yesterday, and certainly not like a man with money. His boots were scuffed and old, his brown pants and white shirt were both worn loose, the shirt untucked, and the sleeves rolled to his elbow.

The coat he had abandoned in the other room had been old as well and stained with dirt. A mortician by trade, he'd said. His magic must be extraordinary for his father's friends to appoint him the position of professor. They weren't the most relaxed people when it came to associations and appearances. Which only made Harlen all the more curious and cautious about precisely what the man was capable of.

"I see you take after your father with your conversational skills," Jacques offered after a long moment. He'd lit another cigarette now that the door was closed. The smell of it filled the small room quickly, and it left a haze hanging in the air.

Harlen didn't supply an answer, and Jacques blew out a cloud of gray. "So. You're kind of shit with magic, right?"

The abruptness startled him, which seemed to amuse Jacques, who grinned. "Just based on what I've seen. If you've been hiding some incredible talent, then, by all means, feel free to correct me."

"No," Harlen said. The cufflink's pressure against his fingers helped ease the tightness in his chest. "No, I'm not."

"Fantastic. Well, we know where we're starting." Jacques tapped the cigarette on the edge of the table, scattering the ashes carelessly on the floor. "From square one then."

He stood up, and Harlen watched him stroll over to the corner of the room where a row of cabinets stood with cobwebs stretching between the handles.

Oblivious to them, Jacques dug his hands into them and threw the cabinet open, revealing rows and rows of jars, bottles, and neatly tied bundles of herbs.

Alchemist's ingredients. The simplest form of magic: one his father and his friends freely spoke ill of. It was no wonder it sat unused in a place like this. But Harlen straightened in his chair.

Alchemy dealt strongly with remembering measurements, ingredients, and long incantations. Of every element of magic that had ever given him trouble, memorization had never been one of those things. It was precisely why that branch of magic had always interested him, but the topic could simply not be breached with his father without it being quickly shouted down as lesser and undignified. It had taken years for him to stoop to allowing him to try runic magic.

But perhaps Jacques had a different view. Maybe he would be able to accomplish something.

Jacques took a bowl from the cabinet and walked it over to the window. He pushed open the glass and held the dish outside for a few moments, collecting a fair bit of rainwater before dropping it on the table between them.

He gestured to it with his cigarette and spoke with a heavy drawl, "The basest form of magic detection, and the thing that usually tips parents off that their kid's got something weird going on, isn't intentional. It's emotional. Kid gets mad you won't let him have a cookie before dinner; next thing you know, the bed's on fire—that sort of thing. I damn near blew my brother into the ocean when my parents figured something was up with me. To be fair, he had it coming for throwing sand in my face."

Harlen tensed. That sounded similar to his father's method, but Jacques made no move to touch him. He began wandering away from the table again, back towards the cabinet as he continued. "We're going to leave that right there just in case something kicks in with you. Rather you freeze that than me if you get riled up."

"What are you going to do?" Harlen asked, shifting to see past Jacques into the cabinet. He didn't know what all was in there. It could be more tools like his father used for all he knew.

Jacques looked over his shoulder at him. "You know, you need to calm down because you're making *me* jumpy," he said and walked back over with his arms full of what Harlen realized was nothing but various ingredients. He dropped them unceremoniously on the table, and Harlen had to quickly grab at a glass jar of what looked like dried rose petals to keep it from rolling away and smashing on the floor.

You strike me as a bit of an intense fellow. That's all. Figure it might not be a bad idea to keep an eye on that," Jacques said, nodding to the water bowl.

Jacques sat back in his chair in his supremely casual way and tossed a book off the stack onto the table that landed with a thud so loud it made Harlen jump. It called back to mind his father slamming his hands on the dining room table, and he nearly twisted the cufflink on his sleeve clear off.

"Now, let's have a look at that." Jacques wedged the cigarette in the corner of his mouth and waved for him to open up the book.

Harlen pushed down the uneasiness and tried to focus as he flipped through the first few pages, and quickly the feeling faded to a dull thudding in the back of his mind. It was not truly gone but diminished dramatically by seeing the lovely illustrations in the book of various components, measurements, and outcomes.

It was quite different from magic and followed some slightly different rules, but Jacques allowed him to read uninterrupted until he found something that caught his eye and seemed simple enough to be doable. A straightforward frost spell.

If the description was any indication, it was a beginner's recipe that was frequently only used in cooking or as a party trick in real-world applications. There was a far more powerful version of it on the next page that could shatter glass and kill crops, but he thought it better not to be too ambitious. Even though for the first time in a long time, he felt excited.

The feeling slowly worked its way over his uncertainty as he read how simple it was. Magic was hardly mentioned in the instructions; most of it was left to proper measurements, preparation, and incantation. Anyone with the smallest magical abilities could do it.

"Alright," Jacques said, clapping his hands together. He gestured broadly to the table of ingredients and said, "Have a go."

Harlen wasn't sure what would happen if it didn't work but decided it was best not to think about that. It was better to enjoy the moment of hope while it lasted, which was easier while he focused on sorting through the bottles and counting out the exact measurements for the few ingredients needed. It was a process that was quite calming.

His only trouble came when he tried to slice a bit of bark off a small branch that had come from one of the little bundles of twigs. As it turns out, the only instrument in the cabinet capable of cutting anything was a very, very dull knife that looked as though it hadn't seen the light of day in decades. It was dull, rusted, and Harlen felt he would have more luck trying to cut with the handle.

Jacques watched him struggle at it for a few minutes before growing bored. "Here," he said, pushing back his sleeves. "Hold that out. Let me take care of it."

"How?" Harlen asked.

"You're full of questions, aren't you, Vostesk? Just let me have a moment of suspense, please."

Harlen reluctantly held up the branch, and Jacques quickly indicated he should move it away from his face. "It's unlikely that I'll miss, but just in case, it's better not to have your head just there."

"What does that—" Harlen started to ask, but Jacques was tired of questions. He closed one eye and made a quick, sharp gesture with his fingers. There was a high-pitched whistling sound, and Harlen felt like the air had been sucked out of the room. And then everything happened at once.

A whistle of wind shot past Harlen. It cut through the branch, slicing off a section of the bark. It also sliced through his sleeve, up his arm, biting into the skin underneath. He felt the invisible blade zip past the side of his face, narrowly missing his cheek. Jacques cursed.

"Shit! Shit—sorry. Might have overestimated that."

But Harlen wasn't listening. The wound wasn't deep. He felt the faint sting on his skin and saw the blood seeping out, but that wasn't what concerned him. What was concerning him was the skin itself. He was exposed from wrist to shoulder.

His entire arm, covered in scars, was in full view. Panic swept through him so suddenly and so strong that he forgot himself entirely. He stood up so fast that his chair clattered back onto the floor. His sleeve was hanging off uselessly. Anyone who so much as glanced at him would be able to see it, and he heard a faint ringing in his ears that nearly drowned out another curse from Jacques.

"What the hell is that?" he said, and Harlen saw he'd gone ghostly white. His freckles stood out like a spray of ink across the center of his face.

He didn't wait for Jacques to recover to tell him otherwise. He ran out of the room and didn't stop until he'd reached the washroom. He had no idea if there was even anyone remaining out in the hallway to see him.

He closed the door, stood over the washbasin, and turned the water on, scrubbing at the blood on his shirt. He felt like the inside of his brain was nothing but an empty ringing growing steadily louder. No emotion. He felt dazed and worked the blood out with frenzied hands and an odd numbness.

"Don't come in!" he shouted when someone began to open the door, and immediately it closed again. Then, Jacque's voice came through.

"It's me. It's just me—are you sure you don't need some help?"

He sounded shaken. Harlen could hardly blame him. He'd startled him enough for the ringing to begin to fade, and he felt his throat begin to close as hot tears pricked at the back of his eyes. He could see his reflection in the sink, his ruined shirt. His ruined skin. Everyone who saw it would know. Know his uselessness in magic and know what a ruin his body was. Never had he felt so ugly as he did at that moment.

Uselessly, he tried pushing the shoulder of his shirt back into place. There was no helping it. No hiding how pathetic he was.

"Harlen?" Jacques called again from behind the closed door.

"I can't go home like this," he said, dazed but somehow still shaking. He couldn't walk through the street like this. Even if he did and made it home, what would he tell Millie? She hadn't seen it. She didn't know what he looked like.

All at once, she was the only thing on his mind. Millie with her impish smile and wild hair. He couldn't let her see this. It would terrify her.

"My wife—" he started, then realized the thought of her reaction made his throat too tight to say it. "What am I going to do?" he asked.

There was a brief silence where the question hung heavy in the air, then Jacques shouldered through the door. "Get in one of those stalls and give me your shirt," he said gruffly.

"Wh—"

"Shut up and do it, Vostesk."

Harlen slunk into the furthest stall and did what he was told. He had no idea what else he was supposed to do.

"Don't you dare tell anyone about this, yeah?" Jacques said as he passed him his shirt and jacket beneath the stalls' door and waited. He listened and heard a tin popping sound, followed by rattling noises, then the sound of a thread pulling through fabric.

"You can sew?" Harlen asked.

"Shut up," Jacques snapped, but after a few more picks of the needle, he sighed and said, "My mother didn't just teach me about magic, alright? She, uh, wanted me to learn a few practical skills. Can't cook without near burning the house down, so she got me sewing instead. Plus, you have close a corpse's mouth somehow."

Harlen thought for a moment. He was moved by his kindness and wanted to say something profound, but he had a feeling that if he touched too forcefully on emotions, Jacques might just get up and leave. So instead, he settled for, "It's a good skill to have."

Jacques sighed, but his voice was less gruff when he spoke again. "Yeah, well, at any rate, it's useful here. Can't send you back to your wife not looking your best, right?"

"Thank you," Harlen said because he didn't know what else to say.

Jacques cleared his throat. "It's nothing. Hey—don't think I can't hear that tone. Don't you dare get sappy on me."

After what had to be the better part of an hour, he was done. It wasn't a flawless job, but the shirt and jacket were wearable again. Harlen put them on and stepped out of the stall gratefully while Jacques passed a hand back through his coppery hair and breathed a sigh of relief.

"Sorry. I thought I had a better direction on that. I'm out of practice if I'm honest." He sounded genuinely apologetic and was still quite pale. He rubbed the back of his head, searching for words, then gestured vaguely to Harlen's entire person. "Feel free to ignore me but, well. . .what's all that about?"

"Physical duress," he said, his voice taking on another unwelcome tremble. "Physical duress is supposed to bring out dormant magic. Magic in the blood will rise to protect the body it inhabits. I've heard my father mention that a lot of noble families use it with. . .problem children."

Harlen watched Jacques run his hands down his face, then shake his head and produce a cigarette from his pocket. He began pacing and didn't stop until he lit the cigarette with a shaking hand and burned away half of it in one long breath. His reaction was not what Harlen had been expecting.

"I thought," he said, flinching out of habit as Jacques rounded on him. "I thought you knew."

"Knew?" Jacques exclaimed, clearly annoyed. "No. Hell no. Vostesk Senior happened to leave out that particular detail."

Harlen would have thought for sure his father would have at least mentioned it to the one supposedly training him. But the expression on Jacques's face told him that, no, he hadn't. Harlen could practically see the man's brain firing a hundred questions at once, and the one that happened to emerge came out stilted and confused.

"Your wife doesn't know about this?"

"No," Harlen admitted.

"No offense but," Jacques used the smoking cigarette to gesture vaguely to Harlen's person once again, "Does she not question. . ? Those? At all?"

"She hasn't seen them," he said. "We—we haven't. . ." he trailed off, too embarrassed to say it out loud fully. "I just don't know how to explain it. And I don't know what she'll think."

And for the first time, he gave voice to the full extent of that particular worry. "It's too much."

He realized he was getting choked up again and tried to clear his throat discreetly. Jacques pretended not to notice by tapping out his ash into the washbasin. When he spoke after too long a pause, Harlen was glad he changed the subject.

Jacques offered the same grin he'd been wearing earlier. He plastered it across his face in an attempt to make the situation less unbearably heavy than it was.

Harlen was grateful for his effort, even if the smile was utterly hollow. Because there was nothing that could be done, they both knew it, and neither wanted to mention it.

"Well, how about we go to work on that spell to shut him up, huh?" Jacques said with too much forced enthusiasm. Even so, Harlen did his best to return the smile. It was easier. Easier than addressing what was under his shirt and all it implied.

CHAPTER 13

Millie woke up, not knowing what time it was. The perpetually gray sky made it so easy to lose track of time, and when she finally heard the clock chime, it was nearly nine in the morning.

Millie rolled herself out of bed with a grumble, dressed quickly, and noticed the sky didn't look quite as dreary as it usually did. She looked out the window with the tiny constellation beneath it and saw the rain seemed to have slowed.

She glanced over at the trunk at the foot of the bed where she still kept a good deal of her things. It was ridiculous after so long, but the place didn't feel enough like it was hers to leave her things scattered around. It was precisely why her letters were inside, buried beneath clothes and books and not stored in the drawer of Harlen's desk.

Maybe this would be as good a time as ever to try and send them home. After the events of last night, she felt she could use any advice her mother and sisters had to offer.

She knew there was not much they could do to change her situation, but she would gladly take it even if they had only the smallest advice to offer. In all truth, even if they had nothing to say about any of it, it would be everything just to hear from them again.

She fished them out from her journals, ribbons, and other heaped-together things. Altogether she had written about five. She thought sending them all at once in a bundle should be enough to make up for the time she had missed, though she was sure Roslin at least would consider her not having written every day a crime. Millie did hope she wouldn't be too upset.

A creak from the great oak doors downstairs drew her attention while she was still crouching beside the trunk, and she glanced up toward the sound. Was Harlen home early? According to the great clock ticking away down the hall, he wasn't due home for some time.

She stood up curiously and began to make her way towards the door for a look, and almost didn't notice the cup of dirt on the bedside table with the green branches sprouting from it.

She picked it up and held it to the light in confusion and felt her breath hitch in her throat when she finally realized what it was. Lavender.

She glanced back at the bedside table where it had been left and found a little scrap of paper tucked under it. She unfolded it and couldn't help the smile that tugged at her lips when she saw that it had a small ink drawing of a bumblebee in one corner.

"I still don't think I'm much of an artist, but I hope this is close enough to what you had in mind."

Millie felt her smile widen, and before she could think of a more dignified response, she found herself folding the paper very carefully and sliding it into the pocket of her dress.

She already had a remark about it ready on her lips when she left the room and hurried to the end of the hall, expecting to see him at the bottom of the stairs. Instead, when she reached the top of the stairs and was able to see the foyer, she saw none other than Vostesk Senior hanging his coat beside the door.

She felt her stomach grow cold, just as it had when she'd seen him for the first time at her wedding. But she did her best to keep her face neutral as he glanced up and spotted her. She even managed a small, polite smile and forced her legs forward. She wasn't going to hide from him like a child after he had spotted her. But she did clasp both her hands behind her back before he could see the letters.

"Lord Vostesk," she said pleasantly as she could, looking into those cold, pale eyes. She searched for any indication that he had spotted her last night. Some flicker of anger or irritation, but she saw nothing. "I didn't think you'd be home so early."

He inclined his head toward her with curt politeness. "Good afternoon. I do hope I'm not interrupting any plans by doing so."

She fought to keep her smile from faltering. There was no way he could KNOW she was planning on sending anything home. It had to be a trick of some kind. Needling at her to see if she would respond with guilt, he didn't know if she was up to something, but he was sniffing around to see if she was.

"I was just going to have a look at the garden. Harlen brought me some lovely flowers this morning. I realized it's almost the time of year when ours would start blooming back home. I was going to wait until the rain let up, but. . ." she trailed off and let her eyes wander to the window where the perpetual rivulets of rain were streaming down the glass.

As soon as Vostesk Senior glanced in the direction of the window, she quickly hid the letters in her pocket, not taking her eyes off him. As she watched, she couldn't be sure if the smile he gave was real or mocking. Either way, it didn't reach his eyes.

"Yes, I suppose if that was the idea, you might be waiting for some time. We have about two or three truly sunny days a year. Any other time if it isn't raining, it's rather gray. Not precisely conditions for gardens. I do hope you haven't anything too grand in mind."

"Grandness or lack thereof shouldn't be a problem," she said, clawing back through her mind for every bit of manners she'd ever learned. "I'd honestly just like to see the flowers."

Lord Vostesk nodded, then gestured towards the high, arched doorframe that led into the dining room. "Well, then. Allow me to escort you."

Millie felt her stomach twist, and unconsciously she put her hands together, touching the wedding ring on her finger, running her thumb over the engraving showing their combined family crests. Two mountains and a shark.

She had always thought sharks were something made up for stories until Harlen had told her otherwise. She had also thought ordinary people couldn't make you feel fear until she met Vostesk Senior. "That sounds just fine."

She descended the stairs, and they walked side by side across the black and white chessboard floor, their footsteps echoing off the high ceiling. The house had never felt so empty.

"I understand that this place is a good deal different from your home," Vostesk Senior said. "I do hope the change isn't too jarring. I hope you find this place. . .agreeable," he said, choosing the last word after a moment of careful thought.

"It is different," Maggie said, deciding it may be best to admit to a few truths. Saying she found the place pleasant would be too obviously an outright lie. "It's a lot colder than I'm used to."

"Well. I hope my son does a good job of keeping you warm, at the least," he said, and the sly look he gave her out of the corner of his eye said that he wanted her to be embarrassed. Or, at the very least, he wanted to trip her up in some way. Just like what he had said about not wanting to interrupt any plans she might have had for the day, he was sniffing around to find out. . .what exactly?

It could also be that he just wanted to throw her off and make her uncomfortable because he was an ass. That seemed just as likely.

She made a point of smiling at him with all the calm pleasantness she could muster despite how badly Millie wanted to give him a good slap and responded with confidence she certainly didn't feel but was proud of herself for faking.

"Well, of course. But I hardly thought mentioning that was appropriate. I will say that the cold is more notable in his absence."

She could have sworn she saw him nod. It was so slight she couldn't be sure, but his face settled itself as if he was acknowledging her small pushback. She wished very much that she could push him back physically: right into the wooden doorframe.

"Indeed. I do hope that the two of you will have better luck in those endeavors than my wife and I," he said as they passed through the dining room, through another arched door on its lower end, and into the sitting room furnished with dark wooden furniture covered in blue-green upholstery.

She saw a generous portion of the room where the floor pushed out beyond the ceiling, leaving an entire wall encased in what looked to her like a great glass dome. It jutted out into an area of the vast side yard filled with bushes, waving lavender plants, and a fountain that seemed comically redundant under all the rain. She had seen it several times, but she still thought it looked rather sad compared to the rolling, flowering fields she'd been able to look at from her bedroom window back home.

"We managed only the twins," Vostesk Senior continued, and Millie reluctantly drew herself back mentally to that glass-enclosed room beside him. "After that, she simply could bear no more. She was too frail, I'm afraid."

Right. Children. *This man's grandchildren*, she thought with her chest feeling tight. She had grown up with such a large family that she had always liked the idea of having one herself. But the idea of them growing up here with that small, rain-soaked patch of flowers and this house being the only places for them to play, living under the cold gaze of Vostesk Senior, had her unconsciously touching her stomach. As if that gesture alone could protect them from him.

"I'm sure you're in far better health, though," he continued, with her half-listening, apparently unconscious that she had stopped speaking. "She was from just down the road here, and most that live here are rather sickly by nature. I thought it might be better for someone who had grown up in a place known for raising more robust people to expand the family. That was why I selected you for my son."

Like picking a dog to breed, she thought. Fear and anger competed in her head as she stood beside him.

She kept her eyes on the waterlogged plants outside, afraid they would give her away if she looked at him directly because he was watching her. He was openly staring, cold eyes raking over her. Appraising. Not sexually—it was far more calculating and chilling than that.

"Your mother and eldest sister had some magical inclinations, yes?" he asked, and Millie had to keep from clenching her teeth.

"Yes," she said, fighting hard to keep her voice even. "Why do you ask?"

He folded his hands behind his back and shrugged. "It is important to carry on the magic in a bloodline. The Vostesk family has been a family of proud Sorcerers for generations. I'm simply saying that with such a combination of good blood, it is highly likely that you will pass on magical traits to your children. Even though you do not possess it."

She risked a glance at him, and he smiled. It still didn't reach his eyes.

"You should be excited." He said.

"My biggest concern is happy children," she said, and he chuckled again. She wished he'd stop.

"Of course, it is. You're their mother—it's in your nature. My wife was the same with our daughter. But from a practical perspective, continuing the bloodline is of the highest importance."

"More so than their happiness and health?" she said, unable to keep the incredulous tone from her voice or the revulsion from her face.

He stopped smiling, and his expression settled into one of utter seriousness. "Far more."

He paused for a moment, his jaw tight, as though considering what he was going to say. Or, instead, considering if she was worthy of an explanation. When he finally did speak, it was how one would talk to a child in need of a lesson. "Magic is a living thing. There is still much about it that we don't understand, but we generally know how it behaves. We know that it cannot survive on its own. It needs something to inhabit."

Vostesk Senior raised one hand, smooth and unlined even though he must have been in his fifties. He made a small, swirling motion with his fingers, and in the air above his palm, Millie saw ice crystals form in the air. They glittered in the gray light outside and hung suspended for a moment before dropping to the ground like snow that slowly dissolved back into little drops of water on the tile floor.

"When it inhabits people, it gives them control over the aspects of nature, mind, and man. Or, if they are not as strong, it lets them become a conduit of sorts. Passing on the power through themselves to imbue things like runes and objects with power that they cannot wield themselves. It is a sign that their blood is too weak to take hold of the true nature of magic."

He lowered his hand again, his eyes on the water that had gathered on the floor almost reverently. "Those who chosen to wield magic in its true form—to have it live in their blood— are those who are most worthy of living in this world. To understand and feel its true nature. To those without it—who never feel it—I cannot comprehend how they go about such menial lives."

He turned to face her, and it was like she was watching a snake contorting itself to swallow a mouse. She felt a morbid fascination at the coldness in his voice and the small upward turn of his lips when he looked her over as he finished his last statement. Never in her life had she encountered someone who so obviously derived so much satisfaction from not only his own superiority but from shoving what he saw as the inferiority of others in the faces of whoever he could.

"Harlen has no magic." She saw his eyes flash dangerously, but she continued. Maybe she could at least make him question his strange logic. "What is it that you think of his life?"

"He has magic," Vostesk Senior said so sharply it sounded like a threat. It was such a violent shift from how calmly he had just been speaking that she had to stop herself from taking a step back. "He's a Vostesk. It's in his blood. He just needs the proper motivation and training."

"He seems to want to cast magic more than anything from what I've seen. I don't know what other sorts of *motivation* there is," she said, snapping right back at him, angry that he had taken to raising his voice at her for having the audacity to do something as small as question him.

She knew she was pushing her luck, but he had been so awful she couldn't resist taking at least one last shot at him. "Though I'm sure you're very creative in that regard."

She wasn't brilliant—but she was no idiot. The image of the bandages on Harlen's arms was bright in her mind's eye with every word she said. She had no idea if it had anything to do with magic, but if Vostesk Senior was going to be throwing out blind accusations to see if anything came of it, then so could she.

She knew she would regret what she had just done, but damn if it wasn't satisfying for the moment, it hung in the air.

I know you're doing something *you bastard.*

"Your family has no long-standing magic in its blood," he said with a sneer like he was accusing her of something dirty. "You have no concept of how important this is. Or how deeply rooted magic can become in a family. And I assure you—when it comes to preserving that, I can be very *creative* indeed."

He took a step towards her, his hands twitching at his sides, and she reached quickly back to the table beside her. There was a massive, silver candlestick there, and she seized hold of it, ready to pick it up and swing if necessary. Magic blood was good—but a blow to the head was a blow to the head no matter your breeding.

The moment he saw her take hold of it, he seemed to come back to himself. The anger that had overtaken him eased, and he stood back to the proper distance, fixing his face with another polite smile that did nothing to thaw the ice in his stare.

She watched his hands momentarily clench in and out of the shape of fists before he folded them behind his back again. Not as though he was calming down. More like he was pushing down something that never entirely went away.

"Oh, come now. You don't think I'd harm you, do you?" he asked with contempt, trying again to bring out her guilt. How could she jump to the conclusion that he was going to be such a barbarian as to lay hands on his son's wife? They were only having a civil conversation after all. His face said it all, but she was having none of it.

"I don't know very much about you at all, Lord Vostesk."

His jaw twitched. Millie tightened her grip on the candlestick. She felt as though the air was again glittering with crystals of ice as he said, "If that is how you wish to be."

He gave an exaugurated, mocking bow, and excused himself from the room. He said something about having more important things to take care of and that she evidently wished to be left alone. Millie didn't dare take her eyes off him while he left the room and didn't let go of the candlestick until she heard the door to his office upstairs swing shut with a bang.

Only then did she realize she'd been shaking.

CHAPTER 14

Harlen arrived home to the sight of his father and several of his associates stepping through the front gate, all of them shrouded in cloaks against the steadily increasing rain.

Quickly, he stepped back behind the tall stone pillar that held the gate in place at the far corner of the yard and waited, counting off seconds in his head until a minute passed. Then, he carefully glanced around and saw the figures of his father and the other men vanishing far down the street.

He was quite relieved to approach the house with the knowledge that it was mostly empty. He and Jacques hadn't been able to make much progress after the incident. Despite his attempts at being lighthearted and optimistic, Jacques seemed to have lost the stomach for it and dismissed him almost as soon as they sat back at the table.

Harlen had spent the better part of an hour pacing around the front of the building nervously, rubbing his scratched arm and the lumpy stitches that ran up his sleeve impulsively because he knew he wasn't expected home until late.

Honestly, the entire way home, he had thought that he should have stayed longer. Even if he only managed to wander around aimlessly and acquaint himself further with the old guild house, his father would not be pleased if he knew he had left before he was expected home.

It was a weight off his shoulders to know that perhaps things had worked out in his favor, and he had just missed the lot of them. Now he only had to hope his father decided to stay out for a few hours.

Harlen hurried through the front door and hung up his wet coat beside the door, rubbing his hands together in an attempt to shake off the numbness the cold had left in his fingertips. Every sound he made from the dripping of water from the hem of his coat to the rustle of his clothes seemed to echo off the high ceiling. Harlen thought it was a bit what standing in an empty cave must feel like and exhaled a long breath into his clasped hands, amusing himself by admitting in his mind that he probably looked a bit like one of those tiny, blind creatures that tended to inhabit in such places. If his reflection in the fogged, silver mirror beside the door was any indicator, he was undoubtedly pale enough for it.

"Hello?"

Harlen jumped when he heard a voice from the other room before he realized who it belonged to. Millie.

"It's me," he called back.

"You're early."

Maybe she was just glad it wasn't his father stepping back in, but he thought she sounded happy to hear it was him.

She sounded as though she was in the sitting room, so he walked towards it quickly, unconsciously smoothing the front of his shirt as he went. He wondered if she had found the lavender he left for her—if she enjoyed it or thought it was a bit too much. Did she think the note was charming or silly? And, finally, selfishly, part of him hoped she had missed him.

He found her sitting in one of the chairs beside the window, the very one he had occupied yesterday while his father and Chairman Berkley chatted about his new professor. She was sitting with her legs tucked up under her as was her habit, and when she turned and smiled at him, he felt his breath catch in his throat.

Ever since they had been married, he hadn't been separated from her for longer than a few hours. He had never stopped thinking that she was a lovely woman, but after being gone for the day, he felt as though he had forgotten how she truly looked. How well her long, dark hair that never seemed to lose its wild, tousled look despite her best efforts suited her, just how warm her gray eyes were. How her lopsided smile pressed that dimple into one cheek just so. She stole the breath from him.

He likely would have found himself standing there, fumbling for words, had he not noticed that the smile wasn't quite right. He couldn't name it exactly, but something about it was different from the grin that was never far from her lips.

"Are you alright?" he blurted out before he could think better of it.

In the silence that followed when the smile vanished, he walked across the room, hesitantly sitting in the chair opposite her with the table holding a gleaming silver candlestick between them.

He wanted to stand beside her and put a hand on her shoulder, but he wasn't sure looming over her would help lessen any uneasiness. Instead, he remained on the edge of the green, and blue embroidered chair with his hands braced on his knees, watching her intently as she blinked at him in apparent surprise.

"Of course." She tried another smile, and he realized what wasn't quite right about it. It didn't reach her eyes. The spark was absent. "I feel like I should be asking you about that. I hope they weren't too rough on you on your first day."

"It wasn't as bad as expected," he said, which was mostly right. He certainly had a story he could tell Millie if he chose; having a professor nearly slice his arm open was interesting if nothing else.

She remained silent, giving him room to elaborate, but he couldn't get past how tightly she curled in her chair. It didn't look like an aversion to the chill. It looked more like every muscle in her body had tensed so tightly that sitting any other way was impossible.

She also had one hand perched on top of her knee that was pulling at the silky gray fabric of her dress, plucking absently and repeatedly at a loose thread in an embroidered blue flower. It was...very odd.

The thing that jumped reflexively to his mind was that she was annoyed. He wondered if he had irritated her in the few moments since his entrance but quickly dismissed the thought. This didn't strike him as anger. Everything about how she was sitting and speaking and smiling was indicative of something he was more familiar with: fear.

He dragged his eyes slowly upward from where he had been watching her hand as she worried away at the thread and found her studying him with a nervous expression. It reminded him of the way he looked at her in the first few weeks of their acquaintance when he had been sure that at any moment, she was going to shout at him or slap him.

He was taken aback to see it reflected on her of all people. He was sure he had never seen her look even the slightest bit anxious aside from a few tense moments with his father. He didn't know what to make of it.

He tried offering her his attempt at the warm smile she gave him when he was feeling jumpy. Her lips twitched upward in response, but it still didn't touch her eyes.

So instead, he prodded gently, hoping it would put her at ease and coax her to speak, "Are you sure? That you're alright?"

She looked out the window, the light from outside reflecting brightly off the side of her face. She kept her eyes on the waterlogged garden outside when she spoke, trying to adopt a casual tone and failing when she asked, "Out of curiosity. When we do have children, what exactly are you hoping for?"

Harlen started. He hadn't even managed to kiss her yet, let alone think that far ahead. The suggestion made his face grow hot, which he knew was ridiculous. It was a legitimate question and a subject he knew they would discuss eventually.

However, he thought they would spend a bit more time getting used to each other, and it would come up somewhat naturally. Nothing about this felt natural. It was abrupt and strained, and Millie seemed rather alarmed. It gave him a sinking sensation in the pit of his stomach.

He knew the answer before he finished asking, "Did my father say something to you?"

She didn't have to tell him. The look that passed over her face, she tried hiding by propping her chin in her hand, and turning a bit further away from him was enough.

Harlen sank back in his chair, feeling as though he was crumbling inward. His fingers pressed into the place where his kneecaps met the bones of his legs until it was painful.

Of course, his father would want children from them. It was another chance to have magical offspring to raise. He should have seen it coming a mile away and had no idea why it felt like such a blow.

"I'm sorry." He said, and he meant it.

She looked up at him. First, a glance to see if he was sincere, then a long, steady gaze that burned into his eyes intensely. "I just need to know. What is it you're expecting?"

He hadn't thought about it until now. Never in all his life had he thought he would even become a married man, let alone be in a position where he would have his own child to raise. He supposed that living isolated in this house, absorbed in his books on magic, he thought of himself a bit like Adrian

Vostesk. Alone and always working, searching for answers endlessly with no other company.

Millie's arrival had changed that. He didn't feel quite so alone with her teasing him and smiling at him and breathing beside him at night, lulling him to sleep. As nervous as she made him, it was seldom out of fear anymore. It was a lighter sort that was coupled with something like relief whenever he saw her.

He was never lonely anymore. That feeling had been so welcome, so intense that he had been an idiot. He hadn't even considered *why* his father would arrange a wife for him. He should have known that he had a motive that had nothing to do with his happiness.

Harlen tried thinking of what children of his own would be like, and he couldn't imagine that they would be anything different from him. Small, sickly, and non-magical. Helpless.

He imagined a boy of about ten, a copy of his own younger self with scars and bruises on his skinny arms, looking up at him and asking why he had to be punished for what he couldn't do, no matter how badly he wanted to please Vostesk Senior. Because no matter how terrible he was, there would be a part of them that would still want to make him happy.

Harlen knew it. He knew it would be there, dug deep into them if they were anything like he was. They would never understand why all their work never made them any better or more worthy of love. It would only mean more frustration and more scars on their flesh, and it would be his fault for passing them his burden. For giving them over to his father.

"I want them to be safe," he blurted out. More than anything, he would want them safe. "I don't—" he thought, struggling to put it into words without admitting to too much. Struggling with the image of the little boy in his head that he wanted to snatch up and run out of the house with. To wherever they didn't hurt those without magic in their blood. "I don't want them to feel like I do."

He couldn't read the way she was looking at him, only that she seemed unbearably upset. He could see her still twisting the blue thread from her dress around her first two fingers. Tighter and tighter. Precisely the same as his fidgeting with his cufflink. She was afraid just like he was.

It was enough to push him to reach out through the space between the two chairs and put his hand over hers. The same as she had done to him, pulling her fingers away from the thread biting into her skin and leaving angry pink lines behind.

He wanted to reassure her and tell her she didn't need to worry and that everything would be okay. But she was too smart to believe that. Instead, he stood up and took her hand in both of his, rubbing her fingers to soothe the marks left behind by the thread.

Harlen wondered what exactly it was that his father had said to her. He couldn't imagine it was anything kind. He wished he could have been there to prevent it, but then again, what would he have done? He'd never stood up to him before. He'd always been terrified of the man. But he hoped that if it came down to it, he would be brave.

She was all alone here. She had no friends, no family that wasn't separated from her by weeks of travel. He was all she had.

It was a horrifying thought. He was nothing. But if the way her fingers curled around his as he rubbed the places where the thread bit into her flesh to ease the sting wasn't a plea for him to be more than that, he didn't know what was. And he wanted to be. For the person who smiled at the stars he drew under his window.

She was so scared. And she was alone. He had to do *something*. He knew too well what it was like to be alone and afraid. She was bright. She was kind and warm, and he had never seen her look so small and fearful. It wasn't fair. It was the same thing his father had done to him, his mother, and tried to do to Tansey. He wanted to do it again as soon as he could get a child from them.

It couldn't be allowed. Harlen couldn't sit and watch it happen again.

"What can I do?" he asked Millie, holding her hand tightly.

Let me help you. Harlen thought. *Let me do something, please.*

"I want to write to my family," she said with a hitch in her voice that broke his heart. She cleared her throat immediately after and frowned like it had betrayed her. "Or I did write them letters; I just don't know where to go to send them. And I don't want. . .him to take them I want to do it myself."

An idea came to him immediately, and it was a bad one. Every part of him was screaming that it was stupid at best, dangerous at worst. He hoped Millie couldn't tell that his stomach had turned to ice and that his heart was drumming up in his throat.

He didn't know exactly where the post office was. Only that it was in the lower trade districts. He wasn't supposed to go there, but then again, he wasn't supposed to be home either. His father would be furious if he found him here.

Taking Millie there—or at the very least taking the letters there—would be safer, would it not? At least until the time he was expected to return from The Academy.

Besides, his father was gone and likely wouldn't be back for hours. They could slip in and out before he returned, surely. The thought made his hands sweat, and his throat felt like it was going to close as fear conflicted with whatever new thing he was feeling. He could imagine that somewhere Tansey was smirking at his sudden surge of rebellion as he spoke before he could overthink and stop himself.

"I can take you to the post office," he said.

Millie blinked in what he could only describe as disbelief, and her eyes snapped up to look at him. "What?"

"It'll be fine," he said, not so sure of it himself.

Her smile was like a cloud had lifted from the sun. She was on her feet before he could even blink and threw her arms around him.

He was so startled he took a step back and bumped against the table, rattling the heavy silver candlestick sitting on its top. Millie seemed oblivious to it, and he stood, unable to catch his breath while she pressed her cheek into his chest and squeezed him.

She had begun loosening her grip by the time he even thought to return the gesture. His long, awkward arms found their way around her, and she stepped right back into place, right up against him once his hands touched her. Solid, soft, warm.

How long had it been since someone had put their arms around him? He couldn't remember precisely with his mother, but he knew she hadn't been anything resembling affectionate since he was very young. And Tansey—Tansey had gone years ago.

It had been over six years.

He realized he was gripping the back of her dress rather tightly and made himself loosen his fingers, but he didn't want her to pull away. Not yet.

"Are you okay?" she asked, very softly, muffled against his shirt.

"Yes. Yes, I'm—I'm fine," he said, his breath coming quick and his eyes misting. He felt her rub a small circle between his shoulders, and his knees nearly buckled. It was so gentle, so kind. He had hardly noticed how long he had gone without a kind touch, and it was like all the time that had passed hit him in an instant.

How long had it been for her?

As lightly as he could manage, he ran his fingers through her hair. He felt her grip tighten and heard her breath catch, and knew that no matter what the outcome was, he would be sure they got her letters home.

Finally, he stepped back with great reluctance, clearing his throat and adjusting his glasses to give him a chance to rid himself of the water in his eyes. Millie straightened the front of her dress, sniffing a bit too hard, and when they looked at each other, the silence was awkward.

"Um." Harlen rubbed his arm, feeling the lumpy stitches in the one slightly lopsided sleeve. "We really should get you a coat. Before we go."

The rain had become a downpour, and she would freeze without one. Harlen at least knew the place they were going was near the town center, and she wouldn't make it more than three feet from the door in the gauzy material she wore.

She let him step out to get her something more suitable and cool the burning in his face and neck. He tried taking a moment to stand in the draft of the front door, sucking in several deep breaths that didn't chase away the feeling of her hands pressed between his shoulders or the smoothness of her hair between his fingers.

It was a futile effort, really, but he didn't entirely mind the lingering sensation of her cheek against his chest as he hurried up the stairs to retrieve one of his coats for her.

CHAPTER 15

The coat was long, made of heavy gray leather with black cuffs and a collar, lined on the inside with fur. It was too big to fit correctly, but it would keep her warm, and it seemed to please her immensely when he helped her into it.

"You might never get this back," she said as she secured a few of the silver buttons at the coat's waist. She seemed to be back to herself after having taken a moment to calm down as well, though Harlen did notice her eyes darting in his direction more than usual.

"It never suited me much," he said, unable to keep a smile from tugging at his face.

Watching her sheer excitement did help dull some of his nerves, but he kept an anxious watch in all directions as they made their way to where he hoped he would be able to find the post office.

"I've never seen a place so squished together," Millie observed as they got away from the mostly empty road where the Vostesk Manor stood and entered the town itself.

They moved through the rows of huddled-together buildings, all of them with faded roofs and awnings, their paint peeling from the constant wet and the onslaught of salty air from the sea. The taste was heavy enough to make Harlen's mouth dry despite the rain as they came close enough to the ocean to hear the roar of the white-capped, black waves over the pounding rain.

The only warmth and light came from little orange and yellow lights glowing inside the shop and house windows. Harlen noticed Millie walking a bit slower next to the display windows that shone the brightest of all, looking in curiously at all the strange scenes set behind them to entice customers.

There were two cloth dolls propped up by wire seated at a pink table frozen in a scene with cups in their hands in the window of the tea shop. The baker displayed frosted cakes where the blue, yellow, and green icing stood out brilliantly against the faded colors world on the other side of the glass. The woodcarver had gone as far as creating a small wooden forest complete with a cabin and a pack of glossy pine wolves running between the trees to sit in his window.

Harlen watched as Millie slowed in front of each one, and her head turning of its own volition as she took it in while her feet kept trying to keep her walking.

Tansey had told him about these a few times. He found them fascinating, but not nearly as entertaining or soothing as Millie's reactions.

"I take it they don't have these in the mountains?" he asked while her eyes gleamed at the sight of the polished pine wolves in the trees.

"No," she breathed. "It's mostly open-air markets. I've never seen anything like this."

It was the first time he had heard her sound like she enjoyed anything she saw in Wakefield, and he was glad. He wished he could thank the shopkeepers for making the cobblestone streets a bit less dreary.

He was still on edge. He couldn't keep himself from scanning the crowds around them continuously for a face he recognized as his father or one of his associates. He felt dreadfully exposed, and everything inside him was screaming that they needed to go back before anyone caught them.

But Millie was smiling again. For the first time since he had met her, he believed she was happy.

"That one looks like you." She said as they passed the window of a cramped toy shop. She was pointing in at a painted toy deer with comically long legs and a pointed face. She grinned at him, inviting him to step closer, and he had to press up against her side to peer into the window in the crowded street. He must have made a face when he gave the thing a closer look because she chuckled.

"Well, that looks like you," he said, pointing to the far corner of the zoo-like scene. There was a cat with long, cotton fur quite nearly the same color as Millie's hair in the far corner with closed eyes and a profoundly self-satisfied smile stitched on its face.

She made a noise of mock-offense and jostled him with her shoulder. He very nearly slipped on the icy paving stones but caught the corner of the window ledge, and Millie grabbed the sleeve of his coat to keep him upright. They stared at each other for a frozen moment, then both burst out laughing.

It broke apart the lingering awkwardness from their earlier exchange, and for just that moment, Harlen was glad they were here. It was a fleeting moment of joyful abandon before his fear that they might be spotted by someone who knew his father crept back in, but it wasn't a feeling he would forget. Neither was the feeling of Millie walking beside him, huddled close enough to touch, as they continued on their way.

The post office, luckily, turned out to be easy enough to find. The sign was painted in letters fresh enough to stand out, though POST's red was already fading on its white background. The two of them ducked inside the door beneath it.

The building itself was cramped. There was a small standing space before a massive counter that stood in front of an even more enormous set of shelves. They housed baskets of letters sorted alphabetically, packages from all sorts of places, and what looked like enough quills, ink, stamps, and stationery to stock a small military encampment.

At the front desk stood a rather stern-looking man with very neatly trimmed dark hair and thin-rimmed glasses. He stood beside a blue goblin with equally neat, trimmed hair sorting through one of the baskets of letters.

They appeared to be the only two in the shop, so, despite its cramped nature, it somehow still managed to feel empty and quiet. The only sound was the papers in the basket rustling and an occasional thump as the goblin stamped something.

"Good afternoon," the man said very curtly. "How may I assist you?"

"Yes! Hello," Millie said brightly and rummaged through the coat. She produced five envelopes, already addressed, and set them on the counter. The goblin reached out with his tiny, sharp-clawed hands and pulled them towards the stack of mail he was working on. To Harlen, it seemed like he was admiring the stationary before the man gave him a sharp glare. "Just some outgoing post."

Harlen tried to eye the man behind the counter surreptitiously but was reasonably sure he had never seen him before. If the man recognized him, he did not indicate it. He looked bored out of his mind. His eyes glazed over both of them with hardly a hint of life. He simply asked for the fee and nodded when Harlen stepped forward and passed him several silver coins.

"You don't have to do that," Millie said, slowly putting back a small coin purse she pulled from her pocket.

"It's alright."

He had to make use of the money behind the mirror eventually, didn't he? It had been easy to grab along with the coat, and he had no other use for it. It was more than enough to make sure a few of her letters got home.

CHAPTER 16

The errand had taken much less time than expected. In fact, Harlen thought he was beginning to understand why Tansey had liked this so much. Behind the fear that he knew wouldn't be departing as long as they were outside, there was a sort of rush to it. It was dizzying.

He was half-convinced his father would still find out and that there would be hell to pay, but as they made their way back down the street talking and peering in shop windows together with their fingers now and then brushing between them, he couldn't push away the idea that this was somehow worth it.

The idea that he should have done this a long time ago was contending with the repetitive, loud shouting that he should never have done this in the first place. He was surprised to find that he almost favored the former.

It filled him with a near-giddiness dampened by guilt. What if he had forced himself to do this just a few years earlier? Tansey might still be around.

The feeling settled heavy in his stomach, but it was comforting to know that she would be teasing him mercilessly right now if she knew what had finally pushed him to do it. Or if she could see how he blushed every time Millie's fingers touched his.

If he knew Tansey at all, he knew she would just be happy he had finally done it—even if he *was* scared out of his mind. Perhaps it was that thought that made him suggest they should step into one of the shops whose window he and Millie had paused to stare into.

"I don't know if you would want to waste time watching me look at ribbons and dress pins," she said as she looked at the window of the modest little clothing store. Two mannequins were posed as though they were dancing in party dresses with great puffs of feathers on the hems and sleeves. "Or at what looks to be a selection of dead birds for that matter."

"Maybe not, but maybe we could get you something warm," he said as if he hadn't already spotted something inside in the far back that he thought she might like when she was staring at the displays.

She looked at him with a slow-spreading smile that made his legs feel far less sturdy than usual. He wondered if she suspected he had seen something good, but if she did, she said nothing as they entered the shop.

It smelled like dust and wool inside. Piles of clothing muffled every noise from inside and outside the shop. It was more library than a store, and they both kept their voices low out of principal as they spoke.

"Thank you," she whispered as they walked between the stacks of sweaters and folded skirts made of heavy material. There was no silk and gauze here.

"Well, I was starting to think my father was never going to get around to getting you something suitable."

"No, not that. Well—yes, that. But I meant for listening to me. Overall, I suppose."

He might have been mistaken, but he thought she looked embarrassed. "Why wouldn't I?"

She shrugged. She was keeping her eyes firmly on the clothing and tucking her hair back behind her ear repeatedly. Her own nervous habit Harlen supposed.

"I don't know. I assumed you had bigger things to worry about than letters home and warm clothes and lavender plants. I'm beginning to think I should choose my words more carefully in the future since I didn't think you even paid attention to half the things I talk about."

"They're important to you," he said. They were in a secluded corner of the store, so he felt free to come to a stop. Millie did as well, a few paces from him. She kept her eyes averted for the most part but kept glancing at him in flashes.

"I know being here isn't. . .easy," he confessed. "I don't know much about what other families are like. But I know enough to know mine isn't exactly the most comfortable. And my father is. . ." He trailed off, still looking over his shoulder out of habit. "And I know I'm probably not what you had in mind when you imagined your husband. But I like being around you. You're very kind. I would never ignore you."

Harlen had come quickly to the conclusion that he was terrible at expressing his feelings and that a narrow space surrounded by scratchy sweaters was probably not the best place for doing so. He felt hot and was very aware that his words were tripping over themselves on their way out of him.

Still, he had to get them out somehow. He had to let her know that she made him feel less alone, and he desperately wanted to do the same for her in his fumbling, imperfect way.

"You care about me falling asleep with my glasses on. And you liked the stars under my window," was all Harlen could think to say. It was the only way he could describe it, and even then, it was inadequate. But try as he might, he had no other words for the affection required to notice the things that made him feel, for the first time, seen. Not as an inconvenience or as a failure, but just as himself.

He was fiddling with his cufflink again and only realized it when she reached out and again took his hand. He looked at her and saw that she wasn't looking at his eyes but their intertwined fingers. The gold of their wedding bands gleamed in the dim light that managed to filter through the windows, and she smiled ever so faintly. A different kind than he was used to seeing; this one was soft and almost shy.

"I do." She said.

Then her eyes were back on his. The spark had returned to them, and her smile returned to the impish grin that dimpled her cheeks. "And for what it's worth, I do think you're an outstanding artist. Your bees are spectacular."

He blushed as a raspy laugh bubbled out of him, and she winked. She let her hand slip from his, and he felt the remaining warmth from her fingers send a shiver up his spine. The worry that he said too much too quickly was still present, but not nearly as intense as it had been the last time they spoke. The silence was comfortable as he watched her find what he thought would catch her eye.

It was situated in the shop's back; a nearly floor-length dress with long sleeves in a beautiful lavender color, the hem, sleeves, and collar trimmed with white lace. The material was soft and heavy. As soon as Millie touched it, he saw her eyes brighten.

"What do you think?" she asked, looking at him before outright saying anything about it herself. However, her face said quite loudly that she loved it.

He considered how to answer. She was lovely, and he thought it would be lovely, but was that too forward? Was she expecting something witty?

Thinking quickly as he could, he settled on, "It would be very pretty on you."

Her smile only grew bigger. "I still think your dressing robe might be better, though."

He laughed and had to admit to himself he did get some enjoyment out of thinking she might still wear it even if she had something better.

"If your father asks, I'll just say I got it myself," Millie said as they made their way back, her new dress tucked under one arm. "Though he might think me managing to navigate the city a bit unbelievable."

"I'm not sure he'll notice," Harlen admitted, and that was the truth. As much as the man seemed to know, he never noticed when Tansey had gotten herself some new clothing or decoration from the city.

Harlen had always thought it brazen for her to walk around like that, but over time he became convinced his father paid the women in the family far less mind than he did his son or colleagues.

He would notice if Harlen had the smallest thing out of place or comment on some new broach one of his friends wore. But his eyes seemed to simply pass over his mother and sister as if they were no more than furniture.

He remembered on one occasion he and Tansey had to secure an entire new wardrobe for their mother. She had gone into a fit that lasted days and ruined nearly all of her clothes. Harlen had created the orders through letters and forms, and Tansey had gone to collect them physically from the post office and shops.

He had thought it would lead to some kind of punishment, but the man either never noticed or he didn't care when his wife suddenly had new clothes.

Harlen felt his heart once again leap up into his throat when they approached the front gate of the manor, and their conversation trickled away to silence. He wrapped his hands around the gate, the cold of the metal biting into his hands as he pushed it inward.

Above them, the two separate wings of the house stretched out to greet them. To fold them in like some massive bird of prey.

He had to wonder how Tansey had ever brought herself to come back after her first taste of freedom. He certainly didn't want to step through the doors. The only comfort as they swung shut with an irritated bang that echoed off the high ceiling was that the place was still as empty as it had been when they had left.

CHAPTER 17

Millie felt far more content than she had since her arrival in Wakefield. She sat wrapped in the thick fabric of her new dress, holding a cup of steaming tea in her hands, knowing that by now, her letters home were probably on their way back towards the mountains. She had seated herself on a stack of pillows while Harlen had already fallen asleep on his side of the bed.

He had been reading. In rare form, he had been relaxing with one of the poetry books he was so fond of that he kept on the shelves nearest his bed. It was good to see even if he had fallen asleep with it still in his lap, his glasses on his face again.

She had marked and closed his book, taken off his glasses, and pulled a blanket over the top of him and somehow hadn't woken him up in the process. The most significant reaction she'd gotten from him had been when she was lingering next to him a moment longer than was strictly necessary when she had taken off his glasses.

She wasn't sure what prompted it, but she had brushed some of his hair away from his face, and he turned his cheek into her touch, still fully asleep, letting out the smallest of sighs. It was very sweet. He was very sweet. He was growing on her, and the fact that she hadn't had the heart to move her hand until he had shifted away was evidence enough of that.

She'd spent the last hour or so sitting and watching the rain pour down the street, watching Harlen slowly sink lower into a laying position, listening as he occasionally mumbled something in his sleep. She took that to be evidence that she must be growing on him as well since she had never heard him so much as move or make a peep after he closed his eyes before. She also never had someone cling to her quite as desperately as he had earlier when she'd hugged him.

Her family was very affectionate. There had always been someone leaning against her, propping their chin on her shoulder to see what she was doing, hugging her, or ruffling her hair until three months ago. When she had first put her arms around him, she thought she knew what it was to miss human contact, but there had been such a hunger in the way he responded that it made her chest ache just to think about it.

It was what kept her reaching down as she sat beside him to run her fingers through his hair as he'd done to her. Every time, his hand resting on the pillow beside him would curl a little tighter.

The last time she had done it, she had run the side of her hand down the sharp jut of bone above the deep hollow of his cheek, and he'd released a shuddering sigh that sounded almost like a whimper. It had taken everything in her to push back the impulse to pull him into her arms again.

She wasn't sure why. It wouldn't do much of anything to help with whatever required bandages, and it wouldn't do anything to protect against it in the future. She just couldn't shake the feeling that it was still something Harlen needed regardless.

Millie sighed in contemplation and looked back down the street as she leaned back against the pillows, taking another sip of her tea. There wasn't much to see beyond the darkness and the rain, but as she watched, she saw three figures emerging from the downpour, huddled miserably under cloaks that flapped as they moved briskly down the street.

It wasn't difficult to recognize a familiar white top hat among them. It stood out like a spotlight in the dark, and Millie wondered what Chairman Berkley could be doing coming this way so late at night. If the chimes she heard from the clock down the hall were correct, it was nearly midnight.

Curious, she watched as the figures stopped near the curve at the end of the street, close enough for her to see that they must be arguing. Rather aggressively at that. Their cloaks flapped like agitated bird wings as they gestured wildly, and she wished she could hear what they were saying.

Then, without warning, one of them turned sharply and began stalking toward the house. The other two, including Berkley, lingered at the edge of the street and seemed to share a few more words before they turned and left, vanishing back into the night.

Millie was still following Berkley's hat when she heard the heavy thud of the front door opening and closing, followed by pounding footsteps on the stairs. She nearly fell off her perch as Vostesk Senior's office door slammed thunderously and was amazed it didn't wake Harlen. How often did he sleep through things like this?

Indignant and more interested than she had a right to be, she stood and crept over to the bedroom door. She eased it open ever so slightly and peered out into the hallway lit only by the dim light of the moon trickling through the window at its end.

She had no plans to get closer to the office, where she heard a series of bumps and thuds. She only wanted to take a quick look with the hope Vostesk Senior was the type to mutter when he was irritated so she could learn what the confrontation had been about.

She remained crouched and waiting and straining to hear if there were any words mixed in with the shuffling coming from the office and jumped when a bright light suddenly came to life beneath the office door.

But she did linger and wondered at the odd glow coming from beneath the door.

It was a vibrant orange light that, at first, she thought must be coming from the fireplace. But how would he light it so quickly? Even if he had managed to light it as soon as he entered, it wouldn't be so bright so fast.

What was more, it didn't look like fire. It was a constant, steady glow that offered no flickering. A candle or one of the kerosene lamps would have had a bit of a pulse to it. But as she stared at the pool of brightness seeping under the door, Millie saw no such thing.

Then, all at once, the light was gone as though it had never been. It was followed by Vostesk Senior cursing loudly and the sound of what she thought had to be him throwing everything off his desk or overturning a table. It sounded like a child having a tantrum. In this case, a child with power over the entire house.

Very carefully, Millie eased the door shut and climbed back into bed. The angry banging and clunking continued uninterrupted, but gradually they faded to background noise just like the rain. At least there were no more great crashes.

She lay in bed, stiff with fear, until she made herself take a deep breath. Then another. By inches, she made herself climb down from the heights of fear she leaped to with the sound of that crash.

She wouldn't let him scare her. That was one thing she had control over. She would not let herself be frightened by an overgrown, temperamental child.

She measured her breaths and reached into the pocket of her new dress, and ran her finger along the little folded note with the drawing of the honeybee. She reminded herself that she would hear from her family soon and that if they genuinely thought the situation she'd described was dangerous, they would find a way to help her. She couldn't let herself doubt that.

It didn't solve her immediate worries. But it was a comfort.

Millie tried to ignore the noise out in the hall. Instead, she listened to Harlen breathe next to her, more deeply and evenly than she'd heard since she had met him. She tried to match the sound of it, looking up at the window ledge above her, counting the stars etched into the paint.

She only noticed right before she drifted off that there was one more than the night previous.

CHAPTER 18

"It's quite impressive how long these petals keep their smell, isn't it?" Harlen asked.

He was back in the quiet back room of The Academy with Jacques, half the contents of the component cabinet scattered over the table.

For the last few weeks, Jacques hadn't done much in the way of teaching. For the most part, he simply unleashed Harlen on the books and ingredients after his first few attempted mixtures with them failed. He focused his attention on chain-smoking, filling the room with the bitter smell of cheap tobacco as he occasionally eyed him with a measure of curiosity.

It was strange; Jacques hadn't pointed out that he had failed at such simple magic at all. He acted as if he didn't even notice when he completed a mixture, and an incantation uttered only for Nothing to happen. The most he would interfere was now and again suggesting that he try a particular recipe or criticize that he was holding a new, sharp scalpel that he had brought from his mortuary the incorrect way.

All the while, the bowl of rainwater remained on the table, just in case. It sat between them, the elephant in the room, never so much as shifting aside from when Harlen's leg would bump the table.

Harlen supposed he should have been bitterly disappointed by that. If anything, this was likely the closest he would get to prove that there was simply Nothing magic, Nothing grand, about him.

Even those with the smallest arcane inclinations can master alchemical spells with enough dedication. It struck him as supremely odd that he didn't feel bitter or even disappointed by the, not entirely unexpected, revelation. Perhaps it was because his father wasn't reminding him that he should be, or because he found that he honestly enjoyed the meticulous process of measuring and mixing. as

He had found that he could produce some relatively competent salves and medicine, which they discovered one afternoon when Jacques came in complaining of sore shoulders from an evening of grave-digging. He tried to whip up something for himself when he was sure none of the other professors were going to peak their head in to see what they were doing.

Harlen had asked if he should be doing that. He pointed out what Jacques had pretty strong elemental magic of his own and expressed some concern that it may mix poorly with alchemy.

Jacques wasn't attempting anything magical. The salve was purely ordinary and medicinal, and his magic was unlikely to have much of an influence. Harlen just wasn't sure of another way to point out he was mixing the wrong things without sounding rude.

"How many times do I have to tell you not to worry so much?" Jacques had asked, and promptly the jar he had been shaking his ingredients together in exploded so forcefully that it wasn't so much glass shards as it was dust that they were brushing off their clothes in the aftermath.

Harlen had politely put forth the idea that perhaps he could give it a try instead. Jacques, still holding the lid of the disintegrated jar in his hand, was not too eager to try it again, so he had allowed it.

Harlen mixed three different variations of the concoction before he felt sure it would work. He held his breath while Jacques swallowed the brew that smelled like damp leaves and honey, and Harlen briefly admired his willingness to drink something made by a man who had yet to create any mixture with success.

He watched for his reaction intently, but when Jacques rolled his shoulders and said it worked, Harlen didn't believe him. he had actually been as bold as to say he was lying, which only made Jacques blink at him with his copper brows scrunched in bewilderment.

"Sure, Vostesk, sparing your feelings is much more important than me throwing out my back at twenty-five."

"Show me."

Harlen had no idea what he meant by that. He only knew that he was gripping the table with both hands, staring with such intensity that Jacques put up his hands in surrender.

Harlen had no idea it was possible to communicate sarcasm through gestures, but Jacques managed it as he did a series of stretches with his arms.

"See? Very limber."

Harlen didn't know what to say. He had remained silent for the rest of the afternoon, his head buzzing thoughtlessly. He could hardly come to terms with the idea that he'd been successful at anything.

Harlen had been making him regular batches ever since. He kept expecting them not to work, but each time the result was the same, and since then, he had slowly gotten braver. Whenever he and Jacques finished their attempt at magic for the day, he would slowly explore the realms of his newfound…He wouldn't call it a talent. Not exactly. It was competence. And it was exhilarating. After a lifetime of reaching and reaching inside himself and finding only emptiness, he was startled that his fingers had finally brushed something.

He experimented. He had even found a combination of cooling oils and herbs that helped with his headaches after his father's turn at lessons in the evenings.

Some afternoons he realized he was enjoying himself. Jacques's presence and watchful eye didn't bother him so much anymore. The young professor had given him no reason to be afraid, and he was coming to enjoy the conversations Jacques would strike up with him over the table about things that had nothing to do with magic or his lack thereof. Usually, it was one-sided and consisted of complaining about the nobles he worked with. Harlen was familiar enough with them to understand the complaints and sympathized with them much.

"I swear Berkley could schmooze his way into a position of actual power if he had more backbone than a pastry," Jacques would say.

He said many things, all equally as risky if anyone overheard. Harlen was sure there wasn't a nobleman in the bunch that would let that slip by, but Jacques never seemed to care about it one way or the other. He sat across the table, chatting and smoking like a chimney with seemingly not a care in the world.

At first, Harlen had been too afraid to speak out against his father's friends. He thought they would find out or that Jacques was simply testing him and would go running back with anything he said to his father. But over time, he started to add his own, not insults but observations. He even joined in with empathetic glances from time to time when specific names and predictable actions were mentioned.

Harlen had even initiated a few discussions. He was curious about his position as a mortician and undertaker, and the slightest inquiry could provoke many fascinating stories. He remembered the first time he'd even suggested his curiosity. Jacques's immediately jumped to the tale of his first time seeing a freshly dead body. It groaned when he touched it and nearly scared him into quitting the family business entirely. There was a scientific explanation for it that Jacques glossed over quickly, but Harlen didn't mind too much.

He was, admittedly, quite curious about the more technical aspect of his trade. Still, Jacques seemed to grow bored talking about how to crack ribcages and keep eyes shut and how to avoid the skin slipping off more decayed bodies rather quickly. That seemed to be true of everything Jacques spoke about, though. He didn't care much for anything that didn't make a funny story or couldn't at least be complained about.

That day, though, he had been oddly quiet. Ordinarily, he wasn't silent for longer than a few minutes before he found something to say.

Still, that day he had been working his way through his seemingly endless supply of little white paper cigarettes with hardly a comment on his coworkers or customers. When Harlen pointed out the smell of the flower petals, it only provoked a non-committal grunt. He had been expecting he would at least roll his eyes and tell him he desperately needed a hobby other than books and salves.

"I should ask Millie more about this," Harlen continued. He had become more talkative throughout their lessons, though not nearly as much as Jacques. At that moment, he was just trying to fill the unusual silence. "She did mention they grew quite a few medicinal herbs and flowers back in her home. She probably knows all about these sorts of things. She was telling me some interesting things about goldenrod the other day. Do you know how many insects live on that? It's practically an entire ecosystem in its own right—"

"Hey—you doing anything after this?" Jacques asked as though he'd heard Nothing, tapping out the remains of the cigarette he'd just finished on the table, leaving behind a black stain.

Harlen looked up at him, unbending from above the mixing bowl full of white paste and bits of rose that contested the smell of tobacco in the room, and answered, wondering if it was a trick question. "Studying?"

Jacques didn't assign anything for him to study technically, but he had been taking the medicine books home and reading them at night before bed. If there was any plant in the texts he didn't recognize, Millie could name it and its properties, and he found her insight invaluable to his understanding of what he would try during lessons.

Most evenings, they stayed up together with a candle lit by the bedside and went over the scribbled script together. Millie was an excellent teacher and had even begun compiling him a field guide of sorts regarding medicinal herbs to go along with their nightly study sessions.

He insisted she didn't have to, but she had dismissed his concern and said she was bored out of her mind most days anyway. It was something to do to fill the time, she said, but he was still flattered by it.

He wasn't sure if he wanted to explain all of that to Jacques, though. Telling him how it was to sit next to her with the only light coming from a candle's flame, watching the light reflect in her eyes, the way it felt when she would lean back against him to show him something of particular interest—that felt too personal.

"That's not what I mean," Jacques said with a look of exasperation. "Look. Since we've been at this, I don't think I've seen you do anything but walk between here and that creepy mansion of yours. From what I understand, you're not hurrying back to have a little fun with your wife, and you're not out in that back yard doing sports with those skinny arms—so what is it that you do?"

"Millie is fun," Harlen protested. "She's been trying to teach me some of those dances they do at spring festivals back in her hometown. I'm, ah, not very good, but she says it's because my posture's too rigid."

That was true if a bit embarrassing to admit. But it was easier to talk about than their lessons.

Jacques opened his mouth like he was going to say something but seemed to think better of it. Instead, he said, "Yes. Well, that's all fine and good. Nothing screams fun like folk dances. But what else do you even do?"

Harlen twirled the smooth, silver stirring stick he had been using between his fingers. A single crumbled rose petal still clung to the paste, coating its end.

He and Jacques hadn't talked about the lessons his father gave. Not since the first day when Jacques saw his scarred arm had they even brought it up. He hoped now that Jacques wouldn't make him try to explain the man's nature. And luckily, with his sudden silence and fidgeting, Jacques seemed to get the idea.

Harlen watched his eyes darken as he leaned back in his chair, then saved him from having to respond by breaking the silence himself.

"Alright, then. That settles it. Your wife's right—you're too rigid, and we're going to fix that." He tipped his chair back until he could set his scuffed boots up on the table and tipped himself back so far Harlen thought he might fall. "That traveling troop that does the theater is back. You're going to have a look around at it with me tonight."

"I—I couldn't. I—I don't know what to do. I don't know what to wear or—" Harlen started to say, but Jacques shook his head.

"No, listen, it'll be fine. Nobody cares what you wear, and if they do, after a few hours, everyone will be too drunk to remember it. Or you will be."

Harlen wondered if he should mention that he'd never actually been drunk before or that he hadn't even had hard liquor but thought it might not be the time to say it. Especially considering the much larger problem. "My father would never allow it."

"You're a grown man, aren't you?" Jacques sighed in exasperation.

"Yes," he said quietly. "But. . ."

It was more complicated than that. Much more complicated. Harlen hoped Jacques would remember enough of the scars to put the pieces together and stop pressing him because he began to shift uncomfortably in his seat.

Jacques gave him a long look, and Harlen saw the understanding. Then there was something else; anger flashed behind his eyes.

"Fine." Jacques's tone was flippant as he spoke, but there was a hard and defiant edge to it. "Fine. Let me talk to him. I'm a professor, aren't I? I'll tell him I need you for some professor shit, I don't know. I'll figure it out."

He seemed to be talking more to himself than anyone else, nodding slowly and gaining a kind of self-righteous excitement as he spoke.

"I'm not sure it's that easy," Harlen said.

"Look." Jacques dropped his chair back to all four legs and leaned forward. The bang made Harlen flinch. "You're weird. Probably the weirdest person I've ever met, with a few exceptions. But you seem alright."

Harlen wasn't sure if he should be insulted or not, but Jacques kept going.

"You're the smartest person I've ever met," he continued. "You're a walking encyclopedia with no concept of social skills."

"Thank you? I think?" Harlen said, too confused to be upset.

"My point is you never do anything that doesn't have something to do with studying or magic. And trust me. I get it— it's important. But shit, you have less of a life than most of the people whose ribs I crack open." Jacques shrugged. "I'm saying that once you unclench a bit, you seem like a decent guy. I feel like I would be—what's that word you used the other day— *remiss*. That one. I'd be remiss if I didn't at least try to get you to do *something*."

Harlen twisted the stirring rod between his hands. There was one other problem. And it was something Harlen couldn't budge on.

"I can't leave Millie there by herself."

She tried to hide it most of the time, but he knew she was afraid of his father. It was a perfectly rational fear to have. He hadn't said it to her in so many words, mostly because she seemed embarrassed to admit to being frightened, but he had promised her a thousand times over in his mind that he wouldn't leave her there alone any longer than he had to on any given day. Leaving her there for hours, possibly after Jacques needled him into one of his angry fits, wasn't something he could abide.

He didn't want to argue with Jacques. He didn't even really know how to argue, but he would if he had to.

Jacques shrugged and gestured widely with one arm, a grin tugging up his lips as if he'd just come up with a brilliant idea. "Bring her along. I'm sure she could use a night out if she's as stuck as you."

"Can you convince him to do that?" Harlen asked. This was so sudden and was happening so quickly that he felt disoriented. He highly doubted Jacques would be able to convince his father of anything, but Jacques just grinned wider and seemed again unbothered by the risk.

"Look, if Berkley can schmooze, have a little faith in my skill. I sit on the board with the guy, after all. Might as well put what I learn from him to good use."

Harlen was unsure. He was still skeptical when they left the school at the end of the day, and when they reached his house, he was already beginning to tell Jacques that this was a bad idea. It wasn't going to work; he shouldn't bother. But it seemed Jacques had made up his mind. He just elbowed him and told him to stop thinking so hard about it.

"Just go get your girl and be ready to go," Jacques said as though it would be as simple as that.

CHAPTER 19

Harlen was ready to crawl out of his skin as soon as they walked through the front door. He could hear his father in the sitting room and made one last attempt to stop Jacques, who shook him off with a command to be ready before turning on his heel and walking quickly after the sound of Vostesk Senior's voice.

Harlen stood in the entryway as the end of his professor's coat vanished around the corner, numb with anticipation. Harlen thought maybe he should wait and see if he could hear how the conversation was going, but as soon as he heard Jacques's boisterous greeting, he knew he couldn't stand there and listen.

Instead, he hurried up the stairs and took the fact that he heard no shouting as a good sign. It didn't completely smother the panic curling in his chest until he reached his and Millie's shared bedroom door. There, he was filled with nerves of an entirely different kind.

He took a deep breath to steady himself and smoothed down his jacket. Millie was sitting cross-legged on the bed when he walked in, working away at what he assumed was another letter home.

She looked up and smiled at him, and it made heat bloom in his cheeks. He had never asked her to go somewhere with him. It was silly, but he felt like he was asking her on a date. In a way, he supposed he was.

Before he could lose his nerve, he exclaimed, "Would you like to go somewhere with me?"

She blinked at him. "Well, that sounds ominous," she said, but she was only teasing. Her grin was positively impish, and he could already see the excitement creeping over her features before he had even explained what was going on. She folded the paper and set aside the book she was using as a makeshift desk. "What's the occasion?"

Harlen briefly explained the situation, trying to sound as casual as he could about it. Millie frowned, and he saw his uncertainty reflected.

"It'll be fine," he said. Millie didn't believe him more than he believed himself, but she did smile in appreciation for the sentiment. And she did slide her hand into his to give it a brief squeeze before they got to the grand staircase that would be in view of anyone standing below.

He returned it, hoping it did as much to steady her as it did him, letting his hand trail out of hers with a pang of reluctance. Her hands were nearly hot to the touch, soft on the back, but callouses from years of climbing trees in the sun covered her fingers and palms. He liked the way they felt. He wished he could have held on for a moment more.

Surprisingly, by the time they reached the top of the stairs, Jacques stood beside the door, his hands in his pockets. He gave them a broad smile when he saw them, and Harlen didn't see his father anywhere. They were allowed to walk out without a word.

"What did you tell him?" Harlen asked once the door had shut behind them.

He looked back at the house, expecting to see his father watching them out of one of the windows with his icy stare of disapproval, but he saw Nothing. He would have thought it was empty was it not for the faint flicker of the fireplace burning in the sitting room.

Jacques shrugged. "Like I said. Some shit about needing the both of you for some professor stuff. Don't worry so much."

Jacques had said the last he was going to say on the topic and turned his attention to Millie.

He extended a hand towards her. "I feel like I know you already. Harlen doesn't shut up about you."

"Jacques!" Harlen exclaimed, turning bright red and then several shades darker when Millie laughed and looked up at him slyly.

"Really?" she asked with great interest.

"So!" Harlen exclaimed, reaching up and tugging at the end of his chopped hair on the side where Millie was standing, for the hundredth time wishing it were longer so he could duck behind it. "We should get going, yes?"

Jacques and Millie exchanged conspiratorial grins, and had Harlen not known they'd just met; he would have thought they'd been scheming together for years.

"Certainly," Jacques said.

This is strange, Harlen thought as they moved between the hunched buildings on the cobblestone streets. Strange that he had lived in this place his entire life and knew Nothing about it. By the time they started getting into the business district where he and Millie had been the other day, he was well and truly lost.

Everything buzzed with sound and life. He was sure he'd never seen so many people in one place before. In the dim light of the approaching evening, lamps that glowed like fireflies on their posts between buildings were being lit, painting the world around them in deep shadows and warm, yellow light.

Music was floating out from somewhere, weaving between the threads of voices in the wind and the air itself felt light and vaguely magical. Even the hunched buildings that were so dreary seemed to have an exceptional kind of beauty to them at that moment.

As out of place as he felt, he couldn't help but stare in wonder at all of it. It was the sensation of excitement he had had with Millie the other day looking in shop windows but magnified. Or, rather, without the background roar of fear dulling it.

He was desperately hoping that he wouldn't lose track of Jacques, who seemed to know his way around like the entire city was his home. Harlen wished that the street was quiet enough for him to ask again what he'd said to convince his father to allow something so wildly out of the ordinary. Dismissive as Jacques had been of it, Harlen couldn't help but think even Berkley couldn't have managed such a feat. Even if he used every bit of concentration and magic, he possessed.

It nagged at him. The curiosity tugged persistently at the back of his mind no matter how hard he tried to dismiss it and simply enjoy the moment. There was no way of knowing if he would ever get another chance to wander so freely again.

He walked along the pavement, occasionally stepping in the puddles that always lined the street, even though for that evening the rain had retreated to a patchwork of gray clouds that hung overhead with breaks here and there to show peaks of a brilliant, starry sky. The moon glowed over it all like a lamp in and of itself—a second, silver sun.

He wondered what a perfectly cloudless sky away from all the lamps would look like: what sky Millie saw every night growing up. He knew she had never needed to draw her own constellations, but what did she see when she looked up?

He glanced at her out of the corner of his eye, where she was chattering away happily with Jacques. She looked positively beautiful and so happy, and he wondered what it would be like if their circumstances were different. If he could walk along the street like this every night, and she could see the city like this all the time: the lamps and shop windows and the people buzzing around like bees. Then maybe she would like it here. Perhaps she would be happy walking through it with him, her hand with its warmth and lively roughness in his.

It was a thought he lost himself in. It was a dream with fuzzy edges, and he found himself smiling and laughing along with the conversation being flung back and forth between Millie and Jacques. Until he caught sight of the theater, and his stomach turned to ice.

The Cat's Eye Caravan.

The theater building was wood and stone. Painted on the side was a large, golden cat's eye with the curling gold lettering above it proclaiming the name. He had never seen it before, but he knew it as soon as he laid eyes on it.

"Woah. Everything alright?" Jacques glanced up at him and looked taken aback. Harlen wasn't surprised. He was sure that all the color had drained from his face, and he could feel his eyes growing wide behind his thick glasses.

He tried to say something. To explain. But he couldn't put into words the feeling that had come over him.

Jacques gripped his arm tightly as though he was worried he might topple to the ground and gave him a bit of a shake. Finally, Harlen managed to say, "I'm alright. I'm fine."

Jacques said something else, but Harlen didn't hear him. All he heard was the continued rumble of his voice while he stared at the name. The Cat's Eye Caravan. He knew that place. How could he not? It was the very first on the list. Tansey's list.

She had been talking about finally getting out of the house for days when she had seen the traveling theater troop coming into town through the mansion's windows. It was all music and bright colors, and it had been a final straw of sorts. He could still remember the look of mixed frustration and wonder on her face while she watched them through the library's window, her books and papers abandoned on the floor while he crouched in the middle of them tracing runes with his fingers, trying to block out the sounds from outside.

He remembered the look on her face when she'd turned back to look at him. If ever someone truly had a fire in their eyes, she had it then. They were ablaze with determination, and a smile curled her lips.

"I'm going to see their show," she said.

His stomach had plunged into the depths of his body with sick coldness when he realized that she was completely serious. All the other times she had spoken about leaving the house, it had been with vague wistfulness. It was a dream and Nothing more. There was no wistfulness in how she said this one phrase that changed everything.

He shook his head and tried to protest, but it was like he wasn't even there. She'd walked across the room, heedlessly stepping on the papers she'd dropped, nodding and grinning to herself. He pleaded with her to sit down, to stop making that face, or father would know something was wrong, then they would both be in trouble.

"I'll be back before anyone knows I'm gone," she said, far too loudly for his comfort.

He had begged her not to do it, begged to the point of tears. But she just laughed and told him he was too paranoid.

He hadn't been able to sleep that night. He curled in bed and jumped at any creak or pop in the house's bones, terrified that any of them might be his father tearing through the house after discovering she was gone.

When he had seen her at the breakfast table the next morning, sitting there as though Nothing happened, he thought she'd changed her mind. But as soon as they were alone in the library with the door closed, she told him all about it.

She was so excited, so alive, talking at length about the glowing lamps that lit the street at night and the actors with their painted faces and the glittering costumes. How everything and everyone was so breathtakingly beautiful, all while bouncing around the room like she was weightless. The same weightlessness that could have carried her up in a sea breeze one night and taken her away from all of them forever.

It was the place that started it all. And as Harlen stood on the street, staring up at it, Jacques speaking to him about something he couldn't hear, Harlen knew he had to go inside.

What if there was something there? Someone who had known her? Some clue as to where she had gone?

He'd never seen one of the places on her list before. Not in person. He'd looked at them on the town map countless times, trying to find some kind of pattern in the locations' placement and hoping for it to tell him something though it never did. He had never stood in front of one. He felt Tansey herself had just stepped through the crowd and given him a little wave.

His ears were ringing so loudly he could hardly hear the loud talking and laughing of the people around him. All his senses felt muffled with certain things coming through in bursts of too-bright light and thunderous sound—the golden light pouring from the building and the bright sparkle of it off the polished glass diamonds around the necks of the people inside as they passed through the front door. The sound of harsh laughter. An animal cry from somewhere deep inside.

As they moved forward, he became aware of a stark difference between the people who had come in off the street and the performers who were draped in bright, gauzy clothes with splashes of paint on their faces. They were other-worldly creatures mingling with the guests. The silver eye paint on a woman who brushed past him seemed bright as a flash of lightning, and the smell of her perfume was dizzying. He felt as if he were walking in a dream, searching.

He was jolted as a wave of new patrons hurried in off the street. He stumbled on the red carpet beneath his feet in the long entrance hall and noticed it was stained in places with splashes of something an even deeper red than the fabric.

Wine, he realized as a chorus of cackling laughter rose from somewhere deeper inside the building, from one of the dim hallways spiraling off from this one. Of course, it was wine. He could smell it in the air.

When he finally stopped staring at it and looked around, Jacques and Millie were gone. He peered into the crowd but could see neither of them, not the lavender of Millie's dress or Jacques's bright hair.

No, that's impossible. They aren't just gone, Harlen thought frantically, but at the same time, he felt panic rising in the back of his throat.

How long had he been staring at the ground?

Harlen felt his legs nearly give way under him as someone brushed through quickly, knocking against his shoulder. He caught himself on the arm of one of the men passing by. The man shrugged him off so forcefully he nearly stumbled into one of the tables draped in brilliant purple, holding silver trays of bubbling drinks that glittered in their glasses.

He wondered if he was here often. He asked if the man had ever met Tansey.

"I'm looking for someone," he said to the man, but he just turned back to his conversation.

Harlen imagined reaching out and grabbing the back of his silky, black jacket and spinning him around, grabbing him by the arms and making him listen. But the thought was gone as soon as it arrived, and he moved on.

"Excuse me?" he asked as another woman, a performer. This one with dark eyes standing out like two chips of onyx behind white streaks of makeup shaped like feathers over her eyes, "I'm looking for someone. Tansey Vostesk."

The woman shook her head and moved on, and he kept going. Every person he turned to gave him the same confused, vacant look. They didn't know her.

Eventually, he pushed through a set of glittering curtains and fell into a dark room with boxes cut into shapes covering the lamps so that the light and shadow in the room blended to give the illusion of trees growing up along the walls. Some of the lamps spun, and the shapes of birds flashed across the floor while clouds made of shadow rolled slowly across the ceiling.

Harlen felt like he was stumbling through a dream, and at least three times, he thought he saw someone who looked like Tansey. Or Jacques. Or Millie. It was so hard to see, and he felt like he was chasing a ghost every time he half-turned and nearly called out to someone that looked so familiar only to realize at the last moment that he didn't know them.

Branches of light twisted over his body as he moved through the illusion of a forest. He could hear music drifting in from all directions, and each time he moved, he bumped into a new person he hadn't seen through the alternating light and shadow. All of their faces were blurred and unrecognizable.

He could taste panic in the back of his mouth, bitter and cold. He had no idea where he had come in or where he needed to go to get out of this room. He seized on the first thick curtain he saw and stumbled through, and it was like being tossed from one dream to another with no chance to regain himself.

There were no strange shadows or mingling, loud noises. All sound seemed to stop at once, replaced only by the faint strumming of a harp in a room with pale walls and a floor of polished wood.

At the center of the room, a group of women drifted around in pale-colored, silk dresses like angels was doing some elaborate dance while everyone watched. The women would occasionally break from the room's center to weave between the watching guests, who all seemed thrilled by it. Harlen found them unsettling.

Their white, powdered faces and utter silence felt wrong. It was more unnerving than the disorientation of the shadow room. It felt even more like one of Harlen's nightmares. Lost in a sea of ghosts. Alone.

One of the dancers touched him, and he took a stumbling step back. Some of the observers gave him strange looks, but for once, he couldn't find it in himself to care that people were staring.

He cast around for an exit, and that was when he saw it. Blonde hair vanishing through a door that lead to the outside. Every rational part of his mind shouted at him that that could have been anyone, but the part of him that hadn't seen his twin in years shouted louder.

"Tansey?" he called. He drew more attention by shattering the room's quiet, but he was rushing towards the door that lead to the building's inner courtyard. Where the blonde hair had vanished. "Tansey!"

Come back. I came looking for you—if you wanted me out of that house, I'm here, I'm out! Come back!

She didn't have to come back. Harlen just wanted to know why—why she left without telling anyone. But even if she didn't explain, if she didn't even speak—that would be alright. He just needed to know she was alive.

Harlen burst through the door to the courtyard, where the rain had begun again. There were men twirling sticks of fire, and Harlen stumbled out into the night air, heedless of staying beneath the colorful awnings that stretched out for the other watchers who were lingering beneath them.

Harlen trudged right out into the mud and rain and felt the heat from the performers' fire while he tried to squint and use its glow to look at the other faces gathered there. She had to be here. She had to. She was *just* here.

"Tansey!"

Someone grabbed his arm before he could stray into the path of one of the performer's sweeping gestures and yanked him back under one of the awnings. It was hard to make out features in the darkness, but Jacques's bright orange hair stood out.

Harlen felt like he had been shaken awake and blinked as Jacques turned to look at him. He was so pale the freckles on his nose were standing out like splashes of ink, and his hair seemed to have grown redder in the absence of blood in his cheeks. His brow furrowed in concern. "Where the hell are you going?"

"She was here," Harlen said as if it were an explanation, and he hated that he felt himself tearing up as reality came slamming back down on top of him.

Tansey wasn't here. She likely hadn't been here in a long, long time. His mind had raced so far ahead of him that he was chasing random women through buildings.

Jacques looked confused and alarmed, but instead of asking for an explanation then and there, he dragged him back inside, back through all the rooms until they returned to that front lobby where the performers and attendees were chatting.

He sequestered him in a quiet corner and forced one of the bubbling drinks being offered by servers with silver plates into his shaking hands. It was oddly sweet, and the bubbles made him want to cough, but Jacques wouldn't let him say a word until he drank half of it.

Jacques sat next to him on the bench covered in soft, green upholstery and asked him what, exactly, the hell that was all about.

"Nothing. I just. . ." Harlen trailed off, shaking his head. "I got a little mixed up, that's all."

Jacques snorted. "You call that mixed up? I thought you'd gone completely off your head for a second there." He looked around, eyes scanning the crowd, and raised a hand to someone in the distance who Harlen recognized was Millie.

Before she could arrive, Jacques leaned over and whispered, "Are you sure you can be here? If you need to get out, I can always make an excuse. I've gotten myself out of plenty of parties before, don't worry about that."

"I'm fine," Harlen insisted. Jacques still looked at him with suspicious, narrowed eyes, but Millie was close enough to hear, so he pressed no further.

"What happened?" she asked frantically. She was out of breath and must have been looking all over for him as well. Harlen felt guilt twist at him. He hadn't meant to make her worry.

Jacques waved his hand. "Ah, just got a little mixed up in all the people, that's all. He'll be fine."

"I'm okay," Harlen assured her. She looked unconvinced, so he raised a hand to squeeze hers. "Really."

And he was, mostly. His head was spinning less, and the drink was making him feel a bit less frazzled. Now that he had taken a step back, he could feel his thoughts coming more clearly. Whatever manic energy he had felt was dissipating, leaving a hollow ache in his chest.

Millie squeezed his hand tightly and didn't seem to believe him. She kept her fingers firmly locked around his and sank onto the bench next to him, her eyes never leaving his.

"Tell me what happened," she said. Her voice was firm, but her grip on him was grounding and soothing.

Harlen wanted to shrink away from the question. He wanted to shrink away from her and fold in on himself, but she was so concerned. Her voice was so gentle, and she ran her thumb over the back of his hand in circles, not dispelling his self-consciousness but calming it, smoothing down the frayed edges of his nerves.

"It's Tansey," he said.

Immediately Millie's eyes went wide, but her hand on his remained firm.

"Tansey used to come here. She used to leave the house, sneak out at night, go to all these places. . ."

He stared down into his nearly empty drink and told them everything. Where Tansey used to go, how she would tell him about those places, and finally, the list he had made and kept, she vanished. When he finished, that ever-invading thought that he revealed too much still bit at him, but not as strongly as before. Millie's hand hadn't loosened its grip on his. Her thumb would stroke the back of his hand when he had started to hesitate, and it continued once he had finished.

"I guess I thought I might find something," he said, finally looking up at the two of them. They both looked shaken and a bit paler than they had before. But neither of them were telling him it was idiotic. Neither of them was looking at him with disdain. He saw Nothing but sympathy.

"You should have told me," Jacques snapped, but there was no real venom behind it. Just worry.

"Maybe," he admitted. "But then we probably wouldn't have come in. And I wanted to. I had to—I had to see. I had to look. I don't think anyone else ever did."

Those investigators had come, but after walking out the door that morning, he had never seen them in his father's presence again. It could have been that he met with them elsewhere, but Harlen doubted it. He really, really doubted it. "I should have found a way to look sooner."

He should have been braver. He should have pushed aside his fear. It seemed so self-centered now, looking back, that he had been too afraid of what would be done to him if he tried and got caught. What would she have done if it had been him?

"What if we looked now?" Millie said. She was gripping his arm in earnest. She was looking at Jacques, then back to him. "We could. Even if. . ." she trailed off, but she set her mouth in a straight line and said, "We could even if there's Nothing. It still matters."

We? "I can't ask that," Harlen said.

"I'm not so sure she was waiting for you to ask," Jacques said. "But she's right. If you wanted to, there's no reason we couldn't. I mean, what's the harm?"

Harlen stared at them in disbelief. He wasn't sure if it was the alcohol, but he could hardly believe his ears. They couldn't mean that, could they? Their faces said that they did.

The thought made him dizzy with possibility, and something he hadn't felt for so long resurfaced, and he struggled to name it.

Hope. Hope that something might still be out there. That someone, anyone, might even care enough to help him. To help her. He had never considered that anyone would ever want to.

"Thank you," was all he could say with the sudden lump in his throat.

It was utterly inadequate, but it was all he could think to say as they returned to a mercifully empty house. He said nothing as he walked through the door of their bedroom, let it shut behind them, and looked up to see Millie standing in the middle of the room, wringing her hands.

"Are you sure you're okay?" she asked, although he was reasonably sure neither of them knew how to answer that question. He felt as if he were feeling everything at once to the point where every complex emotion felt like white noise, and he could see the same conflict present on her face. Quite a lot had happened to both of them over the last few weeks.

Somehow, that led them to meet one another halfway across the room and to wrap each other in a tight embrace that's real meaning was simple enough to be clear in the moment of turmoil: both of them were afraid. But neither of them were alone.

He was unsure how long they stood in the safety of each other's arms. Only that when it was over, Millie pulled her head away with her hands still clutching at his jacket as if she were afraid to let go.

He hadn't held back in telling them what had happened to Tansey—vanishing in the middle of the night, seemingly without a sound. He hadn't outright said that he often wondered if his father had known or had been somehow involved: at the very least, he'd never searched for her. But he knew that his tone had implied his suspicions. He could see it in Millie's face as she looked up at him. The fear that the same thing could happen again.

"Do you think we're in danger here?" she asked, hardly a whisper.

It gave him a surge of determination and bravery that he was unaccustomed to—to hear her speak that way. It was just like when he had found her curled up in the sitting room. Only this time, he wouldn't meekly offer to take her somewhere to alleviate her fear. "I would never let anything happen to you."

Whether she believed him or not, he couldn't say. But when the time came to crawl into bed, he took the side closest to the door, so if anyone did come in during the night, they would have to get through him before they could touch her.

They laid closer to each other that night than they ever had before. He faced her, and she had her back towards him, looking off at the opposite wall of the room, having thoughts he couldn't read. Perhaps she was still afraid and didn't want to show it.

He cautiously reached out a hand to touch her back to remind her that he was there watching out for her. His fingers brushed the back of her nightgown, silk warm from her skin, and she took hold of it without a word and pulled his arm around her waist.

It stole the breath from him, but rather than shying back from her invitation; he shifted closer to allow her back to press firmly to his chest. The way her muscles relaxed told him he had made the right decision. As did the way some part of him sighed in relief at the closeness.

It was the most peacefully he had drifted off to sleep in his recollection.

CHAPTER 20

The Vostesks.

Millie remembered the afternoon Roslyn had come running back from listening in on one of her father's meetings. After she'd told them all what was in store for her and once her mother and Beatrice together had managed to soothe her ensuing hysterical crying and screaming at the prospect of being sent away, Millie had asked for time alone. It was a rarity at their house, but it was granted.

She wandered the grounds for the longest time, through the garden outside their house overflowing with every color imaginable through the fields beyond it. She'd looked at it all— run her fingers over every leaf as though she might never see anything beautiful again.

She didn't return to the house until well after sunset when the last rays of pink and gold had faded from the sky. Then she had gone to the library.

It was Beatrice's favorite room, but not one Millie visited often. She associated it with her stuffy tutors and being forced to sit and copy lines of dull poetry while she far preferred to lay on her stomach in the grass outside and listen to the gardeners explain their craft. What each plant was, what it could do. Seeing it play out was always so much more fun than listening to someone drone on and on about something that had happened thousands of years ago and made little difference to her. Still, she had been forced to spend enough time there, so she knew her way around. She knew exactly where to find what she was looking for.

In the very back of the library, there was a heavy, little-used book. Its spine creaked when it opened and coughed dust onto her hands as she pried apart the pages, searching through the names. Every prominent house since the world began—or, rather, since people had started keeping a record of those things as the tutor would always correct her. It was there for memorizing the names of those who thought themselves too important to need an introduction so that when a member of a particular family arrived at an event, they could be shown what they considered the proper courtesy.

Millie had always thought it was a sign of a fragile ego rather than importance. Her tutor had not been pleased with that observation.

But it had what she needed. She flipped through until she found the name Vostesk and ran her hand down the page.

They were an old family with magic and ice in their veins.

The book went on about their magical prowess and incredible feats: an attack on a town brought to a halt by a wall of ice rising around the city, and an entire army lost in a massive snowstorm summoned by one man. A sea frozen over, another town brought to its knees when a killing frost destroyed its crops in the middle of summer. None of it had what she was looking for—nothing except the portrait on the next page.

The man pictured was a thousand years dead, but he matched the description of every Vostesk her sisters had told her about in an attempt to placate her. They were tall and fine-featured and so very refined. They had assured her that they were nothing if not polite and even-tempered. But all Millie saw when she looked at the man in the picture with its old paint chipping was the sharp, ice-cold eyes. Such a pale blue that they were nearly white. There was no kindness or softness in anything about them.

She had left the book on the floor, open on the picture of the man's face. He had sucked out of her any desire to scream and cry: she only felt cold.

It had been almost three months since then. Three months and Millie still didn't like the coast or Vostesk Senior, who had the same eyes as the man in the book. But she did like the person lying next to her.

She was awake, lying on her side and looking at him in the moonlight that filtered through the window, thinking, getting a real look at him for once when he wasn't fidgeting. . . He certainly wasn't handsome in the traditional sense, yet looking at him at that moment made her smile. In his way, he was beautiful. Especially his eyes. She couldn't see them now, but they were nothing like any Vostesk she had ever seen in person or portraits. They were far warmer and betrayed just about any emotion he ever felt, even behind the thick glasses which she carefully eased off for him.

She was beginning to wonder if he left them on purposefully so she would take them off for him once he was asleep, or if he was simply so accustomed to them sitting on his nose that he forgot to do it himself. Either way, she wasn't sure she minded. She had seen the way he smiled too many times when he found them on the table beside the bed when he thought she was still asleep.

Millie wasn't sure if she was in love with him. She had never been in love and had no idea how one was supposed to know. Millie had kissed boys in corners of the hedge maze behind her house and at festivals. She'd had boys she liked very much but never felt like she loved any of them. She knew she liked Harlen, more than she ever thought she would, and far more than she'd liked the others.

She didn't mind being married to him. In fact, she felt an odd sense of happiness at being able to refer to him as her husband. Her only real regret was this damn house. And that his father lived in it.

She couldn't stop thinking about her conversation with Vostesk Senior the other day or the way he looked at her. She had never felt her entire body go cold before just from someone's gaze. Even thinking about it gave her an unpleasant prickle at the back of her neck.

She would call the look predatory, but she had seen foxes and wolves and other predators. Their eyes weren't evil. They were the way they were because of a need to survive, and there was a gleam in their eyes that showed it. Vostesk Senior, on the other hand, had no such glimmer. His eyes were flat and cold, and she could not think of a word for what he was other than monster. Whenever she looked at him, she got the impression that something inside of him had died.

He wasn't home yet. Millie had not heard the door downstairs, and she wondered where he'd gone off to. If she had to guess, she would assume he went to vent his anger somewhere after Jacques's visit. She didn't know what Jacques had said to him. He hadn't answered when she asked, but she couldn't imagine he had taken kindly to someone ordering him around. Unless Jacques was secretly the best diplomat in

Wakefield, she imagined Vostesk Senior was on the warpath right now.

Slowly, carefully, trying her best not to disturb Harlen, she slipped off the bed, wincing as her bare feet touched the cold floor. She wrapped Harlen's robe that she had once again commandeered tighter around herself as she approached the bedroom door and stared down at the handle, wishing for a lock.

She had listened to Harlen's story about Tansey, and she had her suspicions. All of it drew back to her last conversation with Vostesk Senior: *"I'm not sure what you're capable of at all."*

Her own words echoed back at her as she frowned at what her mind had immediately jumped to. Would anyone, no matter how cold, really bring themselves to make their child disappear? It was something only the worst kind of person would do.

Or a monster, her thoughts added, unbidden, and she felt a chill that had nothing to do with the cool of the room.

She wasn't entirely sure what that implied. She didn't know if she thought he had sent her away somewhere or if she thought he had murdered his flesh and blood. But for what reason? No matter how badly she wanted to jump to the conclusion that he had done something reprehensible, she couldn't imagine him doing it without some kind of rationality to go with it.

Millie didn't know what to think. All she knew was that she was not going to sleep in a room where Vostesk Senior could walk in at any moment. And not having a lock on her door was not going to keep her from that. One did not need a lock to bar someone from entry.

Millie grabbed the chair sitting in front of the desk and began dragging it, quietly as she could, in small scoots across the floor with the intent to shove in front of the door. She paused every time she managed to budge it a few inches to make sure she wasn't waking up Harlen, which was how she heard it. The footsteps and soft crying were coming from the hallway.

Millie let go of the chair and pressed her ear to the doorframe, listening until the sound of sniffling and sobbing passed by again.

She cracked the door open ever so slightly, peering down the long, dark hallway, and at first saw nothing but blackness. The dim kerosene lamps had all been snuffed out for the night, leaving only the light of the window at the hallway's end. It was pale gray and reached feebly into the dark for only a few feet before the house swallowed it up.

Millie squinted into the darkness, and then she saw a figure walking down at the hallway's end, coming quickly closer. A white shape was emerging from the dark.

Millie jumped back and pulled the door with her but didn't let it shut all the way. When the footsteps passed the door again, she eased it open just a crack and peered out, curiosity winning over her heart that was beating painfully up in her throat.

From the moonlight streaming through the window at the end of the hallway, she could see the figure more fully. It was Mrs. Vostesk. Her long hair was hanging limply nearly to her waist, and she was wearing a nightdress that almost matched her skin in whiteness. A pale, silk robe whispered around her ankles with every barefoot step. She looked afraid and confused and was wringing her little hands with tears shining on her face.

Millie took a deep breath and stepped out into the hallway.

The woman started when she saw her, and Millie approached carefully with the best friendly smile she could manage while feeling somewhat unsettled herself. She never realized how small Mrs. Vostesk was.

Millie had seen her at dinner a few times, but she looked so frail outside of her everyday clothing layers. She must have hardly cleared five feet in height since Millie had to look down at her, and her hands and face and what she could see of her legs were thin as a willow branch. She could not imagine how the woman had carried twins.

"Who are you?" Mrs. Vostesk sniffed, looking up at her with eyes that seemed too large for her delicate little face.

"It's me. I'm. . ." she began and saw no spark of recognition in the woman's wide eyes. The blackness had consumed so much of her eyes that Millie couldn't say for sure what color they were, and there was nothing but an animal fear behind them. Instead of coaxing out a memory, she decided to try a new approach and extended her hand. "My name is Millie."

Mrs. Vostesk looked down at her hand and very slowly reached out to take it. Hesitantly. As though she wasn't sure it was real. She closed her fingers around it. Her fingers felt like the bones of bird wings. "My name is Pearl."

"Hello, Pearl," Millie said.

She wanted to ask what had upset her so much but wasn't sure that was a good idea. She didn't want to upset her more since she had stopped crying and was only giving the occasional sniff. She still didn't recognize her, but at least she seemed less afraid after the introduction.

Millie wasn't entirely sure *what* to do. She didn't want to just deposit her back in her room. So instead, she gestured towards the stairs. "Would you like to go to the kitchen with me? I could get you some water, maybe some dinner if you haven't had any."

Pearl shook her head. "No. No, my husband wouldn't like that. I can only eat at mealtime—he'll be cross with me."

A few choice words jumped to mind, but Millie decided to bite her tongue for the time being. "He isn't home. And I won't tell him if you won't."

"He's not home?" Pearl asked, turning her head to the side. Millie nodded, and very slowly, she said in a whisper, "Alright." And reached her hand back out for hers.

Millie felt a pang of pity for the poor woman and took her hand, offering it a comforting squeeze as she guided her down the hallway.

Pearl hesitated when they got to the top step, but she followed when Millie began to go first. Hesitantly at first, then with quick, delicate strides and breathy giggles.

The giggles continued as they made their way to the kitchen, and she kept shooting Millie excited smiles as if they were doing something incredibly secretive. Which only made the pang of pity in Millie's stomach grow to a gnawing, painful twisting.

It prompted her to tell Pearl not to worry about getting dinner and that she should eat whatever she wanted when they got to the kitchen.

The woman's eyes widened, and she asked at least four times if she was sure she should do something like that, and when Millie insisted, and herself reached into the pantry and broke off a bit of a slab of chocolate to help embolden her, Pearl put her hands to her mouth and let out a little gasp. A gasp that was quickly followed by a high, short giggle.

"That's not allowed!" she said but seemed delighted.

"Doesn't matter. What do you like?" Millie asked her.

Pearl seemed overwhelmed. She looked around the kitchen as if it were a candy store, and she was a child who was told to take as much as she could. In fact, she struck Millie as incredibly childish, and she felt nothing but the urge to make her happy, if only for a moment.

"I like sweetbread," she said, whispering it like it was a secret and clapping her hands together. "The one with honey."

Then, Millie determined, she could have all the sweetbread she could eat. They both searched the kitchen for it and eventually found some in one of the cabinets.

They took their collection of treats to the small kitchen table, and Millie set a place for both of them while Pearl sat in her chair, looking pleased, swinging her legs off the bottom of the stool. All the while, the goblins above the stove remained conveniently asleep, occasionally opening one bright eye to peek at them.

Millie had a feeling that they wouldn't be saying anything to the head of the house and determined that she would find out what they were paid and find a way to give them a decent raise. Whatever they were getting now couldn't be nearly enough to deal with what they had to put up with.

"You know your way around here very well," Pearl said as Millie finished setting the plates and pulled herself into the chair across from Harlen's mother.

"You know your way around here very well," Pearl said as Millie finished setting the plates and pulled herself into the chair across from Harlen's mother.

"I've had a lot of time to look around," she said, smiling and trying to keep her tone light despite how she was feeling. She was thinking of Vostesk Senior and what he'd done to his wife to make her eyes look so vacant. She was gripping her napkin tightly to hide how her hands were shaking with anger.

"You've been here long?" she asked, and when Millie nodded, her eyes finally lit up with recognition, and she exclaimed, "Wait! I remember you! You're my son's wife!"

Millie nodded, and Pearl stared at her for a long moment, smiling ear to ear. She gave a long, soft sigh and looked at her plate with tears in her doll-like eyes. "Oh, it's so nice to have a little lady in the house again. It's been so long. My sweet little Tansey used to liven up the place so much—it will be lovely to have that again."

Pearl stopped speaking for a moment to nibble delicately at the bread in her hand. Millie tried to take a bite of her chocolate so she wouldn't stare, but her throat felt too closed and dry to swallow correctly. She couldn't help but wonder: had Pearl always been like this?

Harlen had mentioned she had a reliance on opium, and Millie recognized a few of the symptoms well enough. Was her behavior a result of that? Or was this what living under Vostesk Senior had done to her? She had no idea which prospect made her sicker.

Harlen had mentioned she had a reliance on opium, and Millie recognized a few of the symptoms well enough. Was her behavior a result of that? Or was this what living under Vostesk Senior had done to her? She had no idea which prospect made her sicker.

"My little girl is so sweet," Pearl continued after dabbing her lips with a napkin. "Oh, we used to sit for hours, and I taught her how to make cross-stitch patterns. I do so love those. I'm not sure she found it as entertaining as I do, but, oh, the talks we would have while we did them. And I would brush her hair and fix her up so pretty. I so loved having a girl."

She smiled, and her eyes were distant. Millie could hear the clock ticking away in the other room as her face slowly fell, and her eyes welled up again. "I don't know why he was so cruel. He's always so cross with them. My children never did anything to make him so mad."

"Lord Vostesk?" Millie didn't want to interrupt, but she couldn't help the outburst. Pearl nodded sadly.

"He wanted children gifted with magic. And I couldn't give them to him. After they were born—the twins—Tansey and Harlen. I couldn't give him anymore. Or that was what the doctor said anyway. I didn't understand why he was so upset;

they were both perfectly healthy and so smart. But then again, he said I never understood anything. Which I suppose is true. I never went to school. And he has so much prestigious education, so I suppose he knows what's best—but I never understood why he had to be so cruel about it."

Pearl was back to wringing her hands with tears brimming in her eyes. She pointed out past the kitchen, through the dining hall, and towards the garden's glass windows. "When they were still very small, and he was trying to teach them his magic, he tried to lock them out there in the rain. He said that if they wanted to come back in, they would have to find a way to use magic to do it, but I just couldn't let him. I took Tansey and ran with her up to my room. I pushed my bed in front of the door. He pounded on it for hours, and I was so frightened, but I couldn't let him hurt my little girl."

Tears were running down her cheeks, unheeded again, and Millie picked up her napkin to dab at the woman's eyes. She smiled ever so faintly, and Millie wanted to let her go on doing so, but there was something about what she had said that Millie didn't understand.

She had to ask, "What happened to Harlen?"

She blinked and seemed confused, then looked back towards the window room as though she was watching it unfold. "Oh, I had to let him back in. After his father had stopped pounding on my door and was sure it was safe to come out, I saw him still outside. I don't know what time it was, only that it was very late and very dark. Harlen's lips and fingers were blue. I let him in, and I wanted to get him in dry clothes and into bed because he looked like he was getting a fever. But his father had found me again by that time and told me to leave him and go back to my room with Tansey. So, I did."

Pearl was shaking head to foot and said in a whisper, "It was always like that after that night. He would get cross, and I would take Tansey, and we would hide, but he didn't chase me anymore. And later, Harlen would come to me with the bruises and the cuts, but I couldn't help him. It was an unspoken agreement. I could have my little girl, but the future of our house belonged to him. It was the only thing we ever agreed upon."

Millie had been dabbing the tears from Pearl's face and was now frozen, still half out of her chair, napkin in hand. She hadn't thought she could feel any colder, but her entire body felt frozen in the horror of her realization.

"You just left him?"

"He's a boy," Pearl said, giving her a confused look. "He's a boy. Boys are strong. He could handle it. His father always said so."

Millie thought about how Harlen flinched nearly every time someone raised their voice at him or how he'd cried on their wedding night out of fear that he'd made her angry. It took him ages to look her in the eyes, and every laugh or joke seemed to be followed by an apology. How utterly terrified of the world and the people in it.

No, she thought. *No, he couldn't. Who could?*

Millie had no idea what to say or even what to think. She felt her mouth open and had no idea what was about to come out when Pearl suddenly froze, and her face turned a grayish-white.

"He's back."

Millie heard the front door easing open and grabbed both plates. She grabbed Pearl's hand and hurriedly slid the dishes onto a back shelf in the pantry behind some jelly jars and made for the staircase with her.

They were almost halfway up, and Pearl was repeating over and over for her to hurry in a panicked voice when the door creaked open, and Pearl stopped moving so abruptly that the pull from her suddenly frozen hand nearly sent Millie face-first into the stairs.

Luckily, she caught herself on the banister as the door swung open fully. A cold wind blew in from the outside, and Pearl let out a long, low whimper.

"What's this?" Vostesk Senior stood in the doorway, his rain-drenched coat partially off his shoulders, staring up at the both of them.

Again, Millie thought of all the predatory eyes that were so much warmer than the stare fixed on them, but she was determined not to freeze. That was how rabbits got torn to shreds by wolves. She needed to do something.

Knowing even the smallest details of what he had done to his children—the image of Harlen as a child trapped outside with blue lips—made her want to bare some teeth. But making yourself big and intimidating was how you dealt with predators, with bears in the woods and wild dogs.

If growing up with the gardener's lessons and stories had taught her anything, it was that there was the only way to get around a monster. You had to outsmart it.

Millie didn't know if she could outsmart Vostesk Senior. All she knew was he was one of those men with his name in that dusty book in her library who expected to be known and respected before his introduction. One of those with a fragile ego that she knew how to approach.

Thinking quickly, she did her best to look embarrassed she'd been caught rather than afraid. Fear looked guilty; shame meant he would feel some degree of power over the situation. That was what he wanted to see. "Mr. Vostesk—I'm so sorry. I didn't think we would be up so late. I was just asking your wife a few questions."

"About what?" he was suspicious but not angry. Good.

Mille could feel Pearl's hand shaking. She did her best to give what she hoped was a flustered smile that didn't give away how terrified she was and said, "Well. They were questions of a.. .personal nature."

The frightened quiver in her voice added some believability to her shy act as she cleared her throat and said, "I was asking about certain. . .marital matters. My mother didn't have much time to discuss such things with me. You and I were talking about children the other day, and, well, I was hoping for some womanly advice."

She was nearly gagging on her own words, but Pearl had stopped shaking. She was looking at her wide-eyed as Vostesk Senior's face broke out into a smile that reeked of smugness, and he returned to taking off his coat, giving a chuckle and a shake of his head.

"She may not be the best person to ask about that sort of thing. I can certainly speak to that," he said, and Millie saw Pearl's lip begin to quiver again. She could swear her body felt weightless with how hot anger was burning in her stomach. But she got what she wanted. Vostesk Senior waved his hand at them, sounding amused as he said, "Go on."

Millie began pulling Pearl up the stairs, biting her lip so hard she could taste blood to keep herself from saying something that would put them back in danger. She considered punching a wall and would have if he wouldn't have heard it—her knuckles and the wallpaper be dammed. But once they were up the stairs and out of sight, she felt the anger and fear flood out of her, and the effect made her dizzy.

She had known she was frightened but hadn't realized how bad it was until it was Pearl who was supporting her arm to keep her from slumping down to the floor while her legs turned to jelly. She had no idea what Vostesk Senior would have done if he'd found out what they were doing and had truly gotten angry about it, which was precisely what scared her: the not knowing.

"Thank you."

It took a moment for Millie to hear, but Pearl was whispering it over and over while clutching her arm. "Thank you."

Steady yourself, she demanded and again bit down on her lip to distract her mind long enough for her legs to become her own again. She took a step back from Pearl; the woman looked up at her, pale and wide-eyed.

"You're so brave," she whispered, but Millie shook her head. She was disgusted by how scared she had been. Even more disgusted that she was planning on slinking back to the relative safety of her room instead of running back down those stairs and giving that man a good beating around the head with that cane he carried so pompously.

"Let's just get you back," Millie said. She didn't want to stand in the hallway anymore where she could still her Vostesk Senior walking, and she was sure he would be following them up before long. She had no desire to reencounter him.

CHAPTER 21

Millie led Pearl back down the hallway. She didn't hold onto her hand this time, just listened to the sound of the small woman's feet patting the floor behind her.

She had no idea what to feel towards her. She didn't deserve what had happened to her. Or, instead, what was still happening to her at the hands of her husband. But she couldn't come to terms with the idea of a mother leaving one of her children to fend for themselves against the same awful man.

She simply didn't know what to think and walked in front of her in conflicted silence. She would have slipped back into her room without a word had Pearl not reached out and tugged at her sleeve.

"Wait. Please." Pearl went into her room and motioned Millie to follow her inside, quickly and quietly. Reluctantly, she trudged after her.

There was a hospital back in Millie's hometown that she had gone to once when she was very young. It was a splendid place, with the best doctors the area had to offer. Her room, for the week she'd remained in the throes of a fever, had been lovely. There was just a distinct feeling of heaviness that hung in the air in that place that no amount of pretty decorations could hide. That was how she felt walking into Pearl's room.

It was lovely; everything from the bed to the gauzy, white curtains on the window were finely made. But there was an oppressive air that came from the clothes dragged half from the wardrobe and the window hanging open that was letting in the cold, night air and just enough rain to dampen the curtains, making them hang heavy against the wall rather than float on the breeze. The atmosphere was oppressive.

Millie found herself standing uneasily in the doorway, searching for the smell of strong disinfecting soap.

Pearl tapped her fingers together as she made her way toward the window. She waited there for a moment, and when Millie didn't follow her, she again motioned urgently for her.

Millie didn't want to go inside, but she did. She walked up to where Pearl stood, the rain outside hitting the windowsill, spattering her nightdress with water that she either didn't feel or didn't care about.

She said nothing, so Millie followed her vacant gaze out the window and saw the street below flowing like a river and the faint lamp lights that lined it glimmering through the haze of rain. More importantly, she saw the ornate, metal hairbrush that had been jammed into the window frame itself.

It was jammed into the wood at an angle, forcing the glass to remain open. The wood that had been left to soak up the rain swelled until the brush may as well have been part of the wall. Even if someone removed it from the window would never have appropriately closed again. At the very end of the brush hung what looked like a necklace, dangling and swinging as the rain pelted it.

"It's for Tansey," Pearl explained, speaking suddenly after her long pause.

Millie looked down at her, and Pearl was smiling faintly, fumbling at the collar of her nightdress. Millie watched as her dainty fingers eventually produced a necklace that looked similar to the one hanging outside. A pair of brass hands cupping a little disk of sapphire.

Millie recognized it immediately. It was so jarring to see something so familiar that she spoke without reservation.

"Shareen," she exclaimed, and Pearl seemed pleased that she knew who it represented.

"Yes." She nodded eagerly in her whispery, thin voice. "Goddess of fertility, family, and forgiveness."

Yes, Millie nodded. She knew. Whether it was removing the bustle of cities or the sheer natural oddity that comes from living somewhere so untouched by time, the mountains were a place where gods and monsters were anything but uncommon.

Among them all, Shareen was by far the most popular. Practically everyone worshiped her up there where life depended on crops and the families that harvested them.

Millie had grown up surrounded by her and was startled that she had yet to see a sign of a god or goddess anywhere in Wakefield. She had never seen any religious observance in Wakefield. It had been the first thing to make her realize how truly far from home she was.

Pearl looked down at the necklace in her hand, and Millie couldn't tell what thoughts were passing behind her eyes.

She only knew that a single tear fell from Pearl's eyes and dripped onto the little disk of sapphire before she closed her white fingers around it.

"I've kept that one out there every night for my little girl. So she can find her way home. So she knows I'm not upset with her for leaving me."

"You think she left you?" Millie asked.

Pearl bit her lip. "I don't know. I know she was unhappy here. We're all unhappy here. But I think she would have been the only one of us brave enough to find a way to leave and truly disappear where my husband couldn't find her. Harlen tried to leave once. So did I back when I was very, very young. But he always found us. It was always worse when we were brought back. But she could have done it. Dead or alive, she found a way to leave this place."

She looked back out the window at the charm swaying and glittering in the rain. "Every night, I hope that she'll come back to me. Dead or alive, take me away too."

What about your son? Millie wanted to ask. But for the third time that night, she bit her tongue. Pearl took the necklace off from around her throat and pressed it into Millie's hands.

"Here. You should take this since you're here with us now. It will protect you."

Millie looked down at the metal charm in her hands. She looked at Pearl and tried to hand it back, but she took a step away and kept her hands at her sides. Pearl was shaking her head, and in return, Millie burst out, "What about you?"

Pearl smiled. There were no tears in her eyes this time, but they still filled with unbearable sadness that, despite everything she'd said, twisted Millie's stomach. "There's nothing left to protect," she said, looking toward the window again. "All that's left for me is to wait."

Millie had no words. She stood frozen at the window, being splashed with cold rain just like Pearl had been while the tiny woman wandered back across the floor and sank onto the edge of her bed. She looked all at once, like a child and a ghost that had lived a hundred years in this room.

Pearl stared, her eyes comprehending nothing, her hand eventually wandering as if by itself to the little brown bottle at her bedside.

"You don't need that," Millie said, snapped out of her thoughts by the image of Pearl pouring some of the liquid she knew was opium into a crystal water glass beside the bottle. Her sharp voice seemed to temporarily bring her out of her stupor once again, but only for a moment.

Pearl looked up at her tearfully and said, "Yes, I do."

Before Millie could protest further, she put the glass to her lips and drained it. Millie wanted to do something—to take the glass, the bottle, but would that do anything? Would she not just find another bottle, or perhaps something worse to curb the soul-crushing sadness Millie glimpsed in her? It was Vostesk Senior who kept her supplied. Would he not just give her more?

"You shouldn't let him keep you like this," Millie said. The only way to help would be to convince her she didn't need it, but Pearl was no longer listening.

Pearl's eyes were glassy, and she looked over at the charm hanging from the window. "Goodnight, Tansey," she said as she fell back onto her side in bed.

Millie couldn't be in that room for one second more.

She didn't care about being quiet or unseen. She ran from the room into her own, dragging the chair in front of the door, stopping only when it was wedged firmly in place to catch her breath.

She'd started crying at some point, and as she crouched by the chair-blocked door, she scrubbed her face with the hem of her nightdress before turning back toward the bed.

Harlen was still asleep, though he had shifted around a little. Even with his hair a mess, his clothes twisted; a small line of a worried frown pressed between his brows as if he could sense the unrest in the house.

Who took care of you?

She walked over to the bed, slowly, quietly. The symbol of Shareen still in her hand. She could feel the cold metal pressing into her palm. She looked down at it again, then at Harlen. And then, very carefully, she wound the little brass chain around the bedpost.

Fertility, Forgiveness, Family.

Shareen was a feminine goddess, to be sure. Millie had seen her statues back in her hometown. She was always depicted as a beautiful woman with dark skin and kind eyes, dripping in flowers with outstretched hands. Inviting, warm.

But there was an undeniable strength to her. She was a goddess of blessing and protection. To destroy a family or turn against your loved ones was to invoke her wrath.

He's my family now. If nobody else will protect him, I will. We'll protect each other.

Millie gave the charm one last touch and felt her heart stop beating so erratically in her throat. She felt a sort of calm wash over her, and she bent down towards Harlen and very gently brushed his tangled hair away from his face. He didn't budge, but the worried line between his eyes smoothed as her fingers trailed down his cheek.

As quietly as she could, she laid back down in bed. She stared at the back of his shirt and couldn't shake the image of what a younger version of him must have looked like locked outside that glass wall, crying and begging to be let back in with blue lips and fingers.

She reached forward and wrapped her arms around him, pressing her face into his back, and only then did he stir slightly. He jumped and turned his head towards her, his eyes still bleary from sleep, and his voice slurred as he asked, "What happened?"

She smiled at him. She felt like crying again, for some reason, looking up at him. But she didn't. She just smiled and reached up to touch the side of his face again and said, "Nothing. Go back to sleep. You've worried enough for one day."

You're safe.

His mouth twitched up in a tired grin, and his head fell back onto the pillow. Then she felt his hand reaching blindly up towards the arm she'd wrapped around him. When he found her hand, he intertwined their fingers tightly, and as soon as he'd found a way to hold her, his breathing evened out immediately, and he fell back into sleep.

CHAPTER 22

Overhead, the lightbulb swung. Harlen was seated in a wooden chair, his wrists held in place by leather straps, his nearly naked body shining with sweat that served only to give him convulsive shivers in the cold dampness of the basement.

His hair was soaked in it and hung in limp tangles on either side of his face; a purple bruise bloomed on his left shoulder. On the table in front of him was a glass of water.

The shadow of his father walked back and forth on the other side of the table. Sometimes the lantern would throw his face into a harsh light that gave him a wolf-like appearance, and other times it swung so far that he was nothing more than a prowling shape in the dark. Maybe not even real. The only constant was the pain, the water glass, and the smacking of his father's cane against the flat of his palm as he paced.

"I will tell you again. Your mind is too crowded with unfocused thoughts. Use that pain to block out the rest. Focus." His father's voice echoed on the stone walls.

Harlen had to admit he was right. He was distracted. But for once, his thoughts were refusing to be shut away. They kept drifting back to the events of the day that had passed before his father told him to go down to the basement and await his return.

Millie and Jacques had kept their word. He could still hardly believe it; he supposed he thought that their promises to help him had been idle, comforting words. Beautiful in the moment, but ultimately empty.

But no. Hardly a week had passed since they had made their first trip to the Cat's Eye Theater when Jacques had closed his book during one of their lessons with a broad grin and announced, "Millie's outside. Get your coat."

Jacques later explained that he'd seen Millie out in the garden the day previous and had managed to get her attention from outside the gate. Something about throwing rocks and very nearly earning a solid slap when the one that got her attention bounced off her shoulder with more force than he had intended.

Regardless, the two of them had discussed taking another look at the theater. They had planned a day and a time to meet up and set it in motion without his knowledge.

"The timing was her idea," Jacques had said. "Easier to go when you're supposed to be out of the house anyway, right? Now you head out through the front and don't get caught. I have to grab a few things from the staff room."

You're not going out the front?" Harlen asked, and in reply, he only got another broad grin.

"Hey, you're supposed to be in class; I'm supposed to be at work. I've got to keep this quiet too," Jacques said, slapping him on the back to get him moving. "Now move your skinny ass."

Harlen did as Jacques told him, feeling a bit ill.

Harlen was so nervous he thought he might be sick, but that nervousness was tinged with the same excitement he had felt the day he took Millie to the post office. He hadn't been able to suppress a tiny grin as he hurried out through the thankfully empty halls.

Millie was indeed outside; across the street, she gave him a conspiratorial wink when she saw him coming that made his heart jump into his throat.

"Look at you, skipping class," she said as he got closer, her gray eyes twinkling. "Didn't know you had it in you."

Oh, he'd wanted to crush her into a hug right then and there. To pull her to his chest there and then, not caring who stared. But as soon as he reached her, she laughed and pointed up at the school. He followed her gaze just in time to see Jacques climbing out of one of the second-floor windows.

Jacques hauled himself out, not a simple task given his broad shoulders, and hovered for a moment on the ledge easing the glass back into place behind him. Then he simply jumped off the edge.

Harlen was too stunned even to make a sound of shock. He watched the dust and papers that littered the street stir themselves into a frenzy beneath him, and Jacques landed on a puff of dusty air. He bounced off the invisible cushion and hit the ground with both feet, cigarette still held in his mouth, and gave a theatrical bow to the both of them.

"You know, I've done that a few times, but this was my first time with an audience," he said, walking up to them and brushing a hand back through his thick, copper hair. "Does it look as good as it feels?"

"You're like a bird," Millie said. "A bird plummeting to the ground, but a bird."

Jacques nodded, seeming rather pleased with himself. "I can take being a shitty bird."

They went back to the theater, which by then was closed and inoperative, but Jacques was apparently friends with a few of the performers. When he told him what they were looking for a missing girl, they were more than happy to let them in to ask around with the actors who were present and awake in those early hours of the morning.

At first, nobody they spoke to knew her based on her name and description. Jacques admitted it had been a few years, so it might be hard for them to recall for sure. Harlen had been ready to thank them for trying and leave when the last woman they spoke to recalled her name.

It was nothing special. It was a story about how Tansey had made an impression by spilling a drink on one of her costumes way back in the day. She had been what the actress considered far too tipsy for a girl who hardly looked to be in her teens.

She had sat Tansey down in her dressing room for an hour or two to sober up where she could keep an eye on her. After all, the theater was fun, but it was no place for such a young girl to be wandering drunk and alone.

She had been a pleasant girl, as the woman recalled. Clever despite her intoxication. They chatted now and then when they saw each other, which hadn't been for a long while. She had been wondering what happened to her.

It was nothing really. Nothing that would lead to Tansey being found or offer some clue as to what happened to her, but the immensity of it nearly made Harlen's legs go out from under him. He'd laughed and probably seemed out of his mind to the woman he was speaking to, but it didn't matter.

The things Tansey talked about doing always sounded so foreign and distant. Like they happened in another world, another life. He hadn't quite realized how strongly he'd felt that until he heard a simple story about her spilling a drink from this woman at the theater. Someone other than himself, outside his family, had known her. She'd left footprints behind her, and people could follow. She had existed, here, in the world, she'd told him about. People remembered her.

For the first time since she'd gone missing, he felt hope that it was possible to find where she'd gone.

His euphoria was so immense that he hadn't objected when Jacques suggested they may as well blow off the rest of the day. Harlen had allowed Jacques to take them all to a small, cramped café on the lower side of town that's coffee had been fantastic.

He'd spent the entire afternoon listening to Jacques and Millie crack jokes and tell stories, eating greasy toast and cookies with too much sugar. It all felt so amiable and warm, and eventually, he was brave enough to put his hand over Millie's, where it sat on top of the table so very close to his own.

He held his breath as soon as his skin touched hers. The restaurant's air seemed to still, and he suffered the grim feeling that everyone nearby was staring, but then Millie smiled, and he didn't care if anyone was looking at him. For the first time, he found himself wishing people would look over at their table to see what felt like a dream's glowing happiness—a table serving as a little island on the rainy coast where hope existed.

SLAM.

Harlen's attention jumped back to the room as his father brought the cane crashing down on the table, nearly spilling the glass of water all over the floor.

"You're not trying!" he shouted. "Do you not understand that you're now out in the public eye? You are going to shame this family!"

Harlen flinched and turned his head, bracing for another impact, but it didn't come. He heard his father sigh and only opened his eyes and began to relax when he felt the bonds at his wrists being yanked free.

As soon as they were off, his father grabbed his shirt and jacket from the neatly folded pile he'd placed them in at the corner of the room and threw them at him.

"Get dressed and get out," he snapped, planting both his hands on either side of the table. Vostesk Senior stared down at the glass of water, and as Harlen watched, he saw the water frost, then freeze, and the glass crackled as his father stared at it with more and more intensity.

"I'm so tired of dealing with you," he said slowly. Harlen couldn't tell if he was talking to him or not. He stood with his shirt held to his chest as his father continued, "The very least you could do is make some offspring with some kind of talent if you're even capable. At the very least, you could try, but you can't even manage that, can you? I drop a woman in front of you, and you can't even stop sniveling long enough to take her to bed."

Harlen stared at him and, for a moment, felt as if he couldn't think. He didn't realize what emotion was bubbling inside him until he noticed he was digging his fingernails into the palms of his hands so forcefully they were beginning to draw blood—he was angry.

You can't talk about her like that. Harlen felt part of his mind shouting. *You can't do that.*

But that wasn't all. What had struck him even more, was how odd what his father had just said was. Harlen stared at him questioningly, unmoving.

Perhaps it was the anger, or maybe it was the confusion, but he found the strength to speak without his voice shaking and asked, "How would you know that?"

Millie might not be pregnant, but it had been four months since she'd arrived. How did he know that they had or hadn't done? He could just assume and throw out insults, but that didn't explain why his father's face dropped suddenly. He had slipped, and Harlen knew it.

The anger made him bold. Harlen could hear the indignance in his voice when he didn't ask but instead demanded, "How would you know?"

Millie might not be pregnant, but it had been four months since she'd arrived. How did he know that they had or hadn't done? He could just be assuming and throwing out insults, but that didn't explain why his father's face dropped suddenly. He had slipped, and Harlen knew it.

The anger made him bold. Harlen could hear the indignance in his voice when he didn't ask but instead demanded, "How would you know?"

There was a beat of silence where the room froze in time. The dynamic in the room had shifted, and it was disorienting. He'd spoken back Vostesk Senior for the first time in his life, and he knew he'd struck on something. The scowl that formed on his father's face made him sure of it.

The smack was hard and came so abruptly that Harlen had had no time to brace for it. It knocked him off his feet, and he hit the wall in a daze, bright lights bursting behind his eyes.

"How dare you!" his father roared at the top of his lungs. "You do not ask questions of me!"

Harlen pushed up onto his side and spat blood onto the floor. He'd bitten his cheek in the fall, and the world around him still felt like it was spinning.

There were a million thoughts in his head all rushing at once, and the ground beneath him warped unsteadily as his father continued to scream and berate him.

He said that he was stupid. That he was putting words in his mouth, that he hadn't listened to what he said. But it wasn't right. It wasn't. He had heard what he heard. His father had made a mistake and let something slip—the agony was that Harlen didn't know *what*.

Finally, after what could have been an hour of screaming, his father straightened and ordered him to stand up. He did, slowly, with a pounding ache in his jaw.

His father looked at him with a cold stare and said in a much more composed voice, "I know because I know you. I see how you look at her—you're terrified even to touch her. It's because you're a coward and a sniveling little brat who wouldn't have the manhood to sleep with her if she begged you."

Harlen looked back at him. He always looked at the floor when his father spoke to him, but this time he dragged his eyes back up to his face. He looked into those cold, pale eyes. Harlen didn't say anything; the gesture was defiance in and of itself. And he knew that his father could see what was written plainly all over his face: *I don't believe you.*

He fully expected to be ordered back into the chair, but he wasn't. He was told once again in a frigid tone to go back upstairs. This time, Harlen stared at him for a few moments longer before backing out of the room.

CHAPTER 23

As Harlen climbed the stairs, one thought repeated over and over in his head. *I don't believe you. I don't believe you.*

He didn't stop to rest his aching muscles on the stairs or in the upper hall. He went straight for his bedroom, closed the door, and began to search.

He upturned everything. He tore the sheets from the bed and flipped the mattress. He pulled every book from the bookshelf and felt along every angle of the shelves inside. He yanked the drawers out of his desk and tossed the clothes from his wardrobe.

He even moved Millie's things to feel along the inside of the trunk she'd been given and opened her wardrobe, looking for something—anything—that could be used to see or listen in on what they were doing. He even emptied his hiding place behind the bathroom mirror, but he found nothing.

He had no idea what he was looking for: a rune of some kind, perhaps? He didn't know who his father would have contacted to make them but knew that runes did exist that could accomplish such a thing. He searched diligently for the telling glow that such a marking would emit but found nothing of the sort.

He had read of a few charms that could be performed by either runic magic or alchemists that could be placed on crystals, or glass marbles, or little bits of mirror that would allow for spying—but there was nothing. There was nothing in the room other than the furniture and what he'd put in it.

The furniture itself didn't appear to have been tampered with either. There was nothing.

Standing in the middle of what he'd torn apart, Harlen began to wonder. Was it just something about him that proclaimed his timidity so loudly that others could see it plainly? Was there a sign so apparent that his father could tell only by looking at the two of them that they hadn't done anything? He hadn't imagined that look of guilt on his father's face. He had let something slip. Or had he?

Slowly, Harlen began to put the room back in order. He carefully placed everything back where it belonged, using the process to look over everything one last time. He turned the pages of his books, examined ink bottles and the pockets of clothes—but there was nothing.

He sighed as he slid the last book into place, and in the silence that followed, he heard the humming.

He thought that he had lost his mind for a moment, but then he recognized the voice. It was his mother.

He stood up and walked out into the hallway, slowly approaching his mother's room, careful not to make the floorboards creak. He up to where the door was left open ever so slightly and pushed it in a bit more.

His mother was sitting on the bed. She was sitting up, fully dressed in a purple and white striped dress, humming to herself. Now and then, a faint smile flickered over her face. Then he saw another figure in the room and realized it was Millie his mother was smiling at.

He pushed the door open further to see her walking around, echoing his mother's hum and carrying the stronger tune every time his mother stopped. Millie was picking up the clothes from the floor and putting them back in the wardrobe, straightening the little bottles of perfume and jars of powder on her vanity. Once in a while, she would look back at his mother and smile, and she would mimic it in her delicate, faltering way.

He watched the two of them and felt a smile tugging at his mouth. He supposed that he did love his mother, even if it seemed she never shared the sentiment. Even if he hadn't, he knew he would have taken no more joy in seeing her than he did now in the state she was usually in—a sad, rocking shell of a person who seemed able only to cry and stare tearfully into nothing. Or on her best days, to exist as a distant and confused husk. Lost in her pain.

She had been a good mother once, or she had tried to be. She'd never been happy with his father, and he'd always known that. Even when he was too young to understand their relationship's nuance, he had felt the tension. There was no warmth in the way they looked at each other, and she would always stop smiling when he came into a room. It was like he blew out the light in her eyes whenever he looked at her. But she had tried, in the beginning, to be good to both himself and Tansey even if Tansey was her clear favorite.

She used to clean the cuts and bruises he received from merely being a child and from his father. She would try to explain why he was doing what he did, even if Harlen couldn't understand it at the time. He didn't understand magic or the need for it; he only understood that he was in pain. He would try to explain that to her, but she never seemed to listen. She was absent in a way, even then.

She would just pick him up after she'd bandaged his cuts and bruises, and she would hold him and tell him that everything would be alright. Back then, he'd been young enough to believe her.

Then, one day she'd simply stopped. He had no idea why. All he knew for sure was that she suddenly acted as if he wasn't there at all, and he was suddenly trying to clean his own bloody arms in the bathroom sink.

He always suspected it had something to do with his father. Harlen could never be sure if that lessened or increased whatever distant bitterness he felt towards her, a feeling that never won out over his desire to see her attention return to him again. Or his desire to see her returned to her old self, who at least seemed to feel some kind of happiness and had some inclinations towards motherly affection.

She had no capacity for any emotion but senseless grief as she was now. She had gotten worse and worse as the years passed, fading into a ghost.

When Harlen looked at her, he felt as though he was looking at a portrait. The woman who sat before him looked like his mother, but there was no life behind her eyes.

He was still staring at his mother, and Millie was picking up a hairpin from the floor when she looked up and spotted him in the doorway. She looked startled but smiled at him in that way that dimpled her cheek. He felt his heart flutter when she walked towards him.

"Are you sneaking up on me now?" she asked and opened the door fully, immediately slipping her hand into his like that was where it belonged.

She gestured with her free hand to his mother and explained, "I know it's late, but I thought she'd feel better if we both got dressed up. Right, Pearl?"

His mother smiled again and nodded eagerly while wringing her hands together. "Yes. She let me put a few pins in her hair, and I think she looks lovely."

"She does," Harlen agreed, and Millie laughed.

"You didn't even look."

He wanted to say he didn't need to, but his mother was still watching intently, and despite his confidence earlier that day, he thought that perhaps it was best to reserve some statements for privacy. Instead, he just gave Millie a sheepish smile and looked to see where a few pins were gleaming in her dark hair.

"You look lovely," he said, which, much to his surprise, turned her cheeks a rosy pink and made her squeeze their joined hands.

"Do you mind if we step out for a moment?" Millie asked.

His mother nodded, and Harlen followed Millie out into the hallway, easing his mother's door shut behind them. From behind the door, he could hear her continuing to hum and remarked, "She seems happy."

"Well, when we got back, she waved at me from her room, and I didn't feel right just walking away," Millie said. She looked a bit conflicted, too, though he wasn't sure why. "I thought I could at least clean a little in there. I thought dressing up would be good for her too. She strikes me as the kind of person who enjoys that."

"She does," Harlen nodded. "She used to wear these little diamond earrings every day when I was younger." Millie bit her lip and looked at the ground, and he added, "I think she likes you."

"She worries me," Millie admitted, glancing back down the hallway at his mother's closed door. "How long has she been like that?"

Harlen thought back. After she'd started distancing herself from him, it had taken him a while to stop trying fruitlessly to regain whatever favor he'd lost seemingly overnight. Once he'd come to accept that that was simply the way things were, he had tried not to pester her.

He hadn't noticed many subtle changes in her personality at first; she had always been prone to certain behaviors, and the opium certainly didn't help. But once Tansey went missing, she seemed to come apart all at once. "After Tansey mostly. A little before, but nothing like this."

"Do you think finding Tansey would help her?" Millie asked. She seemed lost in thought, staring at his mother's door with her brow furrowed, chewing her lip.

"I don't know," he admitted. "I hope so. It's not. . .we haven't been close in a long time. But I hate seeing her so sad."

Millie looked back at him, and he reached up to adjust his glasses nervously. "I guess, a selfish part of me hopes that if we get Tansey back, she'll be herself again. That's not the only reason why I want to find her, of course, but I'd be lying if I said that wasn't one of a lot of reasons."

"How is that selfish?" Millie asked, and he shrugged.

"I guess it's because if she gets back to her old self, then, maybe—Maybe I'd get a chance to be close with her again. I don't know."

It was difficult to explain; as neglectful as she'd been, there was an undeniable conflict in him. Part of him wanted nothing to do with her, to neglect her as she had him, but another, larger part of him just missed his mother. It was confusing and unpleasant and sent him back to twisting his cufflink on his sleeve again. Millie reached up and pulled his hand away from it.

She held his hand between both of hers for a moment. She seemed to be studying it: turning it over a few times, massaged it with her hands, and eventually, it stopped feeling so twitchy and lost the sensation that he needed something to occupy it.

"That's not wrong. She's your mother."

She tugged wordlessly on his hand, and he followed her into their shared room. She shut the door carefully, dimming the sound of his mother's humming before she turned back towards him.

"You know she's not the only one I worry about, right?"

Right. He'd forgotten to put himself back together after the basement. He'd been too busy putting the room back together.

He sat on the edge of the bed, level with her eyes. His exhaustion must have been written all over him. He expected questions, but she just put both her hands on either side of his face. It was a movement that startled him and usually would have embarrassed him, but her warm gray eyes were studying him with such concern that he felt nothing but a softness towards her that melted away everything else.

"You look tired." Her thumbs stroked the bones of his cheeks—the hollows beneath his eyes. The sensation was heavenly.

He should tell her what happened down there. But she was right. He was so tired.

The panic and fear were easing away, leaving nothing in their wake like they always did. Leaving him with nothing but lingering pain where he'd been hurt and a dull ache in his bones.

Her hands on his face, by contrast, were warm and gentle. It took everything in him to not bury his face in her palms because he was sure that would ease the slowly encroaching pain behind his eyes where his usual headache was beginning to ramp up.

"Yes, I do," was all he could manage. He looked up at her, and she said nothing. She just bent and kissed the place between his eyes as though she knew that that was where the pain was. And, as if by magic, it began to dissipate.

The pain began to pull away; the bright lights dancing in the corners of his vision began to fade. He had never experienced anything like it before.

He was so surprised and fascinated he didn't even realize he had asked her to do it again until he saw her smile before she another soft kiss between his eyes and ran her fingers back through his tangled hair.

In the absence of the ordinarily head-splitting pain, he was flooded with the most peculiar sensation. It started at the place behind his eyes where the headache was usually the strongest and spread back through his skull, down through his entire body. Not nervousness. Not even the butterflies and warmth Millie usually evoked. This was something. . .else.

He could only liken it to the pins and needles of blood flowing back into a sleeping limb. Like air flooding back into a collapsed lung.

It happened too quickly to decide if it was painful, then it passed. It left Harlen feeling much the same as he had before, except for a single realization. This was the first time he had emerged from the basement, not feeling like the weight of the world and every failing in it was on his shoulders. He felt alright.

No matter what his father said he was, there were people that would joke with him in diners and people who would hold his hand beneath the table. Some people were willing to help him, his sister, and his mother. There was someone who would hold his face and kiss his forehead and run her hands through his hair when the worst came to pass.

He wasn't alone. He didn't *feel* alone.

"I'm happy," he said out loud as the word for the emotion that was eluding him hit him all at once. It was a punch to the stomach that made him open his eyes and look up at Millie. Both his hands flew to the sides of her face while a breathy laugh burst from him.

The worst had happened. He'd been beaten and screamed at. He had left the house; he had talked back to his father, and he would pay the price for it. And it didn't matter because he was *happy*.

He studied Millie's face; took it in like he was seeing her for the first time. He'd hardly been able to look at her when they first met, and now he had no idea how he had been able to take his eyes away—the curve of her brow, the brightness of her eyes, the shape of her mouth. Everything was stunning.

He felt a pull towards her that was akin to how a stone is pulled down to earth. He leaned forward a bit closer to her, again uncertain of what the feeling was exactly, but when his gaze wandered down from her eyes to her lips, he realized what it was. He wanted to kiss her.

"Millie?" he broke out of his trance, suddenly nervous. But he didn't move away. Unless she said no, he wasn't sure that he could.

"Yes?" she'd stopped smiling and was looking at him with a strange glitter in her eyes he hadn't seen before. Everything felt tense, and she was breathing quickly. His heart was pounding.

"Can I kiss you?" he blurted out, his words running together in an effort to get out of him.

She stared up at him, and the glitter in her eyes grew brighter. She nodded, a quick jerk of her head that seemed to startle her, and she said very quietly, "Yes. Please."

Please. The please was what gave him the final push to press his lips against hers.

He understood little of how kissing was done, so it was barely a touch of the lips, but when he started to move back, thinking of a thousand ways he'd done it wrong, her hand gripped the front of his shirt to keep him where he was, and she kissed him.

The feeling was remarkable. His body felt weightless. He thought that if she didn't pull away, he could do this forever.

Eventually, his lips matched hers in their movement, and he wrapped his arms around her waist to pull her close. Her arms wrapped around his neck and one hand slid up into his hair, and he shuddered against her.

"Still happy?" she asked, pulling back just enough to ask with that impish grin he loved so dearly.

"Yes," he said, and this time he was the one who pulled her closer—for once, not thinking—doing nothing but feeling a sense of hot euphoria consuming him like fire.

He wanted to be closer to her. There was a pit in him that left him wanting like he never had before. Never in his life had had he been more aware of a body that was not his own, and he wanted to press his body against hers, to feel her kissing him like this.

She was soft. His hands could not find any sharpness to her as he slid his hands down over her shoulders and back, mimicking the path her hands took down the length of his spine. Her hair was silk between his fingers, but he had no objections to her leading his hands to her hips.

One thought made him shiver: alone. They were utterly alone.

Or are you?

He remembered what his father had said. And all at once, the feeling of being watched was overwhelming.

He broke away from her and looked at the door, a ball of ice in his stomach. Nothing. Nobody.

You're just paranoid.

"What's wrong?" Millie asked, her breath coming quickly, her cheeks flushed. He knew he was red, and he felt like he was struggling to breathe past the hard pounding of his heart. He wanted more. But he couldn't shake the feeling.

"It's nothing," he said, his voice sounding more husky than usual while he brushed the hair out of her face.

Should he tell her what his father said, or would it be scaring her for no reason? She was already frightened of the man—was there a reason to scare her further for what seemed to be nothing so far as he could see?

He swallowed as he thought about it. How unbearable it would be for her to stay here alone if he put the thought in her head that there might be eyes peering over her shoulder. It could be that all his father was trying to do was make him uneasy. He didn't want to help him by making Millie feel the same.

Instead, he allowed his mind to return to what had just happened and felt himself blush all over again. He couldn't steady his heart that seemed to be trying to beat out of his chest "It's, um, that's intense," he breathed.

She laughed, and he tightened his grip around her waist.

Maybe she would believe him anyway, even if he were paranoid. He would tell her, yes. But not here. If someone was watching them, this was no place for it. The next time they left with Jacques, he would tell her. Until then, he would advise her to be careful and would keep as close an eye on her as he was able. Yes, that was what he would do.

"Would you be offended if I said that was much better than the one from the wedding?" she asked.

He winced, but his smile couldn't retreat for long with her curled up against him. "No, I would be inclined to agree with you on that."

No, he wouldn't scare her. He would climb into bed with her for the night, and he would hold her like he had the night before. He would feel his arms around her and bury his face in her hair; he would kiss her between the eyes as she had him to soothe her to sleep. And even if only for that night, they would be happy.

CHAPTER 24

The bed was cold in the morning. Millie woke up, still curled over where she had been the night before. She reached out with one hand, feeling only tangled blankets, hearing only the sound of the rain pattering against the roof and the sound of the clock ticking far down the hall.

Everything was as it had been the day, the week, the month before.

Maybe that was why she was surprised at how disappointed she was to feel the bed beside her empty.

She sat up, brushing back the nest of tangled dark hair from her face while looking around the room. Beside her, on the pillow, she saw a folded scrap of paper, and she smiled before she opened it.

She read it lying on her back, her legs propped on the headboard as she would have done back home. In a way, the bed was beginning to feel like hers.

It was long, rambling, and absolutely perfect. It went on and on about wanting to tell her good morning but not wanting to wake her. And about the kiss. He sounded like a dizzy teenager, and it was hard to pretend she didn't return the sentiment. Especially considering that while she read it, she had unconsciously raised a hand to her mouth where she could still feel the ghost of his lips.

After she finished reading the note several times over, she stretched out in the sheets to listen to the sound of rain. As she lay there, she caught one other sound through the white noise she'd grown accustomed to—a faint humming coming from down the hallway.

Millie stood, walked to the bedroom door, and opened it just a crack. The door to Harlen's mother's room was half open, which Millie had never seen, and from the inside, she could hear her humming away to the same tune as yesterday.

Millie had found herself in Pearl's room yesterday because she'd heard her crying through the door. Harlen and his father had vanished to the basement again, and she was told she could return to her room. She'd been standing in the hall debating whether or not to follow them to see if she could discover what was going on when she'd heard his mother shriek.

Millie had forgotten her manners, burst through the door, and found Pearl sitting on the ground in her nightdress, her hair a tangled mess, sitting over the remains of her water glass that had fallen and broken on the floor.

She had evidently been trying to pick up the pieces and had succeeded only in cutting her finger open. She was holding her hand to her chest, rocking and crying, and no matter what Millie felt for the woman, she hadn't had the heart to leave her like that.

Millie had spent the next half hour using a pin to dig the glass shards out of Pearl's fingers. Luckily, Millie had broken enough glasses and vases in her life to know how to get all the little bits out with as little pain as possible.

The entire time Pearl had stared at her with her big, wet eyes like she was trying hard to place who she was, which was unnerving. At least she didn't seem to be hurting her. In fact, by the time she'd finished with her hand, washing it and wrapping it in a scrap of linen, Pearl seemed to have forgotten she'd even hurt herself, to begin with, and asked why there was glass on the floor.

"I'm not sure," Millie had said, forcing a smile. "Why don't you let me get that up, so nobody steps on it."

Pearl nodded, still looking lost, while Millie dusted up the glass into one of the fireplace scoops and threw it in the bin. By the time she did that, Pearl had placed who she was and started mumbling about Tansey again. About how nice it was to have another girl in the house. It was all the things she said the other night, and Millie wasn't sure if she knew she was repeating herself.

Millie tried to listen, but when she again began explaining how her husband had let her keep her little daughter safe, she couldn't just stand there.

She started to tell her that she shouldn't have just left her son to fend for himself, but Pearl's eyes were so vacant that

Millie was sure it wouldn't make a difference no matter how eloquently she expressed her point. Shouting at her probably would have just made her more frightened and confused, so instead, Millie closed her mouth and started cleaning the room.

She hoped it would get rid of the oppressive air of the place. And that it would give her a way to vent the frustration she felt on something physical.

At some point, while she was doing so, putting clothes in the wardrobe, Pearl stopped talking. Millie hadn't thought much of it. Pearl drifted in and out of the conversation at random, so she continued untangling and hanging dresses until the silence was broken by gagging.

She turned to see Pearl lying in bed with her opium bottle in one hand, being sick all over herself. She must have tried to drink directly from the bottle while on her back and had seized like a dead spider. The sound as she tried to gasp for breath past her own sick was awful.

Millie had dropped everything and ran to grab her, too startled to think of shouting for help. She had no idea what to do other than haul her onto her side to stop her from choking. She turned her over, so her head dangled off the bed where her vomit dripped out of her mouth like drool, her head lolling like there were no muscles in her neck at all.

Her first breaths were wet, raspy gurgles, and Millie fully expected them to be followed by a scream. She knew she would be screaming in her situation. She might start screaming and not stop until she collapsed, but Pearl had done nothing but stare blankly the entire time.

Her glassy eyes rolled aimlessly in their sockets, eventually wandering up to look at Millie, where she asked in a daze, "What happened?"

Mille couldn't remember if she told her or not. All she remembered was spending the next hour getting her changed, bathing her, seeing where her bones poked out through her white skin.

She then redressed her, feeling as though she were caring for a very young, frightened child rather than a woman twice her age.

What she had done to her son was wrong. Not stepping between Vostesk Senior and her children was wrong. She probably deserved to be left alone as she'd done to Harlen, but Millie couldn't bring herself not to help her.

She hadn't mentioned the incident to Harlen when he'd come back upstairs. As much as he tried to act like he was fine, he looked pale and worried already, and she could tell he was in pain in some way, though he never mentioned it. She didn't think she needed to add to that.

She tried bringing it up again after the kiss when they had been lying down to rest. That was when she noticed the shadow of a bruise forming on his cheek.

In the end, she said nothing about either. Just as she had been deciding what to put forward first, he looked at her with a beaming smile. And with all the gentleness in the world, he kissed her between the eyes. She hadn't had the heart to mar his happiness after that.

Both worries remained, but Harlen had at least gotten his rest and was off for his classes; it wasn't quite as cold as usual, and Pearl was humming in the other room. For the moment, things were as peaceful as they could be.

CHAPTER 25

Millie washed in the bath, soaking, letting the water warm her from the chill that always seemed to creep down to her very bones when she slept. She was convinced the bath was the only truly warm place in the house.

She lay in the water, staring up at the ceiling—at the patterns of waves and sea creatures etched along the molding. There was a painting of a great shipwreck in the center of the ceiling where men were clinging to boards, faces frozen in horror as great sharks with open mouths and gleaming teeth emerged from the black water.

Millie still hadn't quite been able to look at it without feeling an unpleasant shiver. She knew the shark was the symbol of the Vostesk house, and as such, the creatures were depicted everywhere. She just wondered what the hell was going on in the mind of the person that decided it was a good idea to put that particular piece over the bathtub.

She tried to put her eyes anywhere else and saw the evidence that Harlen had already been in here that morning; the bottles of oils and cologne he used were still on the counter where he always left them, lined up in a neat row by height. He was the only person she ever met who left a room more organized than he came into it—and the only person she knew who folded his clothes before he put them in the hamper.

In the clothing basket, he'd folded the towel and washcloth he used before putting them in. His clothes from the other day, as well, were folded neatly inside. The only thing that could be considered partially out of place was his pale brown jacket hanging on the back of the door.

When Millie climbed out of the bath and pulled on her clothes, the lilac-colored dress with the lace at the collar and sleeves, she took the jacket and pulled it on, smiling to herself. He wouldn't mind if she kept it warm for him while she was away. It gave her another layer of warmth, and she supposed that by now, she could admit she missed his absence, and this helped dull it.

She left the bathroom, tying her damp hair back away from her face with a scrap of purple linin and sat down on the bed, crossing her legs under her, fumbling over the side of the bed for the next letter home she had been working on and had abandoned on Harlen's desk the night before.

Millie propped an ink bottle on the nightstand and considered what to say in light of recent events, touching the end of the pen to her mouth, occasionally tapping it with her teeth. She had a good deal to say and tried to think of how to put it all into words. All the while, she listened to the humming from the other room, unconsciously chiming in herself until she heard footsteps on the stairs. Vostesk Senior's footsteps.

She sat bolt-upright immediately and shoved the half-started letter under her pillow. She reached for the ink as well but succeeded only in knocking the glass stopper resting atop it to the floor. She swore under her breath as it hit the ground with what seemed to her like earth-shattering loudness.

She held her breath; the bottle still clutched in one hand as the footsteps drew closer, then stomped right by her door. She let out a breath of relief that choked her as she heard the door to Harlen's mother's room bang open. Millie dropped the entirety of the ink bottle onto the desk that was, luckily, already stained with countless other ink spells that may very well have happened in the same way.

"WHAT THE HELL ARE YOU DOING?"

Millie froze in place, ink dripping off her fingers as she heard Vostesk Senior roar in the other room. She had heard her father angry, even heard him shout on a rare occasion. But she had never heard a man scream like that.

Straining her ears, Millie couldn't hear Pearl's reply if she made any.

"EITHER SHUT THE DAMN DOOR OR SHUT THE HELL UP! I'M TRYING TO WORK AND I CAN'T MAKE ANY PROGRESS WITH YOU MAKING ALL THIS DAMN NOISE!"

The door slammed. Millie heard Vostesk Senior's stomping down the hall to his office, followed by another slamming door. In the echoing silence that rushed in to fill the booming of his shouting, she could hear Pearl's faint sobbing.

It replaced Millie's fear with a kind of pure lividness that turned the edges of her vision white and freed her from the frozen trance she'd been in. She jumped off the bed and hurried down the hall to Pearl's door.

She pulled on it, and it gave ever so slightly, then was yanked shut by the woman behind it.

"Please! Please, go away!" she sobbed on the other side.

"Pearl! It's me! It's Millie!" she hissed in a whisper.

"Please! I'll be quiet! Please, just go!"

Pearl's voice was ragged, and without even seeing her, it was clear she was on the verge of hysterics. Millie tried the door again, but it may as well have been locked with all the force that tiny woman was desperately putting against it to keep it shut.

Or maybe she'd pushed the bed in front of it again like she'd talked about with Tansey. Either way, Millie wasn't going to get in.

"It's Millie—I'm not going to hurt you!" she tried whispering through the door one last time, but she was met with nothing but more broken cries and pleading to be left alone.

Millie stood for a moment with her hand still wrapped around the doorknob, then let it drop. She took a step back, but she only took off her shoes rather than return to her room in defeat. She threw them into the open door of her and Harlen's shared room, leaving her in her thick gray socks.

It was a trick her older sister Lily taught her for sneaking down to the kitchen at night. It served her well as she crept soundlessly down the hall, staying close to the walls to prevent the floorboards from creaking as she crept slowly towards Vostesk Senior's office.

The door, when he'd slammed it, hadn't locked. He'd banged it so hard off the frame that it had bounced swung partially open.

Like a child throwing a tantrum, she thought again.

She got down on her hands and knees so she wouldn't be seen at eye level. She crawled forward and very slowly peered around the door.

She had no idea what she was doing. She couldn't confront him; he was bigger and undoubtedly more callous than her. She doubted he'd have any qualms about hitting or beating a woman. Not to mention, he had magic. There was no way of knowing what that made him capable of.

It wasn't as if she could count on Pearl to come to her rescue should she need rescuing. But she just couldn't slink back to her room. She had a sinking feeling it had something to do with Harlen and the basement, and at least a quick look may do something to chip away at the constant sense of unknowing that made her skin crawl.

Vostesk Senior looked more disheveled than she'd seen him previously. He abandoned his suit jacket on the back of the chair, and under the black vest, his white shirt was a rumpled mess. His sleek ponytail of long, pale brown hair looked as though it was falling out of place in long strands around his shoulders, and he had an unusually twisted scowl on his face as he dug through his desk drawers, tossing papers aside.

However, what caught her eye was when he went to the bookshelf and picked up what looked like a fist-sized glass ball. It was orange and sitting in a little iron cradle, and when he picked it up off the shelf, he stared at it for a moment with a long, thoughtful frown.

It could be a trophy of some kind or nothing more than a decoration for all she knew. She'd never seen anything like it.

As Vostesk Senior stared into it, his eyes became distant—almost hazy—and the room filled with faint orange light. The same orange light she had seen the other night. She was struck by it, but her attention was quickly drawn away by what was on the sleeve of the arm he was using to hold up the object. Blood.

Not fresh; it looked as though it had been left to dry for hours, but the spatter was unmistakable. All she could think of was that several hours ago, he had been in the basement with Harlen.

That was enough. She had to know.

Keeping on her hands and knees, Millie waited until he'd turned to place the object back on the bookshelf and crawled past the door. Once she was on its other side, she stood and walked on her toes, keeping near the wall once again as she made her way down the stairs to the kitchen where the door to the basement stood waiting.

She was, again, overcome by a sensation like her mother's voice in the back of her head, telling her she was doing something stupid. Millie agreed. Unfortunately, she had to ignore it no matter how badly she wanted to give in to her urge to run. She needed to see. She *had* to know.

Thunk.

She pulled on the door, and it wouldn't budge. It was locked. She pulled again.

Thunk.

Slowly, she felt her entire body go cold. This door hadn't been unlocked the last time she'd tried it. Just a few days ago, she had tested the handle but hadn't been able to push past the fear to go down. It hadn't been locked then. What changed?

She dug back through her mind, trying to think of something, anything, that could have made Vostesk Senior lock a door he had never seen the need to lock before. She couldn't see a man like him changing his habits without reason, but she could think of nothing severe enough to make an impact. *Unless.*

Millie let go of the doorknob and took a step back. She whipped around, but the kitchen behind her was empty. Millie crept to the door and peered out into the dining room, but the entire lower floor was empty. She was alone with the sound of her heart pounding in her ears and the sound of her breathing, which suddenly seemed too loud.

The only reason he would have locked it is if he knew she had tried to go down there.

CHAPTER 26

"Harlen."

Harlen stared at the rune he was tracing over and over below the mix of dried berries and rainwater he had made.

"Hey, Harlen."

"What?" He looked up at Jacques. Through the haze of smoke in front of his face coming from the cigarette, Harlen could see his green eyes and coppery eyebrows set into a look of tired resignation. He felt his stomach sinking before he even opened his mouth.

"How long do you want to keep this up?"

He didn't ask it cruelly; it was a genuine, tired question.

"Look," said Jacques, running a hand back through his messy, curly hair. "It's not that bad, alright? Lots of people don't give a shit about magic and get on just fine without it. I know it's supposed to be your thing, but maybe it just. . .isn't. It's not the end of the world. Sometimes things just don't work out the way we plan."

Harlen knew he meant well. He had been thinking the same thing over these last few weeks. There was just something about hearing someone else say it out loud that made his stomach sink.

His sullen demeanor didn't amuse Jacques. He was straddling a chair with his chin propped on the back and reached over to stomp out the cigarette on the side of the table in frustration, staining the already stained and warped wood with another black streak.

"Look. You're smart—you know more about this shit than I do—I shouldn't even be the one tutoring you. You could probably tell me more about this than I ever bothered to learn. Do you have any idea what else you could do if you put your energy into literally anything else—"

"How did you know?" Harlen asked suddenly, turning towards him. "I've always wondered. What does it feel like when there's magic in your blood?"

Jacques blinked at him, surprised that he cut him off but pleasantly surprised that he'd spoken up. He took the cigarette out of his mouth and smirked. "Well, I'm not sure, seeing as I've never been any other way."

"What did your family do?" Harlen prompted. That was his real curiosity. What was it like to live free from expectation?

Jacques sighed and shook his head. "Don't think they knew what to do with me at first, to be honest. I'm not an old magic family; please suppress your gasp of horror. They didn't do much of anything for a while, until I hit the teen years, of course, and it became a problem." He chuckled.

Harlen gave him a questioning look, and Jacques pointed at the bowl of rainwater. "It's hard to explain—most of the time; it takes a lot of concentrating to make this magic nonsense happen. But other times, it comes with strong feelings. Which, you may know, a moody teenager has a lot of. This is why places like this exist. To help teach others to keep that shit under control."

Harlen nodded but didn't speak.

"But you're dodging my question. I'm asking if you want to do this. Do you want to spend all day staring at something we both know isn't going to work, or would you rather we spend this time out looking for your sister? I feel like you think that's a bit more important to you, right?"

"My father—"

"Your father's a piece a' shit, and we both know it."

Harlen stared down at the table and instinctively reached up to grip his upper left arm where a good chunk of the scarring was. In some places, even though his clothes, he could feel the twisted, raised flesh. Usually, the sensation of it beneath his fingers was enough to scare him into silence. It made him think twice before making rash decisions. So, he was surprised he instead felt a spark of the same anger he had felt yesterday when he had demanded to know what it was his father wasn't telling him. He was even more surprised that he found himself agreeing with Jacques aloud.

"Yeah. He is."

"That's the spirit. Now, tell me. What would you rather be doing? What's important to *you*?" Jacques asked, letting the question hang in the silence that followed.

Harlen wanted to say something profound. He felt like he was standing at a crossroads he had been idling in front of for ages. He needed to make a decision. But for once, he wasn't thinking. Or at the least, he had no coherent thought. His ears were ringing, and every thought was passing too quickly to comprehend. He couldn't say for sure what it was he even felt, but it must have lead him to shut the book of alchemy he had spent the last weeks bent over without realizing because when Harlen could see the world around him again, he was staring at the cover.

"Atta' boy." Jacques slapped the table and stood up, grabbing his bag from the floor. "Let's go."

"Don't we need to be careful about this? You went out the window last time," Harlen said, scooping his things up in a rush and following as Jacques stormed toward the door, pushing it open with an elbow.

"I might have exaggerated how sneaky I needed to be. I've always wanted to try that trick," Jacques said with a grin as they walked down the empty corridor and into the chilly, damp air outside.

It wasn't raining, but the air was filled with a thick mist that dampened their hair and faces, and they walked. Harlen had to wipe his glasses as they made their way towards the busier section of town.

"Aren't we going to get Millie?" Harlen asked, dodging carefully through the people swarming around them.

Jacques didn't answer, and in the crowd, Harlen assumed he must not have heard him. He repeated the question, but Jacques only waved his hand dismissively.

"Yeah. How do I put this?" Jacques grimaced. "The next place is the Crow's Nest; you said—right?"

Harlen nodded. He had made Jacques a copy of the list, and evidently, he had been studying it.

"Right. Well, it wouldn't look good. Millie going in there with two men. It also might not be the safest place for her to be in general—appearances aside."

"I don't understand," Harlen said flatly.

Jacques put a hand up to his face and ran his hand back over his hair. He looked uncomfortable. "Yeah, you wouldn't," he muttered. Then, louder but not by much, he said, "Listen. The Crow's Nest is a, uh, rowdy place, let's leave it at that. You really don't want her in there."

Harlen frowned and slowed his pace. They were out of the middle of the street, slinking along the sides of buildings so he could do so without being trampled over. "She's supposed to be a part of this. I can't just leave her at home. I made a promise, and my house isn't exactly safe either. You know that."

"This is a different sort of unsafe, believe me." Jacques snorted. "Trust me when I say she wouldn't mind sitting this out."

"You don't know that," Harlen insisted. He had stopped walking entirely, and Jacques stalked back to him, glaring.

"Why is today the day you decided to grow a spine?" Jacques quipped, clearly annoyed.

"I told her I wouldn't let anything happen to her, and I meant it," Harlen snapped back.

The tone of voice felt strange to use. Harlen was afraid of what it might evoke from Jacques, but the memory of cupping Millie's face in his hands and asking her to trust him was stronger—especially when he thought his father might be keeping a closer eye on them than he was comfortable with.

"It's a place for prostitutes! Harlen—The Crow's Nest has lots of prostitutes and very aggressive, grabby men that don't really take no for an answer," Jacques exclaimed in exasperation. He grimaced and blushed as several passersby gave him strange, confused looks, then lowered his voice and grumbled, "Trust me, I may or may not have spent some time in there myself, and I think bringing her there would be a bad idea."

Harlen blinked at him. He was stunned, to be sure. He thought of the times Tansey had come back smelling like smoke and alcohol. She would want to go right to bed when she returned those nights after telling him about her long night out, and he would have to plead with her to wash up first, so their father didn't smell it on her. She would reluctantly drag herself into the washroom and would complain of headaches all the next day. Was this where she'd been those nights? She had hardly been fifteen the first time she'd told him about it. Had she gone there alone?

Very aggressive, grabby men that don't take no for an answer. He didn't doubt his sister's bravery, but bravery would only go so far for a petite young girl on her own. But she had never talked about it like that. She had never come back in a mood that suggested anything bad ever happened.

"It's a beautiful place. Not the building so much—not on the outside anyway," she'd said. He could remember her laying on his floor with her hands behind her head, still smelling like smoke and strong alcohol, her eyes glazed and far-off. "But the inside looks like a real palace. It's full of all these beautiful people. Every single one of them looks like they were made to be there, a bunch of painted dolls in their little doll palace. Nobody ever stops smiling and laughing. The drinks make your head feel like a dream, and everyone there is just happy to be alive. It's stunning, stunning."

He had believed her. But what Jacques said still made his stomach twist and his throat close.

"Hey, before you give me that look, I don't know why she came," Jacques said. "But, hey—they also have some really great drinks there. Maybe that's why."

Harlen nodded and hoped it was convincing. Jacques gave him a worried look that replaced the irritation, then began walking again. Much less enthusiastically than before.

They made their way into the lower town section where the cobblestone was more uneven, and the buildings huddled closer together with their awnings crossed over one another like the canopies of trees. It left the corners of the streets dark with occasional streaks of light in whose path tangled weeds too tough to be stomped out by the people walking over them grew between the cracks in the stone.

The Crow's Nest itself was a surprisingly small place. The outside truly was not much to look at. He might have missed it entirely if Jacques hadn't pointed it out, but the inside was not what Harlen pictured when Tansey talked about it.

The floor was stone and didn't suffer from the rain-warped wood that plagued most of the buildings. The light inside came from very dim lamps on the walls whose flames were surrounded by pink glass that did very well to give the place an other-worldly feel and helped cover the stains of spilled drinks on the floor you could see beneath every table if you stared too long. There were little yellow designs painted on the walls, meant to look like gold, beginning to flake off. Harlen supposed that when night came, and the light wasn't coming in so brightly through the soot-stained windows, it would look better. More like she'd described.

He tried to tell himself as much, but it still left an ache in his chest. It was not because it wasn't how she had said; it was because he had always imagined that she was perfectly happy when she left. Why would she change her story when she told him about it if that had been true?

The place was mostly empty since it was the middle of the day. A few men in waistcoats sat at a table in the far corner, smoking and playing cards, who glanced up as they came in. He and Jacques must not have been enough to hold their interest as they went quickly back to their game.

Harlen vaguely recognized one of them as the son of one of his father's friends and felt a brief spasm of panic, but the young man seemed just as eager not to be recognized as he was. He was trying very hard to cover his face with the cards in his hand. His friends and the young woman seated on the lap of one of them were laughing at him as he sank deeper and deeper into his chair.

There were a few other women seated at the bar. They weren't what Harlen imagined when Jacques told him about them. Yes, their dresses were far more low-cut than he was used to, and many had their skirts pinned up to their hips, so their legs were almost fully visible. But he supposed he had imagined something similar to what he read in books when he heard the word prostitute. They were always smooth, sly, almost other-worldly seductresses in stories and poems. But most of the women he saw just looked tired.

They were sipping coffee and rubbing their eyes. A few were chatting with each other, complaining about the food. One of them appeared to be asleep, her head on her folded arms, her straw-colored hair splayed over the counter while the woman beside her rubbed her back.

A few of them had glanced up as they walked in. A woman with curly black hair and a faint smudge of red lipstick remaining on her lips grinned and waved. Jacques recognized her and was trying very hard to pretend he didn't, which she seemed to find rather funny, as did the other women seated around her.

"They seem friendly," Harlen offered.

"Oh, now you have jokes," Jacques grumbled at him.

He hadn't meant it as a joke, but from the look Jacques gave him, he supposed it was better not to try and explain.

Jacques knocked on the bar's counter to try and get the bartender's attention. While he did that, Harlen looked over to see the woman with black hair looking in their direction and whispering something to the girl he thought was sleeping. Now that her face was visible, he saw that she was startlingly young and blinked at them with bleary but curious eyes. She didn't look like a seductress at all: she looked like a teenager.

"Do you think they would have known her?" Harlen could imagine Tansey starting up a conversation with anyone. If they were here every day, he couldn't imagine her not speaking to them at least once. The girl with the straw-colored hair must have been practically the same age.

"Do you think they would have known her?" Harlen could imagine Tansey starting up a conversation with anyone. If they were here every day, he couldn't imagine her not speaking to them at least once. The girl with the straw-colored hair must have been practically the same age.

"Alright—you got your joke, now piss off," Jacques grumbled, still trying to get the bartender's attention. Harlen let him be and stood quietly behind him when the women with red-smudged lips approached. She looked to be in her late twenties; her black hair pulled back into a sloppy bun that hung down at the back of her head, and she had pale green eyes. Her dress was red, black, and covered in lace.

"Is he being a little rough, hun?" she asked, her voice a deep purr. "Maybe there's something I can help you with?"

"Yes, actually, that would be great," he said. "Thank you. . ."

"Magnolia, dear," she said with a wide smile.

He smiled back. "Magnolia. I'm looking for my sister," he explained. "Ah—she would have been about sixteen or seventeen the last time she was here. Uh—"He dug in his pocket and produced a rough sketch he'd made of her face.

He wasn't a fantastic artist, but he knew how to do measurements and did his best to replicate the shapes in the family portrait. As a result, the sketch did look quite a lot like her. "She had blonde hair, blue eyes. Very small—about this tall?" He measured with his hand.

Magnolia stopped grinning. She took the picture in one lace-gloved hand and looked at it. She didn't quite frown, but Harlen thought her eyes looked sad despite there being no spark of recognition in them.

"Sorry, we see a lot of girls that come through here, I'm afraid." She lowered the picture from her face and looked up at him. Her voice had lost the purr, and he noticed she had a heavy accent that he couldn't quite place. He also noticed in the bright light from the window behind them that there were faint bruises on the side of her neck, and a deep purple one welled on her arm, just below her sleeve.

He understood why Jacques didn't want Millie here. He wished Magnolia and all the women watching their conversation with intense curiosity out of the corners of their eyes weren't there either.

She sat down on one of the bar stools, still taking glances down at the sketch, and Harlen sat down on the seat beside her. She set the paper on the bar and, without looking, managed to pull a cigarette from the front of her dress along with a tiny matchbox. Her eyes never leaving the paper, she lit it, stuck one end in her mouth, and asked, "How long she been gone?"

"A few years," he said, and this time she did frown.

"A few years is a pretty long time. Not sure how many folks will be able to help you."

"I know," he admitted. "But I can't not try."

She turned her pale green eyes that were smudged all around with black kohl up at him, and he couldn't name the expression on her face. There was a twitch of a smile on her red lips, but she still seemed to be sad.

"Tell you what. I hold onto this—" Magnolia tapped the paper, "And if I see her come through here, I'll tell her you were looking. Who knows? Sometimes just knowing you're missed can be enough to get you to go home, right?"

"Would you?" Harlen smiled and didn't understand why she chuckled and shook her head.

"Sure, why not? What's her name?"

"Tansey."

"Tansey?"

Harlen heard someone echo the name from behind the bar counter. Jacques and the bartender stopped mid-argument over what Harlen had no idea. There was a young man with a mop of black hair and dark eyes crouched over a crate of glasses staring at him. When Harlen blinked at him, the man said, "You said you're looking for Tansey?"

Harlen felt as if all the breath had been sucked out of him. The young man put the crate down. "Yes, do you know her?"

"Yeah, I know her," he snapped and wiped his hands slowly on a rag while looking him up and down. "How do you know her?"

"Donnie—relax," Magnolia said, her tone exasperated. "Guy says he's her brother. Lay off."

The young man, Donnie, snorted. "Tansey didn't have a brother. Or at least not one she ever bothered mentioning to me."

Harlen felt like he'd been slapped and opened his mouth to respond, but Jacques reacted instead.

"Alright—and who are you?"

"Her boyfriend." The man glared at Jacques.

"You haven't been her boyfriend for years," Magnolia said. Donnie snapped at her to shut up. Then he shrugged.

"Yeah. She said something was going on, and she had to lay low for a bit. Not two weeks later, she's gone. Been gone for a long time."

"You sound pretty accusatory," Harlen said, not loudly, but Jacques gestured back towards him to emphasize what he'd said.

Donnie narrowed his dark eyes at him. "Yeah— because she seemed pretty scared when she told me. And I didn't see her around after."

"That sounds like a you problem," Jacques snorted.

Donnie dropped the rag he was holding and started to march up to the counter. Magnolia and half the women at the counter got up and took a few steps back. The bartender finally intervened- he shot out his arm to block him and barked at all of them to calm down.

"What did she say was going on? Did she say she was leaving?" Harlen stood up as well, but he stood to take a step toward Donnie.

He pressed his hands flat to the counter and leaned forward as if that would pull an answer out. This was someone who had known her. Someone who could have some idea of where to go. Someone who had just implied that she could be very much alive.

"Go to hell," Donnie spat. The bartender barked at him again.

"Come on, let's go." Jacques grabbed the back of his arm, but Harlen refused to let himself be pulled for once.

"What did she tell you? What was scaring her?"

Again, nothing but a scowl. Harlen stared at it and felt something still practically foreign flare up in him. Anger.

Harlen stared hard back at the young man across from him and spoke with venom in his voice. "Did you even listen when she told you? Or were you just angry she left you?"

"Bastard—"

Donnie tried to rush him again. The bartender struggled to hold him, and Jacques repeated that they needed to go, tugging on his arm, but he couldn't leave.

"You didn't even know she had a brother," Harlen continued. "Now someone's looking for her, and you won't tell them anything out of spite? That shows a lot of care, doesn't it? You must have really loved her."

Donnie had gotten away from the bartender. Harlen felt the back of his hand connect with the side of his face and stumbled to the side, braced for more when he heard a howling of wind followed by a cry of surprise and the breaking of glass. Harlen saw Jacques had blown Donnie backward over the counter, and he had taken several cups with him.

He struggled with the bartender to right himself, and Magnolia turned to both of them with wide eyes. "Back door," she said.

She grabbed them both by the shoulder and pushed them towards the shop's far end, which led to a long, dim hallway.

"Fourth on the left," she said in a rush, and this time Harlen let himself be pushed. The hall was long and dark and smelled like heavy perfume and tobacco. He could hardly see, but Jacques seemed to know his way well and yanked him stumbling along until they reached the door that led to a bright burst of light from outside.

CHAPTER 27

Harlen followed Jacques into the back alley, confused and trying to puzzle in his mind how Tansey might have gone on purpose and that she could still be alive. Jacques was busy muttering to himself about never being allowed back in. Maybe that was why neither of them heard the door open again and why Harlen didn't realize someone was behind him until he'd been slammed against the far wall and punched square in the face.

His ears rang, and he saw white, only returning to reality to see Jacques had picked up the person that turned out to be Donnie and had returned the punch with one of his own. The young man hit the far wall and stumbled.

"Are you okay?" Jacques grabbed him roughly by the shoulders and shook him.

"Yeah—yeah, I'm fine." The hit hadn't been too bad, and for the record, he had worse. Donnie didn't seem to have quite the same experience, though, because the one punch had sent him reeling.

"Good, let—" Jacques turned to push him out of the alleyway, but he was suddenly gone. Harlen turned and saw he'd hit the ground, and his leg was tangled in a knot of those weeds he had seen growing out of the sidewalk. Donnie was reaching out and squeezing his fist. Harlen realized he was making the weeds wind tighter around Jacques' ankle.

"You little shit!" Jacques spat blood from hitting his face on the stone pavement, and with a gesture, Harlen felt the air hum as Jacques shaped it into the sharp blade he'd felt once before.

Blood sprayed from Donnie's cheek. The plants fell limp, and Jacques scrambled to his feet, motioning for them both to run, but Donnie raised himself again and clapped his hands together. Jacques made it only a few steps before he was entangled in the vines growing up the wall of one of the buildings. They reached out as though alive and pulled them both in—a tangled, green net.

Harlen was only caught around the waist, but the vines were squeezing tight, and he watched in horror as blood began to seep out of his skin where the smaller roots tried to push their way in. He tried pulling at it and tried digging his fingers into the vine itself to rip it away but to no avail.

Jacques was far worse off. He was pressed flat against the wall with his arms splayed out at his sides, and Harlen could already see the blood bright on the side of his face where sharp roots cut into his cheek.

Panic. Harlen felt nothing but panic and anger as Donnie walked up to him with a smirk on his face, blood dribbling down from the cut on his lip where Jacques punched him. He spit the blood at him and said, "Apparently, she didn't tell you too much about me either. I was the one she told that she was scared, that she was laying low. She didn't tell you anything."

Donnie looked him over with his dark eyes, and his smirk widened. "I bet she didn't even tell you she came here. You wouldn't believe how much of a tease she was. I'll tell you, though, it was nice to see a rich girl begging for it."

Harlen threw himself against the vines. He grabbed Donnie by his collar and pushed, ignoring the pain of the roots ripping through his flesh as he shoved himself forward blindly and smashed Donnie into the opposing wall.

He heard Jacques shouting behind him, dully, as if it were coming from miles away. He couldn't listen, not even if he wanted to. All he could see was white at the edges of his vision, and all he could hear was the ringing in his ears.

"How dare you," he demanded. "What have you been doing since she's been gone? Have you looked for her, or have you been sulking? You've been free to do what you want. Did you even BOTHER to look? How DARE you talk about her like that—how *DARE* you?"

Donnie was shrinking back from him, and Harlen suddenly felt his body being consumed by a cold, prickling sensation that seemed to roll outward from his chest where the ball of anger was burning. Burning cold enough to feel as though it were frozen fire, burning the inside of his chest where it sat, covering bones with frost until they cracked and turned his blood to ice.

Donnie stared at him, mouth open, and Harlen thought he was beginning to black out. It seemed as if a black fog was rising in his vision, but then he realized that it wasn't behind his eyes. It was real. A thin, black mist rose from Donnie's open mouth and leaked from his eyes and into his own, blocking his vision and gagging him. He dropped Donnie, who crumpled to the ground like a stuffed doll.

The world went white. Harlen's head pounded. The ringing in his ears rose to a deafening pitch. He clawed at the sides of his face, desperate to escape the sound, then all at once, it was over.

Jacques had escaped the vines and was crouching in front of him, holding him up from where he must have fallen to the ground. His mouth was moving, but for a moment, Harlen couldn't hear him. Then, slowly, ever so slowly, his hearing began to return.

His head still pounded. His thoughts were swimming, and nothing made any sense. The only thing he was sure of was that he could feel blood pouring out of his nose and dripping hot off his chin as his eyes struggled to focus.

"Shit," Jacques was mouthing, grabbing the front of his shirt and wiping at his face with it. "Shit, that's a lot of blood."

"What was that?" was all Harlen could say. Hadn't Jacques seen the fog? "What was that?"

He repeated it over and over dully. Dazed.

He didn't feel as hysterical as he probably should; he felt strange and detached. His skin was prickling with the needle sharpness of blood creeping back into a sleeping limb, and his thoughts swung around in lazy circles. Other than the pain pulsing behind his eyes, he could hardly feel anything.

Harlen looked out of the corner of his eye at Donnie and saw he was still lying on the ground, a crumpled mess. Breathing, but gasping and writhing as if he were in pain.

Instantly, fear lanced through the haze, and Harlen started shouting his repeated question. He couldn't hear himself, but he was aware of the strain on his throat until Jacques slapped him across the face.

It seemed to snap him back into his body. Harlen blinked and saw that Jacques had gone white with panic. His eyes were so wide; his pupils seemed to be nothing more than pinpricks of ink on a green sea.

"We need to go," he said, hauling him to his feet and pushing him towards the street. "Buddy, you're bleeding bad; we need to go."

Did he not know? Did he not see? Or had he imagined what he just saw?

"What about him?" Harlen looked back at Donnie.

"Forget him. He'll sort himself out. Let's GO." Jacques grabbed him and began physically dragging him out of the alley because Harlen's legs were numb. He tried to stand on his own, but his entire body felt frozen. Like whatever cold had filled him was still clinging to his bones to keep them from moving.

Jacques kept both of them moving forward, the one thought running in screaming circles around Harlen's head, only picking up speed as they ran.

What was that?

What was that?

CHAPTER 28

Millie sat in the hallway that overlooked the house's grandest window, which looked down onto the street. Sitting with her legs curled to her chest and her dress pooled around her on the checkerboard floor, she watched and waited as thunder rumbled in the distance and white sea birds drifted over the rooftops. She was waiting for Harlen to come home.

She had spent the day hiding. Not in their bedroom—she couldn't stand staying trapped in the same hallway as Vostesk Senior. She'd found different places in the house to tuck herself into where he wouldn't see her. Deep in the library shelves, the pantry, behind one of the lounging couches in the sitting room, were a few such places. She only dared to sit in the open now because Vostesk Senior had once again gone out for the day, vanishing with two other polished, sharply dressed men into the approaching evening.

She had tried to get into the basement when he was gone. She'd even gone into his office to see if she could find a key once she was sure he and his smartly dressed friends weren't coming back.

She'd been cautious about leaving everything just as it was and had only dared touch the desk—she didn't want to get too ambitious—but there was nothing there. It was somewhere else in the office, or he'd taken it with him. She didn't want to think too much about the latter. That meant he was anticipating her curiosity and felt too much like he was reading her thoughts.

She knew it wouldn't make her situation better, but it wasn't as if she could leave. That was something she'd come to realize over the last few weeks, especially after the few talks she had with Pearl. She and Harlen had both tried to leave at different points. Both had been returned one way or another. If he wouldn't let his own family leave, there was no way he was going to let his chance at a magical heir go.

That wasn't just speculation on her part either. She didn't consider herself smart by any means, but she knew a few things.

She knew she had sent her letters home weeks ago and no reply had arrived. She had been surprised she didn't find any correspondence from her family hidden in his desk drawers, but she doubted he would keep them somewhere so obvious. He likely didn't keep them at all. He probably threw them into one of the many fireplaces. She wondered if her letters had even left the post office.

Knowing what was in the basement was not going to help her. But the not knowing was eating her alive. There were so many unknowns in this house—this town—this terrible, cold place. She needed to have an answer to something. Or she'd probably have a breakdown like Pearl.

She was determined to fight that if nothing else. Dammit, she would not let this place drown her. She was not going to be miserable or just lie down and let things happen. She was going to fight. And she was going to find out what happened in that damn basement.

She saw two figures approaching, and through the rain-blurred window, she first thought it was Vostesk Senior and his guest returning. But she wiped the fog from the glass with the back of her sleeve and saw Jacques' bright copper hair. It looked like he was dragging Harlen. Something was wrong.

Her footsteps echoed through the vast, empty house as she ran down the stairs and threw open the doors. She ran out into the rain and pried the gate open, demanding to know what had happened.

"Long story," Jacques said. He had what looked like grass and dirt stains all over his clothes. His face and lip were bleeding, and Harlen was white as a ghost and covered in blood. It dripped down his chin to the waist of his shirt.

She grabbed Harlen under his right arm while Jacques held the left, and he explained.

"We went looking at another place on the list. Long story short, we met an old boyfriend of Tansey's, and he wasn't too happy with us. Really knocked the shit out of us, to be honest, but I think your husband put him down for a bit."

"I'm fine," Harlen said, protesting as they got him through the front door and closed it behind them. "I'm fine—no—Jacques, we can't talk about this here."

"Shut up, we're helping," Jacques said and turned Harlen's face to the side. He grabbed his jaw hard, feeling for a broken bone.

"He could be watching us," Harlen insisted. "The other day—he knows things he shouldn't. I think he's watching us."

Millie was taken aback and felt her heart drop, but Jacques shook his head.

"That's not possible. Your family's deal is ice magic, right?"

"But what if it's something else?" Harlen continued. "It could be runic magic or some kind of object. "

"Harlen, he was probably trying to freak you out," Jacques said, shaking his head as he and Millie struggled to get him up the stairs. "Doubt it'd be the first time. Besides, if he knew what we were doing during class hours, don't you think he'd have put a stop to it?"

Millie looked at Harlen, who didn't seem to have a retort for that. She had no idea how most magic worked, but she knew Jacques did. She had more significant worries on her mind right now than something that was just a possibility.

They got him upstairs and into the bathroom of her and Harlen's bedroom. She sat him on the edge of the bathtub, and Jacques stood back, wiping his hands on his shirt.

"I need alcohol," Millie said.

"Shit, me too," Jacques said, but when she shot him a look, he turned and started rummaging through the cabinets. Millie pulled some clean towels from the linen basket. She had already wet one and used it to scrub Harlen's face until he took it himself.

"Harlen, take your shirt off," she instructed, looking at the blood staining his white shirt.

She frantically set out the towels and only noticed the silence that had fallen over the room when she looked up and saw Jacques had frozen with a glass bottle in one hand already outstretched towards her. He and Harlen were exchanging a worried, knowing look.

"What?" she asked, looking between them.

Jacques handed her the bottle and cleared his throat awkwardly. "I'll, um, I'll see myself out, alright?"

He gave Harlen one last apologetic look and slipped out. Millie felt dread eating away at the pit of her stomach when Harlen wouldn't look at her.

"Is. . .something wrong?" she asked.

Harlen sat on the edge of the tub, his hands on his knees, gripping them so hard his knuckles were white. He was silent, and she felt her dread mounting, and nearly jumped out of her skin when he spoke again, barely above a whisper. "Just don't. . .be scared."

Nothing good ever comes after a phrase like that. Millie thought, clutching the glass bottle of alcohol in both hands while he slowly set his jacket to the side and unbuttoned his shirt like it was physically painful. She thought he must be hurt worse than she'd been led to believe, but when she saw his chest, Millie realized what it was, and she had to bite her tongue to keep from gasping.

His chest, no, his entire body, as far as she could see once it was off his shoulders, was covered in a patchwork of scars. Some were long, even lines that left silver marks behind, and others were deep, twisted, and red, like gnarled tree bark that grew around the scars left behind by a woodsman's axe. There were burns as well, things that looked small enough to have been the size of a cigarette's tip and others that looked as though he'd been sloppily branded.

She felt lightheaded, and her hands were shaking. She knew she'd gone as white as Harlen. He looked at her, his big, sad, dark eyes pleading for her to say something, but she couldn't. Not without crying. It all looked so painful. Without even having to ask, she knew. This was what happened in the basement.

She needed to say something. He'd stopped looking at her, and his hands had gone back to grip his knees. But if she cried and made him feel like a monster, she'd never forgive herself. So she clamped her teeth down on her lip and knelt next to him with the cloth and alcohol.

She caught his eyes for only the briefest of moments, just long enough to see he too was holding back tears before he looked away again.

Silently biting her lip and blinking her eyes quickly, she examined the cuts on his side. His skin felt uneven and twisted, and she felt her stomach drop when she touched it—not for how it felt but thinking of how painful these must have been to receive.

The cuts, the new ones, at any rate, weren't deep enough to need to be stitched shut. Millie cleaned them, and he didn't so much as flinch. She bandaged them to the best of her ability, her fingers lingering on the bandages when she finished.

"Physical trauma," Harlen said suddenly.

She looked up at him, but he was still looking away and speaking in monotone with only the slightest of tremors to his voice.

"Physical trauma will, in some difficult cases, bring out dormant magic in a subject's blood. This is believed to be because it seems to have a desire to protect its host and or vessel. In the past, trauma varying from minor to the extreme has been shown to bring dormant magic to the surface. Notes by Lancon Vesh. Student of magic and the body."

Harlen dragged his eyes back to hers. She hadn't stopped staring up at his face as he spoke, and as soon as their eyes met the monotone he'd spoken in, and the blankness of expression that had come with it broke.

His voice cracked as he said, "I should have told you. I should have told you how bad this is." He picked his shirt back up, the one still covered in blood, and began pulling it on quickly and closed it tight over his chest. "You shouldn't have to see this."

"Harlen," she finally said but bit her lip again as she felt the tears welling in her eyes. She reached out to touch him, but he flinched, and she drew her hand away. "Please. Please, let me at least get you something clean to wear."

He'd closed his eyes, clutching the collar of his shirt, but nodded. She didn't want to leave him. She wanted to put her arms around him and somehow let him know that it was alright, but she knew it wasn't. Nothing about what had happened to him, and probably still happening, was alright. And she couldn't say anything to make it go away or stop.

She got to her feet and left the room. Only when the door clicked shut behind her did she allow a few tears to slip out, biting her sleeve so he wouldn't hear her crying.

CHAPTER 29

It was hours before he came out. It had to have been.

Time felt like a blur as he sat on the floor, his back against the wood of the door after Millie had handed him his new clothes, still untouched on the ground beside him. He was curled in on himself, still holding his shirt closed as if that could undo what had been done.

He'd watched the color drain from her face when she saw him. She hadn't cried out. Hadn't said anything. He'd stunned her speechless, and it made him sick.

It was probably the best he could have hoped for, but it made him want to claw his way out of this disgusting skin all the same. Still, somehow, that wasn't the worst. The worst was realizing as he sat there and she'd knelt next to him, was he had wanted so badly for her to know about this for so long.

He wanted her to know and understand. He couldn't ask her to ignore it; it wasn't something that could be ignored. It could only be understood, and then maybe it could exist as something he could be loved in spite of.

He wanted, so badly, to be loved. He loved her. And in turn, he wanted her to know him and to love him, but he couldn't ask for both.

He dressed again, finally, slowly, and considered sleeping on the bathroom floor. He couldn't get into bed with her. He couldn't press up close to her with her knowing what he looked like.

The only thing that made him emerge was the knowledge that she would sit up and worry all night if he didn't come out. So he eased the door open and was relieved to find she'd fallen asleep on the bed. On top of the covers. It would be easier that way to sleep at his desk.

"What are you doing?"

He froze as soon as he'd sat down, facing away from her, and couldn't bring himself to look back at her. "I won't make you share a bed with me."

He heard the bed creak and hoped she was laying back down, but instead, he listened to her footfalls on the floor, and her voice came from right beside him.

"Harlen, get up."

Her voice was quiet, pleading, but there was a strength in it that demanded his attention, and he did as she asked.

"Look at me."

He did. Slowly, painfully, he dragged his eyes over to her. Her hair messed from lying in bed, one cheek was rubbed pink from resting it on her arm. She was so breathtakingly beautiful that he felt he was trying to stare into the sun looking at her.

"You should go home," he said.

It broke his heart to say it out loud. He couldn't imagine being without her, but he loved her, and he could not make her stay. "It might be hard after so long to convince people that we haven't. . .finalized our marriage. But we haven't. And you could. You could go home where it's not so cold and damp, and you could marry someone kind and good, and you could be happy."

She was smiling at him. She hadn't said anything, but the tearful smile was all it took to silence him.

"How can I leave?" she asked. She wrapped her arms around herself and gave a laugh that was half a sob, and Harlen wanted to pull her to his chest and make her feel safe but, how could he? "We both know your father wouldn't let that happen. And how can I just leave when your mother is a mess, and we haven't found anything about Tansey—there are too many things. I can't just drop it and go home and act like everything is like it was before."

I'm so sorry. Harlen lowered his gaze.

"And how could I never see you again?"

He looked back up at her in disbelief. Tears were staining her cheeks.

He reached up to wipe them away without a thought. His hand touched the side of Millie's face before he could think better of it, but she didn't cringe out of his touch. He hesitantly brushed her tears with his thumbs, whispering every soothing thing he could think of whether it made any sense or not.

She allowed him to worry over her for only a moment before she reached for his face in turn. He thought she meant to push him away and began taking a step back, but she found the collar of his shirt and gripped it tight, tugging him down. Close enough to feel her breath.

Through her tears, her eyes were bright with something he couldn't name. He remained still as he could manage, afraid to break the strange tension of the moment. Even when she leaned closer and kissed him, first brushing her lips over his with aching tenderness, then again, more firmly, shaking her head.

"I won't do it," she said, her hand sliding from his collar into his hair. He trembled but didn't move a muscle though he felt like his body was burning beneath his skin. Her lips pressed his cheek, his mouth, his neck. He feared any sudden movement might scare her away until she whispered into his ear something familiar and sweet.

"Please."

He kissed her. He pulled her tight to his chest, hands gripping at her waist, and before he knew it, he was sitting on the bed, tasting the sweetness of tea on her lips and leaning into the warmth radiating from her.

She sat in his lap, holding his face and kissing him as though letting go meant she would die. He felt that if he let go of her for even a moment, he would never be able to breathe again.

"Take your shirt off," she said when she'd pulled back long enough to speak.

"Millie—"

"I don't care," she said, looking up into his eyes earnestly. She tightened her arms around his middle as she spoke. "I don't care. I want to see you."

Her eyes were pleading. He hesitated, but the damage was done, wasn't it? She had already seen. She already knew.

She placed both her hands on his chest, where she would be able to feel the raised scars through the fabric. Then she'd started kissing him again.

He wasn't sure when he started crying between her gentle touches and kisses, but when she broke away to ask if he was alright, all he could do was tell her to come back.

Her touch was warm, and he could taste both of their tears in his mouth when she placed hers back on his. When she pulled away again, she took his hands and put them on the back of her dress. Harlen felt the cold, silver buttons beneath his fingers.

"What are you doing?"

"We're here together. Whatever comes of it," Millie said.

He was stunned momentarily into silence. "Millie, are you sure? There's. . .there's no going back from this."

"I know. That's the idea," she said with a glint in her eyes.

"I just. . ." he swallowed. "I don't want you to feel trapped. With me."

She shook her head. "I'm trapped here. In this place, this house. But you are not something I'm trapped with. Even if I do go home, I would want you to come with me."

He looked down at her, his heart shaken to the core, his hands trembling. "Yes. Yes, I—I'd go with you anywhere," he whispered, touching her face with his hands, hardly able to believe she was real.

"Good." She said gently. He was again unable to move as she drew back just far enough to unfasten the front of her dress. He knew what she meant to do but was still confused by the action until she began to slip it off her shoulders, and he felt his face flame with heat as he averted his eyes out of habit.

She paused, still covered. "Harlen. I want this." She said, picking up his hand once again and squeezing. "Do you?"

"I do." He said it with a sincerity he hadn't been able to offer on their wedding day. He brushed back her hair, watching it slip back over her bare shoulder. He followed its path first with his eyes, then spurred on by her certainty, he leaned forward and placed a kiss there. Lightly, shyly, then when he heard her breath catch, he kissed it again.

He tasted her skin, felt the curve of the bone beneath it, thinking of all the times he had seen her shoulders gleaming in the firelight in one of her summer dresses. The way they slid upward when she laughed. He never imagined touching that skin, but now the desire nearly choked him as he pressed his mouth to it until he could feel her tremble.

He would have stayed there all night if she hadn't moved his hands back to the buttons. He managed to undo several and allowed her to unfasten the buttons on his own shirt. He wondered only briefly if the sight of him would destroy the energy crackling between them, but for all the world, it was like she didn't even notice. Her hands went right to his belt, and she stopped only to look up at him, voicing another quiet please with her eyes.

His surprise aside, his throat was so tight he was amazed he could speak. "I've never really. I want to, but I... I don't really know how."

"I know." She grinned and again pushed him back onto the bed. "I suppose we'll learn."

A kiss. Gentle, warm. Harlen closed his eyes as she dipped her head downward and felt himself unfolding as her lips touched his. Any nervousness he felt didn't last long in the strange calm that descended.

"I love you." She said, and he believed it.

"I love you too." He said, his face inches from hers. He didn't want to be any further ever again. "I do. I do."

Desire turned to need as he kissed her again, and when she found her way to him fully, it was utterly blissful. No part of him felt ugly or unloved.

She was beautiful, he was beautiful, and for a moment in time full of ragged breaths and hands gripping flesh, they were the only people in the world who had ever loved. Who had ever felt so alive and magical. He was hers, she was his, and they held each other through a night that was not cold or dark but glowing.

CHAPTER 30

In the morning, he woke. He felt warm and contented as a cat sitting in the sun. For once, the clouds had parted, and he could feel warm sunlight falling across his bare back from the window overhead.

He propped himself up on one arm, naked entirely with his lower body beneath the blankets where Millie was still snuggled. He didn't feel shame. For the first time in his life, when Millie opened her eyes and gave him a shy little smile, he felt loved. Loved entirely.

"Not feeling any morning regrets, are you?" she asked as he continued to stare down at her wordlessly, a smile tugging at his lips.

"Not at all," he said, his voice heavy and rumbly from sleep. He couldn't help leaning down and placing a kiss on her forehead, her lips, her cheek. "Never."

She giggled as he nuzzled into her neck, breathing the smell of her, wrapping his arms around her, grinning ear to ear. His love. His darling. His wife.

"You don't have class today, do you?" she asked as he settled in with her pulled close to him. She was running a finger up his arm, tracing the line of one of the long, jagged scars in a way that made it feel beautiful.

"No," he said. Even if he did, he was sure he wouldn't have been able to pry himself away. The bed had never felt so warm. He'd never felt more content. "I'm yours."

She let out a chuckle and shifted in his arms, so she was facing him. She reached one hand up and brushed the hair out of his face, letting her fingers trace down his cheek and bringing a fresh shiver to his skin. "And I'm yours."

It was less urgent but no less wonderful as she took him in her arms again. After, he laid beside her until the clock at the end of the hallway struck nine and would have remained right where he was all day had she not coaxed him out of bed with the promise of a bath together.

Harlen spent a good deal of time washing her hair and peppering her face with kisses. He fussed and doted on her in a way she seemed to find comical, but the way she treated him, in turn, was no different. If anything, she fussed more. As if she could undo any pain he had ever felt with her touch.

It was impossible, though not from lack of effort. And it meant the world to him anyway that she tried.

When he stood to dry off and caught a bit of his reflection in the steamed mirror, he didn't see any ugliness at all. He only saw Millie looking at him from the tub and turned around to chuckle at her, feeling just the slightest bit bashful.

"What?"

"Don't mind me," she said, waving a hand. That impish little grin he loved so much on her face. "I'm just admiring."

He laughed. Really laughed. He laid a towel beside the tub for her and wrapped his loosely around his waist as he returned to their room to fetch clothes for both of them. He scrubbed at his hair and picked up his glasses from the bedside table, slipping them on so he couldn't stumble over anything while getting their things together.

As soon as they were on his face, he glanced around the bedroom and saw the teacup with the sad, wilted lavender branch she had managed to keep alive. Only, they didn't look sad or wilted. They seemed brighter. Fuller. In fact, it looked as if they'd bloomed all over again and somehow flourished in the little cup to the point that they were almost spilling over.

How odd.

"Harlen?"

He looked back towards the bathroom and smiled. "On my way."

There would be time to think about such things later. But for now, the house was quiet, the rain outside had stopped, and all was right with the world.

CHAPTER 31

"Alright! Right up this way, watch your step."

Jacques shouted back at them as he walked ahead of Millie and Harlen, up to the highest point in town. It was the furthest from the sea and the air held only the faintest trace of the smell of saltwater, but the wind was even harsher than on the shore. It turned Jacques' neatly messy hair into an angry bird's nest of coppery curls.

They had been out all afternoon, all three of them in the only green place in town. A park with a gate in the middle divided it from the cemetery. The town's only tree sat hunched and wind-bent astride the iron bars, twisting its trunk around them and growing up right in the middle.

"There it is. The old hanging tree," Jacques said as they stood in the grass beside the fence.

"They hang people here?" Millie asked. She didn't see any bodies or leftover ropes. Morbid curiosity had her searching the branches for either.

"What? Oh, no, not really," Jacques replied while pulling a set of keys out of his pocket.

His family owned the cemetery so they would be spared having to climb the fence. Jacques had insisted on searching the cemetery when Harlen had mentioned the park was on Tansey's list, because according to Jacques no teenager in their right mind would rather spend an evening strolling around a park than drinking in the cemetery. He had to chase too many teenagers off in his time for it to be otherwise.

Millie wasn't entirely sure what they were expecting to find. But they were working their way down the list, and it didn't feel right to skip anything.

He put the keys in the lock and said, "Nobody's ever actually hung from it aside from my own great-great-uncle. My family always called it that and the name just stuck."

"Oh. I'm sorry," Millie said.

Jacques shrugged as he pushed the gate open. "Ah, it wasn't exactly a great tragedy. He was a shit who hit his wife so one day she hoisted his ass right up there."

Millie considered making some kind of joke about Vostesk Senior but decided against it. Harlen stood right next to her, looking up at the branches, and she wondered if he was thinking along those lines.

She looked him over while he stared upward. He stared at the branches overhead, his hair blowing in the wind, like he was trying to memorize each leaf. He only stopped when he caught her staring, then his face broke out in a smile. He didn't avert his gaze. He looked at her, unflinching, his eyes dark and bright and it made her heart beat faster.

She hadn't been sure if the affection she felt for him could really be love for quite a while. But that night, now almost a month ago, the idea of being separated from him had made her sure of it. She'd meant it when she told him so and found the idea rushing to her at the strangest moments. As she looked at him with his wind-blown hair and the open affection of that smile it came jumping back to her thoughts.

I love you.

Jacques continued speaking about his uncle as Millie drifted back to the conversation.

"Some people down in the park saw and told the town's guard but story goes that the family got him down and hid him long before they got here. I'd guess he's still buried out here somewhere."

"Unmarked, I'm guessing," Harlen said as they stepped through the garden of headstones.

All of them were shades of gray and white. Some of their engravings stood out clearly, others were worn away into nothing by the near-constant rain. Millie stared at the odd chunks of carved stone and wondered how long it took for them to be erased completely. Why would anyone want to be buried like this?

Jacques raised an eyebrow. "Honestly, wouldn't surprise me if they did end up marking it so they could piss on it later. The guy was a real nasty bit of work. Not that I ever met him, of course. But just about everyone who did has a bad story or two to tell."

Harlen raised one arm and pointed off across the hill. Millie squinted in the same direction where more stone shapes were rising out of the ground. They were bigger than the ones on this side of the grounds, but she couldn't make out what they were.

"Oh, that's your section," Jacques said with a dismissive little wave. "That's where all the fancy people go. Stone angels lamenting their death, big epitaphs written by the families—very glamorous place to decompose."

Millie grimaced. "This is ghoulish."

"Not really. I find comfort in the fact that we're all the same soup in a coffin one day," Jacques said with a sigh, lighting one of what seemed to be a constant line of cigarettes. "Of course, that could be a side effect of growing up in the family profession. I'm sure it's different for other people."

"I meant the part about the coffins and headstones. Not the decomposing bit," she said as they began their walk over to the other side of the cemetery. "Back home, when you die, they just wrap your body up and bury it with a tree sapling. That way something living gets to come out of it. People say that way they aren't really gone. As long as the tree's alive, that person is still there watching over the people they loved."

"That's beautiful," Harlen said.

Jacques snorted. "What if you want to complain about Aunt Vern's griping and her ghost happens to be hovering nearby because her tree's out back? Can she just smash all your glassware or something?"

"Well, that's why you're not supposed to speak ill of the dead, right?" Harlen asked with humor in his eyes.

Jacques took the cigarette out of his mouth to point at Harlen so the glowing tip could punctuate his point. "I reserve my right to complain about anyone—dead or not."

As they walked over the uneven ground, Millie began to feel a bit nervous and squeezed Harlen's hand. She had held Harlen's arm as they walked on the street, but when they'd veered into the park, she'd let it slip down to his hand instead. It was a gesture that was far less formal, and it was a habit she'd formed with him over the last month. Ever since she had made up her mind to stay.

At first, he'd treated public affections with the chaste blushing of a schoolboy stealing a kiss between classes. But he quickly warmed up to showing little gestures like brushing her hair away from her face, kissing her cheek, and even circling an arm around her waist in relative public. Every time he'd beam, and she felt like he was genuinely glad people saw them together. She felt like the wall he had constructed around himself had come down and he had climbed out to her with open arms.

That really was the thing: thin as he was and as much as he had a tendency to stutter his words, there was an odd, undeniable safety in his arms she'd come to take comfort in, especially at night when they were alone. He would hold her tight against his chest and every worry in the world would be consumed by the smell of him fresh out of the bath and by the kisses he'd place on top of her head.

In fact, the last weeks had passed in an odd state of calm that Millie hadn't experienced since she'd arrived in Wakefield. The air in the house itself felt lighter. Vostesk Senior seemed to have lost interest in screaming at his wife and son. He wasn't kind to them by any stretch, but he hadn't been glaring at Pearl across the dinner table. And it seemed he'd stopped calling Harlen to the basement. Millie had even seen the man very nearly smile at her several times when she was in a room with him.

Had she not known what a snake he was, she might have found it pleasant rather than eerie. As it was, she couldn't shake the feeling that something wasn't right about his sudden shift in demeanor. She still kept that chair jammed against the door every night.

Harlen sensed it as well. The calm seemed to place him on edge, and he had taken as many measures as his slight freedom allowed to make sure that she was rarely alone with Vostesk Senior. Whether that meant making some excuse for her to be out while he was at his academy or making sure he was always with her when Vostesk Senior was home in the evenings.

It was a comfort, but she always found herself the most relaxed when they were out of the house together. Both safely out of harm's way. Even considering the circumstance of their outings.

"Everything alright?" Harlen asked, looking down at her.

She was being silly. She was very aware that she was being silly, but the gravestones made her feel uneasy. So, she made herself smile like she was making a joke and said, "It feels just a bit haunted, that's all. I'm wondering about Aunt Vern."

Harlen smiled back and let go of her hand to instead put his arm around her waist. She was glad he didn't make a big show of it or comment on her being afraid. Especially around Jacques, who would no doubt start making good-natured jokes about it that would still sting her pride just a bit.

She pressed up close against Harlen's side where she could feel the curve of his ribcage through his jacket, glad to feel something warm and full of life when they reached the first great gravestone that looked more like a monument of some kind. There was a great stone angel draped across it, its face worn away completely by time and rain to a blur of gray marble.

"I would have thought there'd be more people here," she said to break the silence and the whistling of the wind coming through the branches of the hanging tree far behind them, weaving around the statues. She made a great effort to take her eyes off the faceless angel that sent a chill down her spine.

She really did think there would have been more. At home, there were always people in the cemetery groves. People took food there to eat under the trees. Children climbed the branches and spent time with old family. This place was empty. There was nobody but the three of them and the statues.

"There's usually not many visitors. Especially in this section," Jacques said, gesturing to the stone monuments where statues were either standing beside them, sitting, or leaning on graves with stone tears frozen on their faces.

Jacques let out a long, smoke-filled sigh that was carried off by the wind and placed a hand on his hip, looking around and clicking his tongue. "It's a shame really. These take forever to put together. There's a stone masonry not far from here, but this marble is special order and takes months to get here. Even longer to wait for the carving to get done. There's usually a big show for the funeral itself but after that…" he shook his head and tapped the ashes off his cigarette with his finger rather than tapping it on one of the stones. "My little sister used to come out here and put flowers on them. She said they looked sad."

Millie was inclined to agree with her. Though, she couldn't imagine coming out here alone around all the statues.

She herself was trying very hard not to look too closely at the stone faces, knowing they would likely make an appearance in her dreams that night anyway. That was how she spotted what looked like a burned circle of blackened grass between the headstones not too far from them.

"What's that?" She pointed it out.

Jacques craned his neck to see where she was pointing and cursed under his breath. "Remember what I said about teenagers?"

"Could they really start such a big fire with nobody noticing?" Harlen asked.

Millie's curiosity had been piqued enough that she wandered out of her husband's grip and he let her go so she could investigate. He followed not too far behind, with Jacques reluctantly bringing up the rear.

"You would be surprised," Jacques grumbled. "I wouldn't get too close- there's probably broken glass. I find so many smashed bottles out here you wouldn't believe it."

Millie carefully squeezed between the graves blocking the way to the charred dirt and ashes. It was almost a perfect circle. A bonfire in a graveyard admittedly did sound like something her and her sisters would get up to, but she couldn't imagine they would ever make something so neat. She also didn't see any glittering bits of broken glass, though she did watch out for them carefully. All she saw was the single log that remained in the center of the fire, surrounded by ashes.

It looked like it had to have been a pretty big pyre and the log was the only survivor. It was blackened and still smoking faintly but mostly it looked intact. She gave it a closer look, mildly interested until something struck her.

"Kids really drag wood all the way up here?" she asked.

They had just passed the hanging tree and it seemed fully intact. It would have had to come from somewhere else. All the wood she had seen used in the fireplaces back at the manor was delivered from further inland in big bundles. Hauling stacks of wood uphill seemed like a lot of effort for a little get-together where they could be chased off by the owners at any minute.

"Again. You would be surprised," Jacques said. He seemed annoyed, kicking at the edge of the ring with one boot. "What a mess. Hey—"

Jacques called over to her as she stepped over the blackened grass into the circle of ashes. She thought she had seen something on the log.

She shouted back that she would step out in just one minute and brushed at the log with her fingertips. Her hands came back covered in ash, but she had dusted enough of the soot away to see the rest of the strange pattern she had noticed. There was something carved into the wood.

"Is that a butterfly?" she asked, stepping back to give Harlen and Jacques a look.

"I think it's a swallowtail," Harlen commented.

Only he would be able to tell the species by a crude carving. She looked back at him and he explained sheepishly, "Tansey used to like them. You can see the dips at the ends of the wings."

"Well, that's quite a coincidence," she said. And it could be. But it struck her as something worth mentioning. Unless carving things into firewood was a common occurrence here along with the unsettling graves.

Millie looked at Jacques to confirm if this were as strange as she thought it was, but the words died in her mouth when she saw he'd gone white. His jaw was set tight and he was staring intensely, seemingly unaware of her and Harlen's presence anymore.

"What is it?" she asked, and it jarred him. He blinked and shook his head.

"It's, ah—It's nothing, it's stupid. A bunch of kids being funny." He shoved both hands in his pockets and seemed reluctant to continue. His eyes kept trailing back to the butterfly carved into the wood. Whatever kind of joke it was, it seemed to have spooked him.

"It's this old superstition. Most people who know it think it's nonsense, but people in my line of work put a lot of stock in it." He rolled his shoulders like he was shaking off a chill as he answered reluctantly.

"Are you one of those people?" Millie asked.

Jacques snorted. She didn't believe him for a moment when he said, "Me? Of course not."

Harlen raised an eyebrow at him that Jacques chose to ignore, and continued, "It's about the goddess of death. Butterflies are sort of her thing. Caterpillars turn into butterflies, death and rebirth, it's all very poetic, trust me. Putting her symbol on something is supposed to get her attention. Sort of like ringing a bell." Jacques rolled his shoulders again, trying to hide the shudder that passed over him. "Eyes I'd rather not have on me."

Millie decided to forego teasing on this one occasion. She had never seen him look quite so unsettled. "Should we get rid of it? Break it or something?"

"No!" Jacques exclaimed so sharply it made her jump. He apologized, running a hand back over his face and through his coppery hair. "Sorry. It's bad luck. Very bad luck. Just please- please get away from it. You're making me nervous."

Millie stepped back from the charred log, the butterfly standing out pale gray where she wiped away the soot. Once she had gotten out of the circle of ash, Jacques stepped forward and picked it up gingerly, the way one might pick up a live spider.

"You have to bury it. It's the only way to close the line so to speak."

"Should we find you a shovel?" Harlen asked, but Jacques shook his head.

"Nah. Dirt around here is mostly mud and it doesn't have to be deep. Just give me a few minutes, alright? There's a bench not too far up that way for you two if you want to go do your disgusting couple thing for a bit while I take care of this."

Jacques pointed them in the direction they were to go, and Millie watched with concern while he walked off, holding the wood like it would explode in his hands. Once he was gone, she looked up at Harlen and was relieved to see him wearing the same perplexed expression.

"He didn't strike me as the religious type. Did he ever mention that to you?" Millie asked, and Harlen shook his head.

"Not that I know of. It could be something he was brought up with—part of his trade maybe. I've read a little bit about a death goddess before, mostly in the abstract, of course. I honestly thought it was more of a metaphor. People describing death as a beautiful woman with a still, stony face and cold skin just seemed like a poet's thing. I wasn't aware there was a religion to go with it. It must be very old."

He produced a small square of linen from his pocket and helped her wipe the soot off her hands, but they agreed not to wander down to the bench. Something just didn't seem right about walking off to relax after the strong reaction Jacques just had. Neither of them said it out loud, but it had placed them both on edge.

They stood, or rather Harlen leaned against one of the high sculptures with his arms folded while Millie stood, careful not to touch it. They listened to the wind whistle through the hanging tree far in the distance and the faint scraping sound that Millie assumed had to be Jacques trying to dig in the dirt with his bare hands. It was eerie.

"It's odd that I never heard of the connection," Harlen said after a moment, mercifully breaking the silence. "I did some research on butterflies for Tansey back when we were teenagers. The garden outside—she wanted to make a butterfly garden. She actually managed to get a hold of some caterpillars somehow, no idea where she got those from. But she had me help her look into caring for them and what sort of plants they liked and, well. . ."

"I assume you got carried away and ended up reading half the library. And that you can now tell me anything that has ever been written about them," she said, a grin creeping up her face. Harlen laughed and a dusting of pink rose to his cheeks. It was a good laugh, though. Not like the nervous ones he had done at the beginning that hardly masked how fearful he was. This was relaxed. Happy.

"Possibly," he confessed. "And you've seen how extensive the library is. It's odd that I never heard of the connection. How does anyone overlook an entire religion?"

"Do you think Tansey knew?"

"I can't imagine she would. She wasn't really into research as I. . ." He trailed off and frowned. "No. She could have. If she heard about it in town. But she never mentioned it. And a goddess of death sounds like something she would have loved. The idea is terribly exciting and frightening."

Harlen looked thoughtfully at the gravestones spreading out around them. Millie could see him turning something over and over in his head like he was examining a broken bit of pottery and wanted to ask what was weighing on him, but then Jacques came hurrying back. His shirt and arms were covered in smears of dirt, but the color had returned to his face.

"Well, that was a bit more excitement than I bargained for when I offered a tour," he said brightly. "But if it's all the same I would rather we head out. I could honestly use a drink after that."

Harlen agreed but was still mostly lost in thought as they departed. They went to the same bar Jacques had been dragging them to regularly and sat together huddled in a corner table. Harlen remained quiet throughout the meal, sipping at his drink only occasionally, absently twirling his fork over and over between his fingers.

Millie had a sneaking suspicion why. She certainly had a few thoughts preoccupying her as well, but hers were mostly focused on Jacques's bizarre behavior. He was so forcefully conversational that he hardly touched his food. Hell, he hardly seemed to breathe as he kept the conversation from stalling for even a moment for her to fit in any questions.

When she eventually cut him off mid-sentence to try and get some answers, he made an excuse to leave and bolted for the door. She considered making a grab for his arm to stop him but instead simply called after him, "We'll see you soon."

It was both a question and a goodbye that he didn't acknowledge. He simply turned up his collar as he stepped into the rain outside, looked furtively up and down the street, then hurried in the direction of the markets.

By the time they finally returned home the sun was beginning to fall beneath the horizon. Long beams of the watercolor sunset were stretched across the floor of the foyer from the thin windows and once the door banged shut the only noise was the ticking clock upstairs.

As they climbed the grand staircase, Millie stared at the giant portrait that watched them silently. Vostesk Senior's cold stare hadn't been softened by the artist, but it was Tansey that she focused on.

The small girl demanded as much space and attention in the image as her father while Harlen and his mother shrank to the background. There was just something about the smile, really more of a smirk, on her face. That knowing smile. Millie couldn't shake the impression that she knew more about whatever was going on in this house than any of them. Even if she was no longer in it.

Harlen seemed to be in the same mindset. As they passed Tansey's room, he gave it a lingering stare.

"Did you want to go in?" Millie asked.

The house was quiet. His mother was probably sleeping and there was no usual sound of his father pacing around in his study. They had time.

Harlen started to shake his head. "I won't make you wait through that. It's probably going to take me ages. I do tend to get a bit. . .lost in things like this."

"So we'll go in together," she said, giving their joined hands a swing.

He smiled at her warmly and thanked her by bending his tall frame over to give her a kiss on the cheek. No words were exchanged; she didn't need them to know that even the offer meant the world to him. He was easy to please in the way that only those that have been truly deprived can be, and it worried her sometimes.

Harlen pushed the door open slowly. She allowed him to take the first few steps inside on his own before following. She wasn't sure how long it had been since he'd last set foot in his sister's room but gathered from the haunted look in his eyes it had been a very, very long time.

He put one hand on the bookshelves covered in layers of dust where her books and collections of trinkets hadn't been moved in years. He looked over at the messy bed and the desk with its ink bottles lined up so neatly. He looked distant, lost in memory. She watched his throat bob as he swallowed and glanced back over his shoulder at her quickly. He seemed relieved to see her standing there.

"Ah, I just want to see if I can find the jar she used to keep the caterpillars in. I have no idea how that worked out, but she did tend to keep, well, everything." He gestured to the shelves with a reminiscent grin.

"I'll help. If that's alright." She walked deeper into the room hesitantly. She didn't want to intrude but his hand reached out to her almost unconsciously it seemed. She grazed his fingers with hers and he smiled, his eyes a little less haunted.

"Yes, that's fine. She named them, so if you find a jar with two names printed on it, that's likely it. I'm not sure how much would be left of them, but I would like to see it," he said, then frowned. "That's not too strange is it?"

She shook her head. "No, not at all."

He seemed reassured and they went their separate directions to search. Millie knew it wasn't possible with how full the room was, but she could have sworn their footsteps echoed. Every sound that came from moving each dust-covered object was magnified by the absence of the one they belonged to. It was made her skin crawl even more than when she had been here hiding from Vostesk Senior. The light of day shining bright through the window and bringing everything into view made the space feel so much emptier.

"I remember once," Millie spoke to try and chase off some of the awful quiet. She wasn't sure if it were appropriate given the circumstances, but she couldn't stand the sound of them quietly shuffling around the abandoned bedroom. "Roslyn lost this locket of hers when we were playing down by the river. See, I made her think it would be a good idea to try to climb up this tree that hung over it because I wanted to see if we could jump over to the other side from up there."

"Did you talk her into that?" he asked. She glanced over her shoulder at him and was relieved to see him smiling faintly. Apparently, the levity was appreciated.

Millie moved aside a lace curtain hanging over part of one of the bookshelves and admired the large collection of white and gray painted bottles behind it. "As a matter of fact, no. Beatrice did. Although, I might have helped with the convincing."

Harlen gave one of his breathy laughs while he pushed open the door of the wardrobe very carefully. She saw him put one hand on the shoulder of one of the dresses and pause, then quickly pull back and close the door. He asked her very quietly with a slight tremble in his voice to continue. Millie turned back away from him to give him the courtesy of privacy and occupied herself with Tansey's desk.

"So, she climbed all the way out on this branch—the longest one there—and somehow her locket came off. It was something she'd gotten for her birthday from all of us, so the poor thing was crying and carrying on and we had to get her back like how you get a cat out of a tree. I had to climb out there myself to get her back and Beatrice being the oldest had to be the hero who dove into the river to get the necklace back."

Millie grinned to herself as she remembered. She had hardly gotten Roslyn down without the both of them falling into the river, and Beatrice had come out of the water with her dark hair matted to her head, her clothes a dripping mess, and the most triumphant smile Millie had ever seen with the locket dangling from her fingers. The way Roslyn hugged her, Millie would have thought she had brought back a lost child.

Millie wondered what she would do if either of them one day disappeared without a trace. The very idea sent a cold shiver down her spine.

All at once she wished she had heard back from any of them. Maybe one of these days she would take a real look around Vostesk Senior's office to see if he was hiding their replies to her letters somewhere.

Then, something on the desk caught her eye and brought her out of her thoughts. A small, darkly colored note wedged beneath an ink bottle made of thick cardstock that was strangely familiar. "Harlen?"

Harlen walked over behind her, reaching past her to pick it up, the dust that covered it smearing beneath his fingers.

"Evaluation," Harlen turned it over, frowning.

He had the same card. Millie had seen it on his desk. He had put it there when he returned from that first day at his academy and it remained there still. She had been using it as a coaster to put her tea on for weeks.

"Why would she have one of these?" Millie asked, and Harlen had to shake his head.

"I have no idea."

Hadn't the chairman said at dinner once that she had practically begged to be evaluated and he had had to refuse her? Had he given in after all to humor her or perhaps her father?

"Maybe Jacques would know?" she offered.

"Maybe," Harlen said skeptically. "But Jacques has only been teaching there for a year. This would have had to have been several years ago."

Harlen's eyes were narrowed and a thin line appeared between his furrowed brows. Millie watched as he tucked the card into his jacket pocket, and the temperature in the room seemed to drop, sending chills up her spine. They didn't need to be in this room anymore.

"We should go."

He'd spoken in a whisper and Millie was glad of it. They weren't forbidden from coming in here as far as she knew, but she felt very strongly as though they'd seen something they weren't supposed to. Millie only felt like she could breathe properly again once they had the bedroom door securely closed behind them.

This time, as they entered their own room, it was Harlen who dragged the chair in front of the door.

CHAPTER 32

"What are these?" Harlen asked.

He had come into the room to show his sister about a new book he was reading on alchemy. Tansey hadn't been inside when he ducked through her door, but he had seen movement in a jar on her desk, and curiosity drew him forward to look at the worm-like creatures inside.

He knew what they were, or at the very least, had an idea. He had only ever seen drawings of them in books. The question wasn't from ignorance as much as it was him trying to express his excitement at seeing something from the page brought to life.

He asked again as she hovered in the doorway, evidently surprised to see him. Her dark green dress and blonde hair were a bright splotch of color in the corner of his vision.

"Caterpillars," she said after a momentary pause. Harlen turned to see a grin spreading over her face as she walked into the room, her black heels clicking on the floor. "Aren't they cute?"

They were wonderful. There were two of them: fat, bright, green things with little yellow spots and short stumpy legs crawling over a twig. They were working away at three big green leaves that certainly didn't come from anywhere nearby.

"Where did you get them?" he asked excitedly.

"In the garden," she said, generously referring to the sad patch of waterlogged flowers she'd been trying to grow under the constant onslaught of cold rain. "Remember? I kept telling you I'd get some butterflies yet."

Harlen blinked at her, his dark eyes very bug-like themselves behind his thick, round glasses as he saw them reflected in the glass on the jar. Glasses he was still getting used to since his father had only recently decided he could wear them.

Harlen supposed he'd grown tired of watching him hit his head on things and knock things over as his rapidly changing height and poor vision combined to make him a walking danger to any valuable, delicate object and to himself. But he didn't need them to see she wasn't telling the truth.

"I've never seen any butterflies here. How did they lay eggs? Moreover, with how cold it is outside, I can't imagine any that did manage to hatch growing this large—"

"Harlen—" Tansey cut him off mid-sentence. Her voice was unusually sharp. "You're over-thinking things again; you know that?"

"It's just. . ." he fidgeted with the book he was holding, pulling a loose thread coming from the binding, twisting it over and over his finger. "You wanted me to research them, and according to what I've read about them, it doesn't seem likely, that's all."

Tansey reached forward and took the book out of his hands. She tossed it on her bed and smiled at him, giving him that look that only she could give. One she'd developed only recently.

Ever since she'd decided to start testing the limits of what they were allowed to do and he hadn't been brave enough to join her, something had changed in the way she smiled at him. He didn't know what to call it exactly. But every time she made that face, he got the distinct impression that she was talking down to him.

"You need to relax," she said. Just like the smile, there was an edge to how she spoke. She had said the same thing to him a thousand times before, and it never bothered him because it was always just a joke. But there was something at that moment about how she said it that time that made him feel stupid.

"You're probably right," he mumbled, reaching up to adjust his glasses just to have a reason not to look at that smile and for a place to put his hands with the book gone.

He didn't see her reaction but heard her sigh. She picked up the jar and placed it in his hands, and for a moment, when she grinned at him, she was herself again. Her blue eyes were bright and excited, and she raised her eyebrows at him conspiratorially.

"I'm going to raise them in here," she said confidently. "They'll have more eggs, and I'll make an entire room full of them. I'll even let you have one if you want it. I feel like you'd like watching them make their cocoons."

Harlen offered her a twitch of a smile that he hoped looked unaffected as he looked at the little creatures inside again. He knew he should keep his mouth shut. He probably just needed to relax, like she said. But the longer he looked, the more it nagged at him, so he tried to phrase it as casually as possible when he asked, "Where did you get the leaves? I didn't think we had plants like that around."

The grin vanished, and she lowered the jar. Harlen quickly said, struggling with his words, "It-it's just. . . I—I don't think I've ever seen plants with leaves like that here. It— It looks like it's from a tree, and we don't. . .we don't have those."

"Can't you ever just enjoy anything?" she snapped, putting the jar down on the desk with a thump. Harlen winced as one of the caterpillars fell off its branch and hit the bottom of the jar, its little legs waving in panic. "Can't you ever just do anything without worrying? I swear you're just like mom."

Harlen had slumped back and hunched his shoulders. He couldn't stop looking at the caterpillar out of the corner of his eye as it thrashed around on the glass bottom of the jar. He answered in a voice so small he wasn't even sure she could hear. "I'm sorry."

"You always question everything."

"You're right," he mumbled, looking at the floor, hating that he asked. Hating that he made her mad. Hating that he thought so much and didn't just know when to shut up. "You're right; I'm sorry."

Tansey sighed, and though he could feel all the anger coming out of her, he still stared at the floor. When she put a hand on his shoulder, he flinched.

"No. I'm sorry. I shouldn't have said that. Look, just—" Tansey looked around the room and gestured to his book on the bed. "Come on. Let's go to the library, and you can tell me all about whatever it was you were going to tell me. Alright?"

She smiled and moved her head, trying to get him to meet her eyes. He did, briefly, and forced a quick smile and a nod.

It seemed to satisfy her. She gave him another pat on the shoulder before turning and heading out of the room, leaving him to collect himself and retrieve his book. He listened as her footsteps faded down the hall, then turned back to the jar.

Very quietly, he unscrewed the lid and reached down into it. When he carefully touched the one still struggling at the bottom with his finger, it flinched. Harlen watched in fascination as two stalks of bright yellow shot out of the top of its head in irritation. Then its legs gave his index finger a few experimental taps.

It seemed to decide it was safe and, slowly, it crawled up onto his finger. Harlen felt a smile tug at the corners of his lips.

"There you go," he urged quietly and placed his hand up against the twig in the jar. It took ages, but the caterpillar crept from his hand back to the branch to join its friend.

Something is wrong.

It was the middle of the night, and something had brought him up out of the dream with a jolt. Millie was sitting up beside him as well, wide-eyed. The room was dark. The rain was pounding. The clock at the end of the hallway clanged the hour, and his heart pounded in his throat. *Something is wrong.*

Then there it was. The sound that had woken him. His father's fist pounding on the door and the metallic scrape of him shoving the chair back.

"Go to the bathroom," Harlen grabbed Millie's shoulders and started pushing her back off the bed. Go. There was no time. "Lock the door."

He didn't know what was happening, but there was an alarm screaming DANGER over and over in his head.

"Harlen—" Millie said in a half-awake panic as they ran towards the bathroom. "What's happening?"

"Something bad."

Before they could reach it, the chair crashed to the side behind them, and his bedroom door flew open. His father was standing there, his pale eyes glinting cold and livid. They locked on his and turned Harlen's blood to ice.

It was a look that had been enough to bring him, even as a scared child, walking slowly towards him with his head down to accept the inevitability of what was to come. But Millie was looking at him, white and wide-eyed and afraid.

I won't let anything hurt you.

He stood his ground between them as his father approached. His heart was pounding, his legs felt like they were made of rainwater, but he wouldn't move. Even when his father came closer, towering over him, glaring down at him.

"Where were you this afternoon?" he snapped.

"Lessons," he said, and Millie let out a cry when he felt the slap connect with his face. He saw bright bursts of light behind his eyes, and it snapped his head to the side. He stumbled but wouldn't move. He wouldn't.

Millie made like she was going to intervene, but he pressed a warning hand against her as he steadied himself.

"Don't lie to me, boy." His father spoke with disdain, curling up his lip. "I know exactly where you were."

He had a dangerous glint in his eyes, and when he went to step forward, Harlen put an arm across Millie and took a step back. But he wasn't coming for them. He went over to the bed, and he and Millie exchanged confused, fearful looks while he snatched up Tansey's evaluation card from the desk.

Millie whispered something behind him, but he hardly heard it. He could barely even hear the sounds of the various ink bottles his father sent tumbling to the floor. His mind was spinning. *How was this happening? How did he know?*

He was reeling, but there was no time. No time to process, no time to understand. His father was standing back up to his full height with the card in one hand.

He turned it over and glared at it as if it had offended him in some way before tucking it in his pocket. He turned back towards them and kicked a bottle out of his way that leaked ink like blood.

"We'll discuss this later." He said. "As well as your recent behavior."

Then, without another word, he began to stride towards the door. His business was done. But Harlen's wasn't.

"What happened to Tansey?" Harlen spoke without even realizing it. His father stopped and turned back towards him slowly like he couldn't quite believe he dared to speak to him, let alone pose a question. Harlen again felt practically dizzy with the fear that look struck deep into him, but this was too much. He couldn't shrink back from this. When he spoke again, his voice trembled, but it was loud and demanding.

"I know you know something. There's a reason you never looked for her." Harlen took a step towards him. "Or were you just glad she was gone because you couldn't even keep your own daughter in check?"

Vostesk Senior blanched but drew up tall. "You have no idea what I've done."

What happened next—there was no thought behind it. Harlen saw his father raise his cane. He heard Millie scream. He raised his arms to knock back the blow, but none came. All that came was utter silence and a strange creaking noise.

Harlen opened his eyes and, for a moment, didn't comprehend what he was seeing. His father seemed to have frozen in place, his raised arm straining against what looked like white string wrapped around it. Not string—roots. Roots that were connected to the lavender plant now flourishing in the corner, dominating the far wall. It was rolling and writhing as though it were alive and angry. Like it was *breathing* in time to the pounding of his own heart.

He was so shocked that it must have broken whatever spell was keeping it in place. The roots went limp, and his father took a step away. Harlen had never seen him look like he did then.

There was fear on his face. But there was a blazing triumph in his eyes.

"Fascinating," he said.

His father brought his arm down, but not with the cane. It was a quick flick of his fingers, and Harlen felt a sharp sting in his shoulder as a shard of ice grazed it. He stumbled back just long enough for his father to get out of the room and slam the door. The metallic scrape that followed indicated he locked it.

"I'm fine," Harlen said as Millie ran up to him. He drew his hand back and saw blood on his hands, but it didn't hurt. Not really. The faint sting was nothing compared to how his head was spinning. Nothing compared to how angry he was or the shock of what he had just seen.

"How did you do that?" Millie asked frantically, then shook her head and said, "Never mind—we can't stay in here."

"My thoughts exactly."

He stood up and went to the plant now covering the far corner of the room, heart racing. "Stay behind me," he instructed. "I don't know how this works."

Harlen touched the plant. He sank his arm between the thick branches until he found the center and gripped it tight. He had no idea how he'd accomplished this, but there was no time to wonder.

"Let me out," he said aloud. Maybe he had to tell it what he wanted. He felt it. A faint tremble in the leaves. Not enough.

Millie was standing behind him. Waiting. She needed him.

I promised. The thought echoed thunderously in his head. *I promised. I will keep her safe. Never again. Never again are you going to scare her in her own house.* The plant beneath him was shaking, rolling. *And you are never going to lock me up in this house again.*

He could feel the plants growing, thick, and angry. He could feel the tendrils of roots snaking past him and heard the wood of the door creaking.

He fanned the feeling, let it pass through his body like a shudder, blinding him. Pain blazed in his head, and his veins felt like they were all filling with liquid fire. He had no idea if the screaming he heard was himself, or Millie, or if it was all in his head. But when he finally snapped free of the trance and stumbled back, the door was hanging in two pieces.

It had cracked in half and torn from the frame, wrapped and suspended in the air by the thick tendrils of the stalks and flowers and roots curling around it. It was beautiful and horrifying, and it changed everything.

Magic. This was magic.
But there was no time.

"Harlen," Millie breathed behind him, staring at it, shocked as he was. He took Millie's hand and pulled her out of the room with him, and both of them ran down the hallway toward his father's office. He shouldered the door open, but it was empty.

"Where is he?" Millie asked.

"I don't know," Harlen confessed, looking around, frantic.

He couldn't be hiding. He wouldn't do that. He could have left the house. Could be anywhere. He looked around the office, and a bright flash of light caught his eye.

He couldn't be hiding. He wouldn't do that. He could have left the house. Could be anywhere. He looked around the office, and a bright flash of light caught his eye.

It was coming from a small object at the center of the desk. A small, orange globe glowing with light, held in a little iron cradle, with strange runes etched into the iron. Harlen had seen it in here before but never glowing. In the darkness of the room, it stood out like a beacon.

He looked closer at the shape of the runes on the side and realized he recognized what it said: *Remember.* Beside it was his initials, HV III.

How did he know that?

He thought back to his old suspicions. His father was watching them somehow.

Harlen reached down, almost robotically, to pick it up and examine it. As soon as his fingers made contact with the warm glass of the orange globe, he felt a shock go through his body, and his vision went black.

CHAPTER 33

That was it. He'd fallen into some trap, he thought, and then the room around him began to collect itself in his eyes like bits of snow, drifting together to form a full picture. But it wasn't the office that he was standing in when it all came together.

He was standing in the washroom in his bedroom. And in front of him, he saw himself standing at the mirror.

He saw himself looking into the glass, tugging at his hair that had just been chopped off. Before it had begun to grow out again, it still looked ragged and uneven, and he was trying desperately to make it look alright. Willing it not to look as awkward as it did because of the important day it was. This was the morning of his wedding; he realized as he looked around at the blurred edges of his surroundings. And at his former self.

Harlen watched himself in the mirror, muttering as he adjusted his glasses and stared hopelessly at his reflection. He was standing directly behind this image of himself from half a year ago, but he was apparently invisible. If his former self could see him, he gave no indication.

"It's fine. It's fine. I'm sure it's fine," he heard his own voice say. He watched his own hands fiddle nervously with his cufflink. "I'm sure she. . .gods, I don't know her name. This is not fine."

Millie.

As soon as he thought of her name, the image around him dissolved and returned at the wedding. Hours before, he'd just arrived and was standing behind his father as a man and a woman dressed in bright colors introduced their daughter, a young woman with dark hair and gray eyes who was clearly nervous but lovely. She was trying very hard to be serious, but she had a smile that couldn't seem to resist playing at the corners of her mouth.

As an observer, he saw himself stumble over his words in their introduction, his face bright red as he gripped her hand and shook it. She laughed, and he let her go quickly and shuffled back, embarrassed. It was astounding how much better things had gotten. As he thought it again, the image swirled.

"Can I be honest with you?" Millie's voice said as the image came into focus. This was new, from a month ago. Early morning surrounded him, and cool gray light was spilling over the bed where they were lying covered in nothing but sheets. One of her hands was absently tracing a scar on his leg as she spoke.

"Of course." His eyes locked on her. He had never seen his own gaze look so hazy and pleased as he studied her face. Never seen such a burning intensity in his eyes.

"My mom used to tell me that if I kissed a boy with tongue, I would get pregnant, and I believed her until I was sixteen."

He chuckled and said, "Well, you were kissing at sixteen. I didn't. . ." he trailed off and looked away, fiddling with his glasses, and she grinned. She perked up like a fox sensing the presence of something good.

"You can't leave me off on that."

He'd blushed and looked at her shyly and admitted, "I hadn't seen a naked woman before you."

"You're teasing me," she said, then as he fiddled with a loose thread on the blanket and said nothing, she prompted, "Alright but pictures. You have an extensive library—I'm sure there's a tasteful, artistic drawing of a naked woman in there somewhere."

"There is but—" he started, then stopped himself again, and again Millie prodded at him until he sighed and mumbled, "I always got too embarrassed to actually really look at them, you know?"

She laughed and curled over until she was leaning her forehead against his shoulder. He was red to the ears but smiling.

"It's not that funny."

"It's sweet," she said and raised herself and planted a kiss on his shoulder. "So, what's your verdict then? Was it worth all the dramatic poetry? Because pictures or not, I've seen some of that poetry you read, and some of it is quite scandalous."

He rolled onto his side so he could kiss her. When he drew back, the softness in her eyes was heart-wrenching. "It doesn't compare."

"If you're trying to flatter me," she said, "It's working very well."

He knew what came next. And as it evoked the thoughts in his head, he saw flashing quickly before him every night, every moment where they'd held each other. Every touch and shudder right down to the very first time when they were both so shy but so sure that this— that each other—is what they wanted. Where they'd shared themselves entirely with each other, alone.

He'd watched them. That was how he knew.

Harlen dropped the globe, and the images left his mind. He heard it hit the carpet and stared down at the vile thing.

He had been right. He had been right, and he wanted to put it back. To put everything he'd just seen and learned back, but it was there. He'd seen his memories laid out, and he felt violated. No, it wasn't just him. Vostesk Senior had violated them both.

That's how he always knows so much.

That's why he's eased up so much. He thinks he's getting the grandchild he wanted.

"Harlen!"

Millie shouted, and Harlen felt a hand close around his arm. He felt his head hit the side of the desk, and when he hit the ground, he saw his father glaring down at him. He was shouting. He was angrier than he'd ever been. But Harlen couldn't hear him. And he didn't care.

He closed his hand around the iron cradle of the glass orb where it had fallen beside him and swung it up with all the force he could manage. He felt the impact of it hitting the side of his father's face and felt only one thing as all sound and motion abandoned the world, and time slowed to a crawl.

Satisfaction.

He was fully ready to do it again when his father turned back to look at him, eyes glowing with anger when another blow came from behind and knocked him off the top of him. Millie was standing behind his father, her face as white as her nightgown, holding the iron fire poker she'd bashed across his back with shaking hands.

"Get off my husband!" she screamed like a mountain lion, bristling and showing her teeth. Harlen had never felt such pride. But it was short-lived as his father turned on them both.

Harlen managed to get himself off the ground and tackled her back out into the hallway. He felt the scrape of the blast of ice that sailed over their heads. He hit the ground with his shoulder as the shard hit the opposite wall of the hallway, embedding itself in the wallpaper.

"Run." He pushed her up and ahead of him, but she wouldn't let go of his hand and dragged him behind her as they ran out of the hallway. They skidded around the corner of the stairs, and Millie screamed as another shard of ice hit the empty vase on the railing, exploding it into a hundred fragments of ceramic that showered down on them.

I have magic. Harlen's mind raced as they ran. *But how does it WORK?*

There was nothing he could use. Not in here. Not unless they got outside, and he could find something like the lavender bush. Lavender bush. . .

"Garden!" he shouted as they flew down the staircase. Another shard of ice flew past them, scraping Harlen's neck. He felt the burn of it as it sliced through the collar of his shirt and into his skin. He felt the blood dribbling down his back, but it didn't hurt.

Four shards in quick succession smacked the wall behind them as they rounded the corner into the dining room. One hit the wall inches from Millie's face, and she barely ducked out of its way as they slid across the tile into the sitting room.

The moonlight fell through the glass wall as the rain pounded on it like thunder. He pulled on the door that wouldn't give way and had evidently been locked. Seeing this, Millie didn't hesitate to grab the silver candle stand from the table beside it. She swung it and smashed through one of the panes of glass.

The rain was coming down hard and blew sideways into the room, drenching them quickly with a spray of freezing water as the glass splintered and shattered. Harlen shoved his arm through the jagged hole it had created, reaching blindly for the bushes below, but his father had already strode into the room. He was laughing.

He raised a hand, and the water outside began to solidify and seal the window, blocking them in. Harlen snatched his arm back before it could be trapped. The water on the floor around them froze almost instantly into a thin layer of ice that was slick to the touch.

His father took a step towards them and jerked his head at Millie. "Get out of here, girl. My son and I have some things to discuss."

She was still gripping the silver candlestick. His father moved closer, and she raised it over her shoulder. Harlen could see the frost covering her fingertips and the blue beneath her nails, but she held firm.

"Touch him, and I'll break your hand."

Vostesk Senior sighed, exasperated. "I should never have gotten you a woman from the country. She has no manners." He raised both hands, cold mist gathering around them. "Fortunately, I am an excellent teacher."

Harlen threw himself at his father.

He grabbed him by the collar and hurtled all his weight into him, sending both of them tumbling to the ground.

He didn't expect him to hit his head on the table on their way down. Didn't expect the blood. It was just a small spatter across the table at first; then, when he landed on the floor, it began to grow from underneath his head as soon as he hit the tile.

Harlen hardly noticed. That rage, white-hot: a burning cold exploded inside of him. He was screaming at the top of his lungs.

Don't you ever, ever threaten her. You will never lay a hand on anyone again, do you hear me? Bastard! Evil bastard!

His father's cold eyes rolled and stared up at him, and suddenly Harlen felt it again. That rolling beneath his skin. He saw those black tendrils of smoke creeping up from his father's open eyes and mouth that opened and shut like the gasping of a fish as he tried to speak.

Harlen fought to keep the world from being drowned out in the bright, white ringing that filled his ears and felt the hot blood trickle from his nose. But he didn't surrender to it. He kept his eyes on his father as the pool of blood beneath his head spread, and he suddenly went limp in his arms.

He was dead.

It wasn't possible. Harlen touched his arm that had gone so inexplicably slack, expecting it to be a trick. Expecting him to reach up and grab him and beat him within an inch of his life for what he'd done. He braced for it as soon as he touched his shoulder—but there was nothing.

A beat of silence. Rain drumming through the window, pattering off the half-formed wall of ice that was melting beneath it. He didn't move. He was gone. He wasn't going to hurt anybody now.

It was so sudden. So unthinkable. Harlen started laughing. Because it had to be a trick, it had to—another one of his lies.

But it wasn't. Not this time. He was gone. He was really gone—just like that! And something about it was so funny and so horrific and so gut-wrenching that he sat on the floor beside him laughing and sobbing, unable to tell the difference between the two.

"But. . .wait. No," Harlen said after what could have been a minute or an hour. Something was dawning on him in his reeling mind. "No. What did you do? No! What did you do! Where's Tansey! What did you do!"

He grabbed the front of his father's jacket and lifted him an inch off the floor, shaking him while his pale hair turned slowly red with the blood pouring out of the crack in his skull. *No. No, this isn't right. This isn't fair.*

"Tell me!"

"Harlen." Millie's voice was small and shaking, and somehow it broke through his screaming and anger and tears. She put a hand on his arm, gently tugging at his sleeve. "You have to stop now. Okay?"

She's afraid. You're scaring her. Stop it.

He lowered Vostesk Senior back to the floor. He uncurled his fingers from around his jacket and sat back on the ground beside Millie. The rain, the ever-present rain, fell behind them.

Millie wrapped an arm tight around his waist to keep him back, away from the body, and she pressed her face into his chest. She was shaking.

"He knew," Harlen said, feeling hollow as all the anger dimmed. It had eaten up everything, and now he felt empty.

"I know," Millie said.

And what was left unspoken didn't need to be said. He had known what had happened to Tansey, and anything he'd known about it had died with him. It was all gone, just like her.

PART TWO

METAMORPHOSIS

CHAPTER 34

Harlen Vostesk, third of his name, buried his father four days after his death.

The casket was closed beneath a spray of white flowers across a lid carved with the image of a shark with the mouth open wide; every pointed tooth etched in mahogany.

It wasn't Harlen's own decision; the funeral was arranged by several of the other nobles who claimed to be family friends. They claimed it was to keep Harlen from having to worry. It sounded far too kind for him to trust, but he didn't have the energy to question their motives when they had come flocking to his house the morning after the city guard removed the body. He hardly knew any of them well enough to judge anyway.

Jacques had done the technical work. He sat with Harlen and Millie during the service, held in a house that Harlen had never been to by a family he barely recognized enough to name.

None of them spoke much, and when it came time for Harlen to place a flower on the coffin, he felt as though he were standing in a dream. That any moment, he would wake up and find his father still alive and still cutting apart his skin in the basement. He had mindlessly crumbled the flower in his hand and found he didn't care about the strange looks he received.

He listened to empty condolences of people he didn't know who didn't know him. He and Millie stood with clasped hands while Jacques politely asked everyone to let them leave early, to give them time alone, to give them room to breathe, and he was grateful. He knew his blank, staring face was unnerving them all.

He knew *he* was disturbing them all because they all knew what had happened. But nobody said a word about it. They shook his hand and offered apologies like Vostesk Senior had passed after a long and tragic illness. But they knew. It was why they didn't meet his eyes.

He had contacted the town guard after it happened. He told them everything the way he hadn't been able to when Tansey vanished. He expected to be taken away, put in a cell, then executed in some form or fashion. But he wasn't. They took the body, cleaned up the glass and the blood. Then left. And nobody said another word about it. And that was what unnerved *him* more than anything.

After the funeral, it took weeks for him to stop feeling as though the entire world had turned on its head. Like he was living in a waking dream. He could come and go in and out of the house as he pleased. He no longer had to jump at the sound of slamming doors, though he still did. He and Millie were no longer being watched. There was nobody to take him down to the basement, nobody glaring at him across the table.

He had dreamed of this strange someday many times in his life and had always thought it would feel liberating. But in reality, he felt even more nervous than usual. He didn't trust that it was real. It didn't feel real.

But gradually, over the days and weeks, his nerves began to ease. He stopped slowing his steps to walk more quietly outside his father's study. He could kiss Millie again without feeling like there were eyes on them. And the terrifying but fascinating question faced him: What was he supposed to do now?

"Anything you want," Millie said when he finally posed the question to her.

They'd started to grow accustomed to having full run of the house and were having tea together in the kitchen when he had asked. They still couldn't quite bring themselves to use the sitting room in spite of the fact that there was no evidence of that night left.

The house had been repaired, the window and the doors. They'd even had the locks taken off all of them, which had been his first action as the new head of the Vostesk family— something that still felt strange to say.

For the time being, they took their meals in the kitchen. Millie liked being able to just grab things from the pantry since it was her first time having free reign of a house as well, and he enjoyed seeing her pace up and down the line of shelves, carefully selecting her snacks.

"What do you want?" he asked.

She placed the spoon she was using to stir honey into her drink in her mouth and squinted at him. "Are you really asking, or just redirecting the question?"

He chuckled. "I don't know. Maybe both."

"I appreciate the honesty," she said with one of her contagious smiles.

"The way I see it, you have a few options. Become the new head of the household, get very distinguished, start wearing tight jackets, and start smiling less."

He chuckled as she continued, dropping the joke as her face settled more into a look of soft concern. "We're now free to search for your sister and whatever may surround that. A much larger undertaking. Or we could figure out what. . .that was." She reached out and tapped a small vase on the table that held two stunted daises from outside suspended in water.

"Right. That." Harlen looked down at his own hands. He began to twist at his cufflink.

They hadn't talked about what he'd done since that night. He was sure she had questions—he had no shortage of them himself. He had been very upfront with her that he didn't understand any of it.

"I don't know how it happened. It just did. I've tried all my life to do that, but now that it has, I don't know how I don't know why—and it—"

Millie reached out and stopped his hand from twisting the link on his sleeve. He jumped at the initial touch but relaxed into it after a moment and blurted out what he'd been hesitant to even admit to himself: "It scares me."

She nodded. Harlen was sure he'd scared her that night, and not just with the magic. He'd apologized many times over and had told her that with his father gone if she really wanted to, she could go home. He wouldn't blame her, and he would never dream of keeping her here. But she'd stayed.

She said that it wasn't his fault, what had happened. His father very may well have killed them had he gotten his hands on them, and he'd meant to do no more than shove him. It was an accident that had probably saved their lives, but he still couldn't stop feeling both glad and guilty in turns that the man was gone by his hand.

"Then we'll get you used to it," she said. "Or we'll pretend it never happened and ignore it forever. Whichever you prefer."

"Aren't you glad I'm finally useful, though?" he asked, only half-joking and laughing nervously.

She pursed her lips, and her eyes gained a distinctive, mischievous twinkle. "I don't know. I thought you were pretty useful already.

He tried to laugh, but it became stuck in his throat and sounded more like choking. He couldn't help it. Millie squeezed his hand tighter.

"I don't understand a lot about magic myself, but I'm sure Jacques can help you. And I can help wherever I can."

He stared at her, into those gray eyes that held all the world's warmth and sweetness, and smiled. "Alright."

He turned toward the vase of daisies on the table and put his hand on the silky petals. Like so many times before, he concentrated. He stared at them, studied them, envisioned the roots growing out into the bottom of the glass and their little wilted stalks straightening. But just like so many times before, nothing happened. He frowned.

He dipped his fingers into the water, taking hold of the roots themselves, placing the flower in his hand. He stared at it and tried to summon up that feeling, that anger that he'd felt that first night, but it just wasn't there. It was like it had all burned up, and he felt a pang of fear deep in his stomach. "What if I can't? What if that was it?"

"Then I'll just use it to tease you about that time you broke a door in half," Millie said, once again managing to coax a small twitch of a smile from him as he put the plant back in its place.

He must have been bad at hiding his disappointment because the next thing he knew, she'd gotten up from her chair and stood in front of him.

"Stop that," she scolded him, draping her arms over his shoulders. "I love you as you are. Magic or not."

Do you?

He almost asked, but really, he knew the answer. Millie had decided long before any of this to love him.

He managed a real smile. "I know."

Though he would never understand why.

She leaned close, and to emphasize her point; she kissed him. A gentle kiss at first that deepened until she climbed in his lap.

He certainly had no objection. It had been so long. Weeks since he'd felt her gentle closeness. His sudden desire for it was overwhelming.

Nobody's watching anymore. He thought as she kissed at his neck, sliding her hands up his waist, so they slipped under his shirt and warmed his skin. He all but purred. *We're completely alone.*

It was the shattering of the glass that pulled them apart. Harlen opened his eyes, and he and Millie both looked back towards the table, still tangled in each other's arms. The daisies had grown. Sprung into nearly an entire bush until the roots had burst the little champaign flute serving as the vase.

"So that's how it works," Millie said with a sly grin. Had he not been holding her to keep her from falling off the chair, he would have covered his face as he felt the heat rising up his neck.

"Don't sound so smug."

"So, have I finally discovered how to keep proper houseplants?" she asked, and when his eyes went wide, and his blush deepened, she laughed.

He was sure he'd never wanted so badly for her to kiss him again and had pulled one hand free to cup her chin so he could do just that. She was still grinning ear to ear and giggling, her eyes scrunched up with the smile, and he could swear he felt his heart melt.

Her lips were warm as the afternoon sun, and she tasted like tea and sugar. He was just beginning to ask if she wanted to take the conversation somewhere where the flowers wouldn't give him away so clearly when there was a knock at the door.

He jumped, though there was no way for anyone at the door to see them from there. Millie laughed before hopping up and straightening his collar, which included several buttons she'd undone.

"Don't worry; you look very distinguished."

"I thought you liked me," he said, smoothing her hair and fixing the laces at the front of her dress he had begun to tug at. When they both looked suitably appropriate, they approached the door, and Harlen opened it.

CHAPTER 35

The rain was pouring outside. As soon as the heavy oak door was open, the fine mist rising from where the rain hit the street drifted inside. The man standing in the doorway had his top hat pulled on low and the collar of his coat turned up, but Harlen recognized the expertly twirled mustache immediately. And nobody else he knew dressed in all white.

"Chairman Berkley?" Harlen asked in surprise.

"Yes! Hello, my dear boy! Would you mind terribly if I stepped inside for a moment?"

Right. He was the one who was supposed to invite people in now. He stepped quickly back from the door and gestured inside. "Oh, not at all. Please come in."

He wasn't sure if there was any other formal greeting he was supposed to give, but if there was, the chairman didn't wait for it. He ducked his head and hurried inside, letting out a sigh of relief once he was out from under the rain. He quickly shrugged out of the wet coat and hung it beside the door, where it promptly began forming a small puddle beneath it.

"I'm so sorry to drop in unannounced," the chairman said quickly, "But I haven't seen you at the school in quite a while, understandably so, and I thought it might be best if I simply came in person rather than just sent you a letter."

He took off his hat, hanging it neatly beside his coat before he turned and blinked in surprise. Apparently, he hadn't noticed that there was another person in the room.

"Ah! Miss. . ."

"Millie. My wife," Harlen said, placing a hand on her back and ushering her forward.

Berkley smiled pleasantly and gave her a formal kiss on the back of the hand. "Oh, of course, how forgetful of me. A pleasure to see you again."

She stepped back close, and Harlen noticed his hand found itself rather naturally resting on her waist as she stood beside him. It was nothing overt and was still very formal, but there was a familiarity to the gesture that felt intimate.

"What can we do for you?" Harlen asked, clearing his throat and speaking slowly to quell the nervous tremble his voice usually held. It was beginning to lessen without his father's presence, but he knew that after years of silence and stammering apologies, it was going to take some time to perfect his speech.

"Oh, it's just matters of your father's that I have to discuss with you," he said. "It's nothing too dreadfully serious. Just finances and the like. And a few other things—simple but important to the maintenance of your estate."

"Right," Harlen said, pulling a smile across his face. "Well, we can discuss things in the office, I suppose."

Harlen had no desire to move into the sitting room. It would undoubtedly have been more comfortable for the three of them. Mostly since the "office" Harlen was currently making use of was not his father's, but an old room that had been used for storage, he had moved a desk into it from the library.

Berkley climbed the stairs behind them, looking around at the house, and commented, "It certainly does look brighter in here."

"I prefer open windows. Even if it is raining," Millie said.

He seemed surprised she'd answered, but pleasantly so, and the two of them kept up a light conversation as they reached the office doors, which Harlen was grateful for. There was no need to linger in awkward silence, and their talk seemed pleasant enough, which was why he was confused when they stepped into the office, and the chairman stood, waiting as if expecting her to leave.

"Is everything alright?" Harlen asked.

"I was just wondering if you wished to discuss these things alone," the chairman said. "These are matters of the house."

Harlen blinked. "She is part of the house."

Chairman Berkley looked uncomfortable and glanced at Millie. "I mean to say matters concerning the family."

"She's my wife," Harlen said, straightening up and feeling something that he wasn't accustomed to. Indignance. "She is part of the family."

In the last few weeks, he and Millie had been doing their best to make sense of his father's papers together. She wasn't a fan of the figures, but she was excellent at deciphering contracts.

He had done so because he was determined that she be aware of what was going on. There had been so many secrets in the marriage between his mother and father. He had no desire to repeat it.

"It's alright," Millie said, raising a hand as tension grew in the room. "I'm sure I can find a way to occupy my time for a few minutes. Gentlemen."

She politely inclined her head to Chairman Berkley and smiled at Harlen. He saw that familiar glint in her eyes, and as she walked outside, closing the door behind her, he had to restrain a smile. He could see the shadow of her shoes remaining just outside, listening. His wife, indeed.

Chairman Berkley made no move to apologize but instead busied himself unloading his briefcase on the desk. Harlen walked behind him, his eyes sweeping over the neatly written pages while Berkley began to prattle on about finances, which Harlen was already relatively familiar with.

His father may have hated him, but he had taught him the basics of what he needed to know about running the house and his affairs in trade. After all, it wasn't as if he had any other options. And he supposed the man had held out hope that one day he would be worth something. Harlen was just glad he didn't have to listen too intently to the chairman.

As his eyes swept over the paper and he let Berkley's words fade into the background, something that caught his eye. A note on a particular account he'd never seen before.

"What's that one?" Harlen asked, pointing to it.

The chairman blinked in surprise, and Harlen realized he'd cut him off mid-explanation. He opened his mouth to apologize, then realized that no. He didn't want to, not after how he'd spoken to Millie.

With an almost dizzying rush, he realized there was nobody who was going to reprimand him with violence for returning rudeness with rudeness. So he closed his mouth and stared at Chairman Berkley until he glanced down, cleared his throat, and explained.

"It's a donation made to the school. It's done by all noble houses in the area. It's not required, but it is an informal thanks for assisting in the rearing of their children."

Berkley stared at him, igniting a prolonged silence where the air in the room shifted and grew taut as the strings of a violin. It made the hair at the back of Harlen's neck stand on end.

"Did your father ever discuss the nature of this donation with you?" he asked, a little too brightly. A little too curiously. The chairman's eyes widened, and he raised his eyebrows as he smiled, his face far too friendly. If Harlen hadn't felt on edge before, he certainly felt it then.

"No," he said, feeling for a moment like he was again in his father's presence. His voice came out small and shaky, but he forced himself to press for more, "Why might that be?"

The unsettling, exaggerated smile faded back to normal beneath Berkley's mustache, and he began re-ordering his briefcase, leaving certain papers on the desk for him and scooping others back into the case. "Oh, I'm sure it's just something he forgot to mention."

Harlen glanced at the papers Berkley seemed eager to get back out of view. It all looked ordinary enough, but he did his best to memorize what he could anyway.

"Right. Well. I should be back later in the week. I'm sure there will be more to discuss by then. I'll be meeting with some of your father's old colleagues this evening, and I'm sure they'll pass on whatever it is you may need to know to keep the place going."

"Should I just go to the meeting?" Harlen asked, confused by the abruptness of his exit. Berkley simply shook his head.

"Perhaps you will in the future, but not this time. They're dreadfully dull, I assure you. All politics and philosophy without philosophers." He laughed, smoothing the front of his pristine jacket with nervous fingers. "Best not to let it concern you. Not now when you've had such a dreadful fright. I'm not one to gossip, but I've heard my share of what happened with your father. I haven't the faintest what got into him."

"I don't know if anything got into him. Nothing that wasn't already there." Harlen said, surprised by his boldness.

He expected Berkley to look displeased by the comment, but he simply sighed and shook his head. "He was never an even-tempered man. His anger and impatience got him into plenty of unpleasant situations that much we all knew. I had hoped he'd had enough of a taste of what it could bring on that he would learn to show some reservation, but...alas." Berkley shrugged and spread his gloved hands.

"I can't imagine what other trouble it got him into," Harlen said, hoping to urge more out of him.

"It certainly earned him a scar or two; I will say that much," Berkley said, sighing and twirling the ends of his curled mustache.

It looked like he was going to say more. Harlen waited, gripping the edge of the desk curiously while Berkley considered launching into a lengthy story about whatever it was his father and his associates got up to. He opened his mouth to speak, then closed it and shook his head once again.

"Ah. I shouldn't go on. I'm sure you've got plenty of things to get in order."

CHAPTER 36

Millie had moved from behind the door by the time the chairman opened it and had vanished seemingly into thin air. As soon as he started hurrying down the staircase toward the door, Harlen saw her emerge from one of the nearby closets she'd apparently ducked quickly into.

She and Harlen both stood at the top of the stairs and watched as he put his coat and hat on quickly before he walked back outside into the pouring rain.

Once he was gone, Millie said, "I hope you found that as strange as I did."

"Most definitely." Harlen nodded. "I don't know what's going on, but I don't like it."

"Do you think it has to do with your sister?" Millie asked, voicing what he was beginning to wonder.

Harlen bit his lip, thinking. "I don't know. I don't know enough of anything to say, and this just adds more uncertainty."

"What does your gut say?" Millie asked.

Harlen felt as though a chill had descended on the room. "My gut says, yes."

"Then, we agree," Millie said. "And luckily, you're in a position where we'll actually be able to look into it."

Millie was speaking optimistically, walking backward as they made their way back toward the office, and jumped so badly she nearly tripped over her own feet as the door at the very end of the hallway slammed.

They both looked to see it was his mother's door that had flown shut, and without needing to even look at one another to confirm their next action, they started moving towards it.

His mother had been leaving her door open since his father's death. She remained in her room as always, but typically she left at least a crack open to the rest of the world.

As they approached, Harlen wondered aloud, "Do you think he scared her?"

"He was one of your father's friends. Maybe," Millie said, knocking softly when they reached her door.

There was no response, but when Harlen touched the doorknob, it gave easily. His mother made no protest when he slowly eased it open.

She was sitting on her bed. Millie had dressed her earlier, but her hair had fallen out of its pins and hung down her back. She sat on the bed with her knees to her chest, balling and un-balling her hands around the skirt of her pale blue dress. Her wide eyes fixed on the opposite wall, and her cross-stitch sat abandoned on the bed beside her.

"Mother." Harlen sat down next to her, putting a hand on her shoulder. She didn't look at him while her bones, fragile as a bird's, pressed against his palm. "It's okay. He's gone. You don't need to be afraid; the chairman left."

She stared at the wall, rocking as if she didn't even know he was there. Millie, who was standing in the doorway, spoke up.

"Pearl."

She blinked and seemed startled to see Harlen sitting beside her. She shrank back for a moment before she recognized him, easing up only slightly even then. Harlen felt his stomach twist but still squeezed her shoulder gently and said, "It's okay. Chairman Berkley left."

"I don't like him," she whispered, her big wet eyes looking up at him imploringly. He wanted to wrap his arm around her and assure her that nobody was going to hurt her, but he knew she wouldn't have liked it. He forced himself to remain at arm's length.

"Why not?" Millie asked, and again, his mother responded to her. Her eyes darted over to Millie, then back to him, and she whispered her reply.

"He was one of your father's friends."

"I know," Harlen assured her. "But he's not staying here. I can meet him somewhere else next time if you—"

He almost gasped when she grabbed the hand he'd placed on her shoulder. She squeezed it so hard; her little fingernails dug into his skin with enough force to hurt, enough to bring bright drops of blood welling in the shapes of tiny crescent moons. He was so shocked he didn't even move while she hissed, "No! Stay away from him. Stay away from him and anything to do with them."

"Mother, I—"

He struggled with whether or not he should say anything about his sister. He was trying to pull his hand back from her iron grip, afraid to let her hold on and afraid to hurt her by yanking away with too much force.

There was no telling how lucid or frantic she was, and he wondered in a panic if it might help calm her if she knew *why* he would want to talk to people his father knew.

"It might help us figure out what happened to Tansey."

"Tansey's gone! Tansey got away from here!" his mother shouted, tears rolling down her face. It wore an expression that was manic in a way he'd never seen while her grip tightened and tightened.

"Let go!" Millie grabbed his mother's hand and pulled her back. Harlen nearly fell backward off the bed as she dragged her nails across his arm in an attempt to hold onto him. Blood trickled down his sleeve while she thrashed in Millie's arms.

"Mother, stop!" Harlen scrambled up as soon as he could and tried to help Millie hold her while she kicked and screamed in protest.

"Tansey's gone! Tansey got away!" she shrieked, her hair flying. "She got away!"

Harlen managed to wrap his arms around her and pinned her hands at her sides. She was as small and frail as a china doll, but she kept kicking and thrashing with a truly staggering amount of strength.

He was familiar enough with these fits to know that these were the dangerous ones. They were the only things his sister was ever really afraid of, and he could see her clearly in his mind's eye, standing white-faced in the doorway while he held their mother as tight as he could. Afraid now that if he let go, she might hurt herself or Millie in a blind fit of rage that was just as terrifying but far more animal than his father's.

It was as if she was trying to claw out of her flesh and raging against her life itself whenever she had these fits. He had seen her smash up furniture and tear things apart, and he could never get out of his mind the one time she'd gotten her hands around Tansey's throat the first and last time she'd tried to intervene.

It was why he didn't dare let go of her until whatever storm was in her passed. And it always went as quickly as it came.

All at once, it was as if his mother had no weight at all. Her muscles went slack in his arms like a puppet with cut strings, and her screaming turned into a high, pitiful wail that twisted his heart.

"Why did she leave me?" she sobbed.

Harlen squeezed his arms around her and dropped his cheek onto the top of her head. Once again, she was his mother, and he walked her over to the bed so he could set her down.

Millie picked up the pillows she'd thrown onto the floor and set them behind her so he could lay her down on her side. He maneuvered her into position and knelt on the floor beside the bed so he could look into her face. So she would know that somebody was there, even if she didn't recognize him completely.

He held one of her tiny hands, and Millie stood beside him with one hand on his shoulder, one on his mother's back. The same mixed emotions of wariness and pity he felt written clearly in her eyes.

"She didn't. I'm sure she didn't," Harlen said, stroking the hand he held while she laid limply across the pillows. She stared past him. "I'm sure there's a good reason; you know she wouldn't just leave you."

Her eyes focused on him as he spoke. For a moment, she saw him and recognized him, and for the first time in years, he saw real light behind them. When she spoke, her voice didn't shake. It was steady and firm, and she said each word with certainty. "Why couldn't it have been you?"

He stared at her. He felt as if all the air had been sucked out of him. "You don't mean that."

She continued to stare at him. She knew him. She knew what she'd said. Her face was expressionless, but her eyes were accusatory. *Why wasn't it you?*

"You don't mean that," he repeated, his voice higher as he felt himself getting lightheaded and dizzy. He felt as though someone had shoved a blade between his ribs. "You don't."

Her eyes were slowly sliding out of focus once again, and the light was dimming. She was gone, but Harlen gripped her hand as tight as he could.

"Mother!"

"Harlen."

Millie's voice was soft, and he felt the hysterics that had been rising in him come to a sudden stop. He felt himself dropping down from the heights those few words had pushed him to, and as he crashed, there was no closing of the throat. Tears simply started pouring out of his eyes and dripping off his cheeks with no sound. No real crying to accompany them.

He was shocked and had it not been for Millie's hands on his shoulders, easing him back to his feet, he was sure he wouldn't have been able to stand.

"Come on. Let's go."

He let himself be led out of the room, back to his own. Millie sat him down on the bed and held him while he dripped soundless tears onto her shoulder.

It was strange. Harlen hadn't cried at his father's funeral. He hadn't cried about him at all since that first night, and even then, it wasn't him he'd cried for. His father had felt like an absence, but never a loss. This was different. This was death. The death of an illusion he'd built even after everything she'd done, everything she'd left him to, that his mother still cared for him.

Part of him had hoped that once his father was gone, she would be able to return to herself enough to treat him like a son again, but now he understood the truth. She'd stopped caring for him long ago.

He'd known it for years. Deep down. Even so, he'd tried to ignore it, and being confronted with it was still excruciating.

But he wouldn't let it cripple him, not after everything.

He allowed himself an hour to come apart. To let Millie hold him and whisper comforting things to him. Then he'd sat up, dried his eyes on his shirt, and smiled at her.

"It's alright," he said while she watched him, clearly worried and unconvinced. "Really. It'll be alright."

He reached over and brushed Millie's hair back from her face.

He wasn't lost. He wasn't unloved. Everything about the worried way she looked at him, and the way she used her sleeve to dab and fuss at his already dry eyes, spoke of love. He felt like part of his heart had been ripped out, but it wasn't gone. Not entirely.

"We'll be our own family, then. You and I."

She stared at him with incredible intensity and reached up to hold his hand against her cheek, nodding. "You and I."

The world was quiet, and his chest ached, but he would survive. They would survive.

She and I.

CHAPTER 37

Millie was concerned about Harlen.

She spent the night beside him in bed, close to him, skin to skin, watching him for any further signs of the damage that must have been done.

It had hurt him; he made no attempts to hide that. He admitted to it freely.

She couldn't imagine how devastated she would be if her mother said something like that to her, but somehow, he was carrying on—still talking about caring for her himself since she was so terrified of strangers.

"Nobody would ask that of you," she had told him. "Nobody."

She had been sitting up on her side, looking at him, the scars pulling at his flesh in the corners of her vision. She focused on his dark eyes that shone as he looked back up at her, a smile playing on his lips despite everything. It was almost painful to look at.

He had one hand raised, stroking the curve of her hip with a feather-light touch against her skin. His hands were soft, but his thumb and first finger each had a permanent rough spot where he spent so much time holding a pen.

"I'll be okay. I promise," Harlen had said with what she had initially thought to be amusement at her worry, but his voice was so soft. His eyes glittered so brightly that she understood it was just near-disbelief that brought the smile. He could hardly believe that she was so concerned. Like so many times before, it made her heart ache for him.

A skeleton with skin stretched across it. Millie had once thought. *That must be what he looks like underneath his clothes.* He truly did, but the fact remained that he was *her* skeleton. He was hers.

Even after they'd made love, she had kept her arms wrapped firmly around him all night to remind him that she was there: that she cared about him. That, someone loved him.

She knew the gesture wasn't lost on him. He had pulled her close to his chest where she could smell that familiar woody scent of the oils he bathed in and could feel his heart beating quickly between his ribs. She could count each bone with her fingers and felt each beat of the rabbit-quick pulse that fluttered against them.

He spent half the night pressing kisses to the top of her head, and when he had woken in the morning, it had been with a smile at the sight of her fully awake but still clinging to him as though she could protect him from all the hurt and sadness in the world.

"Ah, good morning, my guardian." he had said.

Had it been anyone but him, she would have thought he was mocking her. But she understood it as the thanks it was meant to be. And she saw the unabashed look of love in his eyes.

How he managed to feel anything so tender after what had happened was completely beyond her, and despite her best efforts, she'd asked him again if he was sure he was alright.

"I'm not sure." He confessed, gripping her hand tight. "But I will be."

They spent the morning quietly, but in the afternoon, she invited Jacques over to help take Harlen's mind off the lingering hurt she knew was still there.

Besides, they had had no real time to see him since the funeral. Millie thought that it would be good to have someone with a talent for making light of things over for a while. She could certainly use the levity and couldn't imagine Harlen wouldn't benefit from it.

Just as she hoped, he arrived shortly after noon. He showed up in true form, with a cigarette already half-burned in his mouth, covered in dust and dirt, and without pausing to say hello as he strolled through the door, he waved a stack of cards and said, "Shit, it's quiet in here. You should invest in some records or something."

They all took up residence in the kitchen. It was a bit crowded for all of them to sit at the small table; the sitting room would have been far more comfortable, but she and Harlen were still avoiding it. Even though there were no physical traces of what had happened there, Millie knew for sure it made both of them uneasy. She certainly couldn't look at the spot where Vostesk Senior had fallen without the air feeling colder.

He hadn't been a good man by any stretch. She would be lying if she said she missed him in any capacity. Or that what happened to him didn't feel like some kind of justice. But the look of his eyes staring blankly at the ceiling still haunted her.

Jacques didn't seem to mind the arrangement. He sat on the other side of the table from herself and Harlen, the smoke from his cigarette rising and filling the air as he shuffled the cards.

Millie enjoyed the calm simplicity of it, and the jokes shared almost as much as she enjoyed watching Jacques try to explain the rules to Harlen repeatedly. Who, for all his talent for memorization, couldn't seem to grasp them.

"What does this one do again?" Harlen turned the cards he was holding towards her, and Jacques smacked his forehead.

"You can't show her! You're supposed to keep them to yourself!" Jacques reached to take Harlen's cards from his hand, re-shuffled the deck, and passed him five more, facedown. "I swear if you've been doing that this whole time— that's how you keep winning, isn't it?"

Millie grinned over the top of her cards. "You say that as if I need to cheat. Maybe you're just bad at this."

"I call bullshit," Jacques muttered as he sat back in his seat.

He pushed the chair back on two legs, cards in one hand, cigarette wedged between his lips as he spoke out of one corner of his mouth. "So, you said Chairman Berkley was here yesterday? What did that prick want?"

"Other than being incredibly rude, he seemed like he wanted to discuss business," Harlen said, frowning. Millie did enjoy that he still seemed ruffled by how he'd spoken to her. "Talking about donations to the school and all that. He said it's something all the noble families do on a regular basis."

"As someone who works for the school, I'll have to thank you for and encourage that time-honored practice," Jacques said, slapping another card onto the table.

Millie turned her head to the side, looking at him curiously. "You know about that?"

Jacques shrugged. "Like I said, I haven't been there very long, but I've been there long enough to know everyone with a big name or big money makes a huge show of it."

"But do you think there might be some less than scrupulous things going on there?" Millie asked, laying one of her cards down on top of his.

"I think everyone's got the capacity to be less than scrupulous. Nobles especially. Wouldn't surprise me if there's something they're hiding. People persuading the board to take on their kids that have no right to be there, no offense Harlen. But it is how you got in. Speaking of—your turn, mate."

Harlen put down his card, glancing around to see if he'd done it right. Jacques tapped the ash from his cigarette into the water glass beside him and shuffled the cards in his hands. As he did, Harlen sat back in his chair, but Millie saw him frown before speaking again.

"We did find something else relating to the school," he said slowly and seemed just to be remembering it himself as Millie realized what he was talking about. She wondered how on earth she could have forgotten.

"The card," she finished.

Jacques blinked at them and raised his coppery eyebrows while Harlen explained.

"We found a card. An evaluation card like the one I got. It was in Tansey's room. We found it just before—" Harlen paused and nodded toward the doorway, towards the sitting room. "Well. Before that."

"Huh. Alright, that is odd. I thought you said he didn't put as much effort into the whole magic thing from her," Jacques said.

"He didn't. That I know of," Harlen said, adding the last sentence slowly. His fingers drummed on the table thoughtfully. "But I don't know. I can hardly imagine he would tell me everything. I never gave much thought to it before, but there are a lot of things I didn't know he was willing to do."

There was an angry undercurrent that grew into his last statement that was gone just as quickly when he suggested, "It would probably be a good idea to go through his things. I haven't quite gotten to it yet, considering. . .but I should. There could be something there. I just wanted to ask if that sounded strange to you."

"It does," Jacques admitted. "That was before my time, but if she did get an evaluation, there should be a record of it. I could look into it for you. Dig around, see if I can find anything."

"Would you?" Harlen asked, and again Jacques shrugged.

"Couldn't hurt. I've been tutoring this thirteen-year-old since you've been gone, and he's a pain in the ass. That would give me something better to do, at least."

Harlen smiled appreciatively, then rejoined the game. He set down another card—the wrong one—but neither Millie nor Jacques was going to tell him so.

Then there came a crash from upstairs.

As Harlen began to stand up, Millie put a hand on his arm. "I'll go."

"Are you sure?"

"Yeah, I'll be right back. It'll give one of you a chance to actually win a game," she said with a smile and a quick kiss on the cheek that made his face turn red.

"Disgusting. Both of you," Jacques said from his side of the table and flicked a card at them. "No affection at my card table. You take that shit outside."

Millie flicked the card back at him as she walked off into the deeper, cooler part of the house. She climbed the main staircase and could hear the sound of thumping coming from the far end of the upstairs hallway.

Just as Millie suspected, the sound was coming from Pearl. She was standing at the end of the hall beside its one window, staring out of it. She'd managed to get it open, and the thumping was coming each time she pushed it open, only for the wind to blow it back shut. She was staring out the window, her face and dress soaked from the gusts of rain. Her hair hung down, limp and dripping.

"Pearl," Millie said as she approached her.

Millie walked with deliberate slowness towards her and touched her shoulder hesitantly. It was easy to tell this was not one of her moments of lucidity from the stiff and repetitive motion.

Millie couldn't help the sharp intake of air when she saw Pearl's face. She wasn't just staring as she usually did; she was so pale her lips were gray, and her face contorted into a fearful snarl, tears streaking down either side of her twisted mouth.

"Pearl, what's wrong?" Millie tried to turn her away from the window, but she wouldn't be budged.

"There's a man outside," she said, not moving her eyes from whatever she was staring at through the glass.

Something about the way she said it made Millie's blood run cold. She looked out the window as well, following Pearl's gaze. But there was nothing. The street and the lawn leading up to the house was empty.

"I don't see anything."

"He was there," Pearl insisted, her voice trembling. "He was down there looking at me."

Millie slowly dragged her eyes from the lawn back to Pearl. She was shaking head to toe in what looked like a mixture of fear and anger. Without warning, she raised a hand and banged it hard against the glass and shouted. "Go away!"

Millie grabbed her arm before she could do it again. She could just imagine her putting her hand through the glass and cutting her arm to shreds on broken glass.

Pearl struggled, but only for a moment before she became limp and passive as a doll once again. Just like the other day, the anger was gone as quickly as it had come. She lowered her head and started to cry quietly.

"I don't want them here. I just want them to leave us alone. He was always bringing them here."

"Vostesk Senior?" Millie asked.

Pearl flinched but nodded. In her little, whispery voice, she said, "He was always bringing his friends here. I don't like them. I don't. And they won't stop coming; I know they won't. I don't know why. I don't know what they want."

The confusion and fear on the poor woman's face and the lack of lucidity in her eyes was what made Millie swallow her dislike and pat her hands. Pearl gripped them back tightly and looked up at her imploringly, begging for understanding.

Millie genuinely wished she had something to offer. But all she could do was try to coax her back to her room. "You might feel safer in there."

Pearl nodded with that distant look in her eyes and let herself be guided back to her room, back down to a sitting position on her bed where she reached blindly for the bottle on her bedside table before being perplexed by its absence.

Millie and Harlen had been working on taking her off the opium. It was a long process, slowly giving less and less. The doctor had said it was the only way to do it safely, but Harlen still seemed agonized every time he had to give it to her. No matter how small the dose. Pearl asked where the bottle was frequently, but luckily this time, she didn't. She only looked at the empty table for a moment, her pale blue eyes uncomprehending.

"Who did you think you saw?" Millie asked. It was probably best not to pry. But curiosity got the better of her.

Pearl blinked up at her, turning her head to one side. She stared at her for a long moment before saying in a dreamy voice, "One of his old friends. I don't remember what his name was." She frowned and said, "He has a very strange face."

Millie nodded, hoping she hid her disappointment and the shiver that had passed down her back well. She didn't know what else she expected.

Once Pearl was settled, Millie stepped back out into the hallway, easing her door shut behind her. She put her hands up tiredly to her face and backed away from it slowly, only stopping when her back touched the opposite wall of the hallway, and she slumped against it. The only sound now was the whispering crackle of the kerosene lamps and the rain on the glass that still bore Pearl's handprints.

Millie peered past them, through the smudges and rain into the yard below, still empty. Empty and silent as the hallway she stood in. The world outside, from the yard to the street, was completely empty.

She thought of what it might look like, a lone figure standing in the middle of the lawn. Unmoving. Staring up at the window.

It filled her with a fear she couldn't name. The quiet and emptiness terrified her, and she found herself running like a child from the dark back down the stairs towards the kitchen.

CHAPTER 38

"**I**'ll look into it. I promise." Jacques stood beside the door, shrugging back into his tattered brown jacket. Harlen thanked him, as did Millie, who stood behind him.

She had come back from upstairs looking shaken but hadn't wanted to explain why. She only mentioned that she would like to take a look through his father's things, the sooner, the better, after falling back into the card game with the help of a bit of Jacques' joking and prodding.

She was quite nearly herself again by the time Jacques had to leave, but Harlen had been watching her closely enough to notice the tension in her posture that was never so rigid. As soon as the door was closed, he asked what had happened.

"Nothing," she said, tucking a strand of mahogany hair back behind her ear. She folded her arms over her chest and shifted uncomfortably, studying the checkerboard tile until she caught him still staring at her and smiled in defeat. "Not getting that past you, am I?"

"You don't have to," he said, putting a hand on her shoulder. The muscle beneath her skin was tight as new upholstery. "What happened?"

She gestured back up towards the stairs. "Your mother. She was just. . .really upset." Millie chewed her lip, her brows furrowed. "She thinks someone's watching her. She seemed to think it had something to do with your father."

She wouldn't be wrong. Vostesk Senior had been watching them. But this sounded different. "She thinks people are watching us?"

"Sounded like," she said, a little too quickly. She had been frightened and was fighting hard not to show it, as always. "I'm sure it's nothing, really."

Harlen stepped forward and pulled her into an embrace. She sighed again and said, "Come on. It takes more than that to scare me." But she didn't pull back. He felt her grip the back of his shirt tightly.

She remained close, his arm around her shoulder and hers circled his waist, as they ascended the stairs. It was a closeness he was sure they were both grateful for as they opened the door to the office neither of them had been in since that night.

Behind the door was a scene from one of the town's shops windows: a perfect picture of the aftermath of chaos. The things that had been arranged on the desk neat as a pin were scattered across the floor. Books, papers, a smashed ink bottle that left black ink like a spatter of blood across the elaborately embroidered rug. His father's cane lay discarded, the white carved handle clattering against the floor as Harlen pushed the door open and knocked it to the side from its place against the wall.

He bent to pick it up without thinking. His hand closed around the cool handle, and the texture of the carvings, the sharp pinpricks of teeth from the open-mouthed shark, and the wave it sat on that made him realize what he was doing.

How many times had this left bruises on his skin? How many times had this slammed on a table as a threat—no, a promise—of future pain? He could remember exactly how the carved handle felt when it impacted flesh.

He picked it up, feeling the heaviness of the carved ivory, and waited. He waited for nausea and dizziness to hit him. He froze as he braced for the fear to sweep over him, but it didn't come.

Confused, he straightened and lifted it to study the cane closer, the carvings of the waves and shells along the sides supposedly made by the hands of one of his great, great grandfathers. Something beautiful to help contain the powerful magic in his blood that, according to rumor, still clung to the carvings themselves. Lingering like the smell of smoke in hair.

His father always said he could feel it. The hum of magic pulsing beneath his fingers when he held it. But Harlen couldn't bring himself to agree.

He felt nothing. *It* was nothing. Outside of his father's hands, it was nothing but a hunk of ivory and wood.

The thought brought with it an unexpected rush of confidence. Harlen felt himself straighten. Shrugging off a weight he hadn't realized was pressing down on him. Suddenly, the office was no longer foreboding. It was just a room. The one responsible for the oppressive air inside of it was gone. Gone and never coming back.

"Everything alright?" Millie asked.

He nodded. There was a place on the wall for the cane, two gleaming silver hooks above the mantel to display it, and the lovely craftsmanship that went into it. It was a family heirloom, after all—part of the great Vostesk family line.

Harlen propped it against the wall behind the door and left it there.

Further into the office, he saw the remains of the only thing he had returned for after his father died: the orange globe and its little metal cradle. The globe itself lie broken in several pieces where he had bashed it against the desk, leaving a permanent mark in the wood. Even broken, it made his stomach turn as he picked up the remaining metal cradle and ran his finger over the markings on the side: *Remember. HG III.*

His father had been an awful teacher. But if there was one thing he had learned as a result was the ability to tear through books and do excellent research. In the days following his father's death, he had put that to use.

He had wanted to know what this object was. What had let him violate the most intimate moments between himself and Millie. Despite all the times and ways his father had called him useless and stupid, it certainly hadn't taken him long to find out what it was.

It was something called a Recollector. They came in varying sizes, varying strengths, and had slight differences in how they worked based upon design. But the overall purpose of the crystal was the same: to collect and store the memories of the person to whom it was attuned.

The attuning was really just a process of carving in the proper runes and the intended target's name, then keeping it near the target for a week. It wouldn't have been difficult for his father to ensure that it was attuned to him. He was never allowed to leave the house.

He had no idea how long his father had it. He didn't want to go back and see everything his father had spied on. He wasn't sure he would be able to keep himself together if he found out.

"I'm not sure exactly how he organized things in here," Harlen said, letting go of Millie and stooping down to pick up the broken bits of crystal.

There was a waste bin near the door that he dropped them into, along with the heavy, palm-sized metal cradle that thumped to the bottom. "Feel free to rummage around anywhere, I suppose. I don't even know what's in here."

"Do you mind if I start with a fire if we're going to be here for a while?" she asked, pointing to the fireplace full of gray ashes. She looked the way he was used to feeling when he walked through the doors of his father's office: as if she felt she was an intruder who wasn't sure what she should touch.

Harlen offered a smile and said, "You know, despite what Berkley thinks, it is your house too."

It succeeded in getting a laugh from her. Her posture eased as she crouched in front of the fireplace, her new blue dress pooling around her.

He had taken the liberty of getting her several sets of warmer clothes and had managed to find this one with white lace flowers around the hem of the skirt. He thought they looked like seafoam as she formed a nest of the material around herself and set to work.

He brushed his hands off on the front of his jacket, looking at the floor to ceiling bookshelves lined neatly with heavy volumes. The shining display cases were filled with trinkets and trophies of family members long gone, who he knew his father couldn't have ever met.

It gave the place the feeling of a museum without any of the curious comforts of a real museum to dull the sharp edges of distant history staring at him from behind polished glass. Relics of what their family had represented in the distant past watching from all sides. The weight of a great legacy he had never upheld.

It was suffocating. He wondered if deciding not to simply seal the door of the office had been a mistake.

It reminded him of Adrian Vostesk's journal. That ragged volume jammed into the lowest shelf in the library. It was impossible to count the number of times he had read it over the years, memorizing the words of the only person in their great family who had understood him.

"May you feel the crushing weight of the impossible expectation you have placed on me. I hope to live to see you fall from the pedestals you've placed yourself upon and break your backs. Then when I tell you to run, will you understand what you, you giants of history, have asked of me."

Harlen had always wondered if it was true that Adrian had somehow placed a curse on the family. If he'd discovered his magic or if spite alone had been enough to pull the magic from the generations to come. He also wondered, looking around at the collection of artifacts boasting power and control, if they hadn't deserved it.

"It's all rather vapid, isn't it?" Harlen asked.

"I was hoping you would say it, so I didn't have to," Millie said, giving him one of her impish looks over her shoulder.

Encouraged, relieved from the slow-building tension in his throat, he continued and said what he would never have dared otherwise. "He never even met these people. He had no idea who they were. They could have been. . .they could have been assholes who just managed to accomplish something worth remembering. They probably were if the only one of them who ever kept a journal is to be trusted!"

His hands were shaking as he spoke. He fixed his eyes on one of the silver statues depicting a man holding a spellbook high in one hand, a swirl of ice in the other. "What's the point of all this? Is this really what he put us through hell for? So I could be this?"

He hadn't realized how bitter his voice had become until he spoke the last words and could practically taste them on his tongue. He swallowed and stopped, unsure of what he would say if he continued.

He could feel Millie watching him and wondered if he had upset or concerned her, but before his fingers could even touch the cufflink at his wrist, she said, "You could break it, you know. If you wanted."

He blinked at her. She raised her eyebrows and shrugged. "I'm just saying. I bet if you threw it out that one window looking over the street, it would break. Just make sure nobody's coming, so you don't give them a concussion with one of your ancestors."

Harlen gave a nervous laugh. "No. I can't. I—"

Except he could. He could if he wanted.

He reached out and lifted it off the shelf. It was far lighter than he expected as he turned it over in his hands. His father would have smacked him senseless for touching it, and there was liberation in just being able to turn it. To really look at it. To know that he could do whatever he wanted with it.

He would be lying if he said he didn't give Millie's suggestion serious consideration. But in the end, rather than throw it out the window, he set it down on the desk. It was a nice art piece regardless of what it had been made for. Besides, it looked better there anyway. When he voiced these thoughts to Millie, she gave him an approving nod.

"As someone who has excellent taste, I'm inclined to agree with you," she said, standing up and brushing off the front of her dress. The fireplace was smoking and crackling to life, filling the air with the pleasant aroma of burning wood.

CHAPTER 39

    They set to work sorting through the piles and piles of documents, keeping an eye out for any mentions of the school. Millie started in one of the cabinets in the far corner, and Harlen set to work at the desk. He began by going through the various drawers and cabinets and found, to his surprise, that his father was rather disorganized. There were balled bits of paper; little notes scribbled here and there that he couldn't decipher the meaning of to save his life, and according to the dates he could find, nothing seemed to be in order.

    He did find the book of accounts. He flipped through it and located the record of the odd donations to the school. They went back even before his and Tansey's birth and continued right up until the end.

    He made a note of circling them and sticking a bit of paper in the book to mark them and continued to go through what he was sure was years and years of paperwork until Millie set something down on the desk next to him.

    "I feel like this belongs to you."

    It took Harlen a moment of staring at the blue-painted wooden whale bearing the name "Marty" crudely written on the side in black before he recognized it and laughed.

    "Where did you find this?" he picked it up while Millie grinned ear to ear, still holding in one hand a small mobile covered in seashells that clinked together softly.

    "That cabinet way back in the corner under some boxes of old clothes. He really kept everything in here."

    Harlen was surprised that the old toy was still intact after all these years. He turned in the chair to better face Millie and the box she had unearthed and said, "I used to take him in the bath all the time. I'm amazed the water didn't ruin him."

    "You must have been an adorable little boy," she teased. "I, on the other hand, was an absolute terror."

    "I'm sure you weren't nearly that bad."

    He tried to imagine what Millie would have looked like so tiny, but he just couldn't picture it. She had told him before about what she had been like as a little girl: wild and covered in dirt as often as she could be. He always thought it sounded wonderful. He couldn't remember his childhood in a particularly fond way, but there were small bright things he would gladly share with her if she asked.

Millie set down the mobile carefully and moved to sit on the desk beside him. She picked the painted whale back up and examined it. Her gray eyes flicked up towards him, glittering. "Did you name him?"

Harlen laughed. "Yes. Yes, I did. It was also my idea to paint it on him," he said, very pleased with how that made her smile. "I think my logic was that if I did that, he wouldn't forget what he was called."

"Sound reasoning," she said, setting it back down on the desk between them.

She looked at it for a moment, her head cocked to the side, her dark hair tumbling over her shoulder. He watched her face. Lit from the front by the hall's gray light, her eyes were clear as the sea. From behind, the fire turned her hair into a halo of rich mahogany. A faint, thoughtful smile touched the edges of her lips, and her brows drew together in thought, leaving a small crease between them. She was the most beautiful person he had ever seen.

"Should we keep it out, do you think?" she asked, "I'd hate to bury him again. Seems unfair when we might need him at some point."

The weight of her statement would have missed him entirely if it hadn't been for the way she studied his face as she said it. The intensity in her gaze asked what she didn't voice aloud: would they need a child's toy at some point?

He hadn't given it much thought. Before his father's passing, they had both been in agreement that they didn't want children where his father—where Vostesk Senior—could get his hands on them. Harlen had never wanted any child to be put through what he had experienced. Now that Vostesk Senior was gone, there was that question that had been persistent in his absence: what now?

A child. His and Millie's. What would that even be like? Growing up in this house had been a nightmare, but since Vostesk Senior had been gone, the place felt lighter.

He and Millie came and went as they pleased. They brought tea into the bedroom and library, opened the dark curtains, and Millie had been placing jars of what flowers she could find everywhere. They hung robes over chairs and left things in odd places. In particular, he left books on every possible surface, marked with odd papers instead of carefully placing silk ribbons in them and returning them to their shelves.

Millie had commented that it actually looked like a house now, and he was inclined to agree. It was clean, but a comfortable disorder made it look like people lived in it rather than every room looking like a polished set piece.

He was sure it would be a long while before he felt truly at ease. He still hadn't gone down to the basement. Not even to throw everything in it away. To destroy that awful room. The door in the kitchen remained locked, the key on his desk in the bedroom.

Millie had her curiosities about the place but had left it up to him to decide when he wanted to use the key. She had made it very clear that if it were something he wanted to do alone, she would let him, and he trusted her enough to leave it in the open.

He had spent many mornings staring at it, feeling his stomach turn over and over in uneasy knots. He would debate if that day would be the one when he finally descended back into that dark room, all at once feeling the press of cold walls and the tightness of leather around his wrists. Then Millie would paw at him sleepily because he had rolled away too far from her, and he returned gladly to the warm, sunlit present.

That was just it. In the present, in the life that was beginning to emerge around him, he didn't feel trapped or afraid. He was glad to be where he was. Maybe that was enough.

He worried that he might never be free from the past entirely, but perhaps he didn't have to be. Maybe it was alright to look back and see darkness when the way ahead was so bright.

Maybe this could be a good place. A safe place. For a family who truly was happy.

"I'll take that look as a good sign," Millie said, chuckling. He hadn't realized he was smiling.

He grinned wider and looked down at the little wooden toy on the desk. "Well, I feel like a bit more of an advisor on the subject."

He looked back up at her and sat closer to the edge of the chair. With her on the desk, he was at her eye level. He leaned close, into the soft warmth of the moment, the fire crackling and filling the room with the smell of cedar. He spoke with all the care in his heart and found her hand with his as he said, "What is your desire?"

"Desire?" she asked, quirking one eyebrow, her impish little grin pressing a dimple into her cheek. "That's a bit forward."

Her fingers toyed with his on the desk, but her eyes remained on his. Her voice matched the low tenor of his own. He could hear the catch in her breath as she spoke, and his skin shivered at the intimacy of the moment. A moment that was entirely their own with that crystal laying in pieces at the bottom of the waste bin.

"I may be biased," she said. "But I do like the idea of a bigger family. Bigger than us, I mean. Not that I don't enjoy us, but—"

She flushed as she spoke, and Harlen couldn't help but grin. "Did I actually manage to fluster you? That's rare."

She shot him a half-hearted glare that didn't work well when she was fighting back a smile. "Shush. I have a reputation."

He stood up just to be able to stand in front of her, to cup her blushing face in both hands, and place a kiss on her forehead while she grumbled at him.

"There is one thing, though," she said when she had calmed herself, and he had let go of her face with a bit of reluctance. "If we do, when we do, I would like to. . ."

She trailed off and was pulling at a loose thread in the hem of her dress. One of the white flowers. Harlen placed his hand over hers to still her fingers, just as she did when he started twisting his cufflink.

"I want to have them at home," she said in a rush. "I know it's silly, but I want my mother and my sisters to be there. I've seen childbirth. And. . .I don't. . .want to do that alone." She frowned. "It's a stupid thing to worry about before anything's even happened, isn't it?"

"You wouldn't be alone," Harlen gripped her hand tighter, trying to reassure her. He knew nothing about childbirth, but he did know about fear. And there was a genuine tremble of fear in her voice despite her attempt at a casual laugh. "But yes. I promise. I'll take you there. If and when."

She studied him again and must have understood he was telling the truth. Her laugh then was real, relieved, and she shook her head. Again flustered. "Well, you must think I'm a bit paranoid myself now, don't you?"

"Not at all," he said, brushing her hair back from her face to hopefully draw her eyes back to his while she studied the ground between them.

"Well, there's no telling if they would even let us come," she joked, trying to regain her composure. "They haven't answered any of my letters, so I imagine they must be pretty upset it took me so long to write in the first place. They might not even want to see me."

Harlen blinked. "They haven't written back?"

That was the first he heard of it. He had been slipping out of the house with her to the post office for several months. He had agreed with her suspicions that his father was hiding her family's replies or discarding them, but since he had been gone, she'd written home several times.

He assumed she was getting letters back. She hadn't said anything about it, but he had supposed she simply didn't feel the need to tell him everything said between herself and her family. Or perhaps what they were saying to each other was too personal. He hadn't imagined she was writing as often as she was and hearing nothing.

She shrugged, again, the furrowing of her brows belying her casual response. "Letters get lost sometimes. Or maybe they're making me wait because I took so long to say anything those first months."

He said nothing for a moment. Millie kicked her feet where they didn't quite touch the floor and looked down at their joined hands.

"Maybe," he said, another realization dawning on him. "We should go there in person. See what's taking so long."

Her eyes found his immediately. "Are you being serious?"

He could take her there. No rule stated he had to stay here at this house all the time. Or, rather, there wasn't anymore. "Do you think Jacques would object to watching the place for a few weeks?"

The last he said as a joke to make her smile again. He couldn't tell if it worked or not because the next thing he knew, Millie had left the desk and threw herself into his arms. She was kissing him with a vigor that was unexpected but entirely welcome.

He hurried to get a good grip on her so that they didn't both fall as he stumbled back, one arm around her waist and the other up her back, his hand in her hair. He pulled her closer and kissed her, surprised and dizzy, still stepping backward until his back hit the cabinet Millie had left open.

He heard several things fall from the higher shelves and began to apologize but realized he couldn't be heard over Millie's laughing that had started as soon as they hit the door. His apology ended in a fit of giggles, and he leaned his head back against the door. Happy.

"Did I ruin the moment?" he asked.

"I feel like that added to it," she said before stepping back and bending to look at what they had disturbed. Dust had rained down on both of them, and everything that had fallen was covered in a thin gray film. Several dust bunnies were clinging to Millie's hair as she picked up something round and white.

"Well, this is ghoulish. What is it?"

He jumped as she turned it towards him, and he saw what appeared to be a face. A mask. A round white mask with carefully carved lips and nose with two black holes for the eyes.

"I don't know," he said, stepping closer to get a better look. "I've never seen that before."

Maybe it was a trophy? There was no strap or wire to hold to a person's face, so he could only assume it wasn't meant to be worn. He really couldn't picture his father wearing something like that anyway. His father was not one for theatrics, so even if it were a family heirloom of some kind, he couldn't imagine him putting it on. But, if that was the case, why hadn't he displayed it like everything else? Why was it in the closet with things like his old toys?

Millie turned it over in her hands, and they both glanced at each other at the same time. On the inside of the mask, where the forehead would be, a butterfly was carved into the ceramic. The same butterfly that had been carved on the log they found in the cemetery.

"That's strange," Millie said, and Harlen nodded. "You remember what Jacques said this was. Was your father religious?"

"No," Harlen confessed. "Not that I know of. Not that he was open about anything. For all I know, he could have been."

"Your mother is. Maybe that's why she's so scared of your father's friends," Millie suggested. "Understandably so if she knows they're bringing things into the house that's supposed to call—you know," she said, carefully treading around the phrase "death goddess."

He understood why. The room already felt as though all the heat had been sucked out of it. He felt like asking that aloud would only make it all the more unsettling.

Harlen wasn't sure his father was the religious type. But, then again, Vostesk Senior had done a lot he hadn't thought him capable of. It wasn't beyond belief. He would put nothing beyond that man ever again.

"It could be," Harlen said. "I know the chairman planned on coming over again sometime this week. I could ask. Well, not directly, I'm sure. But maybe if I bring it up, he'll say something."

Berkley did like to talk.

Millie nodded, and the two of them continued to stare at the butterfly. Harlen wasn't sure if he could feel eyes on him or not, but he certainly felt unsettled. When he suggested that they bury it, Millie did not object.

Harlen was certain the strange cold feeling didn't pass until they finished hiding it in the dirt of the garden.

CHAPTER 40

The remainder of the week before Berkley's return visit was spent in relative peace. Millie wrote to her family about the possibility of visiting soon, sure that, of all things, it would elicit a reply. She and Harlen also spent a good deal of time sorting through his father's papers and exploring the city in turns.

Both of them were getting to see it for the first time. They even made it down to the ocean, which Harlen seemed more excited for than her. He didn't even seem to mind the strange looks the well-dressed merchants at their shopfronts gave them as they made their way down from the pier to the pale gray sand.

She shouldn't have been surprised that even the sand and ocean here were in shades of gray. But there was something moodily beautiful about the endless, swirling expanse of white-capped, nearly black water and the rolling gray clouds that leaned down to meet it in the far distance. She had never seen so much water or felt such strong, salty wind in all her life. More than once, she was nearly blown entirely over into the sea.

She hadn't minded that, though, or the freezing foam that clung to her legs while she and Harlen made their way up and down the shoreline, sometimes walking, sometimes running and laughing like excited children. It was fun. Truly fun. The first she'd had in far too long.

She even managed to find some scraps of color that she hoarded. Harlen had helped her carry the armload of shells she found: a rainbow of pinks, blues, and reds against all the gray. She told him she had half a mind to fill the house with them, and he had said that in that case, they should bring a wagon to put them all in next time. She was mostly sure he meant it as a joke but knew if she asked him, he would do it.

He seemed lighter these days. The more time passed, and the longer he was out from under Vostesk Senior, the brighter his eyes got. His voice had grown from the whisper it had been to something far more solid, and his laugh didn't sound like pained wheezing anymore. It was full, and it shook his shoulders and made him rub his eyes beneath his glasses.

He certainly smiled more. He even stood straighter. He was coming into his own, and the intensity of it seemed to overwhelm him sometimes. There were occasions when he was laughing so hard he couldn't stop until there were tears in his eyes, and when he would kiss her sometimes, it was with such passion and declarations of love that his hands would shake.

He had asked her if he was doing too much with all these things that were flooding into him. Things he had never really been allowed to feel, or at least feel in their entirety without the fear of some kind of repercussion.

The strength of his own emotion worried him, but she had assured him that he would adjust to it. That he was one of the smartest people she knew, and she trusted him not to take anything too far. She had also said that if he did take anything too far, she could always just tell him he was being an ass, which made him laugh, but he had made her promise she would do just that if it ever came down to it.

She felt happier too. She wasn't sure if she was just finally adjusting to the seaside or if it was the feeling that she was no longer trapped that made the rainy sky seem less oppressive. She had come to enjoy falling asleep to the sound of it gently tapping the windows and had developed a new love for the feeling and taste of warm drinks. Something as simple as hot cocoa was much better when it was cupped in her hands on a chilly day.

She had also developed a fondness for the very forward white and gray birds that would walk right up to her if she offered them any sort of food. They squawked constantly and swooped down at people's hats and were quite fun to watch.

She also had her suspicions that her happiness had something to do with the fact that she was very much in love with the tall, skinny man with thick glasses and lovely dark eyes she'd married.

When the day finally came for Berkley's visit, she was admittedly a bit disappointed. They had been spending evenings with Jacques either at various places around town that sold excellent greasy food or huddled around the kitchen table talking, joking, and still desperately trying to teach Harlen how to play cards.

The prospect of another formal dinner with a man who had implied she wasn't competent enough to be trusted with account books did not appeal to her in any way, shape, or form.

She was glad she decided to opt out of the meeting. Partially glad. Part of her wanted to show up just to spite him. The thought of him imagining she had learned her place, so to speak, annoyed her.

It must have shown, too, because as she and Harlen were getting ready for his visit, he spoke up about it. "You know you really don't have to stay up here," he said.

He was standing next to the wardrobe in his gray dressing robe that she, for once, had not stolen. She was sitting at the desk, wrapped in a towel, and trying to work a brush through her wet, tangled hair.

"I'm sure he would talk about anything if we could just get him chatting. And you're better at small talk than I am."

"Maybe," she said. "But I want you to get some real answers. And if he's not even going to let me see a few numbers, I doubt he would talk about religious practices in front of me." As much as she resented the idea, she had been the one to insist on it.

She heard rather than saw Harlen walk up next to her and paused what she was doing as she felt his hands touch her shoulders. She leaned back and looked up at him, those rough spots on his thumb and first finger brushing her neck.

A small smile touched his lips as her head thudded into his chest, but his tone was somber when he said, "You know you can still come if you want."

She couldn't resist grinning at him. "You are allowed to say that you'll miss my wonderful company."

That did earn a full smile from him, complete with a softening of his eyes. "I thought that went without saying."

There was one more reason she wanted to stay upstairs. They were having over one of his father's friends, and so far, Pearl's track record with that had not been the best. Millie wanted to keep an eye on her, no matter how she might feel about Pearl. She couldn't just leave her to be confused and terrified. Fitting as it might be for what she had left her son to,

Millie knew she wouldn't be able to live with herself if she left Pearl to the same fate.

Harlen dressed in a dark suit and a red tie that was much better fitting than what he usually wore. She watched him in the mirror and thought he didn't look quite as gaunt as when they first met. When he shrugged on his shirt, she saw less of the bones of his shoulders and spine. His hair was getting longer, too, she noticed. It was down just past his shoulders.

He straightened the jacket and smoothed down the tie meticulously, muttering something to himself or perhaps just holding a conversation with his thoughts. When he glanced up and saw her watching him in the mirror and his ears flushed. "What?"

"Red is a nice color on you," she said, eyeing the tie. It did suit his eyes. The light dusting of it across his face didn't hurt either.

"I'll have to wear it more often," he said, giving her one last smile.

Millie finished raking through her hair and tied it back from her face when he shut the door. She dressed in her lavender gown and a pair of Harlen's thick gray socks that were far too big but were an excellent barrier between herself and the chilly floor as she made her way out of the bedroom and towards the office.

Downstairs, she could hear the sounds of the door opening. The chairman's enthusiastic voice floated up to her, as well as a deep voice she didn't recognize.

"I do hope you don't mind, my dear boy, but I've brought along another member of the board! I think it might be good for you to get acquainted, and Ashby here couldn't wait to meet you in person!"

"Pleasure," the man who must have been Ashby said. Millie was sure she had never heard anyone sound less pleased in their entire lives.

She was tempted to eavesdrop further, but they were moving into the other room, and she had matters of her own to attend to. She carefully looked back down the hall to see if Pearl poked her head out of her room, but if she had heard their guests, she gave no indication.

Millie still left the door to the office open as she went inside. Just in case.

The office was in quite a state of disarray. They had been slowly sorting through everything to search for information and put it in an order that would be useful as they took over running the house. For all of Vostesk Senior's primping and blustering, he had been a horrifically disorganized man.

She planned to try and make a bit more headway in the stacks, but as she sat down at the desk, the painted toy whale caught her eye. They were using it to weigh down the tallest stack of paper, and its smiling face and big black eyes looked down at her while she sank into the deep, upholstered chair.

It was in excellent condition. Aside from the writing, it looked practically new. No chipped paint, no scuffs from being knocked around on the floor. It looked like Harlen had barely touched it. Or, more likely, had hardly been allowed to be touched.

There was something quite sad about coming in and seeing it there, perfectly painted, and she very quietly promised it when nobody else was around to overhear that someday it would have someone to scuff it up properly. It was a silly thing to do, but it made her feel better.

She sat in the chair and picked up Vostesk Senior's heavy cane. The other day, she had spent some time taking in the elaborate detail that had gone into carving the ivory; curling waves and tiny fish with sharp fins. Someone had even gone so far as to etch individual teeth into the mouth of a small shark.

It was heavy artwork. Millie nearly dropped it the first time she picked it up. It didn't seem like it would be useful at all for anyone who actually needed a cane to walk.

Harlen had explained that it hadn't been made as a walking cane. It was a regulator of sorts, like a wand or a staff. It had been made for one of their ancestors to help channel his magic.

According to him, magic casters with incredibly powerful, natural magic require something to help when they want to use more powerful spells. She didn't understand all of what was said, but the general idea was that even for those born adept with magic, it can still be taxing on the body to use it. It can be dangerous to use a great deal of powerful magic without having something to provide a bit of a regulator for it, which was what the cane was for. It placed a cap on the magic before it could burn out its wielder.

It hadn't been needed in several generations, but it was said that it had been used long enough that it had developed magical properties of its own. Of course, that was just a rumor within the family. Harlen said he had never seen anything magical about it, and she certainly didn't see it.

She thought it was a bit tacky, to be honest. But it was heavy enough to be rather satisfying to smack against her palm while she sat behind the desk, which she did as she looked over one of the open records books in front of her and tried to make sense of Vostesk Senior's awful handwriting. Until she heard something small that sounded like glass hit the wooden floor and roll.

Millie glanced down at the floor and saw nothing, then looked at the cane in her hands and swore under her breath. The shark's head was missing. Evidently, she'd managed to break it off with the light tapping of her hand. Some heirloom.

She got down and searched along the floor until eventually, she saw the bright white of the shark's face in the light of the dim room where it had rolled to a stop beside one of the many boxes they had pulled out and emptied. She reached for it and paused in confusion when it felt longer than expected. There was the shark's head. And what felt like some kind of tube behind it. About as long as her pinky.

She picked it up and saw that there was, in fact, a tube behind the head—a glass vial filled with a dark liquid, stoppered by the shark.

She held it up to the light from the single lamp she had lit on the desk and saw that, no, apparently, she hadn't broken it. The edge around the shark's head looked perfectly smooth. When she made her way back over to the desk and picked up the cane, she realized the place where the shark had been left behind a perfectly round hole. This was supposed to come off.

Immediately, she felt a sinking in her stomach along with a prickle of curiosity. What was it?

She stood for a moment, holding the vial in her hands, then very carefully unscrewed the shark's head from the top. It was only about half full, but she knew better than to stick her face over it to smell it or to try and taste it. Instead, she held it away from her face and waved some of the air towards her. She recognized the scent of unripened tomatoes instantly.

Nightshade. There was a stubborn patch of it that used to grow beside the garden fountain back home that always seemed to come back no matter how many times it was pulled out from between the paving stones.

She had been warned countless times not to touch it, but there had been times when she had stepped on it when trying to climb up onto the fountain itself or when hopping down from the ledge. Every time she crushed the little sprig of berries, it smelled very distinctly like unripened tomatoes. The only difference was that the smell was more pungent coming from the small vial. What on earth was this for?

And more importantly, why was it half empty?

CHAPTER 41

Harlen stood beside the fireplace in the dining room, one arm propped on the mantel, staring into the flames that were radiating just enough warmth to take away the sharp edge of the night's chill. He held his hardly touched drink in one hand, and out of the corner of his eye, he watched the two other men who had come into the house. Chairman Berkley had arrived right on time with another of the school's professors and his father's friends.

He had long black hair that lay in a lank tangle down his back and a long, pointed face. Harlen had always thought he looked rather wolf-like. It was something about his mean, dark eyes and the way his lips seemed to curl into a snarl naturally. His name was Tevron Ashby.

He was nodding along to a conversation that Berkley was holding mostly by himself; his eyes fixed pointedly on Harlen's back.

Harlen kept his grip on the glass tight, and his jaw clenched. Being in the room with those two, who used to sit and watch his father berate him, was intimidating, to say the least. He wished not for the first time that Millie had decided to join them so that he didn't have to bear the weight of their strange new affability alone.

They weren't friendly, but he found their politeness towards him unnerving. He had to keep reminding himself that, technically, he was on equal ground with them now, and they probably saw it as a simple social necessity.

That didn't stop the rapid beating of his heart, but he was determined to present a brave face. For Millie's sake, at the very least, he could pretend to be brave until he could muster up the courage to do it for himself.

"Anyway, I do think that Carver's boy has some promise to him. He's already beginning to show signs of magical inclination! And at only eighteen months!" Chairman Berkley said.

Ashby offered another curt nod and went back to sipping the wine in his hand.

The chairman frowned, then turned his attention towards Harlen. "Don't you agree, Harlen?"

He looked back at the two men who were milling around the room. None of them had sat at the dining table yet, which Harlen had no complaint about. He hadn't been able to muster up an appetite.

"Yes," he said, unable to muster a smile. "That does sound fortunate."

"Well, their family's talents aren't spectacular," the chairman went on, swirling his third glass of wine. His face was flushed behind his neatly curled mustache. "But if he's raised properly, he should be able to expand his talents, particularly with the aptitude he's showing."

"He isn't even two," Ashby cut in with his deep, monotone voice. "One can hardly tell that young."

The chairman scoffed. "Have you no optimism?"

"I have realism," Ashby said.

Again, Berkley scoffed and turned back towards Harlen. He smiled, and Harlen did his best to return it with a faint twitch of the lips before asking, "This is all wonderful. But I believe you said you were coming by to discuss something with me?"

"Ah! Yes, yes."

The chairman moved to one of the dining chairs to sit, pausing momentarily before pulling it out and glancing up at Harlen before doing so. Harlen looked at him, confused for a moment, before realizing he was asking for permission to sit.

"Please. Please sit," Harlen said quickly, gesturing to the table and moving to take his seat at the head of the table.

It felt strange, settling into the large chair that his father had occupied. The back and arms were carved with images of waves and glaciers, and he felt as if he were settling into a place entirely too visible as the other two men took their seats on opposite sides of the table.

Berkley looked up at him and folded his hands. "Well, Harlen—or shall I say Lord Vostesk now?"

Harlen felt his stomach clench and a shiver ran down the back of his neck. Would he have to go by that? "Just Harlen. Please."

"Very well," the chairman continued cheerfully. "Harlen. Seeing as you're now head of the Vostesk house, we came to inform you about our society. It is a small club of sorts for the nobles of Wakefield, composed of myself, Professor Ashby here, and others of noble birth and prominent magical talent. Your father was a very active participant, you see, and we thought it only right to ask you to step in."

Harlen looked down the table at Berkley. As far as he knew, nobody knew about his new magical talents other than Millie. He briefly considered mentioning it, but something inside himself made him hold back. "Thank you. But I hardly see how I'd be of any use in such an organization."

Ashby gave Berkley a very smug look, and Harlen wondered how much they'd talked about what his response would be before they arrived. Berkley seemed undeterred.

"It isn't simply a place for those of magical talent. It's an organization dedicated to the study, preservation, and continuation of magic. From what I understand, you did have quite the talent for memorization and documentation. Which is of course of utmost importance," he said, giving Ashby a sharp look over the table. "Isn't that correct?"

"I suppose everyone needs a record keeper," Ashby grumbled. The chairman glared at him.

"You would be given access to things not available to the general public. Ancient books, our personal libraries, items imbued with magic that are kept for study. I've been an average magical talent myself, but even so, I spend most of my time in the archives." The chairman's face had flushed more, but this time with excitement as he explained himself.

Harlen had to admit; it did sound fascinating. He had never heard of this before, but it didn't surprise him that his father wouldn't have discussed such things with him. He would have thought it a waste, probably. But curiosity wasn't enough to get him to throw away caution. Not when he had spent most of his life on edge. And with how secretive the chairman had been about this the other day, his sudden eagerness was more than enough to make him suspicious.

"That sounds interesting. But I must ask, what exactly would this entail?" Harlen asked, letting just the smallest hint of his suspicion color his words. Ashby said nothing, but again Berkley was undeterred and spoke just as cheerfully as before.

"I'm glad you asked. Our other guest, who I hope you don't mind we invited along, should be here shortly and he can explain everything—Corrik Magister. Have you ever heard of him?"

Harlen searched back through his memory, trying to recall if his father had ever introduced such a man or mentioned him in passing, but nothing came to mind. He shook his head.

"I'm not entirely surprised. He travels quite a bit, you see—we have several guilds across the country, and he is the sole owner of all of them. Hard to believe he started so humbly. His father owned a funeral home up in Ruasha. He was never wealthy, but his magical talents are extraordinary. He worked his way into such a prominent position he now gets to mingle with some of the most powerful men in the world."

The chairman prattled on and on about Corrik's many achievements while Ashby poured his second wine, and Harlen listened with feigned interest. Thankfully, before too long, there was a knock on the door. The sound stilled both Berkley and Ashby immediately, and all conversation came to a sudden halt. A log popped in the fireplace.

"That must be him," the chairman said, turning towards the door. He moved to stand, but Harlen managed to get out of his chair first.

"I'll get it," he said with a small twitch of the lips that could pass for a polite smile. The chairman thanked him, and Harlen made his way towards the door, his anxiousness building as he moved towards it.

He used the chance to step out of the room with the two men as an opportunity to take a deep breath and blow it out, hoping to expel some of the inexplicable nerves building inside of him as he pulled the great oak doors open.

Outside in the drizzling rain was not what Harlen had expected. He'd imagined some grandly dressed man with a noble air about him based on Berkley's description. The man at the door was rather tall and appeared to be built strongly, but he was dressed very plainly in pants, boots, and a simple shirt, all in varying shades of brown. The brightest color he wore was a red sash around his waist.

He was clean-shaven with dark hair that seemed like it had been left to grow out for a while, tied back neatly into a short ponytail with a few bits hanging out here and there. He had a broad, warm smile and overall had a far more relaxed posture than Harlen expected. The most striking thing about him was his eyes; they were an intense, summer-sky blue and glimmered with a bright intelligence as he turned his head and smiled.

"Greetings. You must be Harlen." He possessed an accent Harlen couldn't quite identify that made all his words sound smooth and rounded.

He extended one hand, and Harlen took it. His grip was firm, and his fingers were calloused. "It's a pleasure to meet you. I'm Corrik Magister. But, please, spare the formality. Corrik suits me just fine."

"It's—it's good to meet you too," Harlen said and gestured for him to come inside.

Corrik stepped in and took a look around, his bright eyes moving over the main entrance, the staircase, and the painting staring down at them from the top of it.

"It's quite lovely here," he said, then pointed up at the portrait. "I suppose you'll be needing to replace that soon."

"Oh." Harlen hadn't thought about it. The painting had been there as long as he could remember.

"There's no rush, of course," Corrik said quickly. His voice was a warm, somewhat rough one that was a pleasant contrast to the clipped, sharp tones he was used to hearing from most of his father's friends. "Just thought that it might be nice to have something a bit happier to look at. I told your father everyone in that painting looked like they were about to strain something trying to look so formal." He chuckled. "Besides, a new start can be good."

Harlen nodded, unsure of what to say. He wasn't quite sure what to make of the man.

"I mean to ask as well before we get into formal matters: it has been a while since my last encounter with your father. I hope you don't think this too personal, but how is your mother doing?"

Harlen blinked and struggled to find words. Nobody had ever asked about his mother. "She, um, she's alright."

Corrik didn't stop smiling. It just dropped to one that was sympathetic and small rather than wide and bright.

Corrik placed a hand on Harlen's shoulder, which made him jump, but his grip was light. "I'm sorry. The portrait reminded me of her—but I should know to mind my manners. And perhaps it's none of my business."

"No, no, it's alright," Harlen said. Why was he apologizing? He'd never had any of his father's friends apologize to him. "She's fine. My wife and I have been taking care of her."

"Oh, yes! You were married just recently, weren't you?" Corrik's smile grew wide and bright again. His bright blue eyes sparkled. "My congratulations. Where is the lady of the house?"

"She's not feeling well," Harlen said quickly. He wasn't going to subject her to an evening of being condescended to by Berkley and Ashby.

Corrik looked at him for a moment, appraising, then nodded. "Of course. Another time, then. Shall we?"

Harlen led him into the main dining room, feeling disoriented. The chairman seemed thrilled to see him, and even Ashby cracked a smile and managed an almost pleasant greeting.

Corrik sat down at the lower end of the table. As the meal began, he took up the conversation that the chairman had been holding mostly by himself and slowly spread it to include everyone by asking both Professor Ashby and Harlen several questions to draw them in.

"Yes, yes. . .I was telling them all about your marvelous accomplishments," the chairman said once he'd polished off his fourth glass of wine. Corrik smiled and slid a glass of water towards him.

"I'd hardly call it marvelous," he said in his warm, scratchy voice. "I only try to make the best of my circumstances, and it has opened many opportunities for me. Anyone willing to take the necessary risks and do the necessary work can accomplish great things. It's all about determination. And, of course, having a willing mind." He looked over at Harlen and raised his wine glass in a shrug. "Then, anything is possible."

"He's far too humble," Berkley slurred.

"And you," Corrik said with an almost boyish grin. "Are far too drunk to be advising me. No offense, my friend."

Professor Ashby looked over at Chairman Berkley and sighed. "This is why we don't serve alcohol at formal functions until after the meetings are over."

"It may be a bit more fun if we did, though. Could you imagine?" Corrik said, and again Harlen saw Ashby crack a rare smile. "It's alright, though; we aren't going to discuss anything too dreadfully serious tonight. It's not good to make a first introduction weighed down with heavy matters."

Harlen nodded along with Ashby, though he noticed that much like himself, Corrik had hardly touched his drink. He sat casually in his chair in contrast to Berkley and Ashby's rigid postures, but he gave the impression that he was more alert than either of them.

There was one other thing about him Harlen found remarkably strange. He wasn't sure if it was his nerves or a trick of the light, but while Corrik sat closest to the fire, it seemed as though he was cast almost entirely in shadow. Like the dark places in the room had crept up around him. The only brightness came from where he directly faced the fire, his strikingly bright eyes, and a little metal charm dangling off one side of the red sash that glimmered brightly as a diamond.

"What's that?" Harlen asked when there was a lull in the conversation, indicating the charm he couldn't quite see with genuine curiosity.

"Oh, this?" Corrik asked. He held it up to the lamplight, and Harlen felt his stomach flip. A butterfly. A swallowtail. That same crude symbol but this time cast in metal.

Harlen nodded. He did his best to appear only mildly interested and didn't want his voice to give him away. Because Ashby and Berkley had all at once stopped speaking and had fixed their eyes on him.

Corrik seemed amused by the tension. "I see my colleagues haven't told you that I'm a bit of a religious man," Corrik said, shifting in his chair.

It could have been the angle he was sitting at that made the effect so strange, but it was like the shadows shifted with him, sinking back so that he was almost entirely cast in the warm light of the fire. "It's quite alright, Berkley, don't look so stricken. I understand death is not a topic most people broach easily, especially considering the circumstances."

Corrik folded his hands on the table and turned toward Harlen, his smile apologetic. "In light of recent events, I wasn't sure if it was appropriate to mention it. But I'm a worshiper of the goddess."

"The goddess of death," Harlen supplied. Berkley and Ashby both looked uncomfortable.

Corrik nodded. "Yes. I know it sounds a bit morbid. But she has been very prevalent in my life. Her worship used to be quite common in my former profession. Not so much anymore, I'm afraid—people have gotten away from many of the old practices. In their place have become wary of what they do not understand. But most morticians and gravediggers and those that work close to the dead still know the stories."

Harlen wanted to push for more. Corrik's welcome expression invited him to ask as though he could sense his curiosity. But Berkley and Ashby were still staring, and caution pulled him back.

"That's fascinating," he said and left it at that.

Once the meal was over, Corrik stood and wandered around the room, taking in the paintings on the walls and carvings in the molding. Harlen caught himself watching him walk out of the corner of his eye and noticed the others were doing the same.

Something was fascinating about the way he moved. Harlen couldn't quite put his finger on what was strange about it; every step and gesture was just a bit too smooth. Like he wasn't so much walking as he was gliding. His footsteps hardly made any sound on the tile floor.

If he was aware of the attention he had drawn, he showed no sign of it. He acted as if he was utterly alone as he stopped in front of the grand piano that sat, polished to a glossy shine, against the far wall.

Harlen only noticed that everyone had gone silent when Corrik spoke. "Do you play?"

Again, Harlen was startled but this time managed not to fumble his reply. "No. My sister did."

Corrik gave him another sympathetic smile. Harlen felt both Berkley and Ashby's eyes snap back to him as soon as he mentioned Tansey—like the mere mention of her would spoil the calm air that had settled over the evening. Berkley probably remembered what had happened the last time her name had been mentioned over dinner.

"I met your sister briefly. She was a lovely girl. It was right in this room; I believe, while waiting for your father one evening. She was charming. A witty little thing." He smiled fondly, and Harlen felt his throat tighten. Even his father hadn't had such softness in his voice on the few occasions he'd mentioned her.

"Would it be too much to ask that I play it? I would hate to spoil a memory."

"Not at all," Harlen said, hoping his voice didn't sound too choked. The chairman and Ashby didn't seem to notice, but Corrik kept looking at him and nodded solemnly. A quiet thank you, acknowledging what he was feeling.

Corrik sat down at the piano and began to play. The notes were simple at first and very rough. Then gradually, they grew into something more complex. His calloused hands drew beautiful sounds from the piano that hadn't been touched in years. The tune was lovely but almost mournful. Harlen knew he was likely reading far too much into it, but he couldn't help but get the strong impression Corrik was playing it for the last person who had sat at the piano's bench.

When the last note hovered in the air, the chairman and Ashby gave a round of polite applause. Corrik glanced back at Harlen once again with a bright smile on his face and mist in his eyes, and Harlen barely bit back the urge to ask how he had known his sister so well. His curiosity was overwhelming, but there was something so pure about the moment that to spoil it with questions felt wrong. He hardly even wondered why his sister had never mentioned this man to him before.

When it came time to escort everyone to the door at the end of the evening, Harlen let the chairman and Ashby say their goodbyes and go to their waiting carriages. Once they'd pulled out of the drive into the chilly fog that had risen in the night and the street stood empty, Corrik approached him at the door.

"You don't have a ride?" Harlen asked.

Corrik clasped his hands behind his back and shook his head. "No. I prefer to walk. It clears the mind."

He moved to leave, and Harlen hovered in the entryway, biting his lip and drumming his fingers nervously on the door's frame before blurting out, "Thank you. For the music. I'm—I'm not sure anyone else my father knew ever said anything about it when she. . .well, once she was gone."

It was like the world had forgotten about her in her absence. Harlen never said so out loud though he thought about it often. He wasn't sure why he was saying it to a near stranger. Or why it felt so right to do so.

"I heard that the two of you were close. I cannot imagine how hard it must have been on you." He looked at him, considering whether or not to say more. "My father passed when I was sixteen. We were rather close as well. I'm not sure if anyone else can properly understand what that experience means until they feel it themselves. A woman at a funeral I arranged put it perfectly; "All the dead are ghosts to those who loved them.'."

Harlen nodded, feeling the presence of Tansey's stare from her portrait hanging above them all the more acutely. He didn't like comparing her to the dead, not with so much uncertainty, but the sentiment was similar enough.

"It was when I found the motivation to 'do great things' as Berkley put it." Corrik chuckled. "But really, I was simply trying to honor his memory. I thought he would want me to work hard, so I did. I still don't know if he is proud. I don't know if I ever will. But I like to think so."

"I wish I could do the same," Harlen said and again had no idea why he'd said it out loud. "I think all I really want is to make it so my family—all of them—can be proud of me."

As soon as the words were out of his mouth, he felt a spasm of fear and shame for admitting something so profoundly personal. But Corrik just offered another warm smile and placed a hand on his shoulder as he had earlier in the evening.

"I'm sure you will," he said with such conviction, staring into his eyes with such intensity that Harlen would have believed Corrik had read something written on his soul. Then he stepped back, wished him goodnight, and walked off into the fog.

Harlen felt shaken. So much so, he didn't even realize until he was climbing the stairs to go to bed that he didn't think to ask how he knew his sister.

CHAPTER 42

When Millie was very young, about twelve years old, her middlemost sister Lily had talked her into trying the bone collector ritual.

It was something their oldest sister Beatrice had told them about the night before under the light of candles, utilizing the little fire magic that she had to cast leaping shadows on the walls. Under the reddish glow, she told them about the looming figure that would stalk the fields, dressed in ragged white robes with stitched-together skin.

He had no face. No eyes, no nose. Just a mess of twisted flesh and a long, stretched mouth full of too many teeth. He glided silently through the woods and the fields at night, and if you listened, you could hear him twitching the long, long fingers on his hands as the bones beneath his skin clacked and ground against one another. Click. Click. Click.

As the story went, long ago, the bone collector had been an ordinary man who sought understanding. He wanted to understand people fully: to see their pasts and futures laid out before him and see how they fit into the tapestry of life.

Anyone who seeks to become an oracle, a true servant of the blind god Oculus who holds the strings of fate, must give up their own eyes in exchange. Everybody knows that much.

Some are born oracles: who come into the world blind and truly blessed—destined for great things. Some gain the gift later in life, losing their vision as the gift strengthens and their power takes hold.

There are others, of course, who seek the gift. It is said that anyone without the natural inclination who wishes to become an oracle must be willing to put out their own eyes for the right to even ask for such a thing.

Naturally, it is a fate few would throw themselves into willingly. But the bone collector did so without question. And he was brash enough to make his own specific request. He demanded an understanding of other persons in exchange for his vision.

Now Oculus, who saw the ebbs and flows of time, was going to deny him, or so the story went. The man had no respect, no understanding of what he asked. But another god had overheard his request and offered his solution. He was a trickster, and arrogant humans were a favorite of his. He suggested that man's request should be granted, but with specific stipulations.

The bone collector thought of nothing but his ambition. He did not even ask the price of the gift. And he no longer had eyes to see the broad smile on the face of the god that had been his mediator.

They granted his request. And as a gift for his ambition, the trickster had thrown in the benefit of a long, long life. Immortality: as long as the man continued to use the talent that had been so graciously given. He would be able to see the past and future of any creature living—if he sewed one of their bones beneath his skin.

The man was furious. He felt he had been cheated. But soon, curiosity and his lust for knowledge overwhelmed him. Drove him mad. He killed a boy in his village and sewed one of his teeth into the palm of his hand. And just as the god had said, he saw the boy's life and death laid out before him.

He was chased from his village. He was stabbed by the boy's father and limped into the woods to die, cursing the gods for twisting his request. But then he was reminded of the rule. So long as he made use of the gift, he would continue living.

He crawled deeper and deeper into the woods until he found a house where the owner took him in. For days, the farmer nursed him, but the man knew he would die if he didn't make use of his gift. He convinced the man that he could tell him the day and time of his own death and his farm's future if he would only give him one of his bones. And the farmer, being a desperate man with five children and an uncertain future, gave in to his request by cutting off his own finger.

Ever since that day, the bone collector has been wandering the earth as something no longer entirely human. He walks the seldom-tread roadways and the fields at night, waiting to be called by those who seek knowledge. Anyone can know their future if one will only be so kind as to give one of their bones in exchange.

Millie had lost the last of her baby teeth just the day before Lily had convinced her they should go out looking for the bone collector. At first, she had said no. She had hardly been able to sleep after Beatrice's story, and the sound of a tree branch tapping against her window had nearly scared her out of her skin. But curiosity eventually overwhelmed her as Lily prodded her with questions, saying that there had to be *something* she wanted to know.

At first, Millie had denied it for hours and hours. But there was one thing that kept creeping up in her mind.

Their grandmother had been sick for weeks. She lay in her bed, white as paper, and coughed splotches of red into the handkerchiefs she tried to hide beneath her pillow before any of them came in the room—as though they couldn't see the traces of it on her lips when she smiled at them.

Millie had been staying with her often, practicing her prayers to the goddess Shareen, asking her to make her better. She had been keeping watch over her like a hawk for weeks, and she wanted to know: would she ever have to watch someone die?

She had been the one to go to Lily's room after dark. She had knocked on her door with her tooth clutched tightly in one hand, and the two of them had bundled themselves up in blankets against the cold night air as they snuck out of the house, into the fields.

The air was filled with the sound of crickets and leafs rustling as the wind whispered through them. Fireflies winked in and out of sight as they walked carefully between the rows of sunflower stalks and corn, and Millie remembered thinking the night had never seemed so quiet or dark. She felt she could hear every step she made and every beat of her heart. She clutched Lily's hand tight and looked over her shoulder every time she thought she heard something click.

"He won't come until you say it," Lily said after she'd looked back for the third time, but her eyes were just as wide, and she had been watching the distant waving fields for any signs of something moving through them.

Millie hadn't seen anything, but she was sure that something was already watching them. Watching them with the empty sockets of his gouged-out eyes.

Eventually, they came to the well that sat between the cornfield and the grain rippling like gleaming, silver waves under the moonlight. The well sat in a flat, open patch of grass where it would be easier to stand and speak to the bone collector if he came.

Millie held the tooth to her chest and said what anyone who wanted to meet with the collector must say: "I wish to make an exchange. Part of me, for part of you."

As soon as she had finished, she heard several loud, slow clicks. Lily had screamed at the top of her lungs, and Millie panicked.

He would want the bone, so she turned and threw it as hard as she could down into the well, hoping he would jump in after it, and took off running, dragging Lily behind her. They got about ten steps back into the corn before Beatrice started laughing.

She had seen them leave and followed them out. She had picked up two stones off the ground and knocked them together to make the clicking sounds. Millie had been livid for all of about three seconds before she burst out laughing in relief. Lily joined in the giggling through sniffles and tears, so the three of them had all gone back inside and stolen honey cakes from the kitchen to solidify a truce. Overall, it was a fond memory.

Their grandmother died several weeks later in her sleep. Nobody had been there to see. She had gone peacefully; that was what her mother said. She was nearly a hundred years old and had gotten to see her granddaughters growing up happy.

Millie had thought, at that age, that she had in a way gotten an answer to her question. Her grandmother had been the only person she had ever thought about as being able to die. She never thought that someone who wasn't elderly and sick was capable of it, a result of being so young and far removed from suffering.

But the thought had drifted into her mind at other times in her life. It was such an earnest question at the time, and it had worried her for so long when she had first thought of it that it never seemed too far from her. She supposed now it was all the talk about the death goddess had brought it back up.

Millie sat in the library on one of the couches, trying to finish her letter home requesting a visit, and had gotten stuck thinking about it again. *Will I ever have to watch someone die?*

CHAPTER 43

"Everything alright?"

Millie blinked and realized she had stuck the end of the quill she was using into her mouth and had been lightly biting down on the very end, lost in thought. She took it out and set it down on the polished wood wedge that served as her portable writing desk and set it to the side. "Just thinking."

Harlen sat in one of the chairs at the table beside her, surrounded by books. He had been doing the accounts earlier but, at some point, had drifted off into trying to find some mention of this death goddess in his father's old writings.

He had told her all about the strange man, Corrik, and their meeting. Ever since that night, the two of them had occasionally been looking for mentions of the goddess. Or for some sign of the religion his father evidently practiced, but there was nothing so far.

Harlen seemed to think it was just his father being secretive. But back home, where the worship of the goddess Shareen was the most common, even people who were quite casual or secretive about their practices had something around their house that indicated their affiliation. It could be something as small as a charm at their bedside or a flower painted on the bedpost for good luck. To find nothing but that strange mask shoved in the back of a closet was odd to her. Something about it just didn't sit well.

She moved, and Harlen did not object when she squeezed into the large chair beside him and leaned her head against his shoulder. She was reasonably sure that she was beginning to come down with something after running through the icy ocean. She had been trying to fend it off with tea and herbs with little luck and had been feeling somewhat under the weather.

The heat of the fire was lovely, and she closed her eyes like a cat in the sun while Harlen stroked a hand through the back of her hair. She could feel the little smile of amusement where his cheek pressed into the top of her head while he watched her eyes shut under his touch.

"You know, if you wanted to stay here and get some rest, I'm sure Jacques wouldn't mind," he said, lowering his voice to the soft rumble it took on when they were curled up together in bed in the early mornings, and he was complaining about not wanting to get up. He had developed a love of sleeping in remarkably quickly for someone who used to be an early riser by necessity.

She didn't open her eyes. She was too comfortable for that but said, "No. I've already skipped out on one meeting this week. I'm wondering what he's been doing since he seems to have dropped out of existence."

Since their last meeting over a week ago, he hadn't spoken to them or stopped by even once. Millie had been getting worried and had been about to ask if they should go check up on him when they received a letter from him in the mail, which was odd in itself—as was his request that they meet up at the school.

"I'm guessing he must have found something," Harlen said. His tone implied that he believed it couldn't be anything good.

She didn't blame him for thinking that way. She had no clue what to expect, and, again, she just felt something wasn't quite right. His absence could be explained if he found something awful and was debating how to break the news to them, but calling them down to the school added an entirely new layer of strangeness. Her curiosity about what was going on far outweighed a slight headache and tiredness.

She had a million theories on what could have happened, each more horrible than the last, but despite it, she rubbed a hand on Harlen's back and said, "I'm sure he's just been busy."

They both knew it was unlikely to be true, but he appreciated the small comfort all the same. He wordlessly let his arm drop from her hair to her waist and held her tight against his side while the fire crackled beside them, bracing himself for whatever was coming.

She was glad he did. That way, she didn't feel quite so pitiful for burying her face against his neck and pretending for a moment like everything was fine as she did the same.

"Am I allowed to go in?" Millie asked as they approached the looming building that was The Academy.

To her, it still looked very much like a guild house. She could see the faint, sun-bleached outline on the wall where the Silver Sturgeon logo had hung beside the door. Over time, the rain had peeled away some of the paint that had gone on to cover the mark.

"They never said guests weren't allowed," Harlen said. He had his arm looped through hers, which, judging by some of the looks they received from several well-dressed and damp noblemen, was appallingly affectionate by their standards.

"And if they do say something, can I expect to see you fight for my honor?" she asked. The weight of anxiousness about what they were about to hear was heavy between them, and she was glad to coax a smile out of him.

"Of course." He returned her teasing grin, but his eyes were soft, and she could read the gentle thanks in them for the attempt at levity.

They made their way up the steps and hung their coats in the drying room. Just as she wondered how they would find Jacques without being stopped by some other professor, they stepped inside, and she spotted him immediately. He was at the base of a tall set of stairs, smoking, and he looked as though he hadn't slept since they last saw him.

His coppery hair was a mess. His face was paper white, and his freckles practically blazed against it beneath the dark circles ringing his green eyes. He was reducing his cigarette to ash beside the plaque that read "no smoking" in tarnished silver, and Millie watched him shoot a glare at another member of staff who walked by and said something to him in passing. He gave a rude gesture to the man once he passed before he spotted both of them.

He didn't approach them immediately, but he waved towards a door on the far side of the main hall and began making his way towards it. Millie looked up at Harlen, who seemed just as perplexed, and she gripped his sleeve tightly as they followed him inside.

It was a small room with one tiny window and a set of cabinets that hung open to show shelves of disorganized jars and bundles of herbs and other oddities. The table was strewn with them, along with books lying open. A stagnant bowl of water sat in the middle of the mess that Jacques propped himself against, waiting with folded arms while Harlen shut the door.

"What's—" Harlen began, but Jacques held up one hand. He waved for them to step to the side and snapped his fingers.

Millie coughed as it felt like something pulled the breath away from her lungs, and the air around them shifted. She stepped away from the door quickly, where she saw the dust on the floor drifting around the frame and a quiet, high whistling sound coming through the cracks.

"It's an old trick I used to use when I brought girls home," Jacques explained. "It'll give us some privacy."

"What did you find?" Harlen pressed as they gathered around the table.

Jacques raked a hand back through his coppery hair and gave them both a look that spoke volumes of his own confusion.

"Apparently, Tansey *did* come here for an evaluation. I went down to the records room and found it in the Vostesk family file."

Millie looked up at Harlen, who had gone white, but his features had set into stony determination. "What were the results?"

Jacques pointed at him, his green eyes sparkling. "That's the thing! Her name's in the file; it showed when she came in, but the results? Nowhere to be found. Like someone just forgot to put them in there. But trust me, Ashby is the guy in charge of keeping records of evaluations, and he's got a stick up his ass about proper documentation like you wouldn't believe."

"I can believe that," Harlen muttered under his breath. Then asked, "But is that really impossible? You seem pretty. . ."

A grin spread across Jacques's face beneath the freckles. "Yeah, I know. I look like shit. And no—that's not the weird thing, though it is a new feeling for me. The weird thing is my key to the record's room has gone missing. It could be a coincidence, but I think the timing's convenient. It's got me a bit jumpy."

He looked more than a bit jumpy. Every time he raised his cigarette to his mouth, Millie noticed his hands were shaking quite badly, and he kept them tightly folded into his arms to hide it. His entire posture, down to the smile, was far too stiff for her liking.

"Jacques," she said, eyeing him. "You know if anything else has been going on, it's alright to tell us." She gestured back towards the door. "Nobody else is listening."

It was quick, nearly imperceptible the way his face fell before he pulled it into another grin. "Nah. Shit's just weird, and it's really got me on edge. It's why I waited a few days before calling you guys. I was hoping I'd calm down a bit, but I guess not. Guess I'm a bit more paranoid than I thought."

Liar. Millie thought, but not angrily. What had scared him so badly?

"Look," Jacques continued, addressing both of them. "I'm trying to get ahold of one of the board members to ask about it. I'm still trying to figure out what's going on with this evaluation thing. Really."

"I believe you," Harlen said. He was gripping the side of the table very tightly with one hand and seemed to be fighting back a mixture of angry frustration and pure upset. "I just want to know what the hell happened. I just want to know where my sister is. That's it."

"I know. Really, I—"

Jacques turned to address him directly but paused mid-turn. He was staring at the water bowl in the middle of the table. Millie craned her neck to see what had stopped him so abruptly just in time to watch the side of the wooden bowl crack as it turned to solid ice.

Harlen and Jacques stared at each other. The room had gone silent aside from the faint whistling of wind around the door. Harlen seemed even more stunned than Jacques and released the table where a spiderweb of frost had formed around his fingertips.

"How long have you been able to do that?" Jacques demanded. If he had looked on edge before, there was no comparing it to now. He looked like he was going to crawl out of his skin.

Harlen shook his head and again looked back down at his hands. He flexed the fingers. "I—"

"How long?" Jacques repeated.

"That's new," Millie said because Harlen seemed at a loss for words. She knew little about magic. But she knew enough to know that that was not normal.

"I thought I already had—" he started, and Jacque's eyes flew open wide.

"Already what?"

Millie reached up and grabbed onto Harlen's arm, and that seemed to bring him out of the stunned silence where he appeared only capable of staring at his hands. She nodded to the dried plants and seeds on the table, and gently as she could manage with her confusion struggling to pull her towards the door, she said, "Show him."

"I don't know how," he said, panic creeping into his voice.

She gripped his arm tighter. "Yes, you do," she said encouragingly. It would be easier than explaining. "I'm right here." She slid her hand down his arm, stopping at his wrist. She held it tightly and nodded towards the table.

Jacques hadn't moved. He still had the bowl in both hands and was watching intently while Harlen closed his eyes. Millie squeezed his wrist the same way they had taken to squeezing each other's hands when they were uneasy.

Breathe, she thought, watching the side of his face, willing the muscle pulled taut in his jaw to relax. *Just breathe.*

As though he had heard what she thought, he took a deep breath. His eyes remained closed, and he made no moves to pull away from her as he raised one hand over the table. There was nothing like the explosion of life that happened when he was with her alone, but anything that had a root remaining did begin to look greener. A weak little bud at the end of a tiny twig began to open by the time Jacques told him to stop, and Harlen dropped his hand back to his side.

"Okay." Jacques had stepped far back from the table and was running both hands through his hair, over and over. His cigarette stump was forgotten and smoldering on the floor. "Okay. That's something. That is something."

"What is it?" Harlen asked. "That shouldn't be possible—right?"

Jacques turned back towards them and put a hand to his face like he was checking his freckled cheeks for stubble. He paused thoughtfully with his fingers still over his mouth, then gave a shrug and a laugh that didn't do a good job of making him sound not scared out of his mind.

"I have no idea. Ah." He tapped his foot on the floor. "Tell you what? I have a, uh, a lot of research to do. Clearly, the important thing is that nobody panics. And also that you don't tell anyone about this."

Harlen nodded. He pulled his hand out of hers and returned to twisting his cufflink. His brows knitted together, and he and Jacques were both doing a terrible job of not panicking.

Millie knew that she probably looked about as pale and worried as they did, but she tried hard to swallow it if for no other reason than to help calm things down.

"Alright," Harlen said, his voice surprisingly steady. "What should I do in the meantime?"

"In the meantime," Jacques said. "You should probably take it easy. Alright? The Tansey thing going on here—just let me look into it, alright? It's just *very important* that you keep calm."

Harlen nodded, then asked gravely. "Do you think this is dangerous?"

Jacques hesitated. "No. Not at all. Just keeping on the safe side, buddy," he said with a smile.

Liar. Millie thought again. But she didn't resent him for it. She even gave him a sympathetic, knowing look as he snapped his fingers and made whatever had gathered around the door dissipate when Harlen wasn't looking.

They left the building without a word. Once they were out of the front gate, Harlen reached to take her hand again, as was their habit but paused. She stopped as he slowly pulled away and clenched his fingers into a fist.

"I don't, um," he said quietly, looking down guiltily. "I don't know if we should..."

She grabbed his hand where he was, pulling it back towards his chest. She took it with both of hers, uncurled his fingers, and kissed his palm. She did feel a spasm of fear thinking of the frost that had coated the table, but it was overwhelmed by another, much stronger feeling as she looked up at him and saw him smiling at her with misty eyes.

"None of that," she said sternly. "Hear me?"

He curled his fingers again, closing them around her own. "Absolutely."

She could feel the eyes of several passersby on them, but she couldn't care any less. She only cared that nothing smothered out the brightness he had gained over the past weeks. No kind of magic was going to take that from him, even if she had to beat it back herself.

Now, she just needed to keep things moving. She understood Jacques's advice, but she also understood that right now was not the best time for him to go back home and be shut up inside the Vostesk Manor. So, with his hand still in hers, she said, "Didn't Corrik say he wanted to meet me?"

CHAPTER 44

Corrik's house was in a far less affluent area of town than Harlen expected.

The Vostesk manor stood on one of the few hills in town, giving the impression that it looked down on it all where the old noble district used to be. Nowadays, the noblemen's houses were built far closer to the sea, near the ports, where the wealthy tradesman could easily keep an eye on their goods coming in and out. Corrik's residence was still in view of the nicer houses but was located in the artists' district, wedged between a paint shop and a stonemason.

It was a tall, wooden building that was so narrow Harlen got the impression it would have sagged over onto its side with its own weight had the shops framing it not been there to support it. It was an older building that shared the same cold, damp look that every structure fell victim to. The window glass was warped and wavy, and the wooden steps leading up to the door bowed beneath their feet from years of swelling with constant rain.

He knocked on the door hesitantly after Millie told him for sure the address was correct. Corrik left it behind, scribbled on a bit of paper where he had been sitting at the table along with a short invitation stating that his door was always open.

Harlen hadn't seen him write it. He wasn't even entirely sure where he'd gotten the pen and paper.

He only had a chance to wonder about how odd it was for the briefest moments, however, because the door eased open quickly, revealing the man he'd seen the other day standing in the doorway.

Corrik's distinctive blue eyes and polite, quiet smile greeted them as though he was expecting a visit.

"Well, Harlen! What a lovely surprise." He reached out and shook his hand, then turned his eyes toward Millie. "And this must be your wife."

"Millie," she introduced herself and extended her hand. He took it, looked down at it, then up at her. His smile widened, and he clasped her hand between both of his.

"It's wonderful to meet you. Please, please, don't stand out there in the rain. I've just put on some tea. It's wonderful for this chilly climate."

He motioned for them to come in, and they climbed the few stairs that led up into Corrik's home. Any traces of cold vanished as the door shut, and they were greeted by cheery yellow firelight and the scent of Jasmine tea, which Harlen commented on aloud without thinking.

"Ah, you know your teas, then?" It seemed to please Corrik greatly.

Harlen offered him an awkward smile. "Ah, sort of. It's Millie's favorite."

"Lovely."

Corrik smiled with genuine warmth and gestured from the entryway towards the sitting room. It was filled with shelves crammed with books and a hundred other things: little jars of leaves, flowers, dust, bits of what must have formerly been living things suspended in a pale yellow fluid. The polar opposite of his father's shelves that were immaculate but seldom used. Where there were no shelves, the walls were hung with enough paintings and decorations to fill a gallery.

Harlen was fascinated. He slowly walked into the room, took in the collection, and paused when he saw an entire shelf that seemed to be dedicated entirely to alchemy. A strange thing to display considering the opinion most of his colleagues had of the craft. Harlen called through the doorway into what must have been the kitchen where Corrik had gone and asked if he studied it.

He returned with a tray holding a simple white ceramic teapot, three cups, and a tin plate of cookies. "I dabble," Corrik said, setting it on a low table in front of a couch and several worn but comfortable-looking chairs. "I'm not nearly as skilled at it as I would like. It's a newer interest."

Harlen nodded, giving the collection one last look before politely sitting. Millie remained standing, looking at all the things mounted on the walls. She was transfixed by a large, green crystal covered in intricate gold runes painted in excruciating detail mounted just above the fireplace that made the gold seem to shift as it flickered.

"That's from one of my journeys north," Corrik offered when he saw what she was looking at. "It's supposed to bring good luck. Or, as the merchant told me, it's supposed to imbue the environment it's placed in with positive emotional energy."

"Does it work?" Millie asked.

Corrik shrugged and offered an almost boyish smile that somehow didn't look out of place on him. He might have been perhaps in his thirties, but it was impossible to tell. His dark hair didn't have even a touch of gray, and his face was unlined. Unlike Vostesk Senior, who maintained a look of youth from his distant elvish blood, no, Corrik's rough features were entirely human. The only word that came to Harlen's mind to describe it was ageless.

"It depends. I suppose if you feel positive at the moment, then, yes, I'm certain it works. If not, I ask that you simply admire it as a lovely decoration and ignore the fact that I bought something so impulsively."

Millie chuckled, then raised a hand. "Can I touch it?"

"By all means. Perhaps I've been using it wrong, and you're supposed to let the positive energy rub off on you quite literally."

Millie touched the edge of it, and Harlen watched the fraction of a moment where she braced for a physical sensation. He tried and failed to hide a smile when he saw her visible disappointment that nothing interesting had happened.

"You two seem harmonious," Corrik said suddenly.

Harlen felt the heat rise up his neck, and Corrik laughed. "Apologies. It's just that I don't get to see many well-suited matches come out of arranged marriages. Your father mentioned your arrangement briefly to me, and I made it clear that I have no particular fondness for the practice. I'm glad that in this case, it seems I was mistaken."

He gestured toward the crystal on the wall. "To go back to energy—the energy between you two is very, well, positive. Very warm. I noticed the moment I saw you on the porch. Pardon me if that's an unwelcome observation."

"It's alright," Harlen said and risked a glance at Millie. She smiled at him very politely, but there was a mischievous glint in her eyes that made his breath catch in his throat. Then something on the wall caught her attention, and her eyes suddenly went stone cold.

"What's that one?"

Harlen followed her gaze and felt his chest go cold. Mounted on the wall was the same mask he'd found in his father's study. It sat between two bookshelves, the crudely carved eyes staring out at the both of them.

Harlen gripped the teacup in his hands and swallowed past the dryness in his throat as Corrik glanced up from the green-frosted cookie he'd picked up.

"Oh, that?" he offered another amused, boyish smile. "It's a burial mask. I suppose it's a bit gruesome for sitting room décor, but I found it interesting. Pardon—"

Corrik stood, dusting his hands on a neatly folded scrap of linen from the tray, and walked over to the wall. He carefully removed the mask from its mounting and held it out in both hands like a presenter at an auction. "Here. It's much better when admired from up close."

He walked back and sat beside Harlen on the couch. Millie came to stand over Harlen's shoulder, resting one of her hands on his arm so she could lean over him and get a closer look as Corrik rotated the mask and explained.

"It's part of an old, old tradition. Not practiced anymore except for some very isolated communities. This was thought to be a reflection of the face of the goddess of death. People were buried wearing it as an. . .offering of sorts. They were marking themselves, saying that they wanted her to claim them. It was thought that this would prevent the energy that made up your life force from wandering the earth aimlessly after death. Offering it to her meant allowing the energy you had in life to be returned to the earth with a purpose. It was essential for those with magic in their blood. It was seen as a vital practice for magic to continue to exist in the world."

Corrik flipped the mask over to show them the inside. The same butterfly they had been finding everywhere these days was carved where the forehead would be, and Harlen noted one character carved beneath each wing.

"Preserve and reclaim," Harlen muttered aloud as he recognized them. It was a habit from being cloistered up alone in his study, and as soon as he realized he'd done it, he winced. But again, his musing seemed to please Corrik.

"You speak old Ruashan?" he asked.

Again, Harlen was caught off guard and admitted, "A little. Not conversationally, but for the most part, I can make sense of the writing."

Corrik still seemed immensely pleased and continued excitedly. "Yes—yes, that's wonderful. So you understand, it's meant to represent a very hopeful outlook on death. But, ah, I apologize if this is a bit too morbid for your tastes. I know Chairman Berkley finds this all rather distasteful to discuss over tea."

"Chairman Berkley finds a lot of things distasteful in my experience," Millie muttered under her breath.

Corrik laughed. "Yes, I did hear he was rather rude the other day. For a man who prides himself on his deft social skills, he does not know how to read a room. It's a shame, really. He can be a rather pleasant conversationalist if the topic is right. I just wish he had a bit more of a range."

Corrik set the mask down on the table, and Harlen couldn't help staring at it. Corrik moved back across the room to sit in his chair, and Millie took up the vacant space beside him. Once she was seated, Harlen said, "My father has—had—one of these."

He was curious about what Corrik's reaction would be, but his expression didn't flicker in the slightest. He didn't stiffen in the slightest, remaining seated in the same professional yet comfortable posture, his back straight but leaning on one of his chair's arms.

"I would imagine so," he said. "It's a token I like to give all of our society's members once they've officially joined. I'm sure Berkley talked about it at length, but in short, our goal is the preservation and continuation of magic in the world, so I suppose I found it apt. Or it could simply be my upbringing as a mortician's son seeping into my current fascinations. Who's to say?"

He took another sip of his tea and placed the empty cup on the table with a soft click. The fireplace across the room crackled brightly and cast a warm glow on the side of Corrik's face, lighting up his hair in deep mahogany and gleaming red.

"I only took an interest in magic after my father died. I'd had some small talent for it myself, but nothing remarkable. Nothing worth pursuing. But I suppose his death gave me a new perspective, as did a very serious illness I caught at the time that brought me close to joining him. I was very close to death all my life, but I feel I truly stared into the face of the goddess during those few months. That was what lead me to see death, not as an end, not as frightening. But as a chance for something new. After all, it was after my brush with the goddess that I took over my father's business and began my little society."

"I suppose that is a change from mortuary business," Harlen said, and Corrik's polite smile widened.

"Indeed. Although there are days where I miss the quietness such a profession offers. The dead do not offer much in the way of small talk, which I consider one of death's many benefits."

The conversation went pleasantly. Far more pleasantly and easily than Harlen was accustom to with strangers. He still had plenty of questions about more things than he could count, but at least here he was getting some answers. Even if they only lead to more questions, it felt like progress. It was solid, and it was what he desperately needed as he tried not to think about the frost that had formed beneath his fingers.

It was almost easy to do sitting there in the warm glow of the fire with Corrik chatting away pleasantly. It was calming in an almost hypnotic way. He couldn't recall ever feeling so relaxed in the presence of one of his father's friends. He even found himself laughing as Corrik recounted Berkley's joining of the society.

"I thought I killed the poor man," Corrik said, shaking his head. "He drinks like a fish, so I didn't think it would be an issue. Leading the toast in front of everyone was a bit too much for him, I think, but even so, I've never had anyone faint dead away like that after one sip."

"What on earth kind of wine was it?" Millie asked.

"Oh, it's not wine. It's a concoction I came up with in the early days that Ashby started calling ambrosia. It's very sweet: I put honey in it to mask the, well, robust taste. I didn't think it was strong enough to do that, though, so it gave me quite a shock.

"Berkley seemed interested in me joining. Your society that is." Harlen felt like it was a good time to mention it.

Corrik grinned, and his blue eyes sparkled. "If you are interested, Harlen, I would recommend attending a function or two before you decided on joining officially. Despite what the other nobles may tell you, it isn't for everyone. Speaking personally, you strike me as a man who would fit in very well with those who are at least similar taste to me. I would love to have you as a member to save me from all the small talk with the other nobles. But speaking professionally, I can't recommend jumping into something so serious blindly. Or sipping my ambrosia without fair warning, I've learned my lesson there."

"How serious is it?" Harlen asked.

Corrik thought for a moment before replying. "It is a meeting of similar minds, but it is also a great task. It's a great deal of work—even recordkeeping requires patience and attention to detail. You've just had a great change in your life and are being faced with many new responsibilities. Eager as the others may be, I must recommend you think about it."

Harlen was surprised. He'd been expecting some degree of secrecy about the group or the mask, but there was nothing. Nothing but an open and calm explanation. It threw him off far more than shouting or refusing to answer his questions ever would have.

The way Berkley, the professor, and even his father had acted about some issues had him believing something deeply sinister was going on between all of them, but now—now he wasn't sure. The conversation hadn't banished his suspicions: far from it. But Corrik's attitude was perplexing.

"I'll have to drop by sometime then." He said.

"Please do. They're normally held at our guild house, but it's normally held at one of the noble's homes for more casual events. Once the location is decided, I'll make sure to send you a letter."

When it came time to leave, Corrik saw them both to the door and shook Harlen's hand. Then he turned to Millie, clasping her hand with both of his. He looked into her eyes, smiling fondly.

"Please, do take care of yourself, my dear. It's so very important."

It was incredibly polite and in no way inappropriate, but the gesture went on for just a beat too long to be comfortable.

"Right. Of course," Millie said, offering a faltering smile as he let go.

"That was strange," he commented as the door closed behind them. Millie nodded.

"He seems nice enough. But, yes, that was. . .strange."

She gave the house another glance but shook off the interaction quickly. Soon she was talking again at her usual, excited pace about everything they'd just heard.

"Very macabre," she said, pleased. "You have to go to at least one of those meetings and tell me everything. Do you think they wear the masks?"

He smiled. "I can't see my father walking around a ballroom in a mask. And don't think you won't be coming—you left me to deal with Berkley alone once already."

Instead of going directly home, Harlen wandered with her down one of the little alleyways near the school. He was getting used to his new freedom to roam, adjusting to it by taking detours when running errands.

As they walked, arm-in-arm, he savored the feeling. The feeling of new-found freedom. The feeling of quiet buzzing happiness of having her walk pressed against him, dropping her head into his shoulder whenever she wanted to get his attention to look at some window display she found particularly interesting. The feeling of knowing that they had a safe house to return to.

Some part of him believed it wouldn't last. Ever since his father's passing, he felt as though he were bracing for something. It seemed impossible that all at once, everything could be okay; so close to perfect. There had to be something else. Some other danger, some threat that would pull away every bit of peace he had found.

He tried not to dwell on it. Most of the time, he was successful. But in small, quiet moments like these that he treasured the most, it was difficult not to acknowledge the feeling.

To distract himself, he stopped in at one of the only bakeries in town to get some of the sugared rolls that were Millie's favorite. They were warm, lovely for holding in their hands on the way, and it was a good distraction from the worry drumming in the back of his mind to watch as she snuck little bites of hers from the crinkly wrapper when she thought he wasn't looking. The only indication he gave that he noticed was pausing to wipe a small smudge of the icing off her cheek with his thumb when they neared the gate.

"Did you see me that whole time?" she asked.

He grinned. "You looked so pleased with yourself that I didn't want to say anything."

She seemed both affronted and amused, and before he had the front door opened, she'd grabbed the front of his coat and tugged him down low enough to kiss. She tasted like sugar and gave him a delighted smile when he pulled away red in the face.

"I must admire your observation skills," she said, so close to the side of his face that her lips brushed his cheek as she spoke, bringing more heat rushing up his neck.

He opened the door, and as soon as it was closed, he pulled her into his arms, aiming to kiss her with passion but instead slipping on a puddle on the tile brought in by the rain, very nearly taking them both to the ground. He shouted a mixed explicative, and the two of them burst out into peals of laughter, which lead to them sitting cozied up together on the grand staircase, munching on their rolls. And as the two of them sat, his eyes wandered up to the family portrait on the wall.

They all looked so grim. All of their eyes were vacant. None of them were smiling, except for Tansey, who had the smallest of smiles pulling on one corner of her lips. A little, knowing smile that Harlen found haunting.

Perhaps Corrik was right. Maybe he should have that taken down. Replace all those cold, dead-eyed stares with something else. Or perhaps take it down and leave nothing but a bare wall. A clean slate. Maybe it didn't need a grand portrait; just ringing laughter, rain puddles beside the door, kisses that tasted like sugar, and arms that felt like home.

That was the kind of house in which he wanted to live—wanted his family to live. But he knew full well he couldn't take down the portrait until he knew where Tansey and her knowing smile had gone.

CHAPTER 45

The man was back at the window.

Millie found herself back at the end of the long hallway upstairs. All the lamps that sputtered their sooty, kerosene-scented flames were out, leaving nothing but damp cold. The rain pounded down on the roof, streaking the glass, reducing the world outside to blurred shapes lit only by the dim, gray light that made telling the time of day nearly impossible. She was sure she saw the blur of a black coat and hood standing on the lawn below the house.

"Harlen?" she called back over her shoulder, but there was no answer. Her voice rang off the walls and was the only thing that answered her. The portraits on the wall stared.

Could he see her? The rain and the light must have made it impossible to see inside from down there, no matter how close he was. How had he gotten inside the gate? And why was he staring right up at her?

It sent a chill through her, but she still reached out and pushed open the glass with the intent of shouting down at him some sort of threat to get him to leave. He wouldn't know she was alone in the house. For all he knew, her husband could be waiting at the door. But as soon as she'd pushed the window open and was hit with the blast of rain and cold air, the figure turned and started hurrying back towards the gate.

She called after them, but they didn't turn around. After a moment of indecision, she found herself flying down the stairs and out the front door. She wouldn't be made to feel afraid in her own home. Not again.

The night was freezing. The rain soaked her as she ran barefoot over the front lawn and pushed through the gate the figure had left hanging half-open. They were already down the street, walking briskly as she gave chase, ignoring the uneven sharpness of the wet cobblestone on her feet.

They were approaching the main street, and the figure was heading towards the alley between two buildings, making to turn down into it and vanish, so she threw herself forward and seized the back of the cloak. She stumbled through it and nearly fell as the cloak crumbled, and she found herself holding empty fabric. The street around her was empty. There was no sound of someone running off down the alley; they were simply gone.

She looked down at the coat in her hands, and as she unfolded it to get a better look, she heard the clack of something hitting the ground. She looked, and the death mask stared up at her, the rain pattering off its crudely carved open eyes and mouth.

Millie sat up in bed, covered in a cold sweat with her stomach turning. She stumbled out of the blankets, half-falling out of bed as she became aware of the waking world around her and the dream dissolved. She realized she was going to be sick.

She managed to make it to the washroom and grabbed the bucket from beneath the sink before vomiting. The next thing she was aware of was the sound of Harlen's confused shouting in alarm as he too stumbled into the bathroom, staring at her hunched over on the floor in confusion for a moment before his still half-sleeping brain put together what she was doing.

"Millie!"

He hit the ground beside her rather ungracefully and grabbed the back of her hair, pulling it away from her face as another wave of nausea hit her, and she heaved into the bucket. He put a hand on her back and rubbed soothing circles into it as she sat back, gasping for breath and shaking.

"Don't move," he said frantically, fumbling on top of the sink, trying not to move too far from her while he pulled down a stack of towels that scattered across the floor. He ignored them and pressed one to her face, wiping at her mouth and cheeks. "Don't move; I've got you."

He sat with her against the bathroom wall when she finally set the bucket aside. She sat between his legs with her head resting back against his chest, trying to calm the shaking in her body while he muttered nonsensical but soothing things in her ear.

Eventually, after a long moment and much insisting that it would help her feel better, he convinced her to sit up and allowed him to put her in the bath.

He sat beside the tub, fretting like a mother hen, which admittedly did bring a tired smile to her lips. He pinned up her hair, rubbed her shoulders, poured water over her, and did everything but crawl in the bath with her. She had to assure him that she was only sick, not an invalid—which still left him with that worried line between his brows and one arm in the bath, occasionally fussing here and there.

Admittedly, the crisp smell of the soap and the coolness of the chilled water was soothing. It was doing wonders to settle her stomach—as was Harlen's insistence that she let him press a cool cloth over her eyes to calm the pounding headache that was seeping in as the nausea faded.

"What happened?" he asked when he was sure she was coming around.

"I don't know."

She had a brief thought brought on by the dream; perhaps there had been something in the tea at Corrik's house. But they'd all drunk from the same pot, and Harlen seemed to be okay, so she dismissed it.

Vostesk Senior, it seemed, had left her paranoid. She still hadn't stopped wondering why he carried around a vial of nightshade in his cane. Or who he had used half of it on.

"Maybe you're coming down with something," he reasoned, pressing a hand to her forehead, feeling for a fever.

He had a point. Millie suspected she was getting ill the past few days. She should have known the weather here would get to her eventually. She also probably should have known better than to go running down by the freezing ocean.

"I could call a doctor—"

"No, no." She shook her head and pressed his hand between her own. "Really, I'm alright."

It didn't convince him. To try and ease his worry, Millie said, "Listen, if this keeps up, we can call a doctor. Alright? I don't want to bother some poor soul for a cold."

"Alright," he said slowly. "If you promise."

She couldn't resist a bit of a grin and held up one hand, extending her smallest finger towards him. "Pinkie promise."

That managed to break the wall of concern, and he cracked a smile. Millie watched him fight it, but his good humor won out, and he returned the gesture, locking his finger around hers.

"Fair enough. Pinkie promise."

That must have been enough to at least convince him she wasn't feeling deathly ill. He helped her out of the tub, back into bed, and pulled off the shirt he'd been sleeping in for her to wear.

He said it would be better than letting rummaging through her things for a clean nightdress. Which, admittedly, she far preferred. It was already warm from his skin and held the delightful smell of him. She must have looked delighted as she put it on because it was enough to earn another smile.

"I think you wear that better than I do," he said once he'd tucked her beneath the blankets and crawled in beside her, wrapping her arms around her waist. She fit snugly back against him, running her fingers over the scarred flesh of his forearms.

They felt strange, but not in a bad way. She had gotten so used to the pattern of raised skin beneath her hand that she couldn't imagine what it would feel like otherwise. She wasn't startled by the look of them anymore, either, not after that first time. They were part of the map of a body that had become a second home to her. But all the same, there would never be one added to it again if she had any say in the matter.

"Good. I like you better like this anyway," Millie said and looked over her shoulder to fix him with a grin for the sole purpose of watching the blush spread up his neck.

She wished that they still had flowers on the nightstand so she could watch them bloom, but after he'd discovered the connection between his new magic and his emotion, he'd insisted rather sheepishly that they not keep plants in the bedroom. Which, after much teasing, she'd agreed to. But watching the flowers in the rest of the house become brighter and fuller when she would kiss him was never not a delight.

"You are feeling better."

That was mostly true. She was a bit shaky still and wasn't at all eager to sleep again. Something about the dream, strange as it was, left her feeling uneasy.

Since the death of Vostesk Senior, she had a few dreams about him. Those cold eyes staring at her with blood soaking his long, pale hair. He never lost his formal air, even in those dreams. But whatever lurked inside of him—that strange evil and darkness—was always more visible than it had been in life. She could see it through his cracked skull.

Those dreams didn't linger, though. They left her in a panic until she remembered he was gone. Until she could remember where she was. Then she could get to sleep again or could go about her day. This one hadn't been nearly as violent as those visions of Vostesk Senior, but something about how real it seemed stayed with her. She could swear she could still feel the empty echo of the house and the damp of the cloak in her hands.

Yet, she couldn't shake the feeling that it hadn't been menacing. Terrifying as it was, that hadn't been its purpose. She couldn't explain how she knew other than she felt as though something in her was whispering: *be careful.*

It was an odd feeling. It was nothing like when she imagined her mother's voice warning her or when she got a sinking feeling in the pit of her stomach that something was amiss. It almost felt like a real voice, though she knew such a thing made no sense.

"Be careful of what?" she tried asking it. Not aloud, only in her head, directing the question at the odd whispering. But she heard nothing in reply.

Maybe she had only imagined it in the first place.

CHAPTER 46

Harlen woke again in the late morning to an odd silence and an unusually bright golden sunlight spilling across the bed. One of Wakefield's few clear days greeted him with a blue sky, flecked here and there by patches of white clouds that drifted along on the salty ocean breeze.

Through the glass of the window, he heard the calling of the seagulls. Beside him, he heard Millie's soft breathing as he lay with her in his arms, warm against his chest. He dropped his cheek to the top of her hair as the clock ticked the minutes off down the hall. He watched the shadows cast by the world outside move over the bed.

He had been awake for a while. Millie had some trouble falling back asleep and developed a bit of a headache, so he pulled her onto his chest and rubbed her temples. His mother used to do it for him when he was very young that had always worked like a charm, and luckily, it seemed to help her too. She had been out and purring in less than ten minutes, and Harlen hadn't had the heart to move her. He was sure neither of them had slept soundly for more than a few hours anyway.

"Mph."

Millie woke up, and he almost laughed at her squinting her eyes, her squished up face, and the tiny, angry expression she gave the bright sunlight pouring into her eyes. Then she turned and saw him and smiled in a way that made his heart melt.

"G'morning," she mumbled.

"Good morning." He smiled and pushed some of her tangled hair back out of her face. "How are you feeling? Any better?"

She hummed thoughtfully and dropped her cheek back onto his chest. "Is it gross that I'm actually kind of hungry?"

He chuckled and continued running his hand through her hair. "Anything in particular appeal to you?"

"Is sweetbread for breakfast wrong?"

He hummed in mock-thoughtfulness and earned another squinting smile. "You're in luck. I choose to exercise my new position as head of the house to make an exception for you."

"Favoritism, how scandalous," she said. "Next thing you know, people will be saying we're sleeping together."

"Well, then they'll just think I'm incredibly lucky," he said, then laughed as he felt heat rising up his neck. "Oh, that was terrible, wasn't it?"

"No, do go on. I would love to hear how good I am."

With some protest from her, he slid out of bed, telling her he did have to leave to get breakfast. Magic could do many things, but as odd as his seemed to be, he wasn't sure making it appear from thin air was something he could do.

"What's the point of magic, then?" she asked. She held onto his wrist loosely for a moment longer. "Only if you promise to come back."

"Always," he said fondly and watched as she gave a satisfied nod and crawled back under the blankets. He walked to the other side of the room, casting one glance back as he closed the door and was greeted with the vision of her curled into a ball beneath the yellow patch of sun, almost perfectly in its center.

It brought yet another grin to his lips, and as he turned and made his way down the stairs, he realized how light he felt.

The house felt oddly full despite the sound of his echoing footsteps that seemed so much louder in the absence of rain pouring down on the roof. The places in the front room where the curtains were pinned back left the checkerboard floor glowing with light.

The flowers he had grown and kept alive via his magic stood in pots and vases on every surface and filled the house with a light, sweet scent that did something to counteract the ever-present smell of salt. The shells Millie had brought back from the beach were placed gently here and there against the harsh, polished décor. In the morning sun, they glowed softly with their cream whites and soft pinks.

Harlen reached the base of the stairs, fastening the gray robe he had taken from the hook beside the bedroom door around his waist as he went, and a very odd thought struck him. He was calm. He was wandering around the house in the late morning with the full intention of crawling back into bed, wearing in his dressing robe, and feeling as though he had full run of the place. He wasn't afraid. Not even nervous. He was relaxed.

He wasn't sure at what point he had stopped expecting to see his father walk out of some room with a scowl on his face, but he realized it had been a while. A few days at least.

He saw mail in the basket beneath the slot on the door and walked past it without a sense of anxiousness or urgency. He walked into the kitchen, made himself a hot cup of coffee that he sipped as he took the sweetbread from the pantry, and decided to set it in a pan to warm it a bit. As he took the bread out of the pan and set it on a plate to take back upstairs, he glanced at the door he spent his entire life regarding in fear.

Maybe it was the morning light or the hazy, happy state of mind, but it didn't seem as frightening as he stood and looked at it. The worn paint around the handle and the chipped frame looked less imposing and more messy. Sloppy.

Curiously, he approached it and lowered his hand to the bent knob. He expected the fear to snap back into him as soon as his hand touched the cool metal. But nothing happened. It was just a door. He laughed, the sound coming from him suddenly and unexpectedly. Whatever power this had had over him was nothing. Nothing.

It was surreal, retrieving the key. The motion of drifting back up then down the stairs felt dreamlike, as did sliding it into the lock. It fit easily as always, and the door swung open with a familiar creak.

Harlen did feel a little tremble somewhere deep inside him as he looked down those stairs, but his hands didn't shake when he placed them on the walls to descend into the chill and darkness.

Nothing, he reminded himself. *This place is nothing anymore.*

The small tremble worked its way up to a pounding in his heart as he reached the second familiar door. This one was still just as imposing as it had always been, and he refused to light the familiar lantern that would send all the shadows leaping up on the wall. He was sure if he did that, brought the demons back to life, he would have run out and sealed off this room for good.

Instead, he took a candle and struck a match to light it. No smell of kerosene. No tall, flickering flame. Just a soft orange glow to illuminate all the sharp instruments still laid out on the table.

He felt his breath struggling to find its way into his lungs; it felt as though they were going to burst, but he stayed. He still cast a long, slow look around the room and took in everything. Even the book where his father had gotten all his ideas was still lying open on the table.

His heart pounded louder and louder as his eyes fell on the diagram of the human body splayed across the page. A man flayed of flesh, showing muscle and bone. Wide, open eyes drawn in ink stared upward from the book as the candle guttered, like pale eyes staring up at the ceiling while a puddle of blood seeped out to stain paler hair.

Harlen slammed the book shut. The thought that came to him was so intense and sudden he practically spat the words into the darkness.

"I hope you're in a place just like this."

It was wrong. He shouldn't think like that. He felt the guilt freezing him as soon as he said it, but there was something hotter inside of him that contended with it. Hotter and angrier. It was the truth. He hoped that somewhere, someone was turning his skin to a mess of jagged scars, telling him that if he just tried harder, if he really *wanted* to, then he could get away.

He hoped he spent forever thinking about what he'd done to his family. His wife, his children. He hoped that he realized he had made all of their lives hell, and it couldn't be changed. He wished he knew his only legacy was a son who hated him.

Hated him. Another thing he had never allowed himself to think fully, even when he had bashed his skull with that horrible crystal. But he did. He hated him. He hated him and anyone else like him. The thought that there were enough people similar to Vostesk Senior to constitute a book on the subject of drawing out magic made his skin crawl. If he ever found out who they were. . .

His eyes caught the glass of water, where Vostesk Senior had left it behind. The light of the candle turned its surface to gleaming, liquid fire, and already he could see that the first few inches down from the top had frozen without his attention.

The frost was creeping down deeper even as he watched. Far faster than he had ever seen it move when his father stared at it angrily. And as he looked at it, it responded to what he wanted. It froze in a flash and in such a way that the glass shattered. It scattered broken bits of glass and ice over the table.

He realized he was breathing heavily and clutching the side of the table so forcefully his fingers dug into the wood. He made himself step back and take a long, deep breath. The chips of ice on the floor began to shine and melt, and he knew it meant, in some way, he was calming down.

He was alright. Nothing in this room could hurt him. Not anymore.

He blew out the candle and watched the smoke furl and twist up into the darkness. Harmless darkness. And with that, he made his way back up the stairs, back through the kitchen, back into the brightness of the morning.

The bread somehow hadn't gotten cold yet. Harlen must not have been gone nearly as long as he thought. It was still steaming, and it continued to do so as he paused just long enough to grab the letters from their basket while he made his way back to his and Millie's room.

He flipped through them to see if anything had arrived from Millie's family. He imagined she would want to know right away if there was any word from them.

He didn't see anything bearing her former surname, but the name on the envelope closest to the top of the stack caught his eye right away. It was from Corrik.

He dropped everything else in the office to be dealt with later but kept the one letter as he returned to the room. Millie was stretched out on her back with her arms above her head, enjoying the space. When she saw him in the doorway, she grinned and seemed more than happy to surrender some of it so he could sit down.

She sat up to accept the bread with a quick thank you and munched on it while he sat on the edge of the mattress.

"What's that?" She dropped her chin onto his shoulder while he turned the envelope over in his hands.

He explained who it was from, and they exchanged a curious look. Harlen cracked the red wax seal and pulled out a single sheet of heavy, rough paper that bore the same writing as the outside of the envelope. The opening expressed brief pleasantries that were nowhere near the flowery greetings of his father's usual colleagues. Corrik's introduction was polite and straightforward, and the rest of the short letter got directly to the point.

"Our society is having another meeting this evening. It's taking place on Ashby's insistence. He believes it would be disrespectful not to welcome me back into town properly, I think. Though, confidentially, I would much rather spend the evening at home. So, I could not blame you and would take no insult if you wish to do the same. I can always send you an invitation to something that would be more interesting than a gathering of gossiping noblemen. But if you do wish to get a feel for things, feel free to stop by tonight."

Harlen could almost see the pleasant smile through the letter. There was an address at the bottom of the page that he vaguely remembered his father mentioning a few times, which he assumed was Ashby's house.

"Sounds interesting," Millie said with a shrug.

"Are you feeling up to going?" Harlen asked.

She looked like she was feeling better. The paleness that had worried him last night had gone, and the light in her eyes had returned.

"Sure. Though I'm not sure I'll be let through the door if it's Berkley's kind of crowd."

"I'm sure Corrik won't mind," Harlen said.

He doubted any of them would make a fuss about her presence around Corrik. Ashby and Berkley, at least, seemed to respect him. "And if necessary, I suppose it's a chance for me to duel someone for your honor."

That made her smile and pressed the dimple he so loved into her cheek. "Alright, then. I suppose we're going out."

CHAPTER 47

Harlen kept the letter in hand as they made their way down the street towards the town's upper district. Millie watched him glance at it now and again as they walked down the cobblestone street with cloaks and coats buttoned tight over their evening clothes. He had dressed in the dark suit with the red tie again, she in her pale blue dress with the embroidered white flowers along the hem.

She could hear the crashing of the ocean turning from mere distant white noise to a thunderous roar as they made their way closer and closer to the sea until she could glimpse the churning, deep gray waves through the spaces between houses. She could see the docks, the rocky shore, and the salt-encrusted ships with their great white sails against the cloudy sky. Overhead, white and black speckled seabirds circled, screaming to one another, perching on roofs, and picking at scraps of fish bones. She had no idea how anyone could live so close to all the noise.

The district was a far cry from where Corrik lived, only in how large and ornate the houses were. They were still close to one another, still smelled like the sea and wet dirt. All of them still had swollen wood around the bases of their doors from being continually soaked. The constant onslaught of water bloated the elaborate carvings running up the frames.

She thought that she was getting used to the city. The places she had seen, the bright shop windows, and cozy tea houses and bars with their windows fogged from the warmth inside had been growing on her. But something about the upper district was different. It lacked the life she found so enticing in the rest of the city.

The massive houses with their dark, empty windows and the streets that stood nearly abandoned felt hollow. It reminded her of the section of the graveyard where all these people would be going when they died, where blank-faced stone angles would watch over them silently.

"I think this is it," Harlen said as they reached the front of one great, beige monstrosity with a slanted black roof. There stood a dark stone dog with an open, snarling mouth on the stone porch to each side of the heavy-looking wooden door. It seemed to her like great care had been put into their fangs and curved claws. She never met Ashby, but she had heard his voice. And she could very well imagine it coming from one of those creatures.

Harlen knocked on the door, and Millie kept one eye on the dogs until the door swung open to reveal a young woman who Millie could only assume had elvish blood of some kind. Her dark eyes were uncommonly large, her slightly pointed ears stuck out on either side of her short black hair, and her white face had features that would have been delicate had she not been so thin. The skin was drawn so tight over her high cheekbones and narrow chin that she looked painfully fragile. Like she would break apart if someone so much as gripped her hand too firmly.

She gave them both a quick once-over that was almost imperceptible, then lifted the edges of her black and white dress into a polite courtesy.

"Good evening. You must be Lord Vostesk," she said in a whispery voice. Millie felt Harlen flinch ever so slightly and would have missed the glance over his shoulder had her eyes not snapped up to him the moment the girl used the title. She wondered how long it would be before she was able to hear it without tensing. "And your companion for the evening?"

Harlen had his arm looped through hers for their entire walk. It was sweet and practical as they braced against the wind and tried to retain whatever heat they could between them.

Harlen lifted their joined arms ever so slightly in response to the question, and the boyish grin that pulled at his mouth was contagious. "My wife. Millie Vostesk."

Again, the surprise on the young girl's face was hardly there for a fraction of a second. "Oh. Of course." Another polite incline of the head sent her short hair gliding smoothly forward.

She folded her hands in front of her and gestured with a nod for them to enter. Every one of her movements was unnaturally smooth. Puppet-like. "Please, follow me. I can take you to the others."

Their coats were taken at the door by a tall man with slicked-back silver hair. Millie could see that Ashby certainly had a preference for the colors represented outside of his house. The floors were solid black marble polished to such a degree that Millie could see the reflection of every person and object in the room inside it. It was somewhat disorienting, actually, especially with the wide, crystal chandelier that dominated the ceiling and sent brilliant flecks of light scattering in every direction.

The walls were the same beige as the outside of the house but far less faded, thanks to the heavy black curtains. She was sure they kept out any bit of sun that threatened to make its way in. What was also clear was that Ashby had a particular fondness for black dogs.

They were everywhere; every variation of any creature that looked large and wolfish was hung in paintings on the walls, carved into the stairs' handrails, or as part of some standing artwork. And sitting and guarding what must have been the entrance to the main room, if the sound of music and garbled speech was any indicator, were two of the largest living animals she had ever seen.

They certainly looked like wolves but were possibly bigger. Their fur was raven black, their eyes even blacker, and their great yellow teeth flashed every time they opened their mouths. They eyed her as they approached, and her hesitation to pass between them must have been noticeable because the girl said, "It's quite alright. They're rather docile."

They certainly don't look like it, she wanted to say but held both her tongue and her breath as they walked between them. Only one of the creatures turned to sniff at her curiously.

She was still glancing back over her shoulder to make sure it didn't change its mind about being docile when a familiar voice jolted her back to a room that was full of people.

She saw noblemen dressed up like peacocks and women in slinky silk dresses clinging to their arms. Women she assumed—both by the girl's reaction to being told she was attending as Harlen's wife and just because of how young most of them looked—they were not married to. Was that why Berkley had been so adamant about keeping her out of even talking about this?

It seemed like an unreasonable amount of nervousness and secrecy to cover up the simple act of being an unfaithful asshole. Besides, she couldn't imagine most of them were very worried about what their wives would think if they found out if Vostesk Senior's treatment of his wife was any indicator.

"I didn't know you were coming!"

Speaking of Berkley. He practically materialized beside them—sans top hat, but with a brilliant green handkerchief accenting his white suit in its place. He truly was cutting loose this evening.

"Corrik didn't tell me he had extended the invitation. How delightful! And you've brought a guest!"

His bright voice had dipped down slightly as he indicated her. He gave her a nervous glance to go along with it, and she offered her most pleasant smile in return.

"Oh, but I assume you aren't without a guest for the evening? I'm sure your wife would be pleased to see you helping to educate all these young women on your society's ideals."

It was probably pushing a step too far, but it was satisfying to watch him flush and glance back at the ladies hanging around the men who looked nearly old enough to be their fathers. She saw Harlen almost choke on a suppressed laugh out of the corner of her eye while he cleared his throat to cover it.

"Yes. Well," Berkley said, adjusting the smart green handkerchief and trying to regain himself. "It is important for all our members to be kept abreast—up to speed—on our most recent functions."

I'm sure you see them as such respected members, she thought with internal sarcasm, but outwardly, maintained her pleasant smile.

"Who is this?"

The voice she had thought of when she looked at the growling wolf-like statues came from uncomfortably close to her left. When she turned, she couldn't help thinking that the man she assumed was Ashby really did look like a wolf.

His entire face had a snarling, pointed look to it and his hair hung down his back in a wild, black mess. He was taller than even Harlen and had a lean, sharp loon to him that was not eased by the most intense eyes she had ever seen. When they had fixed their attention on her, she certainly felt like a wolf was staring her down.

"Millie Vostesk," she said.

She felt Harlen's hand squeeze her arm, his hip nudging hers ever so slightly, encouraging her to continue. It filled her with enough confidence to offer another bright smile and to extend a hand toward the man who she was pretty sure would have bitten it off had he been able. He certainly looked like he wanted to. "I don't believe we've had the pleasure."

He glanced at her outstretched hand and ignored it completely. Then turned to Harlen and spoke as though she hadn't said a word. "This gathering is open only to those who have been invited."

She had only ever heard Vostesk Senior make such an ordinary statement sound like a threat until that point. She felt her second chill of the evening at yet another unpleasant reminder and expected to feel Harlen pull her a step back from the huge man. She thought that was precisely what he was doing when she felt his arm slip out of hers until she felt it move to her waist.

Harlen circled his arm around her middle and pulled her flush against his side. She gave him a glance she was sure she didn't cover her surprise and saw he was meeting Ashby's stare with a bright glint in his eyes she had yet to see. She could still see the familiar set of his jaw that indicated he was anxious, but his voice was calmer and smoother than she had ever heard it when he spoke.

"Which is exactly why I invited her to come with me. I think you'll find I understood the rules just fine."

She was surprised, to say the least. She saw Berkley blink, and Ashby looked like he might really be about to sink his teeth into someone. He tried to move closer when it was like an invisible force pushed him back several steps, and a calm, smiling face appeared between them.

"I see you two are making our guests feel welcome."

Corrik stood there, dressed better than she had seen him so far but still very simply: a black suit in a very ordinary cut. He still wore the red sash around his waist secured by the butterfly pin, but somehow it managed to look elegant rather than out of place. "That is very kind of you, gentlemen. Harlen, Millie, so good to see that you both could make it."

He smiled brightly at the both of them and shook Harlen's hand, and pressed a kiss into the back of hers before clasping it tightly. "I was so hoping Harlen would bring you along. After our conversation the other day, I have wanted another chance to discuss matters. Such as they are."

He paused and glanced back over his shoulder to see Berkley and Ashby had wandered off. Several others who had been giving them dubious looks since they came in had returned to their conversations. Corrik released her hand and chuckled before speaking to both of them.

"I think that should chase them off for the evening. Or for the time being, at the very least."

He clapped his hands together and offered an almost sheepish look. "I'm very sorry for their behavior. I'm afraid most of the people here are rather stuck in their ways. And I'm grateful that you didn't punch Ashby in the mouth. I'm not sure I would have been so gracious in your position," he said to Harlen, who seemed a bit surprised by his own reaction. "Truthfully, though, I'm very grateful the two of you came."

He did seem genuinely pleased. He was smiling practically ear to ear, and his look was one of unabashed fondness. "And I would be open to any conversation that would separate me from chatting about noble gossip for a while. If I must hear about Abernathy and his new mistress one more time, I will pack up and go right back to Ruasha."

"Actually," Harlen brightened, "This death goddess you had mentioned. I've been trying to look into her, but I haven't been able to find anything. I was wondering. . ."

He trailed off because Corrik's blue eyes began to positively gleam. When he spoke, he sounded nearly breathless.

"Yes, yes, I understand. No, there would not be much modern work on her, I'm afraid. But I would be delighted, absolutely delighted to tell you more. I do have a few other guests arriving that I must see to, but, please, I will find you within the hour."

They exchanged more polite handshakes and nods before Corrik walked back into the crowd. Millie glanced back at Harlen once he had gone, and they began to move further into the room. "I think that's the most assertive I've ever seen you."

He laughed and relaxed, and she was glad to see him returning to the man he had become since Vostesk Senior's death. Even amid all these nobles, he didn't seem quite as nervous as he had before. She wondered if it was due in part to her presence or because some part of him was changing.

No, not changing. Emerging. Easing into who he would have been from the beginning, if not for Vostesk Senior and his cold eyes and even colder heart, it was fascinating to see. The things about him she loved the most were gradually becoming brighter and brighter.

CHAPTER 48

"Do you know what this is?" Harlen asked as they were offered drinks in glasses with delicate stems on a silver plate by a stern-faced man in a waistcoat like the one who had taken their coats at the door.

Millie glanced at the brown liquid with a faint, rosy tint and didn't recognize it on sight. She gave it a brief sniff and curled her nose. Harlen chuckled.

"Can I take that as a yes?" he asked.

"I think it's rum."

It was an odd way to serve it, though. And it had a very strange, almost fruity edge to the scent that she couldn't identify. She wasn't a fan of rum under the best circumstances, but as she lifted the glass and gave it a curious taste with a long sip, she decided that, no, this was worse.

She scrunched up her nose at the lingering taste that coated her mouth. There was the burning of rum and the taste of something like cherry perfume that remained on her tongue. She watched Harlen take a much smaller sip of it as well to satisfy his curiosity, and his expression as soon as he did was so similar to her own she couldn't help but laugh.

"That tastes like the cough medicine I used to take when I was a child," Harlen commented, tilting the glass and eyeing the liquid inside warily. "Eerily similar. It would put me out for hours."

"Best be careful with it then," she said, and the two of them decided it would be better to carry the glasses around rather than have someone approach them again. They didn't want to feel obligated to take more polite sips.

She kept her eyes on the room, the groups of noblemen and the women on their arms who honestly looked rather bored at a close glance. Now and then, one lady would look at the other, and they would exchange a look that she recognized as a blatant eye-roll behind a pleasant smile.

She could hardly blame them. She had no idea what she had been expecting, but it hadn't been a bunch of businessmen standing around talking about their trade sipping on awful drinks.

Corrik had said it would be dull, but when she had imagined a party welcoming back a colleague, she had expected at least a little dancing. From the way the chairman and Ashby had tiptoed around the subject of the society when they had come over, she practically expected there to be an orgy of some kind. But the small band that stood in the corner playing away on their instruments seemed to know only one terribly slow song and nobody seemed to be discussing anything beyond petty gossip.

"It's not what I expected," Harlen agreed after they had made the trip around the room, eyeing all the groups and casually dropping in here and there to listen to what was being said.

"Why bother being part of a secret club if you aren't going to do anything fun?" she asked, and he cracked another smile. He seemed just as perplexed and shook his head.

"I guess I was thinking there would be something of consequence going on," he said. He swirled the still nearly untouched beverage in his hand and looked into it, watching the rosy liquid sparkle under the candlelight. "I suppose that could be my fault partially. It's just—we've been looking at this for so long I thought that there would be something here. Some obvious hint at what my father was up to, or what happened with Tansey. . . Maybe there just isn't anything. Maybe I've been putting too much thought into it. I do have a way of overthinking. Maybe I made this out to be worse than it is."

She squeezed his hand, and he turned his dark eyes to hers. He gave her a smile that tugged up the left side of his mouth and softened the sharp angles of his face. "Maybe there's something here; maybe there isn't," she said, keeping her voice low to give them some relative privacy as they hung in the far corner of the room. "But I don't think she would blame you for trying hard as you have been."

His smile warmed, and his hand that was squeezing hers tightened. The arm around her waist did as well, and he bent to bring his face close to hers. The intense gentleness in his eyes made her breath catch in her throat, and the flutter it gave her heart made her giggle.

"You know people are watching," she said, but she was smiling.

"I don't care," he said, and she honestly believed him. She didn't find it in herself to care much either. Not with his lips pressed into hers ever so gently, and his hand pressed flat to her back.

If their holding hands in the street drew sharp looks, she could only imagine what this must be doing. But maybe that was the point. Perhaps he had been growing tired of the looks gradually increasing since Corrik had vanished, and he was asserting that he wanted her there, and there were to be no more questions about it.

Her suspicion was all but confirmed when he drew back and gave her a brief, tender look before glancing back over his shoulder at the noblemen nearby who paused their conversation to stare.

Millie felt the temperature in the room drop at the sharpness of Harlen's returning look. She wasn't sure if the sensation was physical or imagined, but she felt a chill sweep over her. A few of them blinked and rolled their shoulders as though they felt it too before slowly going back to their conversation, this time ignoring them pointedly.

"If this is all it's going to be all evening, we can leave," he said, turning back towards her. "If you want."

"I'll stick it out," she said, keeping the closeness between them by leaning into his side. She did want to hear what Corrik had to say. Even if there were nothing here, that, at the very least, would be interesting. And it might satiate some of the lingering questions she wanted to ask about the death goddess who they had been able to find so little about. Harlen nodded and settled with his back against the wall.

They remained there for quite some time, uninterrupted, chatting quietly until Berkley appeared and moved across the room towards them again.

"Any chance he'll just say hello and move on?" she asked.

Apparently not. He stopped and looked rather flushed with sweat shining on his forehead beneath his perfectly waved, gleaming hair.

"Excuse me. Harlen. My dear boy," he said, dabbing at the sweat with his green handkerchief. He sounded out of breath. "I'm afraid I might need some assistance. Ashby has gotten into a bit of a, well, exchange. Again. I would understand your reluctance, but do you think you could help me?"

Harlen didn't seem thrilled by the idea. He was considering it; Millie could see it on his face. She wasn't thrilled either but did give him a bit of a nod to go on. After all, if the wolf of a man had cornered some other poor soul, she couldn't blame them for wanting help.

"I'll be able to fend for myself for just a few minutes."

"Ah, thank you, my dear," the chairman said, suddenly remembering his manners. He must really have need help.

The shift didn't go unnoticed by Harlen, who had detached himself from her with marked reluctance and smoothed down the red tie. He only paused once, and she watched a dawning realization on his face that made his shoulders sit straighter.

Before following the chairman, Harlen stopped and said, "I'll go. But first, I believe you owe Millie an apology. For tonight and for how you spoke to her in our house during your last visit."

Berkley blinked at him and at her. She was sure she looked as surprised as he did, though she tried quickly to cover it. She would be lying if she said she didn't get some enjoyment out of watching the man offer a quick apology with a few uncertain glances in her husband's direction.

It was very odd; she couldn't quite place the way Berkley looked at him. There was uncertainty, yes, but there was something else. Anxiousness, curiosity. . .something of that ilk. It drew her attention and made her very nearly ask Harlen to stay as he turned to follow Berkley once his apology was made.

It set her on edge, and she watched them make their way through the crowd, Berkley's bright white suit, and Harlen's black. She remained waiting, uneasiness stirring in the pit of her stomach, watching even after disappeared for their return.

For the first time in not nearly long enough, that little voice inside her was whispering again.

Something is wrong.

Chapter 49

Harlen followed several paces behind Berkley as he led him through the main room and into what he assumed was some kind of sitting area separated from the hall by a curtain of deep, deep gold. The room behind it contained several small, round tables where a few men were scattered, sitting in high, spindly chairs of shiny black metal.

All of them seemed transfixed by a heated exchange between Ashby and a man Harlen recognized as Bonnadin. At least, that was his last name; he had never been well-acquainted enough with his father for Harlen to have learned his first. He was a tall man with slick blond hair and a thin, rat-like face that was flushed with either whatever he had been drinking or with indignation. The young man beside him was his son. The one Harlen had spotted briefly at the Crow's Nest.

They stood beside a chair that had been knocked onto the floor and a pile of glittering, shattered glass. From the relative silence of the onlookers, Harlen guessed they had just missed whatever had caused that.

"If you hadn't brought him here in the first place, this wouldn't be a problem!" Ashby shouted. "Everyone knows about it—I don't know why you act as though it would be shocking for us to hear."

"He has no business running his mouth about it!" Bonnadin shouted back. "You know what would happen if the wrong people heard! I'm teaching him to mind his manners! And he was my son last time I checked—don't presume to tell me how I should remind him!"

Harlen's focus drifted away from the two of them to the young man who was the spitting image of his father. He had his face turned downward and was making the kind of face Harlen recognized all too well as an attempt not to humiliate himself further by crying. The reason for which he assumed was the screaming, the staring of the other patrons, and the massive red mark on the side of his face in the shape of a handprint.

It had been forceful enough to break the skin, and a small trickle of blood was oozing from just under his eye.

Harlen was amazed he was still standing. Or maybe he hadn't been before they got here. That would explain why the chair was knocked over.

Harlen felt himself pale and looked to Berkley for an explanation. Berkley was wringing his hands, his eyes darting between Harlen and the arguing men as though he was waiting for him to jump in the middle of them. "What happened?"

"Oh. Well. The subject of The Academy came up, and Avery—that young man there—might have mentioned that he was struggling. With his spells. Their family has been having difficulties with it for some time. It's a very sensitive subject."

Harlen felt his stomach twist. Yes, he was all too familiar with that. He had been in the same position too many times to count.

He knew Berkley had brought him back to help pry the two men arguing apart, but those two could scream at each other until they were blue in the face for all he cared. His concern was Avery, who everyone seemed to be watching, but nobody was bothering to help.

Harlen slipped away from Berkley and approached the young man, well aware he was now the center of attention. Again, that wasn't his concern. He pulled a square of linin from his pocket and offered it to him for the blood running in a fat drop down his cheek.

Avery looked at him with wide, suspicious eyes. It was another look he had worn far too many times himself, but he accepted the linin all the same and pressed it to his face.

"Maybe we should step back over there for a bit." Harlen nodded towards the far corner of the room.

He knew Avery would never leave the party, not without his father's permission. He wouldn't have only months ago. But he might be able to convince him to get out of swinging distance before the fight between the two men escalated.

Avery's eyes darted back to Berkley and the two men fighting. He didn't seem to know what to do but nodded all the same.

"Alright."

Harlen ushered him out of the middle of the room. He could still feel eyes following them, but now the men were taking up most of the attention. Harlen heard another glass break behind them and didn't breathe again until they were in a secluded far corner of the room where there were a few empty tables and a small, narrow window that looked out onto the street. Avery seemed relieved to have a bit of cool air to breathe, though his narrow shoulders were still slumped and shaking.

"Don't let him talk to you like that," Harlen said.

Avery looked at him in surprise. "I'm sorry?"

Harlen kept his face stern, but not enough to be threatening. He wondered if Avery could see the desperation in his eyes as he spoke. "Don't let him. It won't get any better. You'll never make him happy. You need to make him understand that you won't be pushed around, no matter how little magic you have."

How old was he? Harlen thought, if he remembered correctly, Avery should be about eighteen. He was out of his depth in a place like this, holding conversations with noblemen, and it showed. He looked terrified.

Avery lowered his eyes when Harlen spoke and didn't seem to know how or even if he should respond. When he finally did, he was shaking so badly that Harlen would have put an arm around him if he didn't know it would have terrified him further.

"I. . .I mean, it—it was my fault."

"It wasn't," Harlen insisted.

Avery looked at the ground. He seemed to be on the verge of tears again, and Harlen tried not to look at him. He looked out of the window but kept him in the corner of his vision, watched as he screwed up his face, and said in a voice that was hardly a whisper, "You're very kind."

"Please," Avery said in a stiff-lipped whisper, "You shouldn't have come back here—"

His words were cut off as Harlen felt a rough hand grab his shoulder, digging in their fingers. His entire body went cold, and when he was forcibly turned, it took him a moment to understand why he was looking at Ashby's snarling face and not his father's.

Ashby was barking something at him that he hardly heard in his momentary confusion. He was sure it amounted to something about not interfering. But all he understood was that Ashby almost immediately yanked back his hand with a shout of pain. A hand that Harlen saw had turned purple and blue in the fingers. Frozen.

Magic will defend its host.

Those with magic in their blood must learn to keep their emotions in check.

Harlen watched Ashby pull away from him and clutch at his injured hand. His barking had become a low keeping groan of pain, and slowly Harlen tore his eyes away from the sight to look around at the gathered faces.

There was no more curiosity. No quiet smiles of approval that he had seen when he first walked in. No subtle nods at what Bonnadin was saying about his son. No more staring at Avery and doing nothing. There was only stunned silence and eyes fixed on him.

There was momentary fear. They would get up; they would attack him. He would pay for disrupting what he had no business interfering with. Then there came the slow realization that they wouldn't do anything. He wasn't going to be hurt because he was just the same as they were now. The evidence was all in Ashby's frozen hand. They weren't going to go after someone who could strike back at them.

Earlier that night, he had been confident because of Millie. He was determined nobody was going to make her feel out of place or unwelcome. Over the last few weeks, he had been pushing himself to be more confident for her sake, for the sake of the small family that was now his job to protect. It felt good. It felt right. But he had never considered pushing back against something done to him specifically would feel the same.

He didn't mind the eyes on him. Let them understand he wouldn't be pushed. And neither would anyone else they deemed as less. Not in his presence.

"You will not put your hands on me," Harlen said. He spoke low to keep the tremble of exhilaration and indignation out of his voice, but they heard him.

Harlen turned to Bonnadin and pointed back to Avery with blood still seeping through the cut under his eye. "How could you do that to your son? Do you think that's going to make him want to please you?"

He was walking closer to Bonnadin, getting louder as he spoke. The corners of his vision were red and fuzzy. He was angry. He was furious. This was wrong, and none of them cared.

"He's going to resent you. For the rest of his life, no matter what he does. Magic or no magic, he is going to hate you. Do you hear me? Do you care, or are you too selfish and stupid to see beyond what you can brag about to your friends? As long as you can say he knows his spells, everything is just fine, isn't it?"

He was freezing and burning all at once. Harlen felt like he was floating in a fever dream as he grabbed Bonnadin by the shirt collar and his black suit immediately began to form a delicate, lace-like pattern of frost that spread outward from where he'd balled the fabric in his fist. "I thought the same thing of my father—tell me where he is now."

"Harlen—Harlen. My boy. Please." Berkley's voice broke through as the anxious man grabbed his arm. A bold move considering what had happened to Ashby. Harlen didn't fail to notice that he mostly held on to his sleeve as he attempted to pull him off the man whose collar he had in a vice-grip.

Harlen glanced at him, and Berkley widened his eyes. He pressed a forced, pleasant smile into his face beneath his curled mustache and gave his voice an almost sing-song lilt as he said, "It's time to calm down, don't you think?"

The shift was immediate. Harlen felt the odd, red fog begin to lift from his eyes, but the fuzzy quality did not clear. Rather, it became soothing in a way. He was aware that he was slowly letting go of Bonnadin as he stared into Berkley's blue-green eyes.

"Yes, yes, do that. Calm down." Berkley nodded. His voice was soothing, but there was visible strain on his face. Harlen saw the beginnings of red seeping into his white mustache as the man's nose began to bleed with the effort of doing what he was.

Magic. He was using magic. Harlen blinked as he realized it; he could feel it like an invisible hand had slithered into his skull and was squeezing his brain. Forcing out the anger, unclenching his fists, convincing him to take a step back.

"Stop," Harlen managed to say though the word took too long to come out of his mouth. His tongue felt heavy as stone.

"Please, understand," Berkley said, still nodding. Invisible hand still squeezing. Nose still bleeding. "This is for your own good."

No, it isn't. He wanted him to sit back and let this happen like the others. He wouldn't. He refused. Not while he could finally *do something* to stop it.

He managed to arrange his face to glare at Berkley, which made his nervous smile falter momentarily. It took nearly all his focus, but he managed to mumble out, "Let. . .go."

He didn't. Berkley shook his head and only repeated, "Trust me. This is for your own good. Calm down."

No. No, he had spent too much time being quiet and calm. He wouldn't.

He pushed back, back against the squeezing hand inside his skull. Spent all that focus that had been drilled so hard into him on prying the fingers loose and shoving back.

Berkley could feel it. Harlen felt his struggle to push it back into place, but once the grip had been loosened, Harlen's anger returned in full force. He bent the invisible hand back until he imagined he heard the bones inside it snapping, and Berkley cried out in pain. Then he grabbed Berkley's real, physical hand from off his sleeve and shoved him back against the wall.

The impact was jarring, but through the red haze, Harlen hardly felt a thing. All he could see was Berkley's blurred face. And the smoke that began to pour from it. The smoke he had seen twice before from his mouth and eyes. Rising into him and filling his ears with a ringing, humming sound, obscuring the last of his vision.

But this time, it lasted only a moment. Either Berkley managed to shove him off, or someone pulled him away, but the only thing he knew was he felt as though the breath had been sucked out of him as the smoke pulled away. His vision went white as he staggered back, and he felt as though his skull was going to crack open from the force of the pain.

When Harlen's vision finally cleared, he realized he was lying on the floor, staring at the ceiling. His entire body felt as though it was on fire. He was gasping, trying to get breath into his burning lungs, and everything was bright. Far too bright.

"Move—no, move!"

Harlen heard only one person speaking—shouting—over the muttering crowd looking on in horror. Then suddenly, a familiar set of pale green eyes and blood-red lips filled his vision. Magnolia.

"You. Hey, buddy, hey."

She was dressed formally for the party, but her lipstick and the black around her eyes were still smudged. The intensity of the color stood out so blindingly that for a moment, it was the only thing he could focus on.

She grabbed his face roughly, and her sharp nails dug into his skin. "I swear if you make me watch someone die tonight, I'll beat the shit out of you," she hissed in her heavily accented voice, turning his face left to right. "Ashby, what the hell! You're throwing people now?"

"Shut up, whore."

"Yeah, whore, very creative. You hired me, asshole—what does that make you?" she muttered, shaking her head, her grip still tight on Harlen's jaw as though that would keep him alive. It was painful, but it did draw him back enough to reality to finally sit up.

Magnolia let go of his face and sat back on her heels, her glittering red dress pooling around her. She heaved a heavy sigh of relief.

"What are you doing here?" he asked, his head still pounding and spinning. He felt like he had just run across the city. His limbs were shaking so badly that she had to help him stand. She looped one of his arms over her shoulders and lifted him with surprising ease.

"I'm working; what's it look like?" she asked, helping him stagger out of the room.

Once they were on the other side of the gold curtains, she lowered him to the ground where he sat, clutching the side of his head. White spots pulsed like stars behind his eyes.

Magnolia crouched in front of him again, watching like a hawk. "Shit, you really banged your head, didn't you?"

No, that wasn't what happened. Harlen hadn't felt his head hit the ground. He hadn't felt any of the apparent fall actually, but he knew that wasn't what the pain was. He had felt the same thing after he'd encountered Donnie in the alley behind The Raven's Nest. It was how he felt after his father's death when that black smoke had poured from him.

This was similar enough for him to guess that this must be the same, but something about it was different. He ached. And he didn't understand why.

"I need to find Millie," he said. He needed to get her out of here. He needed to get them both out of here. "My wife."

"Yeah, sure." Her dark brows furrowed with concern. "I can get her. What's she look like?"

His thoughts felt like swirling, dark water, and nothing made sense, but he could describe Millie. His words slurred as he spoke, but after a moment, Magnolia had nodded and stood up.

"Wait here."

CHAPTER 50

Millie kept her back to the wall and listened to the wailing of the slow music. People were talking, shooting glances in her direction, laughing amongst themselves. Glasses of that horrible rum were clinking.

Too long. This is taking too long. Something isn't right.

She pushed herself up and began making her way across the center of the room, weaving between the groups, trying to follow the direction Harlen had gone. She wouldn't interrupt if she found him and something serious was going on, but she needed to see him.

The glances from the women as she hurried across the floor were curious, but the glares from the men were sharper without Harlen standing there. She tried not to feel them and the hot, unpleasant prickle they sent down her spine.

Was she overreacting? It was entirely possible. She ordinarily didn't feel quite so nervous about things. But now, she felt like her heart was beating up in her throat, and her vision seemed far less clear than usual.

Everything was too bright. Not blindingly so, but just enough to make her feel like things were slightly off-kilter. That drink couldn't have been that strong, could it? She had seen everyone here working on one; if her one gulp was enough to make her feel unsteady, everyone here should be positively plastered by now if that was the case.

"Watch yourself!" a nobleman she didn't recognize snapped at her as she tried to slide past him and knocked against his arm. She made some kind of apology and felt her stomach roll.

Not right. Something isn't right.

She was going to be sick, she realized. She hurried her pace, cursing under her breath, and cast her eyes about for an exit. She wasn't going to make it across the room to go back between those wolf-like dogs.

As the fuzziness in her head increased, so did the rolling of her stomach. Her heart pounded faster, and that sensation grew to a fevered shouting in the back of her head.

This isn't right. This isn't right.

She spotted an empty-looking hallway that led further into the house and plunged into it. She hit the wall hard with her arm as she rounded the corner, though Millie could have sworn she'd given herself plenty of space to make the turn. But had she? Her vision was beginning to worsen.

Was this more of what had happened last night? Or was this something else entirely? She didn't know. She couldn't think. Her breath was sticking in her throat, and she thought the sheer blind panic would choke her. She had never felt anything like it. It possessed her, shoved her forward until she very nearly collided with a figure that she first recognized only by the red sash.

"Millie." Corrik's voice was concerned, and he put a hand on her shoulder to steady her. "Are you alright?"

"No," Millie managed to get out. She was breathing so heavily she was sure she was difficult to understand but somehow managed to convey that she was going to be sick.

Corrik's hand vanished from her shoulder for a moment, but her vision was too clouded and fuzzy to see where to. It returned a moment later, this time on her back, and he held something in front of her.

"In here," he said.

As soon as the command left his mouth, what felt like the entirety of her insides upended themselves. She could taste the cherry flavor in all of it, and it choked her, but once it was done, she felt her balance returning. The panic inside her faded; the voice that had been screaming at her moments ago quieted down as her vision began to clear once she could no longer taste the bitter cherry in her mouth.

"Oh, shit," she said aloud as she saw what she'd thrown up into. Some sort of vase or flowerpot. She then raised a hand to Corrik and said, "Language. Sorry."

He chuckled. "That's just fine."

She wasn't sure embarrassed was an adequate term for what she felt as she straightened and pushed back her hair. Corrik set the vase aside, and she grimaced. "I ruined that, didn't I?"

"Honestly? It wouldn't be the first time someone has used one of these to throw up in, though that usually happens at Ashby's wilder parties. Trust me, I'm speaking from personal experience," he said.

"I don't think the drinks agree with me."

"Ah, I see." He nodded, and she didn't know why it didn't sound right. "Please, you should sit."

She didn't even know where they were; the room she had stumbled into looked like a library. There was a grand piano glistening black in the far corner beside a tall window, and bookshelves were holding heavy novels that all seemed to be red, black, or gold lined up in perfect rows on their shelves. And bell jars. There were at least ten that she could see, all of them holding little branches from trees where butterflies perched, wings spread—monarchs, cabbage butterflies, swallowtails: quite the extensive collection.

"Lovely creatures, aren't they?" Corrik asked in response to her staring. He approached one of the jars with two monarchs suspended neatly inside the glass. When he touched a finger to the outside and ran it down the jar, she noticed the slight frown on his face. "It's a shame that they're preserved."

They weren't alive. None of them moved from their fixed positions, Millie realized. "How did he manage that?"

"I'm unsure," he said, letting his hand drop from the glass, but his frown remained as he studied the creature and its autumn fire wings. "Despite my early career, I never did much in the way of embalming. I'm sure this is a bit different, but I'm unfamiliar with such things on even the basics. I find it. . ." he trailed off, searching for the correct or perhaps the politest word for something he clearly had some level of discomfort towards.

"Disgusting?" she offered to break the quiet contemplation he'd fallen into, and he returned with a chuckle.

"That is a good way of putting it, yes. Unnatural is another," he said, giving her a fond smile. "You're from the northern mountains, yes?"

That perked her interest. "Have you been?"

He nodded. "Indeed. I'm far more a fan of the burial practices of your homeland. Allowing the dead to pass and bring forth new life. All those lovely forests that offer shade and shelter and places for children to climb on the bones of their ancestors. Far better than doing things like this." He nodded back at the bell jar. "It is. . . an upset of the natural order. Life is a beautiful thing. What comes from its passing should not be wasted."

"Even something so small?" she asked with a genuine curiosity that he seemed to appreciate.

"Especially," he said.

He moved across the room and sat smoothly on the couch beside her, and she was aware that every bit of uneasiness had left her body. Millie remembered she had been looking for Harlen, but now she was almost sure she had been jumping to conclusions, or the drink had caused her paranoia in some way. She felt so exceptionally calm that she couldn't imagine why she had ever been worried as Corrik smiled at her with those intensely blue eyes.

Though, it was strange. Her vision was clearing, but it remained slightly blurred at the edges. In the center, his eyes stood out with brilliant clarity.

"It is the smallest things that can have the largest impact. A small act or small gift given in the right way can result in things beyond imagination."

"Is that part of the death goddess thing?" she asked. Her thoughts were sluggish, and his amused smile in response to her question was contagious.

"It is indeed."

"And the butterflies?" she said. She propped her cheek on her hand; her arm braced on the back of the beige couch with its curling black frame. Her interest in the bell jars had gone, but it was fascinating to watch him look at them. He was only turning his head, but there was something hypnotic about the movement. "I have to ask. I feel like I'm seeing them everywhere. What is it that's so important about them?"

"It's quite simple," he said. "Rebirth."

"Is that all?"

The smile widened again. "Not entirely. It's a symbol of the goddess because she represents not just death but what comes as a result. New life. New energy in the universe. A butterfly represents what she offers—life, death, and rebirth. A caterpillar goes into a cocoon and is reborn as something stronger and more beautiful than before. Like your forests in the far north."

She could see it in her mind so vividly as he spoke. It was like it was right there in front of her eyes, those forests on a bright spring afternoon. Leaves rustling in the wind, petals dropping from the blossoms blooming along the intertwined branches in the family groves. Millie could see how the sun slanted through the branches. She could picture those two monarchs from the bell jar flitting along and floating lazily on the warm afternoon breeze.

She faded off into silence as she thought about it, and Corrik said nothing to interrupt. He only watched her serenely as she blinked and returned to the present like she was waking from a dream. She could swear she could still feel the sun on her skin.

"That sounds beautiful," was all she could think to say.

"It is," he said, his voice heavy with emotion. "I have seen such wonderful things come from tragedy. And I believe you will in time as well."

Some part of her thought that was a very odd thing to say. But that part of her felt distant. All she could feel was a blood-deep calm and the memory of spring.

She could smell the flowers if she tried. She could clearly imagine the beautiful tree that had sprung up after her grandmother's passing and remembered how it had made the pain she had left behind ease. She could visit that real, living thing whenever she wanted and would spend hours reading her favorite books to it, feeling as though she was heard.

"You strike me as a religious woman. Pardon the assumption," Corrik said. His voice didn't break her train of thought and mixed with memory. It seemed to compliment it. There was a musical quality to his voice that floated on the warm wind. "I understand the goddess Shareen is a popular deity in your region."

Millie nodded slowly. Too slowly. Her words felt heavy and jumbled behind her teeth, and she felt distantly that she should be afraid. Corrik hadn't blinked since they sat down.

"Yes. Well, I was never particularly good at it. I don't think I was as peaceful as I was supposed to be. I'm pretty sure I hold a grudge for too long to be a good follower."

"Oh, I don't think any deity requires perfection—only devotion. People by nature are fallible creatures. Even those who try very hard to make you believe that they are not. In fact, it tends to be those people who are the most fallible." He gestured to his chest. "I simply devote myself to my work, and my goddess, as much as I can. And I understand that I am fallible. Believing your own assumptions to be correct at all times can lead to tragedy."

"Like Vostesk Senior," Millie said, not even knowing when it sprang to mind, amazing herself with the bluntness of the statement. It was unwise to say that right to the face of one of his former friends, but Corrik didn't seem offended. He merely nodded, his face grave.

"Yes, much like Vostesk Senior. He had the determination and drive to be a great man, but he could trust nothing outside himself. Wasted potential."

"Did he worship the death goddess too?" Millie asked.

Corrik sighed. "He tried. I don't think he ever fully surrendered himself to it. I'm not even sure how entirely he believed in it. I think part of him clung to some aspects of her. He was a desperate man that I'm sure you know. I think it was something he tried to grab hold of while he sank. A shark that does not keep moving forward dies; he said something to that effect on more than one occasion. But in the end. . ." Corrik shook his head. "I'm not sure he was ever able to accept anything other than perfection. That was where he went wrong. It froze him in place, and the shark drowned all the same."

Millie wondered how much he knew about Vostesk Senior. If he knew the extent to which the man demanded perfection. But something about the way Corrik was studying her made her think he did. He was trying to decide if she knew as much as he did.

"Do you want to know what I think?" she asked.

"Very much," he said, and she believed it.

"I think he was the closest thing to a monster I've ever met."

Corrik again studied her with his clear blue eyes. The entire room was silent. Even the sound drifting in from the other room seemed to have stopped. "Can you keep a secret, Miss Millie?"

She nodded. Corrik lowered his voice to a whisper. "I think you might be right. I think there are far too many like him who don't deserve the claws they were born with. Then there are so many people I see who do twice what any nobleman has done with half the advantages."

"Too bad there's nothing to be done about it," Millie said.

She felt his smile as well as saw it. She felt it like a wave of warmth rolling over her, like the gesture alone shared with her whatever peace and happiness caused it. She found herself smiling as well and only faltered because she heard another whisper from that tiny voice saying *danger*. He still hadn't blinked.

"The goddess works in mysterious ways. I think in the end, power will go to those who deserve it. I think the death of Vostesk Senior has helped bring about something wonderful."

He reached his hand out as though he was going to touch her. She felt heavy and lethargic, but a sharp, hissing whisper from the voice sent her flinching back.

Corrik didn't seem insulted by it. If anything, his eyes sparkled brighter. "Tell me, how late is your blood?"

The question was so sudden and unexpected that through the hazy state of mind she found herself in, she could only feel confused. "What?"

"It's good that you were sick. You should stay away from the drinks. They do have special properties, but in your condition, you should avoid alcohol altogether. I'll tell someone to get you some water," he continued.

Millie blinked, coming up through clouds of confusion and strange, unnatural calm. "Wait—what are you saying?"

"Shh," he soothed, locking his eyes back on hers and placing a finger to his lips. All at once, Millie felt her heartbeat slow. She fell back limp against the couch where she had been beginning to stand. "It's alright. I know it's frightening, but you must understand that you have been given a gift."

She stared at him. She couldn't have torn her eyes away from him if she wanted to. The way he looked at her made her feel like he was peeling back her skin, examining her blood and bones with great care. With the skill of a mortician and the love of an artist.

"I told you that I don't care for arranged matches. When Vostesk Senior mentioned he was seeking a wife for his son, I had my objections. I had my concerns. But it is as I said: the two of you are harmonious. You make him happy. I believe the goddess's gift will look kindly on that."

All at once, the sound came back to the room. It was so jarring that it made Millie jump as another voice shattered the still air. She could hear the music and polite laughter from the other room again, and it was so loud compared to the silence that it nearly startled her off her seat. She could move again. Her heart was pounding in her throat again.

"Hey." A woman with a mass of curly black hair and smudged makeup stood in the doorway, holding both sides of the frame. Her face was drawn and worried, and she was looking directly at her, repeating her question. "You Millie?"

Millie blinked, already standing up. That sense of foreboding that had fled came rushing back in. Even when she darted a look back at Corrik and he made no move to prevent her from moving away, she felt it. "What's wrong?"

How long had she been in here?

"Your husband's looking for you. Or sent me to look for you—same difference. The point is, he's in rough shape."

She was already hurrying towards the door. Behind her, she could hear Corrik beginning to follow. "Magnolia, dear, what's happened?"

"Ashby's lost his mind. That's what's happened," Magnolia snapped as Magnolia lead them to the ballroom. "Apparently, he thinks he can toss people around because it's his house."

As soon as Millie saw Harlen leaning against the wall with a hand to his face, she rushed ahead to get to him. She had known it. She had known something was wrong.

She grabbed hold of him with both hands as soon as she was close enough, searching for injuries. He was paper white, and there was a pink streak above his lip that indicated his nose had been bleeding. She felt tears pricking at her eyes.

"Millie, Millie, what's wrong?"

He was more alarmed by her wet eyes than his apparent injury. The hands he put on the sides of her face were cold and clammy; the tear he wiped with his thumb felt like a burning hot streak across her cheek in contrast.

She couldn't articulate what was wrong. She just shook her head best as she could with his hands still on her face and hoped he wouldn't object when she looked up at him and said, "I want to go home."

No objection. He nodded and slid his arm around her, pulling her against his chest. She gripped his shirt, pressing her face against his ribs until she could feel the pulse of his heart beneath her cheek.

"Please," Corrik was saying behind her. "You're both in no condition to walk. Allow me to arrange a carriage for you."

"Yeah. You look like shit," the woman, Magnolia, chimed in. "No polite refusals. You're going to pass out on the street if you walk all the way back across town."

Millie had no complaints. Anything that got them away from here faster would be fine. She let the conversation take place around her while she listened to the flutter of Harlen's heart, reassuring herself with it that he was alright. That she was alright. Her only protest came when Corrik offered to ride back with them to make sure they got home safely.

She lifted her head to speak, but as soon as she felt his eyes on the back of her neck, that insidious calm smothered her words. She let her cheek drop back against Harlen's chest, and she felt him reach up and touch her back.

"Are you okay?" Harlen asked quietly. They had moved from the ballroom to out beside the front door to wait for the carriage. He had undoubtedly felt her stiffen then go suddenly limp again.

I don't want to get in a carriage with him. Millie thought, but her tongue felt heavy. She could feel Corrik's eyes on the back of her head. It wasn't the ice-cold stare of Vostesk Senior; this was burning hot.

"She was sick earlier," Corrik explained. "But she should be fine with some rest."

Magic, she thought as they climbed into the carriage that pulled up close to the door, it had to be magic of some kind he was using. Something like the kind Berkley had. Something persuasive.

She kept her face hidden against Harlen's shirt for the entirety of the ride, hoping that somehow that would break whatever spell was over her, but keeping away from eye contact didn't seem to do a thing.

She just felt herself getting slower and heavier until, without warning, she dropped off into sleep.

CHAPTER 51

Millie didn't wake up when they moved her from the carriage to the house.

Harlen carried her in himself. Corrik offered to help, but he insisted. Corrik seemed like a pleasant enough man, but the way she had tensed as soon as he had offered to ride home with them made him wary. Harlen had kept his arm firmly around her for the entire ride and watched Corrik out of the corner of his eye, but if the man took offense, he didn't show it. He made no arguments and simply opened the doors of the house for them.

"Please, which one is your bedroom?" Corrik asked as he walked a bit in front of the two of them up the stairs.

Harlen nodded to the door to indicate it and focused all the rest of his energies on keeping Millie from falling. He was still shaken by whatever it was he had done to Berkley. His limbs felt like jelly, and his head still pounded.

"You're sure you're alright?" Corrik inquired. "She mentioned that she was feeling unwell earlier this evening. I could send for a doctor if you wish."

"It's fine," Harlen said quickly. However, he was considering sending for one himself. "When did she mention that to you?"

Corrik opened his mouth to reply and was met with the sound of his mother's door slamming shut.

It had probably been a bad idea to let Corrik into the house, much less upstairs, knowing how much his father's friends upset her. He was still debating if he should say something to her when Corrik gestured into the open doorway.

"I'll see myself out," Corrik said, and Harlen was immensely grateful to end the exchange. He doubted he would have been able to make much sense out of any complicated conversation.

As soon as he heard the door click shut, he set Millie on the bed carefully as he could and collapsed beside her with a grimace. Every part of him hurt. He felt like the breath had been knocked out of him, and he couldn't seem to get it back.

He laid on his back, staring up at the seam in the window, at the tiny constellation of stars he had etched there what felt like a lifetime ago. There were a few more, he noticed, as he counted them. Millie must have been adding to them. It was so easy to picture her lying on her back, scratching them into place with the tip of a pen.

"Millie," he whispered, reaching out for her. It was odd that she had dropped off to sleep so quickly. He had been thinking about it ever since they climbed into the carriage. "Millie."

She opened her eyes, and the relief he felt was enough to make his knees weak. He didn't know what he had been expecting, but seeing the moonlight outside reflected in her gray eyes as they fluttered open made every muscle in his body relax.

"My head hurts," she said, sounding nearly as out of it as he felt.

"Mine too," he echoed and rolled onto his side to face her.

They were both still fully dressed from the party. Millie still had the shining pins in her hair, but that and his stiff suit could be bothered with later. He slid an arm around her, and she slid across the space between them to lay against him.

Something was still bothering her. Harlen could see it on her face, but she was exhausted as well. Everything from the way she moved to how heavily she let her head drop against the pillow said it. His questions could wait until morning. He would have been perfectly content to let her go back to sleep without a word until she said, "Harlen?"

"Yes?" he looked down at her, but she wasn't meeting his eyes. She was running her finger along the seam of his coat sleeve like she could see the scar beneath it.

"Let's not go back to one of those meetings."

He watched her for a long moment. He waited for her to say more, but she didn't volunteer anything. He considered asking, but she sounded so tired. Any questions could wait for tomorrow.

"Okay," he agreed, kissing the top of her head and pulling her closer. "We won't."

She nodded, and within minutes she was sleeping again, though not deeply. Her breath was light and uneven, and a frown pulled at her lips.

He tried to make her a bit more comfortable. He pulled the pins out of her hair carefully and loosened the tight laces at the back of her dress to give her more room to breathe. He tried pulling his tie out of its tight knot and hoped that lying still for a moment would lessen the ache in his body, but it remained. A dull pulse of pain continued behind his eyes, and his lungs felt like they were straining against his ribs with every breath.

He had a feeling. A creeping, cold feeling. A vague idea that pushed at the back of his mind. What he had done at the party. That sensation he had experienced twice before, once while he looked into his father's dying eyes, once with that man, Donnie, from The Raven's Nest. That overwhelming anger. The feeling of smoke filling his eyes and the blinding pain in his head.

But this time it had been. . .interrupted? Stopped? He wasn't sure. But this felt different than the other times. This was painful. His mind and body were sluggish. The only way he could think to describe what he felt in the aftermath was empty.

The only question was: What exactly had he done?

There was only one way to know for sure. He had a theory he had been considering but was reluctant to look into it. He didn't want to leave Millie's side with her feeling so unwell. He didn't want to drag himself out of bed in the early morning, feeling so exhausted and pained. And part of him didn't want to know. But he couldn't push away the thought any longer.

He would allow himself a few hours of sleep. Just enough to dull the ache in his bones and to curb the worst of his tiredness.

Harlen tracked down Jacques at the small, white house he lived in at the cemetery's edge. He arrived at the door just as Jacques was stepping out for a smoke break he had luckily decided to take outside for once.

He stepped outside, cursing under his breath with the cigarette clamped between his teeth. His hands were shaking as he fumbled with the key to lock the door behind him. Harlen watched as he tried once, twice, then twice more before slamming the door shut and shaking his head. He closed his eyes and let out a long sigh, peering out over the cemetery with either distaste or sadness. Harlen couldn't tell. He only knew Jacques wasn't aware of his presence until the cigarette was half ash in his hand.

"I was just about to come looking for you. Here for a coffin fitting?" Jacques asked, his smile far removed from his eyes.

"Not yet." Harlen offered.

He gestured toward the pitiful wooden fence that's original color was impossible to determine. It was half-collapsed into the grass, but Harlen still chose to walk through the squeaking gate rather than step over the fallen boards.

It would have felt too much like an insult, especially now that the house's shabbiness was striking him for the first time. Perhaps because before he had only glimpsed it at a distance, or perhaps because Jacques was beginning to bear an uncanny resemblance to it that made him hesitate to speak.

Had he looked like this the last time they'd spoken? Or was he seeing this only because he had caught him off guard?

"Auditioning for the role of a statue then?" Jacques asked, raising a brow.

"Right." Harlen tried to shake away his concern and stood beside his friend beneath the sagging roof hanging over the edge of the house and quickly asked if he wouldn't mind staying at the house with Millie for a few hours while he took care of something. "She's sick. I don't want her to be home alone any longer than necessary, and I don't know how long this will take."

"Sure, sure," Jacques said. His face was ghostly pale even in the faint glow cast by the burning end of his cigarette. The shadows under his eyes looked like soot smudges. "Something wrong?"

"No," Harlen said.

He wasn't sure why he didn't tell him. Or why he had slipped out without leaving any sort of explanation in the note he left for Millie to wake up to that would warn her that Jacques was probably in the kitchen eating their good jam. "I just need to take care of a few things."

Jacques nodded and only made him wait for a moment while he grabbed his coat from inside. He shrugged it over his shoulders, which were considerably thinner than the first time Harlen had seen him.

Jacques seemed intent on keeping the exchange brief, and it was only just before they set off, Harlen stopped to ask, "Is everything alright?"

"How do you mean?" Jacques asked, hands in his pockets, eyes strangely bright.

There was a time when Harlen would have let it drop at that, but now he kept his gaze steady on his friend as the rain slowly turned the ground beneath them to mud. "Is that lost key still bothering you?"

Jacques sighed. "Yeah. Yeah, it is," he admitted, and Harlen could feel the words left unsaid hanging in the air. Jacques kicked at a rock lodged in the mud with one of his boots and said, "I'm, uh, sorry. Things have been so weird lately. I've just got a lot going on. And hell, if I don't know, you've got a lot going on."

Jacques pulled the cigarette, still half unfinished, from his mouth and tossed it on the ground. He watched it hit the mud and fizzle out quickly beneath the rain. Reluctantly, he asked, "Are you sure you want me at your house today?"

"I didn't ask because I'm angry," Harlen said, catching his friend's eye only briefly. "I'm worried. You haven't been quite right, that's all."

"I thought I told you, I don't do that heavy emotional shit," Jacques said, but there was a faint tug at the corners of his lips, and when he spoke, there was undeniable hoarseness to his voice. "But, uh, thanks."

He pushed off the wall and started down the road in the direction of the house. Harlen walked a few steps behind him to the end of the road, where Jacques was the one to pause.

"Is your mother still in rough shape?"

Harlen blinked. "Oh, I don't think you should have to worry too much about her. I think Corrik scared her a bit last night, but. She's been quiet. That's about as close to good as she gets these days, but we're working on it. Why?"

Jacques shrugged. He'd trained his eyes on his boots again and was kicking at the road like he was trying to stamp out some invisible embers. Harlen asked if everything was alright with Jacques's mother since he couldn't imagine why else he would ask and was met with a quick, sharp laugh.

"I haven't had to worry about my mother in a long time. She uh. She died when I was a teenager; it was a whole ordeal. She was sick for a while, no idea what it was. Lots of coughing, lots of bleeding. Lots of not knowing where she was. She was hardly a person at the end."

Harlen had no idea what to offer other than an apology. "I'm so sorry. I didn't know she'd passed."

"She passed a long time before things ended. The parts that were here were just gone, you know? Sometimes I wonder if it would have been better if whatever she had had taken her faster."

Harlen stared. Jacques never moved his eyes from the mud covering the ends of his boots. He had never really offered much in the way of any personal information that struck too close to his heart, and Harlen wondered if it made him uncomfortable. He certainly looked uncomfortable.

"Jacques, if there's something you need to talk about..." Harlen offered, but Jacques shook his head and was all at once himself again in every way but his eyes.

"No. No, I just met up with an old friend today, and it's got me all philosophical and whatnot. It'll be out of my system in a few days. Besides, you've got your thing to take care of. Don't worry about me."

CHAPTER 52

Under the rainy drizzle slowly turning to a downpour, Harlen made his way back down to The Raven's Nest. It was early afternoon, and the place was still mostly empty. A few patrons sat at tables in the back with young women in high-hemmed dresses making conversation, and a few other ladies sat at the bar.

The bartender was where he had been last time, and Harlen expected him to tell him to get out, but instead, he merely gave him a sidelong glance. Maybe because he didn't have Jacques, the one who had destroyed a fair number of bottles, along with him.

He didn't see Donnie, though. He sat down at the empty end of the bar and ordered a drink that he didn't touch, searching intently for the dark-haired young man. But nearly half an hour passed, and he was nowhere to be found.

"Well, hey there! Didn't think you'd be on your feet so quick."

Magnolia's husky voice was easy to recognize, as was the bright red of her dress. He smiled at the woman as she approached and accepted the chest crushing hug she offered before she held him out at arm's length, giving him a once-over.

"Okay. I see no permanent harm done," Magnolia said.

"Good to know," he said as she let him go and took a seat at the barstool beside his.

She rummaged in her skirts for a moment, pulled out a cigarette, and borrowed a match from one of the nearby girls. She lit it up, then turned to him, propping her chin in her hand, staring at him from under the heavy black makeup around her pale green eyes.

"That looked worse than a bonk on the head last night. Do you ever get migraines? You strike me as the kinda person who gets migraines," she said, pointing at him as she spoke.

He had suffered a spell of them when he was a teenager, which he freely admitted. It seemed to satisfy her. "Yeah, keep some ginger root on you if it's a problem. This guy, Terry, I used to see all the time, chewed it non-stop. He got them every day. Couldn't stand kissing him, so maybe take that up with your wife, but what do I know? Maybe she'll like it. I know a good place to get some if you're interested."

"Maybe later. But thank you for yesterday. That was probably a bit weird."

She shrugged, the black lace on her shoulders bobbing. "All rick folk are kinda weird in my experience. I don't know what you people get up to, but it's like you make being strange part of your job. No offense."

"None taken," Harlen said. He went back to staring into his untouched drink and glancing around until an idea struck him. He turned to Magnolia again and asked, "Have you seen Donnie around lately?"

She shook her head and removed the cigarette from her mouth, leaving the end stained bright red with lipstick. "No, he's been out of commission since your buddy blew him over the counter. I say good riddance to him, personally. He had a temper like you wouldn't believe. Had a habit of getting a little too rough with some of the girls. Like, come on, we're hookers, not animals. Show some basic human decency, right?"

Harlen nodded as she took another long puff from the cigarette, hoping his silence would encourage her to continue. After a moment of staring at the curling smoke in the air, she frowned and turned her head to look at him. "You don't think he did something to your sister, do you?"

"No, no," he said, shaking his head. Although if he had ever laid a hand on her and he ever found out about it. . . "No," he said with a bit more uncertainty that Magnolia didn't miss. She stubbed out her half-finished cigarette on the counter.

"Tell you what. I know where he lives. Not far from here. I'll take you. Lucky me was supposed to check up on him yesterday and remind him he's still employed." She slapped his shoulder as she walked past. It made him jump, but he got up to follow her all the same.

She hadn't been kidding. He didn't live very far at all. His house proved to be more of what looked like a wooden shed tacked on to the side of a shop that she explained happened to be the place they got a lot of their alcohol from. Donnie's father owned it.

"I wouldn't worry about him, though," Magnolia said as they approached the door of the wooden shed. "He goes on these huge benders and disappears every few months. We happen to be in the middle of one. Perks of running a liquor store, I suppose. Never in short supply when you're in the mood to spiral, huh?"

She knocked on the door before Harlen could express his concern and shouted at the top of her voice for the man who supposedly lived inside to drag himself out here. For a moment, there was no response, but as Magnolia began to knock again, Harlen heard someone inside faintly say, "Get the hell out of here."

"You haven't been to work in ages. We're coming to see if you're still alive," Magnolia shouted back, gesturing for Harlen to keep quiet, which he did. He doubted he would be encouraged to come to the door if he made his presence known. Especially if his suspicions were correct.

"Shut up, bitch."

"Alright, we're doing this the hard way." Magnolia stepped back pulled the pin from her hair that held a small red and black hat to her mass of curly hair. "Hold that." She passed it to him and shoved the pin into the lock on the door.

"You really don't have to—"

"No, kid, now this is a personal matter," she said, and after a few moments of jiggling, Harlen heard the lock click. There was some angry shouting and cussing from inside, but what most struck him was the smell of an unwashed body and what he soon saw were dozens of rotting, wilted plants.

Magnolia wasted no time entering, her heels clicking on the wooden floor. Harlen entered slowly, staring at all the hanging pots and vases set up in nearly every corner and available surface in the little wooden apartment. Each was full of yellow and brown leaves, withered vines, petals curled, and yellow like old books' pages—the entire place stank of rotting plant matter.

"What is all this?" Magnolia said, gesturing around in disgust. She was standing at the side of a bed surrounded in what had to be several days of plates, utensils, and old clothes. But it was the figure in the bed that made Harlen's breath stick in his throat.

Donnie looked awful. His dark hair looked like it hadn't been washed in days and hung around his face, which had turned a sickly, grayish color. His eyes were wild, and he was snarling at Magnolia. He made angry gestures at her, but there was no real threat behind it. He looked weak. Drained.

Harlen was so caught up in their argument he didn't even notice Harlen's presence until he asked the question that was making his hands shake. "Why are all your plants dead?"

Donnie looked up. His eyes changed from wild to positively feral as he took him in. "You," he spat. Harlen had never heard that much hatred thrown into one word. And that was the moment he knew.

He knew he had taken his magic.

"What did you do to me?" he roared. Harlen didn't see him grab the knife from the dish beside him or even realize what was happening as Donnie threw himself at him, aiming for his face.

He only felt the impact of the blade on his glasses, cracking through one of the thick lenses, aiming to gouge out his eye. He stumbled back and felt the wave of freezing cold as a blast of ice shot from him and threw Donnie back so hard he hit the wall behind the bed.

The knife dropped limply from his hand, and he collapsed with a clatter into the blankets and plates, clutching his chest spattered with glittering snow. Harlen heard Magnolia screaming at Donnie—that he was crazy—as she dragged Harlen from the apartment and slammed the door.

"Shit. Shit, are you okay?" she asked, ripping the glasses off his face without waiting for a reply, letting out a sigh of relief when she saw no real damage had been done.

Harlen raised a hand to his face and found only the tiniest of scratches on his nose from where the glass over his left eye had broken.

"I think I'm alright," he said while being far from it.

He pulled the hand away from his nose and stared at the smear of blood on his finger, feeling like a black pit had opened inside of him.

He'd taken his magic. He'd taken his father's too by the look of it. But how? How was that even possible? It *wasn't* possible. He had never heard of anything like that, and yet here he was. Making flowers bloom for his wife while Donnie's apartment filled with rotting leaves. Frost formed at his fingertips while his father lay cold in the grave.

He had almost done it to Berkley too. That thought made him reel while Magnolia was dragging him back to The Raven's Nest in case Donnie decided to follow them out, still muttering to herself about how he had to be fired for this. She sat him down at the bar once they got back and downed a glass of whiskey before saying so much as a word. And as she did, Harlen thought of what that would have meant for him.

Berkley, and not just him. Ashby, Bonnadin, practically every nobleman built their entire lives based upon their magic. Berkley was head chairman of The Academy. If he had taken away his magic, just like that, what would be left for him? His entire life would have been gone in an instant because of him.

"I told you he had anger issues." Magnolia's voice brought him back to the present, and he turned to look at her. Her hands were shaking as she gripped her glass.

"Are you going to be okay?" he asked.

She looked at him and laughed. "You're the one that got stabbed, you tell me." She shook her head, still grinning, and the laughter seemed to help ease some of the shaking. She took a long, steady sip of the burning whiskey she had ordered for the both of them and waited until he had taken a drink from his before she continued.

"To be honest, it's not the first time I've seen something like that. And most folks don't wear glasses thick as a beer bottle, so that was alright. Especially in my line of work. It's a little crazy."

If nearly being stabbed in the eye wasn't the worst she had seen, he had to ask, "So, what qualifies as crazier, then? Between this and what happened with Ashby last night, I would have thought…"

She heaved a heavy sigh and tapped her painted nails on the bar counter. She considered her answer for a moment, then spoke with words carefully chosen in a much lower voice than she had been using. "Some of the stuff I see from you rick folks. It's not outright wild. It's just. . .creepy."

She glanced back down the counter where a few of the other ladies were sitting and chatting together, then looked back at him and said, "They make a lot of us uncomfortable. Last night wasn't too bad. They usually let us out pretty early from those parties. The house calls just kind of give everyone the heebie-jeebies. I've been on a few myself. Those big houses are creepy. The way the wives and kids are so skittish is creepy. Because, you know, that kind of skittishness doesn't come from nowhere."

She sized him up with her pale green eyes. "Kinda reminds me of you. Again, no offense," she said, striking up another cigarette.

Like him, of course. He already knew that there were others, other nobles who treated their children terribly. Hadn't he seen it at the party? But hearing it confirmed from another person's mouth free from his own bias made him feel cold and sent that bristle of anger down his back all over again.

"Who do you see?" he asked. Who else was like his father? Who else was a monster?

She smirked. "Ah, I'm not supposed to talk about my clients. But just ask around with your noblemen friends; I'm sure someone will want to brag about it. They do that a lot. A few of them were at that party."

He already knew of one. The thought that he had been surrounded by more than one that night made his stomach twist. But he wasn't helpless. He wasn't powerless to stand in their way anymore. He could do something about it.

"Anyway, sorry about the glasses," Magnolia said. He hadn't realized she had been speaking. He gave her his attention as she gestured to his face and grimaced. "I don't think that's going to be an easy fix."

Harlen pulled the broken glasses off his face and blinked. Everything around him suddenly gained a soft, blurry edge as he examined the extent of the damage. The left lens was cracked completely across in two different directions, and near the bottom, the glass had been completely broken out, leaving a jagged-edged hole.

"I've had these since I was thirteen," he said.

He hadn't even been fitted for them. He had just woken up one day to find them on his bedside table, and his father had grimaced when he had come down to breakfast. Tansey had tried to find some kind of compliment, but he had known how clunky and unbecoming they were. It wasn't as though he had had another option. He needed to see. And he had gotten used to it. He had gotten used to a lot of things he perhaps shouldn't have.

"Yeesh. Sorry."

"No. It's probably time for a change anyway," he decided.

"An optimist. I like it." She tapped her cigarette into the remaining dregs of whiskey in her glass. "Well, I know where we can take care of that. Come on. It's the same place where you can get that ginger root."

CHAPTER 53

    Millie woke to what she thought were voices murmuring in the next room.

    She opened her eyes, stared up at the ceiling and listened, but heard only the sound of rain on the roof.

    She could have imagined it. She had no idea how many things from last night had been real. She only knew that a heavy sense of foreboding lingered and that her hand wandered to touch her stomach.

    "How late is your blood?" Corrik had asked.

    She had hardly noticed, but thinking back, she realized that she was indeed late. By a few weeks at least. She had contributed it to feeling so ill. But that too could be explained by the same thing.

    She sat up and dropped the fancy dress from the night previous to the floor as she read the note Harlen had left behind for her. It felt much better to pull on a nightdress and commandeer his robe again. Jacques wouldn't mind her looking a mess for a while, and if he did, she at least had a valid excuse.

    "Are you really going to tell a pregnant woman how to dress?" she thought, and the idea of dropping it on him so casually made her smile for a moment before the idea settled in. Pregnant. She could be pregnant right now.

    She should be excited. She wanted to be excited. She had always wanted to have a big family like the one she had grown up with. But all that stirred in her was unease.

    Voices again.

    She turned towards the door and could have sworn she heard someone murmuring through the wall. Carefully, she eased open the door to the hall. There was nobody outside, but she still heard sounds coming from Pearl's room.

    She stepped out into the watery light coming from the corridor's single window and felt a chill up her spine. It felt so eerily similar to the dream she had. The house felt empty. There was rain tapping on the glass, and all the lamps had guttered out. As she approached Pearl's door, her footsteps echoed around her. She didn't want to look out of the window for fear she might see a man standing out in the yard, staring up at her.

She knocked softly on Pearl's door and called for her quietly, and the whispering stopped immediately. Millie turned the door handle and found it locked or held shut. "Pearl? Is everything okay?"

"I'm alright," she responded, sounding faint and dreamy.

Millie tried the door again to no avail. Damn. She must have pushed something up against the other side. "Would you like to come out for a bit?" she asked. "I'm going to have some tea in the kitchen. Perhaps you'd like to join me?"

There was a long pause. Millie waited, chewing on her lip until the woman spoke again, her voice a sing-song whisper. "I'll be right down."

They needed to call that doctor back. Whatever it was he was doing to help her come down off the opium wasn't working or wasn't working correctly. She was reluctant to step away from the door, but she knew Pearl wouldn't do anything until she knew she had gone. And as soon as she started back down the hallway, the whispering started back up again.

She would throw some tea together quickly; perhaps she would get some sweetbread as well, then she would be back. Maybe that would coax her enough to open the door. She didn't eat much, but perhaps the promise of something she at least enjoyed the taste of would be enough to get her to peek out.

She descended the stairs and heard the sound of someone batting around in the kitchen. Probably Jacques if Harlen's note was to be trusted. She could see his coat hanging, dripping beside the door. Sure enough, he was sitting at the table when she walked in. He was leaning forward with his elbows on the table, letting his cigarette dangle out of a window he had propped open beside him, staring at the smoke curling out from it as though it held the answers to whatever brought that contemplative look to his face.

"How long have you been here?" she asked.

She apparently startled him. He jumped, dropped the burning paper, and swore.

"Sorry, I thought you heard me come down," she said, studying him while he ran both hands over his face and back through his coppery hair. He looked horrible. His cheeks were sunken, and he looked as though he might be sick at any moment. His green eyes were abnormally bright and anxious, though he forced a smile when he looked at her.

"You're sneakier than you give yourself credit for," he said.

She raised a brow at him, inviting him to say more, but he was running a hand back through his hair again and looking at the table, at anything but her, it seemed.

"I'm going to make some tea," she said, finally turning and making her way to the stove. "I'll make you some too."

"You don't have to do that."

"You look like you need it," she said, the words not coming out nearly as sharp as she meant them. She was too worried to manage any real snapping. She had never heard Jacques sound so defeated.

She busied herself pouring water and setting out the teabags, but while she waited for it to heat, she couldn't resist asking any longer. "Why didn't anyone at the school want you to look into Tansey?"

"I never said that."

"Not directly, but ever since you looked into her evaluation, you haven't been right." She turned back to face him, leaning her back against the counter. "Who has you so torn up?"

He stared back up at her, his mouth pressed into a tight line. She could practically see his thoughts racing behind his eyes, and he opened his mouth several times as though he wanted to speak before he finally settled on saying, "I did look around more. For what's happening with Harlen. What happened with Tansey. I found something I shouldn't have."

The loud bang from upstairs made both of them jump. Jacques leaped halfway out of his seat, and she froze, hands gripping the counter as the second bang sounded. She knew that noise. That was the window.

"No," she said out loud and took off running for the stairs. She could hear Jacques behind her as she sprinted to the upper hallway, shouting for her to stop or slow down.

All the kerosene lamps that illuminated the portraits' staring faces on the walls had burned low and extinguished themselves so that the pale gray light coming in from the window at its end glowed like a spotlight. Just as she had suspected, it was open. As the wind tore at it, it slammed into the frame, rattling the wood and glass. It bounced back out of place, only to be slammed against the house once again.

Images of a hooded figure crawling through the window came to her mind, wearing the same death mask she'd seen in her dream. She imagined it climbing in like a creature rather than a person. Featureless, boneless, crawling in the window and down the hall on all fours like an insect. It turned her stomach, and she immediately wished she thought to grab something heavy to swing.

Those were the horrifying images that filled her mind until she saw that Pearl's door, too, was open. Then fresh dread filled her.

Millie raced to the window and put out a hand to catch the wet glass from slamming. It was a struggle in the harsh wind but managed to get a hold of it to better look at the world outside.

She could see the empty lawn below and the side of the house. There was an old, wooden trellis that housed nothing but ice and the occasional bird nest that clung to the wall itself, and her eyes glazed over it in her blind panic until something bright caught her eye. It was a scrap of fabric about the size of her hand. Lace-trimmed white fabric brilliant against all the grey. Like the kind on the nightgowns Pearl wore.

She had no idea what possessed her to look up. If it was just chance or perhaps some intuition that made her raise her eyes toward the roof near the front of the house, but there she saw Pearl. Standing right at the edge, her blond hair and torn white nightgown swirling around her thin body in the rain.

Millie opened her mouth to cry out, but no noise emerged. It was like seeing something in a dream, and she was half convinced she still was dreaming. Her body was numb, and it seemed like all sound had gone from the world. She didn't hear the wind or the rain; she only saw Pearl standing there.

"Jacques," she finally managed to get out in a voice that was hoarse and choked and hardly her own. She grabbed for him blindly to get him to look, but he had already seen. He was standing stock-still and couldn't tear his eyes off the roof's edge.

"No," he said out loud finally. "No—no, this isn't—wait right here." He spoke in a rush. His face was flushed, and he grabbed both her arms, squeezing sharply. "Stay here. I'm getting help. Don't move!"

"Jacques!" she finally found her voice and screamed down the hallway after him, but there was no reply. He was gone. She was alone. She had no magic to pull Pearl away from the edge of the roof or stop her, and she wasn't close enough for her to grab her. She was helpless. And she watched in horror as Pearl began moving as though in slow motion, moving toward the edge.

Millie shoved the window the rest of the way open and grabbed hold of the trellis. It was madness. But she still pulled herself out of the window, wrapping her fingers around the rickety wood, kicking off her slippers so their smooth bottoms wouldn't impede her grip. She had spent a lifetime climbing trees, she told herself, this was no different.

The wind tried to pull her off the house, and, for one dizzying moment, she looked down at the yard below. The grass was nothing more than a distant green blanket where she would lay on twisted bones if she fell.

No, it was nothing like climbing trees under the warm summer sun, but at least the practice gave her strong arms to pull herself upward. And experienced hands found purchase in the cold, wet beams where they interlocked. Soon, she scrambled over onto the roof where she stayed at a crouch, keeping on her knees to maintain her balance on the rain and ice-slicked tiles as she made her way over to Pearl.

"Pearl!" Millie screamed over the roar of the wind. The woman finally looked up and back at her.

If she was surprised to see her, she made no sign of it. Her expression was dazed, calm, almost dreamlike.

"You went, didn't you? You went to see those people. You can't lie to me. I saw you with that man Corrik," she said in a little tittering way that hardly rose above the wind but was still somehow accusatory. Millie dug her nails into the roof tiles as a fresh gust of wind tore at her. She was amazed Pearl hadn't already fallen.

"I told you I didn't like them. Nobody listens to me. What do I have to do to make you listen?" She took an abrupt step backward and nearly slipped. Mille launched herself forward, rising to her feet and reaching out her arms to try and grab her, but Pearl found her footing and slapped Millie's hands away with surprising strength.

"We only went to look! We just want to know what's going on," Millie said, one arm out at her side for balance, one reaching forward towards Pearl. She was close enough to touch her hair when the wind blew it between them. "Come inside. We can talk about it there. I'll listen. I promise."

"No," she said, shaking her head. "I won't. I can't. I don't like this place."

"Then we'll go somewhere else!" Millie said, inching closer and closer. Pearl was light. She might be able to grab her. Maybe she could calm her down. Or at least hold her until Jacques returned with the guard. "We're going back to my home soon. It's warm and sunny, and you'll like it much better there! I promise!"

"They won't let you leave," Pearl said, her eyes glassy. "Not with the baby."

Millie would have fallen if she hadn't been so fiercely focused on staying upright. "How do you know about that?"

Pearl didn't answer. She looked over the side of the roof to the street below. Millie didn't dare follow her eyes but heard her as she murmured, "Harlen has magic now because of my little girl. She gave him a present. She was always such a good girl."

"What are you talking about?" Millie was sure she was crying, but in the rain, it was impossible to know. She shook her head, trying to indicate that she didn't understand, that she should come back and explain inside, but Pearl only smiled at her serenely. There was no sadness. No pain in her eyes.

"He told me how to see her again."

"NO!" Millie screamed as Pearl leaned and fell backward. Her arms outstretched, moving in slowed time. Her blonde hair fanning out around her, her face the picture of happiness. Her blue eyes closed; her petal pink lips formed into a smile. Millie ran forward and grabbed for her, sliding on the wet tile until suddenly there was nothing beneath her feet.

She looked down into Pearl's face, feeling weightless, still reaching. Her hand managed to find hers for the briefest of moments, and Pearl's eyes opened. There was no fear. Just the same glazed, glassy eyes that showed she wasn't really there.

But as they fell, for a fraction of a second as they neared the ground and felt the pull of the pavement below, Millie saw them change. She understood. And Millie saw fear.

"MILLIE!"

Millie felt something hit her. It knocked the wind out of her, and she thought for a moment she had hit the ground. She threw out an arm to brace herself against the fall but quickly realized what she'd landed on was nothing but one of Jacque's cushions of air.

He'd returned with the guard and had launched himself forward to be close enough to reach out with his magic and break her fall. He was laying on the pavement; knees scraped bloody where he'd slid forward about a foot, and one arm was still outstretched. He almost hadn't made it in time. Almost hadn't completed the spell as the air cushion hit her like a stone rather than a pillow.

She rolled off the side of it, onto the cobblestone, gasping for breath with a horrible pain all down her right side where she'd taken the full brunt of her weight against Jacques's magic. But she was alive.

She lay there, stunned for a moment, staring up at the rain pouring down from the sky. She felt it hit her face but couldn't understand why the clouds seemed suddenly so far away. Or why she was lying on the street when she'd just been up on the roof of the dead-eyed house, she could see looking down at her.

It was the broken choking that broke her out of her trance—the sound of a dying animal crying out in pain. Millie heard Jacques screaming for her not to look, but she turned and saw that it was Pearl, who had been just an inch too far for Jacques to reach.

She was still alive, but she was a twisted, broken mess. Where her nightdress had been white, and her long blonde hair had been pale against her skin, everything had turned red—Red except for the bones that poked blindingly white through the skin.

It was from the remains of her face that the sound came. Gurgling, whimpering. A high keening noise as she tried to either breathe or cry out in pain and horror.

"Pearl," Millie pulled herself across the cobblestone and grabbed wildly for her. For some part of her, that wouldn't pain her to touch. She found one tiny hand still waving, searching, and she realized that Pearl's pale eyes were still staring at her. Wide and horrified as she waved the one hand that could still move.

The hand latched onto Millie's. Hard and fast. There was horrible clarity in her eyes as Millie leaned over her, hovering, not knowing where to touch. There was blood. So much blood. She could feel it pooling under her while she knelt, and it was streaked up her arm where Pearl was gripping it tightly with twitching fingers.

"It's okay," Millie blurted, nearly blind with panic as the edges of her vision seemed to be slowly blurring out of existence, leaving only bright red and white.

"Ru—" Pearl gasped, trying to speak, broken by a wheezing gurgle and a fresh gush of blood from her mouth full of broken teeth. "Run."

Her eyes were clear. She was there. And she was there until the very end, just moments later while Millie cradled her broken, bloody body in her arms, her last words dying with a final gurgle that was drowned out by the rain washing the cobblestone pink.

CHAPTER 54

The world was much clearer as Harlen made his way back up the long street, hurrying through the rain. He had replaced his glasses and was startled to find he could see far better than he had with the old ones.

The man at the shop had said that the ones he had been wearing were practically antique. The shopkeeper asked where in the world he had gotten them from, and Harlen had to admit that he had no idea. Thinking on it, Harlen wouldn't have been surprised to learn his father had dug them out of one of those boxes in his closet.

Magnolia had helped him pick the new ones. The frames were thin, and brass and the lenses were cut into thin rectangles.

"You've got a hell of a pointy face. Might as well lean into it," had been her words of advice. And he had to admit; she appeared to have been right.

He didn't look at himself critically very often. He was reasonably sure the last time he had done so had been his wedding day. When he looked into the tin mirror at the shop, he was startled by the difference.

He wasn't sure if it was the new glasses or if it had more to do with how he had been eating better, sleeping better, and feeling less nervous at all hours. Still, he looked like a different person from the skeletal man with the awkwardly chopped hair that he had seen staring at in the bathroom mirror before he met Millie. His hair had grown out back around his shoulders, and the awkwardly cut ends had faded away. Some of the hollowness in his cheeks had filled in, and his shoulders were straighter.

Magnolia stopped back off at The Raven's Nest. He had told her to be careful and that if she ever needed anything not to hesitate to come by his house. She had given him a smile that was a strange mix of sad and amused and pinched his cheek, telling him to hurry home before he got sick being out in the cold for so long.

He intended to follow her instruction. Millie was feeling unwell, and Jacques looked even sicker than she did. He wanted to have another talk with him if at all possible, but his mind kept wandering back to what he had spoken about with Magnolia earlier. About the noblemen.

He kept thinking about Ashby and Bonnadin snapping at each other over wounded ego. Bonnadin's son with the anxious eyes. All those people watching over the tops of their crystal glasses. None of them stepping in to help. How many of them thought the horror that boy was going through was acceptable? How many approved?

In his mind, he picked back through every face. He had always been good at memorizing things. He wouldn't forget those indifferent looks. The thinly veiled smiles that had tugged at their lips. He wouldn't forget.

He wouldn't do anything drastic, would he? Not so extreme as taking away their magic. But if there was a way to scare them, to make them as afraid as they made their children and families so that they never laid a hand on them again, if that was within his power, then it was something worth considering.

Especially since they seemed to know that something was going on with him, if they hadn't, the incident with Berkley and Ashby certainly would have clued them in that something in him had changed.

And if they were anything like his father, didn't they deserve a little fear?

He paused and turned into the noble district before completing his walk home. He had one last stop to make. A stop that led him to Bonnadin's door.

He didn't know the address for sure, but much like Ashby, he had the sigil of his house just about everywhere. The twin statues of dolphins were easy to spot from the street. His final confirmation came when Avery answered the door, and the young man's jaw nearly hit the ground.

"What are you doing here?" he asked after several attempts to find his voice. He looked even paler than before. There were dark shadows under his eyes, and his face had a drawn, tired look to it. The angry red mark on his cheek from yesterday had turned into a purple bruise with a red slash across it from where his father's ring had split his skin.

"Can I speak with your father?" Harlen asked, giving him as warm a smile as he could manage. "I have something I want to ask him."

Avery wouldn't say no. He wouldn't have if one of his father's friends came to the door. He was allowed into the house, and excluding the abundance of dolphin imagery, it was remarkably like his own had been a few months ago. Spotless. Cold. Every surface gleamed, and not a single sound came from anywhere aside from footsteps on the polished tile.

"He's in his office," Avery said quietly, shutting the door behind them. He didn't move to stand beside him. He remained several steps behind, fidgeting with his hands.

"Don't worry," Harlen assured him, and he meant it. If things went his way, Avery would never have to worry again.

Avery only glanced at him and nodded, quickly looking back at the ground. His knuckles were white where he was gripping his own hands forcefully.

Harlen made his way up the stairs, towards where he assumed Bonnadin's office would be. It was further down the hall than his father's had been: right at the very end. The door was propped open, and Harlen could hear the shuffling of papers inside. He walked up to it slowly and waited in the doorway.

Bonnadin didn't notice him right away, and Harlen took a moment to study him. The office was similar to his father's, right down to the silver tray of drinks gleaming beside the desk. The only difference was that Bonnadin didn't cut quite as imposing a figure as his father had at the desk. Or perhaps he did. Harlen still felt familiar nervousness rising in his throat, but it wasn't as strong as it had been. Maybe it wasn't that Bonnadin was different at all. Perhaps he was the one who was different.

When the man finally glanced up, he started. He must not have heard him come up the stairs after all.

Think of Avery. "I'd like a word," Harlen said.

Bonnadin seemed irritated that he had been startled. He lowered his brows at him and grumbled, "In a moment. I'm busy."

"Actually, I'd like it now," Harlen said before his nerves could tell him otherwise. He stepped inside and sat in the chair opposite the desk.

Bonnadin blinked at him, "You dare—"

"No, *you* dare to strike your son in front of an entire gathering of his future peers?" Harlen paused to catch his breath and was surprised when no answer came. He expected a hand to the face of an argument. But Bonnadin simply stared at him with confusion.

Harlen steeled himself and continued, ignoring the fear gnawing at his stomach, reminding himself that Avery was probably listening from not too far away. "It makes me wonder what you do here. In fact, I think I know perfectly well what you do here if his condition is anything like mine was. Tell me, do you focus more on burning or cutting to try and coax out his magic? Or do you prefer using your own hands like last night?"

"Who let you in?" Bonnadin stood up, knocking back his chair and shaking the silver cart of drinks, rattling the crystal glasses. His face was red with anger. "Who said you could speak to me like this? I'm on the board of The Academy."

"So is half the population of your circle if I kept count correctly during my time there," Harlen said, still seated. He didn't flinch when Bonnadin scowled at him. He refused to. "This isn't about you. I came to talk about your son."

"My son is of no concern to you."

"You made it my concern when you struck him in public." Harlen stood up.

He was glad of his height for once because he had to look down to stare at the man across the desk who was by no means short. He lowered his voice and spoke steadily to make sure none of his uncertainty seeped through in a stutter. "If you harm that boy again, *I* will quickly become your concern."

He was terrified. But at the same time, he was thrilled. Finally, he could do something. Finally, he *was* doing something. He braced his hands on the desk to hide their shaking and ignored the flurry of threats Bonnadin hurled at him.

He wondered what Avery was thinking hearing all this from down the hall and tried to imagine what it would have been like if he had heard one of his father's friends telling him the same thing. The problem was, he couldn't imagine it. He had never thought he was worthy of having someone step in to help him.

Avery was likely thinking the same thing, poised at the end of the hallway with his heart in his throat. Ready to hurry in if shouted for, or run if things escalated.

"I will not be threatened by someone like you!" Bonnadin yelled, moving like he was about to come around the desk. "With no magic!"

"Only that isn't the case anymore, is it?" Harlen asked. He locked on to Bonnadin's eyes, leaning further over the desk towards him and throwing out the accusation to halt him before he could start a physical confrontation. "You know that. You all know that. I think you wanted me in the middle of that argument the other night because you had your suspicions, and you wanted to see what I can do. Well, congratulations. Ashby found it. Part of it, anyway."

Harlen was reaching with his suspicions, but it was a thought that had crossed his mind. The entire situation struck him as odd when he thought back on it. Berkley coming to fetch him specifically for an argument when anyone present would likely have had a better chance of splitting up a fight. The topic of the argument. Avery's apology. It was nothing more than a hunch to go off, but the way Bonnadin's face drained of color told him he had connected with something.

He pressed on. "I don't think you know what I can do. Not really. Ashby was one thing, but what happened with Berkley. . ." Harlen let it trail off and hang in the air.

He had no idea what Berkley's condition was, but if he felt any pain similar to his own after nearly having his magic ripped from him, it couldn't be good. Bonnadin took a step back and eyed him with caution.

Just what did Bonnadin and the others know? Ever since his father's death, his friends had been swarming around him like sharks around a sunken ship, nosing around for. . .what precisely?

If Bonnadin's reactions indicated anything, it was that they knew something about his strange, developing magic. But how they knew and why they were so eager to see it were things he couldn't pinpoint.

He could press Bonnadin for more information. He could. But it would likely be at the expense of the young man listening down the hall, so he decided to end things quickly.

"If I ever see or hear about you harming your son again, I'll show you exactly what I can do." Harlen dug his fingers into the desk to curb the full-body tremble working through his limbs. But he meant every word of it.

"You'd have no way of knowing," Bonnadin said almost smugly.

Harlen leaned forward across the desk again. "Do you know that for sure?" Again, for just a moment, Bonnadin paled. "Then I suggest you proceed with caution. And if any harm comes to him as a result of this meeting, I will come back here, and I will show you the full extent of what I'm capable of."

Harlen turned on his heel and marched out of the office before he could lose his nerve. He allowed himself a deep exhale of relief when he descended the steps and heard nobody behind him; Harlen was fully prepared to see himself out when he saw Avery hovering beside the door.

The young man was wringing his hands and looked nearly gray; he had gone so pale. He fidgeted anxiously but waited until Harlen was right beside him to speak in a hurried whisper, "You didn't have to do that."

Yes, I did, Harlen thought but didn't say as much. He knew they probably only had moments until his father emerged from his office and didn't want to cause him any more stress than he probably already had. Instead, he said, "If he ever lays a hand on you again, you tell me."

Avery blinked at him. "I—I don't—"

"If I see you out, you look at me," Harlen said. He kept his voice low and made Avery catch his eye. "You look at me, and I'll know. I'll make sure he never hurts you or anyone else ever again."

Harlen turned to leave, but Avery grabbed his arm before he could reach for the door. "Why are you doing this for me? Who told you to do this?"

He didn't trust him. No wonder. Harlen could hear footsteps upstairs and knew they had only limited time. Not enough to explain everything. So rather than try to, he rolled back his sleeve to show him the twisted, scarred flesh of his forearm.

He didn't see Avery's reaction. He only heard the young man suck in a quick breath and said in a rush, "Because this can't continue."

Bonnadin was almost at the top of the stairs. Harlen yanked his sleeve back down and reached for the door again. Avery once more stopped him at the last moment.

"Lord Vostesk—Harlen." He called him back. When Harlen looked at him, his eyes were wide and earnest. "I heard your mother isn't feeling well."

His father was standing behind them at the top of the stairs, and Avery spoke loud enough for him to hear. But his father couldn't see the imploring look he was giving him. He couldn't read the warning. "You should go home. Right now."

Harlen felt a cold ball of ice settle in his stomach but didn't let it show. He gave a polite smile and nodded at Avery, then sent a glance at his father. Bonnadin's expression gave away nothing this time, but Harlen added, "I'll be sure to come by again later." For Avery's sake.

Avery gave him one last warning look and shut the door. Harlen walked down the street until he was sure he was out of view of the house from its highest windows, then took off at a run towards his own. Harlen paid no mind to the rain and the wind or the ice puddles forming in the gutter. Every thought evaporated when he rounded the corner to the street that held the Vostesk Manor, and he saw a group of the city guard standing around the gate to his house.

CHAPTER 55

He stood, dazed and confused, until some of the guards shifted, and he caught a glimpse of Millie. She was standing in the middle of the street looking white and shaken, and there was blood all over her.

He ran forward and called out to her, shoving through the guards, pushing aside the hands of the few that tried to get his attention and grab him. He didn't stop until he reached her.

"Millie," he breathed.

The crowd around them was nothing. The voices calling for his attention were nothing. He reached out to hold her arms and sank down to kneel on the street in front of her, looking for injury. As soon as he touched her arms, she looked at him with wide, frightened eyes.

She was still wearing his dressing robe over her nightgown. Both were spattered and streaked red and pink. She was swaying on her feet like she might collapse at any moment, soaked to the bone, barefoot on the cold cobblestone. Her lips and toes were tinted blue from the cold, but she hardly seemed to notice. Why had nobody taken her inside?

He immediately yanked off his coat, put it around her, and pulled her against him. She couldn't seem to form words, but as soon as he'd pulled her tight to his chest, one of her hands curled tight around his shirt, and she pressed her face into him.

"It's alright," he soothed, "It's alright. What happened?"

"Sir?"

The guards had been speaking to him, and he finally heard what they were saying.

"What?"

The man speaking to him was a man in his forties. His hair was mostly gray, and his eyes were dark and worried. "Lord Vostesk, it's your mother."

Harlen looked around the scene. He could truly see it all now that he'd gotten through the wall of guards meant to bar curious onlookers from what was unfolding in front of the house. He now noticed a few people gathered around, trying to peer over the guard's shoulders, but not nearly enough for what he saw unfolding around him.

Jacques was standing with another guard. He was rain-soaked, and the knees of his pants were torn as well as was the skin beneath them. Jacques looked like he was going to be sick and was shaking his head as the two of them spoke. He kept glancing to their side at something covered by a heavy white sheet.

The tarp was thick and bulky, but it couldn't hide the few patches of brilliant color beginning to slowly seep into it. It also couldn't conceal the flowing red and pink puddle the rain spread all over the street.

Harlen knew what it was. The bent shape beneath the sheet hardly looked human, but he knew it was her in some deep part of himself before he even got close enough to catch Jacques's eye. As soon as Jacques saw him, he could see his friend crumble as he shook his head.

"I'm sorry," was the first thing he said as Harlen approached.

Millie remained standing several feet away. She had shaken her head when he started moving closer to the sheet but told him to go ahead. "I'm sorry. I couldn't—" Jacques swallowed and blinked hard. His jaw was clenched, and Harlen realized his eyes were red like he'd been crying. "I wasn't close enough to stop both of them."

"Both?" Harlen looked at the guard standing beside him.

This guard was young. He looked as pale as Jacques as he stammered, "Yes—uh, sir. Your mother and your wife. S— she. . ." He cleared his throat and straightened, finishing in a rush. "They were both on the roof. Your wife tried to catch her, and they both fell."

Harlen felt weightless like everything had been sucked out of him. He balked in horror at the roof of the house. It seemed to grow higher as he looked at it. It was dizzyingly far away.

"Your friend, here." Harlen saw the guard gesture stiffly to Jacques out of the corner of his eye. "We were on our way up the street, and he managed to get close enough to use some kind of magic to try and break their fall, but unfortunately, she was too far away."

"She was so close," Jacques cut in. He was glaring hard at the street and fighting back the tremble in his voice. "If I'd been just a damn few inches closer, I would have had her." His voice cracked high at the end, and he clamped his eyes shut, scowling. Then he looked at Harlen. "I'm sorry."

Harlen had no words. He stepped forward and pulled Jacques into a hug and felt his shoulders heave as Jacques finally let out one muffled cry. When he could finally speak, all Harlen could say over and over like a cracked record was thank you.

"I shouldn't have left," Jacques insisted with a shake of his head. He pulled away, wiping his eyes roughly with the back of his hand. "I shouldn't have. I should have stayed. It would have been different. I should have stopped it."

"You saved Millie's life," Harlen said, gripping his shoulder. His head was spinning. "I'm the one who should have been here."

"No. No, you didn't know." Jacques shook his head. Jacques kept reaching up and swiping angrily at his eyes, but the tears kept coming. "You trusted me."

Harlen tried to assure him, but he wasn't hearing it. Jacques couldn't take his eyes off the crumpled sheet, and Harlen had never seen such a look of pained guilt on anyone's face before. There would be no talking him out of it. At least not while her blood was still pooling at his feet.

Harlen knelt beside the sheet. He could feel the eyes of everyone in the yard on him, and though he knew the full impact hadn't yet settled in, he still felt sick when he reached out to straighten the sheet and felt that she wasn't fully cold. He could still feel the warmth rising off her body, leaving it forever.

He didn't want to pull it back. He didn't want to think about the odd angles and unnatural protrusions that made what was beneath the sheet. He wanted to pretend she was lying beneath it, intact, her eyes closed peacefully.

He had always been afraid he would find her like this. Dead by her own hand rather than his father's. Though, he had always thought it would be from the opium bottle on her nightstand that seemed to give her the only happiness she had left in the world. Not this. Nothing like this. He could imagine her trying to sink into a dreamless sleep, but the image of her crawling through the window onto the roof of the house, the wind pulling at her delicate little body. It was all so strange and horrible.

It was like something from a nightmare. She had gotten tired of years of hiding and being quiet and decided to end everything in the most visible, gruesome way possible. He could hardly believe it was real. It didn't sound like her at all. But the lingering, fading warmth from the sheet on his fingers said otherwise.

He pulled his hand away as more guards approached and winced as they shifted her body. They weren't nearly careful enough, and he heard the sound of bones grinding and the clink of metal on the stone as something fell away from the bloody mess.

He picked it up as the guards didn't even seem to notice and glanced at it. It was some kind of butterfly pendant, and it nearly made him choke. But this one was made of tiny blue jewels, not the crude replication of a butterfly's shape he seemed to be seeing everywhere. It was one of Tansey's.

He had seen it plenty of times in the jewelry box on her desk. A jarring coincidence that set his teeth on edge as he shoved it into his pocket. He would be sure to give it back to her before the funeral.

He spoke numbly to the guards that slowly gathered behind him to ask questions. He watched while they loaded his mother's tiny, twisted body into a cart. He should have gone with her. But Millie was standing there in stunned silence with her blue lips and fingers and her dress covered in blood. He had to take her inside. He couldn't leave her.

"Why hasn't anyone taken her inside?" he snapped at the guard closest to him.

"Sir, there are still questions—"

"You can ask them in the house as well as you can out here," Harlen said sharply, turning from the cart before he had to watch it vanish around the street corner.

Perhaps it was his sudden sensitivity to the color. But he caught a glimpse of the familiar bright red of Corrik's sash as he looked away and spotted him passing the carriage as it neared the bend in the road. Harlen didn't pause to see his reaction to the scene he would be confronted with. He only had one concern now.

Millie was still standing where she had been since he had arrived, but she seemed to be coming around. She was blinking as though the world around her was something strange and new, and as he approached, he saw recognition in her eyes.

"I think my wrist is broken," she said, sounding more perplexed than pained as she held out one hand, and Harlen saw a black bruise wrapped around the lower part of her arm. "It doesn't hurt. But I can't move the fingers."

"Jacques."

Jacques had been moving towards the gate, but when Harlen called, and he turned in time to see Millie's hand emerge from the folds of the coat, he stopped and ran over. He stopped beside her, out of breath, and looked like he might faint.

"How bad is it?" Harlen asked him quietly.

"I can't—" Jacques started to shake his head and took a step back.

"You have medical training," Harlen insisted. The only doctor he had spotted had climbed into the cart with his mother.

Jacques gave him a mournful look, then reluctantly reached out to take Millie's arm. He handled it as though it was more painful to him than to her as he prodded with his fingers, wincing and swallowing hard while Millie stared in confusion at the lack of sensation.

"She's in shock. That's, uh, that'll wear off but. . ." Jacques let go of her arm slowly and flexed his fingers like he could still feel the cracked bone. "Yeah, that's broken. Two places."

"Thank you," Harlen said and took Millie's arm, keeping it up and straight. She couldn't seem to get it to obey her.

He could have one of the guards send for a doctor. Why there wasn't more than one present was beyond him.

He tried to assess any further damage with his eyes, but aside from a few minor scrapes and bruises, she seemed unharmed. He could have cried from relief and from the gravity of what had just happened, but he felt as though he was in some kind of shock himself. The pain was a persistent ache in his chest, and his relief was a light fluttering in his stomach. He was sure it would all come down on him if he let himself pause for even a moment, so he quickly turned to Jacques and said, "You should come in. Let the doctor look at you too."

He eyed the blood running down from Jacques's knees. It was difficult to tell, but some of the cuts looked deep. He could see several places where the skin had been stripped away by the street he'd slid across, leaving nothing but blood behind.

"You can't walk home like that," he insisted when Jacques shook his head.

"He's right," a familiar voice agreed. Jacques stiffened, and Harlen looked up to see Corrik striding towards them quickly, his face grim. Evidently, the guards had had no issues letting him through.

He quickly looked over all of them, pausing on Millie's wrist and Jacques's knees with a deepening frown. "You'll only prolong the healing process. And the lady needs attending. She cannot be alone, and I must speak with Harlen."

"Now?" Harlen asked, pleading with his eyes for Corrik to let it wait, but the man's face remained grim.

"I'm afraid it deals with the matter at hand. I believe. . ." He glanced around at the scene once again and lowered his voice. "I believe I might know something about this."

Harlen felt his stomach drop. He looked at Corrik, then at Millie, who still seemed not herself. Quietly, he said, "At least let me take her inside first."

Corrik's mouth formed a thin line, but he nodded sympathetically. He put a hand on Jacques's shoulder as well and guided him through the door as Harlen picked up Millie and walked her into the house.

"We're going to get you a doctor," Harlen explained. He took Millie up to their room and changed her out of her rain and blood-soaked clothes, taking special care not to disturb her broken wrist. Touching the blood made his skin crawl, and Millie made no protest when he quickly dropped both the nightdress and the robe in the waste bin. He would get rid of it, put it somewhere where neither of them had to look at it.

"I'm going to see what Corrik wants; then I'm coming right back." Harlen dressed her in one of her thicker, long skirts and one of his shirts. It was easier to slide it over her shoulders and button it up the middle than to try to maneuver her broken bones through putting on one of her dresses. It was far too large, but that hardly mattered. All that mattered was that she was alive.

He took her uninjured hand once she was dressed and held it tight. Squeezed it the way she would have his when she was trying to keep him from fussing with his cufflink. When she squeezed back, he felt his eyes mist.

"We'll take you home after this, okay?" Harlen promised. "We'll leave tomorrow. Tonight. Anything just—" He would have promised her the moon if it would have let him stay sitting next to her. If it would have allowed him to keep her hand right where it was, in his and unharmed. "Please, be here when I come back."

She nodded. He wasn't sure what else she could manage after what just happened and was startled when she spoke. "Be careful."

He offered to carry her back down the stairs, but she insisted on walking. She did seem to be coming around, especially when she made him stop at his father's office and asked if he could bring her the cane.

"I just. . .I want something in case. If anything else happens."

He didn't think she would be able to do much with it with a broken wrist, but he wasn't going to deny her some security. He settled her down in a chair in the sitting room with the cane across her lap. Jacques sat beside the fireplace.

Harlen offered him some dry clothes as well, but he just shook his head again. Corrik remained in the doorway, watching the exchange with urgency. He gave Millie's hand one last squeeze before he walked out into the rain with Corrik.

"Alright," Harlen said as they left the house. "What do you have to tell me?"

Corrik walked him past the guards and out onto the road. A few of them looked at them curiously, but none stopped them.

Once they were out of view of the house, he said, "That is something that will require a good deal of explaining."

"Can you explain it to me quickly?" Harlen said impatiently. He felt like a lifetime had passed since that morning. He was bone-tired and wanted to get back to Millie as soon as he could.

Corrik nodded. "Very well. I do have a way of making things a bit simpler to understand. I do wish there were more time to make things clearer. I was hoping for a better moment but. . ."

He frowned and looked conflicted. Harlen tried to press him further, but he simply shook his head as he rummaged in the pockets beneath his red sash. As Harlen watched, he withdrew a pendant composed of something familiar. An orange crystal globe wrapped in an iron circle, attaching it to a long chain.

Harlen blinked at it. It was far smaller than the one in his father's office, but Harlen recognized the symbol carved roughly into the iron. *Remember*, followed by Corrik's own name.

Corrik let it slip through his fingers and caught it by the chain, letting it dangle between them. He took a long breath and leveled his eyes at him.

"It is time I told you why I returned to Wakefield."

CHAPTER 56

Nearly as soon as Harlen and Corrik left, Jacques stood up. He ran his hands back through his thick, coppery hair and swore under his breath, pacing in front of the fireplace. Millie watched him through half-closed eyes as she sat curled in the chair, cane heavy in her lap, wincing as feeling began to return to her wrist slowly.

She wished she had words for him. She had thanked him several times over, but it seemed like he wasn't yet ready to hear it. So, she allowed him to think she had nodded off in the upholstered, high-backed chair and let him be.

She tried to ignore the growing pain in her arm. She tried not to think about what had just happened and was grateful Harlen had changed her out of her old clothes, so she didn't have to smell the blood. She tried to focus on the warmth of the fire and really fall asleep; she was just beginning to drift when she heard footsteps on the stairs. A sound she could have ignored if she and Jacques weren't the only ones in the house.

She almost sat up. If she had been her usual self, she would have shot right out of the chair, but she still felt dizzy and like her body was made of slush. So she remained still and curled over on herself as Jacques shot from the fireplace to whoever was in the other room. Millie heard the sound of a resoundingly strong impact of skin against skin. It had to have been a punch, and whoever it was crumpled to the floor with a clatter.

"What the *hell* was that?" Jacques's voice demanded, echoing off the walls. "What was that!"

"I thought it would be the most effective!" Berkley's voice whimpered.

Berkley?

Millie managed to sit up. She was alone in the sitting room and turned in her seat towards the sounds of the voices echoing from the main hall.

"That was not what we agreed to! It was supposed to be painless!" Jacques shouted back, his voice wavering and cracking. "You're out of your mind!"

"I'm sorry! You said she was taking opium for pain! I didn't find any in the room, so I had to go with the next best option!"

"Sending her off the roof was the next best option?!" Jacques sounded hysterical, but not nearly as hysterical as Millie was beginning to feel.

That whispering she heard. That was Berkley. It had to be. Who else could convince someone to do something like jump from the roof?

"I let you in because you said you could do it. You said you could make it painless!"

Jacques. Jacques brought him here. No, that wasn't right. That wasn't possible.

"How is the young lady?" Berkley's voice came small and shaky.

"She's alive, no thanks to you," Jacques snapped. "You could have gotten her killed!"

"Do you—" Berkley hesitated, trembling. "Do you know if the fall has harmed the child?"

"We'll have to find out, won't we? Someone's been sent for a doctor," Jacques snarled back. She heard him curse again. "She wasn't supposed to get involved. Neither of them were supposed to be involved!"

"Well, she wouldn't have been if you hadn't changed your mind at the last moment!" Berkley piped back, sounding irritated. "Don't think I didn't notice! You ran off!"

"Because you threw a woman off the roof!" Jacques knocked over something that fell to the floor and smashed in a shattering of glass. It masked Millie's cry of pain as she felt the bones in her wrist grind against each other.

She shoved her sleeve in her mouth and bit down desperately to keep herself quiet and stared down, her stomach flipping as she saw the bone shifting beneath the purple and black skin that was rapidly changing color. The black faded to a deep blue, and the blue turned red.

Danger, the tiny voice inside her head whispered. *Danger*.

She clamped her teeth down on her sleeve and felt tears rolling out of the corners of her eyes. From pain, confusion, or anger, she didn't know.

"Jacques, please understand," Berkley was saying. "You've only been with us for a year. It comes with time. You'll see how this all turns out. You've seen how it worked with Harlen. Didn't we tell you? We told you what it took to give him such power."

Jacques didn't say anything. Millie muffled a scream by biting into her arm until she drew blood as a final, sickening crack she was amazed they didn't hear snapped her bone back into place.

"He's not going to join up with us. You know that," Jacques said with his voice hoarse and defeated. "It doesn't matter what Corrik tells him."

"He is a bit unstable, that much we've seen. But with time—"

"I don't think you even know what you did," Jacques snapped, anger rising back into it. "That isn't his family's magic he has! I don't know what the hell that is! If you think anything good is going to come from more of this shit—"

"Do you think Corrik doesn't know what he's doing?" Berkley snapped, the first real anger she'd heard from him.

Jacques let out a long, heavy sigh. "No. But I still think this is all a bad idea. It's a cycle, and it wasn't meant to be messed with. Life and death it's all. . .it's the way it is for a reason. That was what I thought this was all about when I signed on: respecting the cycle." Another long, breathless pause. "What we're doing. It's wrong. You can't trade with death."

"Don't you want to ensure this child's safety?" Berkley said. "If Corrik has indicated anything, it is that this child is going to have magic. Very, very powerful magic. We cannot take the risk of something happening."

Magic.

Millie stared at her wrist. The bruise had faded, and the pain was gone. It was replaced by a warm rush through her body that she could only describe as an attempt at soothing from what was growing inside her. A tiny voice whispering, *"Shh."*

Magic will protect its host.

Pregnant. With a magic child. Which meant that right now, in a way, that host was her.

Millie sat stock-still in her chair. Pearl's death wasn't suicide. It was murder. She was trapped in a house with the two people responsible, and now there was no denying it: she was pregnant. She was pregnant, and she had nearly died.

She had to do something. Who knew what else they had in mind? Who knew where Corrik had taken Harlen? She had to get out. But how to get past two men with magic—one who had just convinced a woman to walk off the edge of a roof and another who could shape the air itself?

She gripped the cane hard as her mind raced; the carved ivory shapes bit into the flesh of her fingers. Then she remembered—the shark.

She found it quickly; the shark with each tooth carefully carved and twisted it. It came away from the rest of the cane with a faint click, and she slid it out of place, revealing the tiny half-empty bottle of nightshade.

Berkley had a fondness for drink, and she had never seen Jacques refuse one. She couldn't imagine he would under these circumstances. There was a cart in the room beside the fire that held an arrangement of pictures and glasses. She stared at the glimmering crystal cups from where she sat and her heartbeat up in her throat.

It wouldn't kill them, surely. Millie wasn't sure how it worked, but magic: magic had protected her from whatever it was in those drinks at Corrik's party. It healed her broken wrist. But it could probably incapacitate them; that was for sure. And that was all she needed—a moment to occupy their magic so she could escape.

There was no time to ponder it. She did feel a twinge of fear; if she were wrong, she could be killing both of them. Berkley, she had little sympathy for; she had seen what he was willing to do. The image of Pearl's broken body was too fresh in her mind for her to feel any remorse over what could happen to him. But Jacques. Jacques was her friend. Had been her friend.

Or had he been?

She squeezed the vial tight in her hand. Jacques had known Pearl was going to be killed. He had *let Berkley in to do it*. The only reason he had changed his mind was that he didn't like *how* he decided to end her, but murder was murder.

She didn't have the time to pull apart her thoughts and feelings or fuss over details. She needed to get out.

They were still arguing in the other room when she got up. Her socked feet were silent on the tile as she slunk over to the drink tray and pulled the top off the bottle. Luckily, Harlen was not as much a fan of drink as his father. Since the dinner party, most of the pitchers stood empty. She blindly dripped the remains of the vial into whatever remained and hoped that the smell wouldn't be obvious while she strained her ears, listening for the sound of footsteps approaching the room.

"Jacques, please, you should sit," Berkley's voice came. Her time was up.

She scurried back to her chair and sat down, hoping to be overlooked. She curled back up in on herself and held her wrist once again, tucking it in the folds of Harlen's shirt that was thankfully large enough to cover it easily. She closed her eyes and didn't dare breathe as the two men rounded the corner, not moments after she had stopped moving.

She listened to the two of them walk past her and towards the window that overlooked the garden. She heard the pop and fizz of fire and smelled burning paper and tobacco as Jacques lit a cigarette.

"You understand why it had to be done," Berkley was saying back in his usual voice. Earnest, worried. "It's not just for the child. That woman would have found a way to interfere."

Jacques made a noncommittal noise, and Millie dug her fingers into her arm to keep from screaming at him. How could he do this?

"She would have seen you with them eventually. She would have said something about your acquaintance with Lord Vostesk, mad rambling or no, and then where would you be?"

This entire time. It really had been this whole time.

"There should have been a better way," Jacques said. "You promised. You, Corrik, the board. You promised they wouldn't be hurt. Millie almost died. How can you justify that?"

"That should never have happened," Berkley snapped, insulted. "If I could have foreseen her climbing up onto the roof, I never would have taken that risk."

Jacques didn't answer. Another puff of tobacco filled the room, and Millie felt like she was going to crawl out of her skin.

"We warned you Harlen would be a difficult case when you volunteered to be his mentor."

"Yes, but you failed to explain the full scope of that, didn't you?" Jacques snapped back. He let out a bitter laugh. "You made it sound like he had some weird, repressed magic. You didn't tell me where he got it."

The two remained silent. Millie's every muscle ached as she sat tensed, ready to spring out of the chair and run. She was torn between hoping they would say more to explain the ringing confusion and betrayal in her mind, some explanation as to *why*, and wanting them to shut up and drink so she could escape. They wouldn't believe she was sleeping forever.

She didn't feel relief when she heard the clinking of glasses on the silver tray—only sick anticipation. Neither of them spoke for what felt like ages. She tried to keep track of the passing minutes from the distant ticking of the clock, but she couldn't think straight enough to count.

"We're a bunch of cold bastards; you know that?" Jacques said, his voice drained of all emotion.

Berkley didn't answer. Millie heard him give an odd little cough, and she stiffened. That was all it took.

"Millie," Jacques said immediately. He dropped his glass back onto the tray, and Millie couldn't see if it was still full or not. She only saw him rushing towards her, a hand outstretched. He reached for her but stopped. The room filled with silence as he saw the angry tears in her eyes.

"Liar," she spat.

Jacques paled, then he coughed. She heard Berkley gag and knew that now was her chance. Millie grabbed the cane in her lap and shoved it forward, sending Jacques stumbling back. Then she was out of the chair and running, cane in one hand, the front door locked in her vision as she rounded the corner from the sitting room into the kitchen.

She didn't dare look back. Even when she heard the sound of vomit splattering the ground and Jacques calling after her. Even when she felt the air around her begin to stir.

She tried to keep running, but the gust of wind swept her off her feet. She tried to grab the wall to keep from falling, but she tumbled down and felt a hand wrap around her ankle before she could get up.

"I'm sorry. I'm sorry, wait—" Jacques pulled her back, away from the door. He was coughing and looked like he was going to be ill but was fighting it off far better than Berkley. Either because he hadn't drunk as much or because his magic was stronger. "Millie, I don't know what you heard, but I'm not going to hurt you. Or Harlen—I promise. That's the last thing I want."

"You were going to kill Pearl," Millie shot at him, rolling onto her back.

"She was dead a long time ago, and you know it! Millie, you knew how she was," Jacques said, pleading. "Please. I've done everything to help you and Harlen. I'm your friend—"

He grabbed her by the wrist. The one he thought was the only functional one. He squeezed it not tight enough to hurt, but tight enough that she couldn't pull away.

Millie could see red veins bursting in his eyes. He wasn't devoting his magic to what he should. The poison was spreading.

"No, you're not." Millie grabbed the cane that had clattered to the floor with her newly-healed hand and brought it up to impact the side of Jacques's head. He stumbled and let go of her.

She reached the door and yanked it open, then turned back to close it behind her to buy her a few additional seconds. She caught sight of Jacques lying on the floor of the entryway, far closer than expected. He looked up at her, pleading in his eyes.

Millie slammed the door. She jammed the cane between the twin handles on the outside and obeyed Pearl's last wish.

She ran.

CHAPTER 57

Corrik hadn't let Harlen take hold of the pendant in the street. Instead, he had walked the both of them out of town, up toward the graveyard. Harlen had reluctantly followed, his trepidation far outweighed by burning curiosity and a strange sensation of dullness that settled gently over him as he viewed Corrik's brilliant blue eyes beyond the swinging pendant.

"Don't you want to understand?" Whether the words were spoken, or if they had simply appeared in his mind, Harlen couldn't have said. He only knew that he hadn't answered aloud.

He had stretched out his hand to snatch the pendant from the air when the world outside the bright, ember glow of the crystal and Corrik's eyes became quiet and blurred at the edges. His body was so heavy, and his thoughts moved so thickly it was as if each word had to swim through mud to make it to his mouth.

His hand dropped back to his side limp as a sack of stones, and his mouth opened, but he couldn't manage any sound. Harlen understood distantly that it should be alarming, but Corrik only smiled serenely and nodded as though he'd said something that made perfect sense.

"Excellent. I will show you everything you need to know."

He hardly even noticed where they were until they stopped, and Harlen realized where they were when he heard the creaking of branches overhead.

The hanging tree.

Harlen looked back over his shoulder and saw the town spread out below the slate-grey sky like a map leached of color. The cold wind pulled at his hair and blew away the fog that had settled over his mind like cobwebs as he's trudged along blindly. He wondered how far he would have walked had Corrik not stopped him.

"Please," Corrik said. "Allow me to show you the full picture. There are..." he trailed off and took a deep breath, looking out over the town. Over and above it. The way he and

Millie looked at the displays in shop windows. "Many things are happening very quickly. I'm sure you must be confused?"

Harlen swallowed, testing his thoughts and the tongue that was his own again. "I have some theories. I know something's going on."

Harlen's eyes darted up and down the man in front of him. He didn't appear to be armed, but in a world of magic, that didn't mean much. Still, even now, there was such an air of calm about him that Harlen wasn't sure what to make of his suspicions.

"I think it has something to do with you."

Corrik smiled benevolently. "I'm sure you do. Your father always said that you had a busy mind, and I'm inclined to agree. You know that something is amiss. There are so many strange things happening, and you know they're connected. But there are too many pieces missing to complete the picture to your satisfaction. Am I correct in this assumption?"

Harlen nodded. For the first time in his life, he didn't feel like running. He remained rooted to the spot, staring at Corrik. Some part of him was afraid that if he looked away, he might vanish and take whatever answers he had with him. The crystal still glinted, suspended on a chain between his fingers.

"It eats at you, doesn't it? It always has. That question: why? Why am I the way that I am, why did my sister leave, why does my father treat me the way that he does." Every word was warm with sympathy. Inviting in the way a fire invites you to step into it in the cold. "Why is any of this happening?"

Harlen swallowed. His hands clenched at his sides, and he could feel frost threading its way between his fingers.

"I understand you're upset," Corrik said and extended the pendant between them. "Allow me to explain."

The thought that this could be a trap went ignored. As soon as his fingers touched the glass, Harlen felt the world around him melt away and felt a whisper of mist as it reformed around him. He was no longer standing on the grass and could no longer feel the rain as he stood in his own dining room inside the memory of several years past, where he saw Tansey sitting at the piano.

His father and several others were talking at the table. She was using the pretense of practicing to listen in on what they were saying, her fingers touching the keys ever so lightly to make the least noise possible while occasionally her eyes flickered over to the others. She was good, very subtle for a thirteen-year-old girl, but not subtle enough to face a room of diplomats.

Berkley was the one who caught her at it. He saw her glancing over at them, and no matter how she tried to play it off as a coincidence, he suggested that the adults move to the library.

The room cleared out, and Tansey slammed one hand on the keys in a huff. Something Harlen was sure would have earned him a good slap across the face, but his father just ignored her. Which he had a feeling caused her more ire than if he had laid a hand on her. She crossed her arms and sat at the bench, stubbornly silent to protest her removal from the conversation: gone in a moment from calm and mature to a petulant child.

Harlen watched from a distance. She looked so real. He was shocked that he had forgotten so many of the small details; the exact shape of her eyes and the actual color of her hair that was just a bit more yellow than their mother's. He hadn't realized he had been slowly replacing features in his head with the ones from the portrait above the stairs.

He called to her without thinking, and for one heart-stopping moment, she turned her head. Then he realized she was just looking towards the person approaching her.

As she sat, brooding, someone eased into the bench beside her. A man dressed simply with his dark hair pulled into a ponytail, wearing a bright red sash around his waist. Corrik Magister, not looking a day younger or older than he was in the present.

"Tansey is it?" he asked.

She seemed surprised that he was talking to her. She blinked up at him, then put her hands back on the piano.

"It is," she said, pressing the keys again. She held up her chin. "I don't believe I've been introduced to you."

"Corrik Magister," he said.

She was being careful not to seem too interested in the conversation. Though, Harlen could tell from the spark in her eyes that she was frantically excited.

"You play very well. Did you have a teacher, or are you self-taught?"

"Self-taught," she said, allowing just a bit of pride to creep into her voice. "Father said that if I wanted to spend my time on something like this, I'd have to learn it myself. So I did."

"As opposed to?"

"Learning magic," Tansey said with a frown. "As if staring at a book all day will improve something nonexistent."

"I thought that you had some magical talent. Your father mentioned it briefly. In a fit of frustration, of course," Corrik said.

Harlen blinked. That would be news to him.

Her hands faltered on the keys, but she corrected herself. "Yes. Well. It isn't much. And it's not like that matters anyway. It's Harlen who he wants to have magic because I can't be heir to the house. It's damn stupid. Oh. Sorry. Language."

"It's alright. I won't tell anyone." Corrik chuckled. "Besides, it's a reasonable frustration. It can be difficult to have your talents ignored."

Tansey lost her air of disinterest. Her eyes were clouded with thought as she shook her head slowly. "As far as he's concerned, it doesn't matter. He pretends that me having at least a bit of magic means something, but he just lets Mom hide me up in her room to knit or brush her hair while he takes Harlen to the basement for real training. And it never works. He just hurts him because he doesn't know when to give up. Sometimes, I wish he'd been born with it instead of me just so he would leave him alone. Is. . .is that wrong?"

"I think that's a very noble thing for you to be thinking, Miss Tansey," Corrik said. "Something I doubt would have even crossed the minds of many others in your position."

Tansey seemed relieved, then stopped playing suddenly and turned towards Corrik with a frown. "You can't tell Harlen, though. About the magic."

Corrik turned his head quizzically.

Tansey sighed and balled the fabric of her green dress in her hands. "If father and I have ever agreed on anything, it's that Harlen doesn't need to know about my magic. He has his reasons, but I just don't want to hurt him. I don't want to have the only thing that would fix his life."

Corrik nodded and spoke earnestly, with a deep empathy in his voice. "I would never betray such a noble thing," he said, and slowly a smile of relief crept over Tansey's face. "And before you worry, I will keep that I even know this a secret from the others. Even from your father if you wish it."

"You would do that?"

"A desire to improve the lives of others should never be punished," he said. "I might even be able to help you improve your brother's position. If that is something you would want."

She again blinked and stared up at him in disbelief. "What? How?"

He glanced towards the other room where the others were still speaking, then back to her, and said, "What do you know of butterflies, Miss Tansey?"

She was confused. "Butterflies?"

He grinned, a row of perfect white teeth spreading beneath his blue eyes. "Read up on them for me. Next time I see you, I'll bring you a gift."

He stood up from the chair, and she stared at him. "How will that help?"

His smile was bright and knowing. "See what you can discover for yourself, and I will tell you more the next time I see you."

The memory dissolved and another formed around him. As it did, Harlen heard whispering voices as the memory descended, taking shape in another familiar room: the board room at the school where he had received his evaluation.

It appeared to be late at night, and all around the small table stood faces that Harlen recognized. Berkley, Ashby, Bonnadin, but most jarring was his father. He was standing almost beside him on the opposite side of the table from Tansey. His arms were crossed, his jaw was set, and his pale eyes were cold as he stared at Tansey, who looked perhaps a year older than last time.

There was a glass of water on the table in front of her. One that Harlen recognized from spending hours and hours staring at it in the vain hope of it turning to ice. But as he watched Tansey staring hard at their father, he saw the frost creep over the top of the water. Then slowly, painfully slowly, he watched the water freeze and pop until it cracked the glass.

"Passable," someone in the room said. His father smirked.

"Barely."

"Potential is potential," Corrik said, appearing from seemingly nowhere. He stepped out from the group that parted for him and stood next to Tansey. "I think she would be a wonderful addition."

"You're kidding," his father scoffed, but there was an undeniable note of genuine interest in his voice. His eyes didn't stop studying Corrik closely, waiting to see if he was serious. He looked strange. Almost what Harlen would call hopeful.

Corrik didn't answer him. Instead, he reached into the bag he had slung over his shoulder and knelt next to Tansey. He produced a jar from the pack, a jar that Harlen recognized after a moment. A jar holding a twig, leaves, and two fat, green caterpillars.

"Those are swallowtails," Tansey said, a pleased smile spreading across her face as he set the jar in front of her.

"So, you have been doing your research on butterflies," Corrik said with an approving nod. "Have you figured out what they mean?"

She hesitated for a moment. "Freedom. Transformation, or rebirth. It depends on where you look."

"Yes," he said, nodding. "Exactly. All of those things. It's exactly how we're going to solve our problem."

Tansey seemed pleased but confused. Then, Corrik instructed everyone to leave the room. "Except you, Lord Vostesk. This matter concerns you as well."

His father stared in a rare moment of uncertainty as the room began to clear out. Once the door was closed, he seemed unsure of what to do as Corrik took a seat at the table.

"Your daughter has a wish," Corrik said. "That we may be able to fulfill." Tansey nodded solemnly. "She has agreed to transfer her magic to her brother."

His father smirked, then paused when Corrik gave no hint that he was joking. The look of uncertainty returned. "You can't be serious."

"It is within the realm of possibility," Corrik said simply. "It has been done before. It is not so difficult in practice if one knows how to perform the ritual properly."

Corrik touched the top of the caterpillar jar. "I must warn you that her magic may change if it is transferred. You see, it is not a direct giving of her power to him. Neither is it a simple release of magical energy into the universe as a whole. It is more complex. He will be receiving new energy that will be given directly to him by the will of the goddess."

"Change how?" his father asked, stock-still as though frozen. His lips barely moved.

"It can change based on what may lie in him already. Just because he has no obvious magic does not mean that there is nothing at all inside of him. He may shape it, just as well as this new power could shape him."

Corrik kept staring at the caterpillars. "I say this as a warning because those with magic blood who undergo this transfer can create something quite powerful."

Harlen's father stared at him. His face was white, and the icy demeanor he seemed to hold all his life had vanished. He looked like a different person; his features weren't nearly as harsh, and there was a tremble in his voice. "And. . .you can really. . ."

"Do you doubt me now?" Corrik asked, not accusingly but rather like he was scolding a child. "After everything I've done and after what you've seen? You have seen the face of the goddess as well as I. You should understand that this is well within her capabilities."

His father lowered his eyes. It was unnerving to watch him cowed by just words from a man that looked to be half his age and was far more soft-spoken. It was uncomfortable to watch.

"There is but one stipulation she requested," Corrik said, holding up one hand. "He must be happy. That is her request, and it must be honored. Only when he finds true happiness will the transfer be complete."

"You agreed to the demands of a child?" his father said, the cold edge returning so quickly that though he wasn't physically in the room, it made Harlen flinch.

"I have communed with the goddess. The stipulation pleases her," Corrik said. "This is the condition."

Harlen knew Lord Vostesk wanted to protest and likely do more than that. If he were in Tansey's place, he would have caught hell, but instead, he said simply, "Fine. As long as it's done."

The room dissolved. When the world took shape again, they were standing in the graveyard beneath the hanging tree.

Tansey was older now. Seventeen, the oldest she would ever be, Harlen realized. Dressed in blue and black, the wind blew her long blonde hair, and she stood facing Corrik. She looked afraid but was trying not to show it while all around her crackled an air of excitement.

"Tansey," Corrik said, "What you are about to do is a brave thing. A kind thing. It is not often that the goddess finds one so willing."

"Does it—" She laughed nervously. "Does it hurt?"

Corrik chuckled. "Only for a moment. Are you ready?"

She bit her lip and nodded. Corrik stepped back from her and faced the crowd.

The world around him seemed to fade. Shadows deepened, and the faint moonlight shining down on the cemetery seemed to focus itself on him. Like the world around him was an illusion or a dream, and he was the only thing that was real. Voices faded. Even the sound of the rain seemed to fade as he spoke.

"Gentlemen! Tonight you will witness the truly extraordinary! The power of the goddess to take, to transform." Corrik gestured to Tansey, and it was as if his direction drew her into focus. She stood out almost as bright as he did. "To do wonderful things with the wish of one with so pure a desire."

Corrik extended his hand toward Tansey. The fear was unmistakable in her stiff posture, but Harlen knew her well enough to recognize the fierce excitement in her eyes. And she took Corrik's hand.

"Your wish is granted."

The knife he took from his belt flashed like a star before it sank into her chest.

Harlen screamed as Tansey's eyes went wide.

Corrik pulled out the blade, and she raised a hand to the wound, staggering forward in silence. Corrik pressed a hand to her face as she crumpled to the ground, whispering something Harlen couldn't understand in some language he had never heard. Tansey stared at Corrik in shock as her blood pooled in the grass.

"What did you do?" Tansey gasped in horror. She didn't know. She didn't know that to fulfill her request; she had to die. Nobody told her.

Corrik smiled down at her. He reached into the darkness around him and produced something round and bright white. He pressed it down over her face, and Harlen could see it: the ceramic death mask. The featureless face with the small, raised nose and mouth. The two holes cut crudely for eyes showed her terrified gaze as she gasped behind it, still living.

"Your request will be granted."

Her eyes looked frantically for help: to their father standing at the edge of the circle of gathered onlookers. They were all cast in shadow, but Harlen could see him. His face was impassive; his eyes were bright. He wasn't going to stop it.

Harlen collapsed to his knees in the grass. He reached for her, but the scene once again dissolved like a dream. His tears fell not on the cemetery's grass but on the wood floor of Corrik's home.

Corrik was at the table, standing and patiently looking at Harlen's father over the steaming teapot on the table. His father had abandoned his chair and was pacing back and forth in front of him, looking incensed.

"Why isn't it working?" he snapped. There were dark circles under his eyes, and his face looked tight with worry and frustration.

"This is not the simple act of moving something from one room to the other," Corrik said, his voice ever calm and contrasting his father's anxious tone. He sounded again like a parent lightly scolding a child. "This is old magic. This is something that takes time."

"I'm doing everything!" his father said, only pausing to grip the back of one of Corrik's dining chairs. His nails dug into the wood, and sweat had broken out on his brow. "I have tried everything to get it to work! It's been a year! He should be showing some kind of sign that he's different by now!"

"You're using the methods dictated in your books again, yes?" Corrik asked. "The ones passed around by your noble friends?"

Harlen saw his father flush angrily. He looked almost ashamed. "Perhaps."

Corrik sighed and invited his father to sit with a gesture. Once he was seated, Corrik said, "While it is true that magic in the blood will rise to protect its host in times of great physical and emotional distress, it is also true that this is no ordinary magic you're dealing with now. This will not be magic he was born with. This will be new and will take time to settle into his body. And given the circumstances under which it was gained, it will likely be very unpredictable. My friend, I must tell you that trying to bring the magic out of him like this could be dangerous. For the both of you. It will likely be very strong, and he will not know how to control it."

"I don't care about the danger," his father said. "I never have."

"I don't doubt your determination, friend."

"What should I do?"

Corrik seemed pleased by his asking. "Get the boy some friends."

His father blinked at him incredulously, but Corrik continued. "You remember, I'm sure, Tansey's stipulation. It is true that this magic will take time to develop in him, but it is also true that she had a will. I made the agreement with the goddess, and it must be honored before the gift can be given. He must know happiness."

"You're not suggesting I let him run free like an animal," his father said. "He's already tried to escape once, and I won't have him doing it again while he's finally got some potential. Not after what we did to get it."

"Then perhaps bring some to him," Corrik shrugged. "Find a way to let him relax in a controlled environment. Whatever you must do."

His father studied the table for a moment in frustration. "So what? Do I buy him a dog or something?"

"Oh, come now," Corrik scolded.

His father fell silent for a moment. The fireplace crackled, and the man who had driven a knife through his sister's chest sat quietly sipping from a cup of hot tea.

"I have been considering something," his father said at long last. "Before we did what we did, I was considering maybe it would be best to just. . .try again. For magical offspring. Sometimes it skips a generation. I have heard that passed around. It's still a sign of dying magic in a bloodline, but with this ritual, it might not be the case anymore. . ." His father trailed off, and Corrik watched him patiently with one raised eyebrow. "I was wondering if he were to have a child, what would be the odds. . ."

"You should be patient," Corrik said with a frown.

"I know, I know," his father said. "But I've been in communication with a family. They have too many daughters, and there is magic in their blood. Nothing too strong, nothing that might prove too volatile. They seemed willing to part with the second youngest."

"Any child that he bears will likely be very powerful from an incredibly young age," Corrik cut him off. "Which means they would be unstable and difficult to control. Dangerous unless cared for very, very carefully. With your current track record, I do wonder if you could manage such a thing."

Harlen's father flushed again and stood up angrily. "You don't tell me how I raise my family! How I maintain the Vostesk family legacy! We're dying! We used to be strong and respected and were at the forefront of magical advancement! My bloodline is dying out with nothing but my simpering, useless son to continue it! Live with that on your head, and then tell me that I need to be patient!"

"If you continue as you are," Corrik said in a grave tone of voice, "Things will not end well for you."

"I'm tired of this cryptic bullshit," his father growled. "I will have my legacy one way or the other."

"You will," Corrik said, setting down his teacup with a sharp clack. "But right now, you will listen to me."

As soon as Corrik spoke, he twitched his fingers, and his father stiffened. His eyes changed from furious to terrified as Corrik stared at him, and his father slowly and jerkily lowered himself into his chair. His limbs moved woodenly, and his lips twitched as though he was trying to speak but couldn't.

"When I let go, we're going to have an adult conversation," Corrik said, his voice once again perfectly calm. "And you're going to apologize for what you put in my tea. Don't think I haven't noticed you've left your cup untouched."

Corrik smiled, and a hint of enjoyment touched his eyes as he watched his father jerk and twitch in his chair but remain rigidly seated. He looked like he was in pain.

"I was surprised you thought that would work. You've never offered to make a drink for anyone. Suddenly, you come here and are so eager to brew some of my favorite tea? I would have thought a smart man like yourself would have come up with something better than a bit of poison. However, your sleight of hand with that cane was admirable. Did you think to reattempt the ritual with me, or are you simply angry?"

Corrik sighed, raising his hand lazily. Harlen watched his father's arm move. It jerked up and slammed onto the table, fingers twitching. The tips were turning a bluish-purple as they scrambled on the wood to wrap around a small fork set on the tea trey.

"If you ever do this again, I'll have you slit your own throat," Corrik said with a simple flick of his fingers. His father responded by slamming his other hand onto the table and driving the fork into it. Once. Twice. Corrik watched the blood well and spill onto the table with a look that could only be described as fascination. The only sound in the room was the crackle of the fire, the sickening thud of the fork into flesh, and the strangled noise as his father failed to manage a scream.

"I'm very glad we could come to this understanding." Corrik sat back in his chair, and Vostesk Senior collapsed.

He fell out of his chair onto the floor, where he curled over on himself and screamed in pain. Corrik reached for the blood that had dripped onto the table. The small puddle crawled up into the palm of his hand as though it were a living creature. He held it up to his face and watched the blood twine around his fingers as his father continued to writhe.

"The goddess and I have a special relationship," he said as though he couldn't even hear him sobbing. As Corrik stared at the blood, what looked like pale purple tears welled in his eyes and spilled down the sides of his face. They dripped off his chin as he turned to stare at his father. "Do you think she would let a man like you poison me? Do what you will with the boy. But the conditions must be met."

The scene dissolved, and for the briefest of moments, before it pulled away entirely, the light in the room shifted. A different time. A different day in the same house. Harlen saw himself and Millie stepping through the doorway less than a month ago.

As Corrik took her hand to shake and his fingers closed around her pulse, Harlen heard and felt what Corrik must have: two heartbeats.

CHAPTER 58

Harlen jerked his hand away from the pendant hanging in front of Corrik's smiling face. He was too shocked to scream, too shocked to cry. Too shocked to move, or at the very least, he thought he was. He didn't even realize he had reeled back until he felt his fist connect with the side of Corrik's face.

His head snapped to the side, and Harlen heard bone pop, but Corrik remained standing. Harlen slumped back against the tree behind him, clutching his chest as he felt his heartbeat stumble over itself. He coughed, and his heart lurched, slowing to a dull thud in his chest that made his limbs feel once again heavy as lead.

Corrik turned his face back towards him, his eyes full of sympathy and his jaw misaligned. There was a spray of ice over the left side of his face, frozen rainwater turning his skin purple and blue. As Harlen stared, the bone shifted and cracked back into place. It tore the skin where the ice held it in place, and a gush of red blood ran down his chin as his cheek stretched upward from the corner of his lip, giving him a tooth-bearing smile.

"I thought you might react this way. This is exactly why I warned your father that nothing good would come from his impatience. I always thought it would land him in the grave, and now that that's come true, it's made everything happen far too quickly. It's made you exactly as volatile as I warned him it would if you were not given time to understand."

Harlen saw the blood dripping down from the corner of his mouth. It stopped before it reached his chin. Then, as though the world was playing in reverse, it slid back up into the cut in his lip and sealed itself back inside his flesh. The ice cracked and melted, and the skin that had blackened with frostbite returned to normal.

Corrik showed no sign of feeling the pain from any of it. He only blinked once it was done, and that calm smile returned to his ageless face. "Luckily, I'm a bit more durable than he was. Thanks to the goddess."

"Where is Tansey?" Harlen asked, unable to think anything else. Still in shock at what he had just seen. "What did you do with her?"

"I have always had a fondness for those groves in your wife's homeland. It's a beautiful tradition. I wanted to give someone who gave themselves to the goddess so willingly a proper burial, but trees do not grow here. With the exception of one," Corrik said with maddening calmness. "I wanted you to be able to visit when the time came to tell you the truth."

Harlen felt his stomach drop. The ground beneath his fingers, the rough bark of the tree he leaned against suddenly felt alive. Like it was breathing, She was here. Right now. This was the place where she had died and been buried for years, and he had never known.

The slow beating of his heart kept him from feeling all of what he had just been told. It might have crippled him otherwise. It also might have allowed him to tap into that well of rage he could feel burning in him that would allow him to put his magic to use.

But he couldn't. He was calm. Calm and useless.

He put one hand against the tree, and his knees buckled, sending him to the ground. Internally he was screaming at himself: *Do something! Do something!*

"It's alright." Corrik's voice was soothing. "Your friend Jacques had a similar reaction when we told him. He, too, learned far faster than he was supposed to. His main concern was whether you and your wife were in danger. He also voiced his concerns about your mother and the health of the baby when I told him Millie was expecting."

"What?" Jacques. That couldn't be right. Jacques was home with Millie.

"I offered a solution to free your mother and protect the child. He was not enthusiastic, but in the end, he agreed. He truly does have your best interests at heart. He insisted on finding a peaceful way to put her out of her misery, but unfortunately, it seems there was a complication in that regard."

Calm. Harlen was too calm. His thoughts that ordinarily would have blurred and made his head spin were slow. As if he were looking over his father's papers, they passed in front of him one by one.

He remained kneeling on the ground, but he felt no wave of panic. No overwhelming dread. Behind his calm thoughts, one thing repeated like the pulse of a second heartbeat as he realized what he needed to do.

Two heartbeats. Two heartbeats.

He needed to get back to Millie. He needed to get her away from here, away from Wakefield. He had to keep his promise to keep her safe.

And Corrik needed to suffer.

Harlen remained kneeling on the ground and dug his fingers into the tree at his side as though to provide balance. He lowered his face. It was no challenge to act dizzy and distraught. It was all anyone expected of him anyway. He was weak. He needed to be taught. He could hear it in Corrik's voice as he continued to explain that this was all for the best.

"She's really here?" he asked, letting his voice quiver.

"Yes, it's alright," Corrik said.

Harlen looked up at Corrik and returned the gesture of a broad smile. "Good. Tansey would have liked this."

He tightened his grip on the tree. The thin branches were easy to move, and concentrating had never been quite so easy. The wind cracked as they snapped downward and grabbed hold of Corrik, winding around his neck, hoisting him up from the ground.

A real hanging tree.

He had no idea if it would kill him. The poison hadn't. This likely wouldn't either. But he wasn't immune to choking for air or clawing at his throat. Who knew how long it would take someone to find him and let him down?

He wanted to take whatever magic Corrik had protecting him, but when he reached out towards him, fumbling mentally along the path he had only taken twice, he found nothing but shadow. He could only assume that Corrik's magic was of a different kind than he was used to. Not so much magic as an agreement with the goddess, as he put it.

The slow beat of his heart vanished as Corrik's concentration did, and Harlen felt it hit him. He felt like someone had just cleaved a hole in his chest, buried an ax in its center. But he would live. He had always been strong enough to endure and now was no exception.

Harlen stood beneath the tree, staring up at the branches as Corrik struggled and kicked against them. He made sure his hold was strong and would remain long after he walked away before he spoke. "If you ever come near my family or me again," he said, surprised at how calm he sounded. "I don't care if you can't die. I will find a way to break you."

Corrik strained to say something, but Harlen had no time for it. He could feel the panic screaming in his ears now to get back to Millie.

He could feel a pounding behind his eyes at the force of the magic he had just used, but Harlen forced himself to remain calm until he crossed the threshold of the graveyard. He didn't dare break his concentration on the vision of the tree until he reached the street again.

Once he was there, he doubled over and vomited onto the cobblestone, a mix of overwhelm and exertion. His nose was bleeding again. Tansey was dead. But there was no time— no time.

He pulled himself up and broke into a run. He had to get home. He had to get to Millie and get her out of here. They had to go now.

The houses, manors, and crowded shops passed him in a blur. He had no idea what streets he took or who he passed. All he knew was that he had to get home. He didn't dare speak to anyone or stop for even a breath though his lungs burned.

As he rounded the corner that lead up to his street, he spotted a figure already running from the house. Millie. He saw her sprinting towards him, away from the fence, and heard the confused town guard who called after her.

She ran right up to him and grabbed him by his shirt front. He put his hands on her shoulders, relief coursing through him to see her safe and alive.

"Jacques—" Millie started to say, and then the street was rocked by what sounded like an explosion. It knocked the town's guard to the ground, and Harlen pulled Millie to his chest, bending double, shielding her as the doors blew off the front of the house and hit the street, splintering as the wood met stone.

Jacques came staggering out of the house, panting from the spell and bleeding from the corner of his mouth. He looked up and locked eyes with the two of them standing on the street.

"Please!" Jacques called, limping out of the house and down the street. The guards were too disoriented or too afraid to interfere as he came towards them.

Harlen stepped between him and Millie. He hadn't missed the way her hand immediately flew to her stomach, and it filled him with new rage. Already the water gathered on the road around them was beginning to fill with frost, and Harlen felt a thin layer of ice crack as he clenched his rain-soaked hands.

"Please, you don't understand!" Jacques yelled.

"Stay where you are!" Harlen shouted back at him.

"Please!" he pleaded, not stopping. "Please—I never knew it would come to this!"

"You knew enough!" Millie shouted, and Harlen had to put out an arm to keep her from throwing herself at him.

"Just come back inside! We can sort this out! Harlen, you know. You know this isn't safe for you! You know what happens when people use too much magic too quickly, it's dangerous! You're going to hurt yourself! And Millie, this stress is bad for her."

"Don't." Harlen warned. "Don't tell me what's safe or good for me. And Millie is the only reason I'm giving you a chance to walk away right now. You saved her, so now you get to disappear. Just like we're going to."

Jacques looked at them miserably. "You can't leave. It isn't safe."

"Because that's what you want?" Harlen said with a laugh. "To keep us safe?"

Jacques winced and glanced back over his shoulder at the roof of the house. "I wanted it to be painless. It was supposed to be a mercy. She would get to pass peacefully, and a new life would be protected."

That was all it took. Harlen ran and threw his weight into him, knocking him to the rain-soaked ground. Jacques's head hit the paving stones, and he swore as he bit down on his lip, breaking it open.

"Why?" Harlen demanded. He grabbed Jacques by the collar, pulling his face up off the ground, screaming the same question again and again. "Why?"

"I didn't know," Jacques pleaded, his eyes wide and truly afraid. Harlen had no idea why he hadn't thrown him back with the wind; perhaps he had drained his magic, or the magic was drained from him.

Jacques looked gray and pale, and his face was shining with sweat. He looked sick. "I didn't know about Tansey when I offered to help you look for her. They didn't tell me until they caught me snooping around. I'm your friend—"

"No." Harlen shouted. "No you don't get to say that."

Jacques closed his eyes. "I'm sorry."

"I don't care," Harlen snapped back and raised a hand over Jacques's face. He heard him cough as black smoke began to roll out of him.

He deserved it. He deserved to lose everything, just like the rest of them. Just like all the others who stepped on those weaker than them. But try as he might, Harlen couldn't bring himself to do it.

He felt the white-hot pain surge through him as he lowered his hand, but this time he braced himself against it. Jacques stared up at him, terrified, and Harlen shook his head.

"You *were* my friend," Harlen said. "I really thought you were."

Harlen got to his feet, and Jacques remained on the ground, blood dribbling from his lip, hands raised. He looked like a scared animal, and it brought him no pleasure. "I never want to see you again."

Harlen turned his back on him and did not look back. Millie was waiting; she never took her eyes off Jacques, even as Harlen could see tears rolling out of their corners. Not until Harlen touched her shoulder and let his hand drop down her arm until it found hers, where he wound their fingers together and squeezed them tight. Then her eyes found him again, and he knew they would survive this.

"Let's get you home," he said.

EPILOGUE

Harlen Vostesk, third of his name, looked up at the stars. He could view them for the first time without looking through a patchwork of clouds.

He wasn't sure if the sky's clarity or the mountains themselves made the stars seem so much brighter. They burned like dripping silver, and he could name every constellation at a glance. They were the same ones that had been etched in gold on the ceiling of the library back home. But he far preferred the ones that stretched endlessly over the horizon.

If he never saw his home again, it would be too soon.

Are you lying on the ground?" Millie's voice drifted out from their bedroom, one her family had been kind enough to let them stay in for a while.

It seemed that they were rather pleased to have them there. Harlen couldn't imagine them even being allowed to leave since Millie's eldest sister Beatrice would protest every time Millie so much as stepped out of the front door these days. Millie insisted she was pregnant, not infirm, but she still sighed in discomfort as she lowered herself to the ground next to him.

"You don't have to lie down here with me," he said, half sitting up, but she waved him off.

"I want to while I can still make it to the ground," she said and settled on the stone balcony with him. It overlooked a rolling field of flowers that perfumed the cool night air that would leave their bedroom smelling like spring. She lay close enough to put her head against his shoulder. "How long does this last again?"

"Nine months," Harlen said, laughing when she let out a long, irritated sigh.

"Magic babies don't grow faster?"

"I'm afraid not," Harlen said.

"At least in the meantime, you know that I will give you anything your heart desires. Without question." He said, taking her hand and smiling at her.

"And here I was under the impression that you would always do that." She laughed. It was beautiful to hear her laughing again, but the way she softened after was even more lovely. "But in respect to my heart's desires, you should consider me satisfied. Completely." She ran her thumb over the back of his hand, and he wondered if she noticed the tightening of his throat. "And you?"

"I'm not satisfied. I'm overwhelmed." He kissed her hand, and the cool of her wedding band pressed against his lips. "I never imagined anything like this was possible."

They hadn't spoken much about that night in Wakefield. And on the balcony, it seemed a crime. The night was beautiful. The stars were bright—they were both safe.

For the first time in a long time, they could both breathe easily.

The End

ABOUT THE AUTHOR

I've only ever wanted to be two things. The first was a zoologist, which I decided when I was six years old, and my first-grade class brought in a woman who had an armadillo and a singing parrot. The second was an author when I was eleven and discovered I could share the stories I saw in my head by putting them on paper.

That's all it was at first—a way to share my imagination with other people. Then as I grew up, it gradually became something for me as well.

I've never had an easy time making friends. Especially in the latter half of my teen years when some medical problems made it pretty difficult to even get out of the house and see people. Then these stories became something more to me. My escape and my friends all in one. It's brought me a lot of happiness, and it's still something I want to share.

This is the first book of what I hope will be many more. Whether one person or many people read my work, I'll be forever grateful that I've had this chance to offer an escape and friends to those who need them.

Made in the USA
Monee, IL
12 May 2021